DISCLAIMER

This book is totally fictional and composed solely from the author's mind and imagination. Any resemblance to real persons, living or dead, places or situations are purely coincidental. All the characters, locations and events are not real. This book was written for the enjoyment of the reader with no other purpose intended.

PREFACE

Have you ever asked yourself, "why me?"

Evie is on an emotional rollercoaster ride that catapults her into a world filled with romance, sexual escapades, loneliness and the upheavals of everyday life.

"I was behaving like such a bitch. I was the one who threw up, not Daniel. Why was I being so nasty to him? Maybe this was my subconscious way of starting a fight so that Daniel would get mad at me. The more I would do it, the less he would love me, until he wouldn't love me at all. Then, he would end this relationship and I would be rid of him. Obviously, I was too much of a coward to just tell him the truth ..."

Brace yourself for constant twists and turns and a most shocking ending where everything comes full circle. You will be surprised and delighted at the same time.

DEDICATION

This book is dedicated to my daughter, Eilleen who has worked tirelessly with me for almost five years as my editor and mentor. She constantly inspired me and gave me hope when I didn't think I could get to the finish line. Thank you for the beautiful person you are, both inside and out.

To my parents, Zlata and Moshe Ickowicz who were Holocaust Survivors. They devoted their entire lives to their children, grandchildren and great-grandchildren. They lived an exemplary and positive life. Their kindness, love and respect for all people was second to none. I could not have asked for better parents. I love you Mom and Dad.

TABLE OF CONTENTS

ACKNOWLEDGMENTS

I would like to thank the following people for making this book possible:

To my daughter, Eilleen Eisenberg, for editing, inspiration, and for working tirelessly with me for almost five years. I could not have done it without you!

To my husband, Alvin Eisenberg, who, no matter how many times I interrupted his online word games, was always willing to critique my ideas so that I could make better decisions.

To my friend, Robert Kabakoff (BigRobtheActor), for all of his help and guidance in getting me through the entire publishing process, while being stuck in Nepal during the pandemic.

To my friend, Donna Poliseo, who helped edit this book for one year, pushed me to meet my self-imposed deadlines, and always took my phone calls.

To my friend, Margie Rocabrunna, who told me that my book was riveting and said she would be the first to buy it.

Thank you! Thank you! Thank you!

CHAPTER 1

Sometimes it's so hard to get up in the morning. My eyelids are heavy and filled with crust. I'm beyond tired because my brain doesn't let me function, no matter how hard I try. Sometimes I don't try at all. It's just easier that way.

I slide the comforter over myself and feel the warmth that engulfs me, as if I'm in a cocoon. I don't want to shed my shell and emerge into that beautiful butterfly called "life." So, I go back to sleep because it's easier ... no need to achieve, make decisions or feel anything at all. It may sound like I'm content to live this way, but I'm not.

What will bring me back from drowning in my own sorrows? I'm so tired of swimming to the surface and being pulled down by forces of which I have no control. I'm all alone in this sea of misery.

Is there any hope for me?

•

This city is too big with its looming buildings blowing acrid smoke from its huge smokestacks. The myriad of stores are calling to the masses that engulf the sidewalks. Every day, people plod like cattle to their cubicles, which serve as an escape from their personal lives.

Sometimes, living in a big city can be all-consuming. It's too noisy with kids crying and adults gossiping loudly as they go about their daily lives. They are oblivious to me as I throw my shadow over their bulging eyes, eyes that see no purpose. It can't always be the comfort of a small town.

What has happened to me? What is happening to me? More importantly, what will become of me? I'm in the belly of the whale and I want to escape, but don't know how.

•

I'm in bed and must get up. I stir slowly, pushing the covers off me. The warmth that had enveloped my being is quickly dissipating. I'm chilly, but it's not cold in here.

Methodically, I move my right leg onto the floor and feel a pinch in my toes. Automatically, I jump back until I realize the sensation is only from the cold floor in my darkened room. I cannot decide whether to try again or retreat back to the warmth of my comforter.

A chill focuses on my back as I realize it's time to bring myself out of this eternal coma that has visited upon me. My numbness is beginning to fade as my legs gain control and movement. Within minutes, my entire body follows. Already the buzzing has started in my head. I can't remember my name!

"What is my name?" I ask as if I'm talking to someone in my room.

I'm very thirsty and need a glass of cold water. As I move slowly to the bathroom, it's hard to decide which to do first. On top of it, my stomach is growling. All I really want to do is go back to bed. This has been my routine for quite some time now.

Why am I sleeping my life away?

•

The sink is filled with dishes that I do not want to wash. I'll probably throw them out, so I won't have to deal with them. There's a carton of soy milk and a half-eaten box of cereal in my small pantry. I guess that will do. I reach for a bowl and grab my only spoon from the drawer.

While gulping down my breakfast, the cloudiness begins to leave my head and so does the buzzing. My thoughts drift to the summer mornings I had spent with Daniel, when I was 25 years old. It was so many years ago.

•

"Blueberries or strawberries in your cereal?" Daniel asked.

"Surprise me, Honey," was my reply.

"Let's hurry up and eat on the deck while it's still cool outside. I don't want the sun to burn us to a crisp," Daniel said in his usual caring manner.

"Okay, I'll get the coffee and the napkins," I responded.

Daniel held my hand while we ate a leisurely breakfast. He always doted on me and tried to make me feel special. I acted as if I was happy with him, and to some degree I truly was. I did love him, but not in the right way. My time with Daniel was comfortable, but that's all it ever was. He never made my heart race at the thought of seeing him. It wasn't upsetting to me when our schedules conflicted so we couldn't get together. I suppose I was accepting of him since I didn't like being alone. So, I stayed in a relationship that wasn't fully satisfying in all the ways that counted.

"Why is it so hard for you to make a decision?" Daniel asked.

"I don't know. You caught me off guard with your proposal," I responded.

"We've been engaged for six months now. I love you so much. Doesn't it make sense that we set a wedding date already?"

"Daniel, I'm just not sure when I want to get married."

"No guy wants to feel rejected, even if they're already engaged. But I understand that you're not ready to set a firm date. I don't want to pressure you," he added reluctantly.

Daniel was such a good guy, but I just wasn't that into him. I couldn't find fault with him as a person however, he was a bit dull. Maybe he was too nice and that was the problem. I probably shouldn't have accepted his proposal to begin with but got caught up in the moment. So, I continued the ruse and became engaged to him. It was very selfish of me. Now that he wanted to set an actual wedding date, I had to face reality, which scared me. How was I going to tell the sweetest guy in the world that I didn't love him?

●

I am drawn toward the sunlight peeking through the curtains. Could there be a person hiding behind them? Maybe two people are waiting there for me? It's happened to me before. At least I think it has.

"Is it safe?" I shouted.

I don't observe or hear any rustling and there are no shoes showing on the floor. Can I trust this?

"No one is here. No one is here. No one is here."

There! I said it three times and that means it's okay. I can proceed because now it's safe.

There are many reasons why I have convinced myself that there is always someone standing behind the living room drapes.

Everyone tells themselves little lies which eventually become big lies. They intertwine in every facet of your life and ultimately become truths. This is the persona I have taken on for the past six months; I had come to believe in my own mistruths and lived accordingly.

Moving slowly towards the window, I notice the bottom of the curtain is frayed and has yellowed. Again, I speak to myself.

"One foot in front of the other, step by step; there is no danger now," I continue to say aloud.

This is one part of my ritual and routine every day. It is very tiring.

Touching the curtain with my fingertips and gently moving it aside is pleasurable to me. Peering out the window, I am bathed in sunshine. There is a whole other world out there with countless people moving about and cars going to destinations unknown.

It must be lunchtime because I can see a hot dog cart. There are a lot of people waiting in line for that one piece of meat slathered with an assortment of toppings. I love a mix of onions, ketchup, mustard and relish on mine. Biting into it is heaven on earth. Wow! I don't remember the last time I treated myself to such a delight.

It's time to step away from the window. I've been standing here too long, but I don't even know how long it's been. There is no working clock to tell me the time. What is it about a ticking clock that mesmerizes me? Well, if I actually got out of the house to buy one, I would find out.

That's it! Tomorrow I'll go to the Tick Tock Plus store and ask the man behind the front counter to help me. He always greets me with a half-smile. His lips open only partway, showing small teeth that have a yellow film and large spaces hollowed out from age. I bet he'll help me find the perfect clock. Sometimes he looks at me strangely, as if he is seeing someone else. When he does that, his brow wrinkles as his face takes on a somber expression.

Why does he look at me that way?

Once, I saw him talking to one of the salesgirls as he pointed in my direction. At least I thought he was pointing toward me. He placed his right hand over the side of his mouth and whispered something in her ear. She then looked at me with a disapproving eye. I was sure that he was filling her head with vicious lies about me. Was I delusional to think that? What could he have said to her? Why did he hate me so much? He has always been nice to me, so maybe he was telling her a secret that had nothing to do with me. I don't know what to think about him anymore. Maybe it's just me.

I might have to put off buying the clock. First, I need to be sure that I can leave my private space. I shake my head back and forth and wave away any bad thoughts about going outside. I realize that I'm still standing by my window. Quickly, I move away and look around my apartment and then a smile comes to my face. I will sit on my favorite couch, my only couch! No one helped me pick it out. I made that decision by myself, but it was not the best choice because it's too small. Three days after it was delivered, I went back to the furniture store. There was a larger one on display that I liked more. It was affordable, but I couldn't make up my mind. Why is it always so hard for me to make decisions? Why do I always doubt myself once I have made one?

CHAPTER 2

My mind is all aflutter as thoughts are racing in and out. I find myself stomping my feet and screaming uncontrollably. My breathing is heavy and my heart is pounding.

I'm in so much pain!

I look at my couch and see my beloved blanket. I can't even tell what color it is, as it is indistinguishable to me at this moment.

Moving toward the couch, I begin to calm down as I lean against the checkered cushions. I wrap the blanket around me to feel the comfort that is missing from my life. Touching the soft fibers and smelling the perfumes I have sprayed on it throughout the years bring back both good and bad memories. I remember who gave this blanket to me.

It was my friend Briana.

Wow! I haven't seen her in a long time. I have always admired Briana and have such happy thoughts when I think about her. She doesn't have a bad bone in her body and is the most genuine person I know. From the first day we met, I wanted to be her friend even though she was five years younger than me. Thankfully, she wanted to be mine too.

Winters here are colder than other parts of the country. Briana always talked about how she loved that time of year. Every December 31st, she would drag me to Rockefeller Center to ice skate, even though she knew I wasn't a fan of the cold. The one time I agreed to go skiing with her upstate, I sat in the lounge drinking hot chocolate while she was on the slopes. She was never affected by the wind or snow, which was so unlike me. Briana gave me the blanket for my birthday many years ago. It was sort of a joke present, a blanket for a "wet blanket." I guess that was me.

This blanket soothes me every time I wrap it around me. It offers me warmth, comfort and above all, it offers me my friend!

Why haven't I seen Briana recently? I need to get to the phone and call her. I don't know where my cell is, and it seems so far away.

I peek out under the blanket and remove myself from its comforts. The air is making me chilly again even though it's warm inside.

I need to find my phone!

The light switch has been turned off for too long. I edge towards it and place my finger on it. The room transforms into luminous crystals. Every crevice and edifice are warmed by the glow. This makes me feel a little better.

I did it!

Okay, now where is my phone? Looking through the kitchen cabinets, opening my desk drawers, and searching under the

couch does not bring success. This seems to close the door to my lifeline. I cannot find my phone!

I need to calm my nerves, so I lay down on the wooden floor. Sometimes, the hardness on my head and back gives me solace. Looking around the room from this angle brings my attention to the light fixture on the ceiling. It reminds me of the time Daniel fell off the ladder and almost killed himself trying to screw in a light bulb. As I continue to think about Daniel, my eyelids become heavy. I drift off into a sound sleep.

•

It's morning again. The same thoughts and feelings resonate inside me from the day before. I do not want to leave my "floor bed."

Again, thoughts of Briana come to my mind. We used to be so close. There were so many get-togethers. I especially loved it when we went to Café Allegra. It was a relaxing place where you could talk for hours, and we did just that! I can still hear her giggling while being serious at the same time.

What happened to all those good times? It's been way too long.

I jump up from the floor, daring myself to stand and feel the cold air as it surrounds me. It negates the warmth from my comforter, my solace.

I splash some warm water on my face and realize that I need a shower. How long has it been - a week, two, or three?

After removing my underwear and tank top, I step on my bathmat and notice the black mold underneath. This can't be healthy, but I'm not going to clean it off right now. I slide open the shower door and quickly turn on the faucets. As I reach for the liquid soap, the warm water streaming down my back comforts me. My stomach hurts because I have to pee, so I let it out. I begin to feel better as it runs down one of my legs. Am I the only girl who pees in the shower? I bet most girls do but don't admit to it.

It seems like it has only been five minutes, but the hot water has already run out. How long have I been in here? Upon opening the shower door, a gust of cold air attaches to me. I start to tremble. I must get my towel, but I'm distracted by my arms. They weren't always so flabby. Well, I am 45 years old, so what am I expecting?

The towel is not as soft as it used to be. It scratches my skin, so I must dry off quickly. Jumping into my clothes brings instant warmth. I sprint to my couch; my comfort zone and safe haven away from all of my demons.

CHAPTER 3

I was only 23 years old when I moved into Daniel's luxurious co-op in Kew Gardens, Queens. It was a large two bedroom with high ceilings yet needed some major renovations. Daniel inherited the place from his Grandma Celia.

Six months had passed by since we were living together, and I was miserable. He wanted what I could not give him.

How long could I go on faking this relationship?

"Ashira and Troy are going on a cruise to the Bahamas. Troy asked if we want to join them. I think it's a good idea. What do you think?" Daniel asked me.

"When are they going?"

"He said something about July 4th."

"I don't know, maybe. It's probably going to be expensive."

"Don't worry about the money. It will be my treat and we'll have so much fun with them."

"You know what, why not? But I'll pay for my share. I'm working too you know."

Daniel came over and kissed me. He was so happy when we were together, that it broke my heart knowing we weren't meant to be.

"Let me check with work. It'll just take a minute," I said.

While I was on hold waiting for my boss to give me the go ahead, Daniel continued to kiss me. He then began caressing my breasts and massaging my shoulders. He leaned against me hard and it was clear that he was ready for lovemaking. Unfortunately, it was only sex for me. I should have felt some type of pleasure, but it was rote. I was only too happy when it was over.

Later that evening, Troy called back.

"I set the cruise up with the travel agent and all is a go. Ashira is really excited to relax and spend some quality time with you guys," he said.

"That's great, Troy! We're looking forward to it also," Daniel responded.

"See you in a few weeks at the pier, or do you want me to pick you guys up? Just let me know," Troy said and then hung up.

Daniel was in such a good mood that I hoped this cruise would turn things around for us. Well, at least for me.

•

July 4th arrived and it was time for us to leave for the cruise.

"My duffle bag is packed and all I need is some extra cash. We can stop at the ATM on the way to the pier. How's your packing coming?" Daniel asked me.

"I'm almost done. I forgot to get sunblock, but I'll pick it up on the ship. Just give me five more minutes and you can take the bags outside. By the way, it was a great idea you had."

"What great idea?" Daniel asked.

"That Troy and Ashira will be picking us up. We don't have to worry about the parking."

"Yeah, thanks. I guess it was," Daniel responded.

A minute later, Troy knocked on our door.

"Hi guys. I need to use your bathroom. I'll just be a minute."

"No problem, you know where it is," Daniel responded.

Troy came out of the bathroom and seemed anxious.

"Let's get this party started and head downstairs! I hate bucking all the holiday traffic," he added.

We ran outside with our bags in hand. Daniel quickly threw them in the trunk of the car and off we went. We were about halfway to the pier when I let out a loud shriek.

"What the hell! I almost had a car accident," Troy screamed angrily at me.

"So sorry," I responded meekly.

"What's wrong?" Daniel and Ashira asked me at almost the same time.

"I feel like such an idiot. I left my ID in the apartment."

Troy turned the car around immediately and just missed hitting an oncoming SUV. He must have been driving at least 90 miles an hour. I was praying that he wouldn't get into an accident and kill us all. I wanted to apologize, but the best course of action was not to speak until I had my license in my hands. The silence was deafening in the car as Ashira and Daniel seemed to be sharing my thoughts.

The mood was somber until we boarded the ship. As the cruise director welcomed us, a waiter holding a tray filled with Bahama Mamas passed by. Troy must have realized that he overreacted, because he offered to buy me a drink. I was so glad that his anger had dissipated and we could move on. I was also glad for the alcoholic beverages.

We went to our staterooms and unpacked our bags. Shortly thereafter, we met Ashira and Troy on the upper deck.

"Thanks again for the Bahama Mamas. They were delicious and I'm ready for some more," I said sheepishly to Troy.

"Works for me," Daniel and Ashira said in concert.

Troy was definitely in a generous mood because it was difficult to remember how many rounds he bought us.

And so the cruise began …

We definitely drank too much within the first few hours, because all of us were slurring our words and we could not stop laughing. Finally, Daniel put a stop to it.

"Ok everyone, we've all had enough for now. It's time to sober up a bit."

"Boo, boo," Troy shouted between laughter.

"We need to eat dinner before we all pass out," Daniel stated.

"Daniel, I don't feel that good," I said.

"What's wrong?" Daniel asked me, as he took his right hand and began to rub the back of my neck.

"You're right. I had too much to drink and my head is spinning. I need to go lay down in the room."

"No problem. I'll take you there right now! See you guys in a few."

Daniel placed his arm around my waist and helped me walk back to our cabin. As soon as we entered the room, I began to feel even dizzier.

"Just get me into bed and let me sleep for a while. Eat dinner without me if I'm not awake."

"I'm not leaving you! You're my fiancé for G-D's sake! I want to take care of you," Daniel responded.

"You're not my father so stop acting like it, okay!" I yelled out.

"What's the matter with you? Why are you acting so mean to me?"

"Just leave the room before I ..."

And then it happened. I threw up all over Daniel. He stood there for a moment motionless until he realized what had just transpired.

"Wow! You should feel better now," Daniel said in a caring manner as he pushed my vomit filled hair away from my mouth. He really loved me unconditionally.

Daniel took a quick shower and I went in right after him. While I was showering, Daniel tried his best to clean up the floor and bed. However, when I came out of the bathroom the stench from the vomit was still present and it nauseated me.

"I can't deal with this awful smell! Get someone in here to clean it up properly!" I screamed.

"I'll call for the maid service to come as soon as possible," Daniel said softly.

I was behaving like such a bitch. I was the one who threw up, not Daniel. Why was I being so nasty to him? Maybe this was my subconscious way of starting a fight so that Daniel would get mad at me. The more I would do it, the less he would love me until he wouldn't love me at all. Then, he would end this relationship and I would be rid of him. Obviously, I was too much of a coward to just tell him the truth.

•

I'm flying in my cocoon of happiness as I lay on my couch. In my mind, I can see the world, but the world cannot see me. Suddenly it hits me. No one cares enough to see what's behind my face, the inner me; the real me. I need to get back out there! I need to remember my name! I need to call Briana!

My emotions are all over the place. My eyes start to blink uncontrollably so I begin to scream, "I can't stop!" Then I do stop, exhausted from the reality that is me.

"Briana, where are you? Briana, I need you!" I scream to no conclusion.

I still have no clue where my cell phone is. It's probably dead anyway and there's really no urgency to charge it. After all, no one calls me and I've had no desire to reach out to anyone. However, there is one person I do want to call, and that's Briana.

The sun must be going down because the light behind my curtain is beginning to dim. Although I do not want to sit in the dark, there is a certain comfort to it. I don't hear any noises and everything is still. Many thoughts enter my mind. I dismiss them all when Briana's face reveals itself to me. I try to concentrate as hard as I can on her.

Memories start to float toward me. I think about all the good times Briana and I had together. I'm worried that those days are probably gone. It has been way too long ...

•

"Hi, Evie, do you want to go to McElroy's Bar & Grill and get some drinks tonight?"

"Hey Briana, I don't feel like it. Work was a bitch today and I'm really tired."

You could almost feel Briana wince on the other end of the line.

"Oh come on! You never want to go out anymore. Let's have some fun, some girl talk," she pleaded.

"Okay, but not for long. I'll meet you there at nine," I said.

But I never showed up!

I never told her I was sorry. Once again, I was a coward, too afraid of what she would say to me. Yet, I knew Briana wouldn't have been angry, because she never judged me.

So, what was I so afraid of?

CHAPTER 4

Years ago, when I was in my early thirties, everything seemed to have been going well for me. The stars were aligned properly and then he had to come into the picture, my almost perfect picture …

I remember it so clearly now. Briana and I were having brunch at Café Allegra, something we loved to do. The waiter placed us in a corner of the restaurant out of view from most of the diners. It was perfect! Our laughter and loud talking wouldn't disturb anyone.

I drank a lot of coffee and didn't want to stop the fun by leaving the table, but I also didn't want to pee in my pants. It was clear to me that a bathroom run was needed immediately.

"I'll be right back, Briana."

"Okay but hurry up! We're having too much fun," she responded.

I stood up and made a dash for the ladies' room. Of course, there was a long line. It never fails! Since I had nothing else to do, I started checking out each person standing in front of me. I tried to be discreet, but people always know if you are looking at them. I couldn't stop criticizing each person in my mind.

"Stop It! Stop judging! Since when are you Miss Perfection?" I whispered to myself.

These negative thoughts of others floated in and out of my head until a stall finally opened. I entered quickly and closed the door. It smelled bad but I had no choice. I usually use a piece of toilet paper to lock the door, but there was none available. All these people touching the same lock with their bare hands bothered me. I envisioned the lock with tons of germs on it, and now I had to touch it. Enough of those thoughts! At least the lock worked. I would usually get one that's broken and have to hold the door shut while trying to pee.

Afterward, I performed my hand washing ritual which lasted about seven minutes. That should do the trick, I thought. I checked myself in the mirror for a moment or two and then left the ladies' room.

While walking back to our table, I stopped cold. My brain could not believe what my eyes were seeing! Dumbfounded, I stood frozen as a wave of nausea and anger cursed through me. Was this really happening? Briana was sitting with a man! Where the hell did he come from? What was going on? What should I do? They seemed heavily involved in conversation, even laughing. This was absolutely ridiculous! I realized that I was getting very angry and had to stop myself from running over and confronting the situation. I should've been happy that some guy had taken an interest in my friend. Instead, I became very jealous and territorial. I needed to compose myself. I stood there and watched them for another few minutes as the waiter brought them drinks.

"Calm down, calm down," I said, hoping no one would notice that I was talking to myself.

As I was trying to figure out what to do, one of the managers came over to me.

"Can I help you, Miss?" he asked in a soothing voice.

"No, it's okay. I'm just heading back to my table."

I didn't realize anyone was paying attention to me. Okay, here I go ...

As I approached the table, neither of them turned around. It was as if they were the only two people in the world. I pasted on a fake smile and sat down.

"Hi!" I said with as much effervescence as I could muster.

Briana was acting like a schoolgirl with a big-time crush on this guy. When she looked at me, it was as if I had never left the table this entire time.

"You will not believe this! What were the chances? This is Paul, my high school sweetheart. We were just catching up," she said gushingly.

"High school sweetheart?" I said questioningly.

"Wow! That was so long ago!" I quickly added.

"I know! Paul is in town for a short amount of time on business," Briana said.

Yeah, monkey business, I thought.

"Paul, this is my good friend …"

The busboy interrupted the introduction. As he began to clear the glasses off the table, one of them fell on the floor and shattered into pieces. Both Briana and Paul broke out into laughter. I didn't think it was funny at all but laughed with them anyway. How could I not? Once the laughing stopped, Paul excused himself and left the table. I faced Briana and looked directly at her.

"Do you still have strong feelings for him?" I asked, hoping for her to say no.

"I think I do. I'm not really sure, but I felt electrified by his presence. I can't believe it! What were the chances that he would show up here?" Briana asked.

"You've always been lucky. It follows you everywhere. I wish some of it would rub off on me."

Briana looked at me in a funny sort of way. It was a disapproving stare that wasn't meant to be obvious. It was clear that I hurt her feelings.

I felt myself falling backward into an abyss, plunging into darkness. I was drowning with no chance of swimming to the top, sinking lower and lower. I could see Briana looking down from the surface, and then walking away.

"You look as though you're a thousand miles away. What are you thinking?"

"I don't know," I said, hoping she wouldn't realize that I was not being truthful.

Paul returned to the table at that moment and saved me from having to think up another fib. Who would have thought that I would be happy to see him again?

Paul placed his hands around Briana's shoulders and gave them a little squeeze. He then sat down and immediately took hold of her hands and kissed them.

Quite the romantic, aren't you? I thought to myself.

"Today must be my lucky day! Unfortunately, I have to get back to work now. I was only supposed to have a quick lunch. Oh, and it was nice meeting you, err, ah …," Paul said.

He began to stutter, a little embarrassed that he didn't know my name.

Funny … I don't even know it myself right now.

"Take care of yourself, Briana. I'll try to give you a call while I'm still in town," he said nonchalantly.

He dropped a few dollars on the table and then left. It was obvious that Briana was not happy at the word "try."

"He won't call," she said with a deep sigh.

I was relieved! Briana wasn't.

"Don't tell me you don't recall the jerk he was. I remember all of the awful stories you told me about him," I said curtly.

"It's been a lot of years, and he's changed. He's more mature, and definitely a lot nicer," Briana retorted.

"Well don't hold your breath. He won't call. He's a loser."

I regretted what I had said but was glad at the same time. I didn't want Paul to call her. If he did, Briana wouldn't have time for me anymore. She would spend it all with him. Then I would be alone. I didn't want to be alone.

It's scary to be alone.

•

A few weeks later, I received a call from Briana. Her voice was very upbeat.

"I have such great news and wanted to tell you in person, but we haven't gotten together since we ran into Paul at Cafe Allegra. He called me the next day and we have been seeing each other since! I didn't tell you sooner because I didn't want to jinx it. He asked for a job transfer to NYC and HR agreed. Isn't this great news?"

I was frozen for a moment. A lump formed in my throat, but I recovered quickly.

"Wow! I didn't expect him to call you at all, never mind so soon," I blurted out.

"Is that all you have to say?" she asked, obviously a bit hurt.

"Ah, um," I stammered.

"Of course I'm happy for you! You just took me by surprise, that's all. Are you two exclusive now?"

"We're going to take it slow and get to know each other again. But this time, it will be different."

"What do you mean it's going to be different? People rarely change. Don't you remember how badly he treated you? You never felt secure with him," I blatantly told her.

"Evie, what is wrong with you? You sound jealous."

Evie!

Holy cow! My name is Evie!

CHAPTER 5

And so it went, just as I expected it to.

The phone calls became fewer and the get-togethers became nonexistent. My relationship with Briana soured and a great friendship began to unravel.

Since the arrival of Paul at Café Allegra, I felt lost and went into a funk.

•

The first two days of the cruise were not happy ones for me or Daniel. I kept trying to pick fights with him and he kept on tolerating my outbursts. This made me even more frustrated. On the third day, I decided to stop behaving badly and tried to make the trip enjoyable.

"Let's sign up for some activities today. What do you want to do?" I asked Daniel.

The expression on Daniel's face read as one of surprise. He must have been shocked by my change of attitude but didn't voice it.

"That's great! Let's go swimming for a while after lunch. Then we could either play bocce ball or take the Salsa lessons they're offering at 4:00 PM."

"Sure, let's do that. It will take me only a minute to get into my bikini."

The smile on Daniel's face absolved me from all my deliberate bad behavior, at least for the time being.

On the fourth day, Troy and Ashira joined us on the lounge chairs.

"Let's get some drinks. What do you girls want?" Troy asked.

"A Mojito sounds good," Ashira said.

"I'll have a Mai Tai."

Daniel left with Troy to get the drinks, and I moved my lounge chair closer to Ashira's.

"We haven't had a lot of time to catch up. How are things going with you and Troy?" I asked her.

"Well, we've been together for a few years now, but Troy hasn't popped the question. Truth be told, I don't know if he ever will."

"Do you want to get married?"

"Yes and no. Sometimes I envision myself as the perfect wife with the perfect husband, a house with a two-car garage and so forth. But other times I like the status quo, a commitment with no real commitment. Truthfully, I don't want to rock the boat, no pun intended, ha, ha. Things are good between us and I don't want that to change."

"That's great for you."

"You say that almost as though you're not happy with your situation, Evie."

I was surprised that she picked up on that so quickly.

"Ha, ha. No, of course not! I didn't mean it that way."

Hopefully, Ashira wasn't aware of my flimsy attempt to cover up that lie, but her women's intuition probably kicked in.

Daniel and Troy came back just in the nick of time. I took my drink from Daniel and kissed him on the cheek. Ashira definitely took notice. Maybe that would squelch any further thoughts on the subject.

"This is very good," Ashira said after taking a sip of her drink.

"Mine is a little too sweet, but it's still good sweetie," I remarked to Daniel.

The rest of the day was pleasant with the four of us swimming, sunbathing and taking our first Salsa lesson. We didn't drink too much this time, especially since we planned on having more after dinner.

Troy and Ashira were fun to be with, but they were really Daniel's friends. It was so easy for Daniel to make friends. He had so many of them, and I guess I was envious. I knew that one day he would make a great husband for a very lucky girl. Hopefully, she won't be a bitch like me.

☐

I have to get up from my couch and look out the window again. It's important for me to feel life as it exists. As I reach the window, I peer around the curtains into reality. The outside world is always the same, yet always different. People are everywhere, yet I am nowhere. It's a stark reality that bites at my very being. Quickly, I turn away from life and go back to non-existence. I realize that I don't want to face my demons, the reality of who I am and what I am. I look in the mirror and see a pile of crumpled old rags.

I'm useless to everyone.

I wish I could cry for myself, but there are no tears that come through, only intrusive thoughts of self. Crying is great to relieve the soul of its discomforts.

I need to get a grip. Where do I start? How do I become better?

It's time to go to sleep again. Can it be evening already?

•

It was the fifth day of the cruise and I became restless again. As much as I wanted it to work with Daniel, my part in it was nothing more than a charade. I couldn't keep it up much longer. Daniel had to have realized that I wasn't interested in him anymore, but he didn't show it in any way. I couldn't understand that. It just didn't make any sense.

Do you want to get a massage?" Ashira asked me as we ate breakfast.

"That's a great idea! Let's go to the spa and see if they have any appointments available."

"Don't worry about getting your purse. You can pay me back later," Ashira said.

"Okay. Let's go!"

We looked at the pamphlet which listed all the various types of massages available. It was hard for me to choose, as I had never had a professional one before.

"I'm getting a 90 minute deep tissue massage, even though it's a little pricey. Which one are you going to get, Evie?"

"I'm not sure."

"Get the one I'm getting, okay?"

"Why not! I'm here to have fun and not to pinch pennies. Let's do it!"

"Do you have a preference for a male or a female masseuse?" the receptionist asked us.

"No preference," we responded simultaneously.

"Do you want a side by side massage?" she then asked us.

We looked at each other and began to giggle.

"No, separate rooms please," Ashira said quickly.

"There's a changing room down the hall. Undress and put on one of the robes hanging by the entry. You can put your clothing in any of the open lockers. When you're done, enjoy some cucumber water in the waiting room until someone calls you," the receptionist said.

Ashira and I did what she said and proceeded to the waiting room. There was a small array of healthy snacks, and red wine on the counter. Both of us took a glass of wine and sat down.

"This wine is pretty good. What do you think?"

"Not bad. I wonder if we're going to get a man or a woman," Ashira remarked.

"I don't care as long as they do a good job."

Within moments, two men dressed in white scrubs came into the waiting room and called out our names. I immediately perked up. This massage was definitely going to be divine.

Very divine indeed!

•

I don't want to go to sleep. I'm wide awake. Intrusive thoughts come into my mind and overtake my brain. Memories float in and out.

What if decisions were made differently? Better judgments of events would definitely lead to better outcomes.

And then Ben materializes ...

Mr. "Wonderful," Mr. "Perfect," Mr. "You Had To Turn My Whole World Upside Down!"

He came into my life quite by accident, or so I thought. I was on the down escalator leaving work. I descended to the main floor of the building and started walking quickly towards the exit. I spotted Ben standing there looking around quizzically. He approached me with a yellow Post-it note in his hand.

"Excuse me, Ma'am, do you know where ..."

Wow! Was this guy hot! He was over six feet tall with striking blue eyes. His bleached blond hair was full on top and close-cropped on the sides. When he spoke, a small dimple showed on his right cheek.

It was difficult not to stare at him. He had this awkward grin while speaking and I found him beyond fascinating. I must have been fantasizing for a moment because he had to repeat "Ma'am" to me.

Who says "Ma'am" anymore? That word is so old school.

"Oh sure, all you have to do is turn right and walk straight to …"

I was beginning to like him and didn't even know why.

Relationships are unpredictable, maybe more like unreliable. There are definitely no guarantees and no promises of happy endings. One minute you're both in love and then the next

minute you can hate each other. It makes no sense to me. How do you go from being so in love to not caring at all?

Ben and I were going to be different, because in my mind, we would beat the odds. Wait a second, what was I thinking? I was already planning our life together. What silly thoughts! I didn't even know him.

After I gave Ben directions to his destination, he left through the revolving doors and went on his way.

I left the office building and headed for Mom & Pop's grocery store around the corner. Going there was part of my routine almost every workday. There was always a variety of delicious homemade foods to choose from. That was the best part, no cooking, no cleaning and no mess.

Amen to that!

The owners at Mom & Pop's knew me and so did the hired help. I loved going in there because they were like my extended family. It was a comfort zone for me as my only family was my sister. Unfortunately, she didn't want to have anything to do with me.

Riding the bus home that night, my thoughts were of Ben. Even though I didn't know his name at the time, I referred to him in my mind as "Post-it Guy." I had never given a man so much thought before actually knowing him. Could it be possible that I would run into him again?

Days passed, weeks passed, and I still did not see Ben. Every time I stepped onto the escalator after leaving work, I immediately looked for him. Holding out hope that he would show up again at my office building was beginning to fade.

•

A month passed since Ben asked me for directions.

"Evie, I need you to come back up here! These papers have to be processed right now," yelled a raspy voice from the top of the escalator.

That snapped me back to reality. I knew my fantasizing had to stop. I realized that I orchestrated a relationship in my mind with a man I had spoken to for only two minutes, if that long.

He was simply a random guy who asked me for directions, nothing more!

That voice at the top of the stairs was Bill, one of my many bosses. I couldn't really complain about him. He was a nice man and a good boss. He was usually fair in his decisions and beneath his hard exterior, he was a good person. I could have fallen for him when I first began working there, but he never showed any romantic interest in me. Bill was always on the straight and narrow and very predictable. He was nice to look at, even though he had gained a few pounds around the middle and in his face over the years. Then again, who hasn't?

That Thursday evening, Bill asked me to work late and I wasn't really in the mood.

"If these files don't get taken care of, we'll have to work on Saturday to finish them," he said.

Of course, I agreed. Let's be real, there was no choice since I wanted to keep my job.

After completing the third file, my eyes became droopy. It was time to go outside and get some fresh air.

"Bill, is it okay if I take a break for a few minutes?"

"No problem; take a half hour," he responded easily.

Going down the escalator, I instinctively looked for Ben. Of course, he wasn't there. Why did I keep clouding my mind with illusions, or should I say delusions?

•

Looking at these two masseuses made me wish that the cruise wasn't ending in two days.

"My name is Fernando, and I will do your massage today, Evie. Do you have any questions?"

Yes, when can we sleep together? That's what I wanted to ask him.

"No, none at this time," I replied instead.

"My name is Kurt, and I will do the same for you, Ashira. Do you have any questions?"

"No, none either," Ashira answered.

Both men had sexy accents but listening to Fernando speak was very seductive.

As Fernando led me to the massage room, I began to check him out. He was about 5'9" with the cutest butt. He had olive skin and jet-black hair. His black-rimmed glasses added to his sexiness.

Very sexy indeed!

I lied down on the massage table where Fernando began performing his magic.

He had the warmest hands. They felt like two heating pads massaging my skin. Fernando was so gentle when he moved his hands all over my body. It seemed that he knew exactly where to apply pressure and where to go easy on me. After a few minutes, my whole body tingled, and I began to feel aroused. I didn't want to leave the massage table, but the appointment was over. It was hard to believe that 90 minutes had passed by so quickly.

I met up with Ashira in the dressing room.

"That was great! How was yours?" I asked Ashira.

"Fabulous! Aren't you glad that you listened to me?"

"You were right!"

We showered quickly and got dressed. I was all set to go back upstairs to meet Troy and Daniel, but Ashira wasn't ready yet, as she was blow-drying her hair. I yelled out to her that I would be in the waiting room until she was ready.

Being the only one in the waiting room was boring, so I took a glass of wine that was displayed on the counter. I drank it too quickly and got a bit woozy, so I sat back down on the chair to compose myself. Just at that moment, Fernando was passing by the room and noticed that I was out of sorts.

"Are you okay?" he asked me.

"I just drank the wine a little too quickly. I'll be fine."

"Let's make sure."

Fernando came into the room and touched my forehead with those warm hands.

"I don't think you have a fever but …"

Oh yes I do! You are making me very hot, I thought to myself.

"Maybe you should lie down for a few minutes. I'll help you to the couch," Fernando said.

My eyes looked directly at his, and he understood exactly what I was thinking. He kissed me ever so gently on my lips and the feeling was exhilarating. This was exactly what was missing from my relationship with Daniel. I kissed him back and the most exciting sexual escapade had begun.

His kisses were hard and quick, almost as if he was in a race to get to the finish line. And that's exactly what it was. He barely touched my breasts and then immediately began to thrust his body against mine. We were finished in less than two minutes, but it was completely satisfying to me. It was so much more exciting than anything I had ever felt with Daniel. Thankfully, no one walked in on us!

Fernando caressed my face with both of his hands and it was so romantic to me.

"I have another appointment in five minutes, but I want to see you again. What is your cabin number?" he asked.

My face flushed as to how bold and up-front he was. I actually liked it and had totally forgotten that Ashira would be walking in at any moment.

"I want to see you but, well, um I feel embarrassed right now."

"You didn't like it?"

"No, it's not that. I loved it! It's just that ..."

"I'm sorry that I took so long, Evie," Ashira said as she entered into the room.

"No problem," I stammered a little.

She looked at me, then at Fernando and then back at me. She knew something had happened; she just didn't know what.

"Are you okay?" Ashira asked.

"I'm fine. I just had a dizzy spell and the masseuse gave me a glass of water."

Fernando did not seem flustered in any way. His next appointment walked in and he immediately whisked her out of the room.

"Ashira, let's get back to the boys. I need to sit and relax for a while. It must be all the rich food that's affecting me," I said nonchalantly.

Ashira gave me a puzzled look as if to say, "something here is not kosher. "

•

On the sixth day of the cruise, the ship docked once again. It was 9:00 AM and we began walking around the island and taking in the scenery. The guys got bored after a few minutes and decided to rent jet skis at the local beach. Ashira and I weren't thrilled with that idea, so we went shopping instead. Afterward, we all watched a short fireworks show. I spent a good deal of time daydreaming about Fernando. It was difficult for me to understand why I didn't feel guilty. Instead, I was trying to figure out how I could meet up with him one more time.

"C'mon Evie, it's time to get back to the ship for some food," Daniel said.

It was at that moment that I decided to make it happen. Why not? Daniel and I were not meant to be. This was my chance for sexual excitement and I didn't want to give it up.

Lunch was buffet style, and I purposely ate so much that it was easy for me to get nauseous.

"Ashira, could you come to the bathroom with me?"

"Sure, what's wrong?"

"I don't feel so good. I think I overate."

We proceeded to the bathroom. Once in the stall, I self-induced vomiting which lasted a moment or two. It was enough for Ashira to hear it and for me to have an excuse to go back to the room by myself.

"Do you feel better now?" Ashira asked with concern in her voice.

"Somewhat. I need to splash some water on my face."

"Are you able to go back to the dining hall and join the guys?"

"No, not now. Please tell Daniel that I'm okay. I just want to sleep for a little while so I'll be good for dinner later."

"That makes sense, but are you sure you want to be alone?"

"Yes, thank you, Ashira."

Once in the room, I immediately brushed my teeth to get the vomit taste out of my mouth and then dialed down to the spa.

"Day Spa," a perky female voice answered.

"Hi, could I speak to one of your masseuses?"

"Who do you want to speak to?"

"His name is Fernando."

"Is there a problem?"

"No. I had a massage yesterday and I wanted to ask him about some products he suggested I buy."

Wow! I was becoming an expert liar!

"I can help you with that. Which ones are you interested in?"

"Thank you, but he was giving me some specific information that I need to speak to him directly about."

"Okay, hold on please."

I thought that was quite convincing as to why I wanted to speak to Fernando.

"He's in with a client right now. Would you like to leave a message?"

I didn't know what to do at that moment. What if he called back when Daniel was in the room? I had to think fast.

"Please tell him exactly what I told you and that I will be in my cabin, #271 for the next hour and a half. Remind him that my name is Evie. Thank you."

I felt a tiny twinge of guilt but waved it away. What if he didn't call in time? I sat down on the bed and stared at the phone.

CHAPTER 6

Since I had to work much later than usual, I was so glad that Bill gave me a half hour break that Thursday evening. I stepped outside and took a long walk. The fresh night air cleared my head and invigorated me. I returned to my office building and chose to take the stairs instead of the escalator. Ascending the staircase, I began to hear what sounded like moaning from the upper hallway. It did not take long for me to realize that the more steps I climbed, the louder the sounds became. It was apparent that some sort of sexual activity was going on.

I should have turned around and walked down an extra flight. In that way, I would have been able to take the elevator back up to my office and avoided whatever was taking place in the stairwell. I chose the latter and it was evidently the wrong choice.

Once I arrived at the landing, I saw two men. One was standing and the other was kneeling in front of him. I should have been able to easily pass them by and arrive at my floor within a minute or two. However, that didn't happen. I began to stare at the man who was standing. I had seen him several times before while riding the escalator. As I was trying to place him, he gave me a very odd look. Was he upset that I was there or just distracted by me? He was dressed in business attire and sported a silver power tie. His curly gray hair covered a small tattoo above his right ear. The other man, who paid no attention to me at all, was dressed casually. He was very handsome with long, wavy blonde hair and a two days growth of beard. I guess "sexy" described him best.

Finally realizing that I shouldn't have lingered, I stepped up my pace. As I was walking away, sounds of footsteps made me frantic. Unfortunately, as I tried to run away, I panicked and froze instead.

"Hey!" One of them shouted.

The "suit" caught up with me, grabbed my shoulders and quickly turned me around. My heart was racing and my throat became dry. I was praying I'd faint but wasn't so lucky. He held onto my arms with a vise-like grip and whispered into my ear.

"Listen, Bitch, you didn't see anything and you better not say anything. Got it?"

His voice was so gruff and his breath smelled of coffee and cigarettes. I was so scared that I wasn't able to answer him. He misunderstood that for not willing to cooperate, so he began to shake me and repeated his threat.

"Answer me, Bitch, or do I have to make myself clearer to you?"

As I started nodding my head up and down in agreement, the other man ran over and pulled the "suit" off of me.

"Leave her alone. It's no big deal and I don't care who sees us. Let's get back to what's really important."

He let me go and I ran up the rest of the steps. I flew into my office and ran directly towards Bill.

"Oh my G-D, oh my G-D," I said breathlessly.

"What's wrong, Evie? You look scared! What happened?"

I so desperately wanted to tell him. I caught myself before spilling my guts and risking that man's ire. I quickly composed myself.

"Some guy tried to grab my purse and I made a run for it. I'm just a little out of breath."

Bill stared at me with that knowing look that said I was not being totally truthful.

"Do you want me to call the police?"

"No! I can't even describe him. It happened so fast. There's nothing they can do anyway."

"I'll be right back," Bill said.

Where was he going? Here I was in obvious distress, and he leaves the room?

A moment later, Bill returned with a large cup of ice water and handed it to me. I gulped it down in seconds.

"Do you need anything else?" he asked.

I looked directly at him and said, "Yes."

I fell into his arms and told him I needed a hug and some reassurance that I was safe. He was clearly uncomfortable and did not return the gesture. The situation was awkward, to say the least, so I moved away from him.

"Wow! I didn't mean to do that. I'm just a bit shaken up," I said with nervous laughter.

Bill took a moment to answer, and then said, "It's normal to feel this way after an incident like that."

He let me off the hook gently. Highly embarrassed, I apologized again and quickly went over to my desk. Thankfully no one else was in the office at that moment.

A few minutes later, Bill approached me and said, "It's time for you to go home. It'll probably be hard for you to concentrate anymore tonight."

I knew he was both angry and embarrassed. He had no empathy or understanding of what had just happened. Then again, I didn't tell him the truth. But still, he knew something had occurred that really upset me.

"I can't leave just now. I'm too nervous and need a few minutes."

He looked through me as if I wasn't even there and said, "No problem, but you should catch your breath and try to calm down."

No problem? Was he kidding? He didn't even offer to walk me to the lobby. What an ass! I wasn't fully together nor composed but did leave the office. It was a short sprint to the escalator. I was glad to see other people going about their daily routines, but still felt uneasy. I guess I was still shaken.

And then there he was!

I couldn't believe that Ben was standing in the lobby! I became so rattled that I almost lost my balance on the escalator.

He did have interest after all! Hooray for me! But then I started thinking that it was almost 8:00 PM, three hours later than when we originally met. Had he been standing there all this time, hoping to meet me again? Wouldn't I have seen him earlier when I took my break? Okay, Evie, enough of this nonsense.

Here I go!

I stepped off the escalator. Since I was still in business attire, I felt good about myself. I quickly opened my pocketbook and put a piece of gum in my mouth. Who wanted bad breath at a moment like this?

I was almost next to Ben when he turned his head in the opposite direction. Startled, I stopped immediately, almost tripping the person behind me. All of a sudden, a beautiful woman appeared and ran into his arms. They hugged for almost two minutes, clearly longer than necessary. I moved closer to one of the kiosks in the building and picked up a fashion magazine. I pretended to be reading it but was actually looking at the two of them. They spoke for a few minutes and then walked to the exit doors.

"Can this day get any worse?" I asked myself out loud.

It was time to leave the building and head out since I did not want to call any more attention to myself.

The evening air felt good. It was a little colder than when I took a walk earlier, but not enough to put a chill in your bones. My decision was not to go to Mom & Pop's. There were many fast food joints and a few small cafes in the area. Going out for dinner seemed like a great idea since I would be around a lot of people.

•

So, there I was on a cruise ship, alone in my cabin, with sexual fantasies twirling around in my head. There was a quick knock on the door which broke the spell. As I opened the door, Fernando stood there with a yellow rose in his hand. He quickly entered and presented the flower to me. I barely had time to accept it when he whisked me around and started fondling my breasts. He then kissed the back of my neck in very slow and passionate movements. There was no doubt that I was turned on but felt a few moments of conversation would have been nice also.

My body was experiencing sensations I never knew existed. He kissed every part of me in almost a teasing manner. Every time I moaned out in pleasure, his fingers would immediately move elsewhere to heighten the experience. His touch was firm yet gentle, and every moment was tantalizing. Fernando was definitely in control, and I wasn't complaining! I tried to keep my voice as low as possible, but the passion was so high that I lost control most of the time. When he slowly caressed my thighs with his tongue, I thought I had gone to heaven. He was a master at lovemaking, but in particular at pleasing me. Fernando edged his way to my inner thighs and then the stars illuminated in the sky with all sorts of fireworks going off. I had never experienced an orgasm that strong, that fabulous, and that satisfying before!

"Thank you so much!" was all that I could think to say.

"Ha, ha," Fernando laughed and I also began to laugh.

"That was beyond spectacular! Too bad the cruise will be over tomorrow. To be honest, I could do this with you all day long," I said.

"Ha, ha, you are a very special lady. I'm glad I could please you. Would you like to join me for dinner tonight?"

And then reality set in. Fernando must have seen that I began to feel uneasy. I lowered my head and told him that I wasn't free to do that. After explaining my situation, he became very angry and quickly dressed.

"You are here with your almost-husband? You should have told me immediately! Do you realize that I could lose my job over this? What's wrong with you?"

His voice was so loud and angry that I started to cry.

"Don't play the crying game for me! I don't like being scammed. If you would have told me this in the beginning, I would have had a choice in my decision-making. At least then I would have known all the facts," Fernando said as he quickly dressed back into his uniform.

Fernando then picked up the rose and ground it into the carpet with his foot. I sat there totally in shock. What was so beautiful a moment ago became so ugly. He turned to leave the stateroom when I heard the key card being swiped.

With all this commotion, I forgot that I was sitting on the bed stark naked. And of course, Daniel walked in!

"Are you okay, E...?"

The shocked look on Daniel's face was unbelievable. It took him a couple of seconds to comprehend the situation before he continued to speak.

"What the hell is going on here?"

I just sat there and stared at Daniel. The scene was frightening and I hoped it would not get violent.

"She didn't tell me she was engaged until a moment ago. You can have that bitch!" Fernando said and quickly exited the room.

"Holy shit! You're fucking the help! What the fuck is wrong with you?" Daniel yelled at the top of his lungs.

He began pacing and flailing his arms as he continued to curse and yell at me. To say Daniel was angry and in shock was an understatement. I had never heard him curse before, nor raise his voice. His face turned deep red with anger and I thought his head was going to explode!

CHAPTER 7

What an evening! After being harassed by that guy in the stairwell and seeing Ben with that woman in the lobby of my office building, I needed a nice dinner to relax and unwind.

I entered Pompidou. It was a small, quaint restaurant with four tables in the front and a large table by the window towards the back. Next to the window was a small alcove with a table for two, otherwise known as "Table Romantica." Every time I had dinner at Pompidou, there was always a new couple smooching at that table.

The hostess was standing by the cash register chatting with one of the waiters. When she turned around and saw me, she immediately came over and greeted me with a warm smile. Just as I was starting to feel better about things, she asked, "Will someone be joining you?"

I wanted to shout at the top of my lungs with a resounding, "No!"

However, in a meek voice, I said, "It's just me tonight."

As luck would have it, all the regular tables were taken, so she escorted me to "Table Romantica." I guess I'll be making out with myself tonight, I thought. The hostess handed me the food menu along with an extensive wine list, which she placed on the glass-covered table.

"Do you need a few minutes or are you ready to order?"

"I need a few minutes, thank you."

She picked up the other place setting and said, "I'll send your server over shortly," and then promptly left.

I began to look at the wine list, which was quite familiar since I've eaten there many times before. This was a place I've always loved. They know you, yet they don't know you. It fits the bill. And then it happened ...

Ben walked in!

He strutted in with the same woman I had seen him hugging in the lobby of my office building earlier. They were immediately seated at a table that had just been vacated. Although Ben sat down with his back to me, his date was in full view. I kept taking tiny peeks at her, hoping that she would not notice my interest in her.

She had that fresh look every woman wanted. Her brown hair with red highlights fit her skin coloring perfectly. She had on makeup, but not too much. Her lips were painted with the nicest shade of mauve. She was dressed a little flamboyantly for my taste, but it worked for her.

The waitress came over and broke my concentration as she asked for my order.

"I'd like to start with a white wine spritzer. I'll order food in a few minutes," I said.

She brought over the wine almost immediately which made me very happy. However, I couldn't stop looking at Ben's "friend." I was jealous and mesmerized by her but wasn't clear as to why. I didn't even know this guy yet felt very possessive of him. How silly my thinking was!

After a few minutes, she noticed my stares and looked back at me questioningly. I lowered my gaze immediately and grabbed the stem of my glass. I began to drink my wine in quick successive sips, and then quickly drained the glass.

The waitress came back and I was so relieved. I gave her my order and handed her the menu. Clasping my hands in front of my face, I tried to think of what to do. Continuously staring at Ben and his date was stressful. It was also obvious and served no purpose. Then it came to me! If I continued to stare, maybe she would mention it to Ben. That would lead him to turn around and hopefully approach me! I would remind him of how we met and then he would ask me to join them. What a fabulous idea! Well, at least I thought it was.

My meal arrived just at that moment. My thoughts were to eat a little bit first and then put my plan into action. The chicken was excellent, although the large oval plate was scant on vegetables since most of it was decorative garnish. After putting the last piece of chicken in my mouth, I looked up again.

They were gone!

 What happened?

"Where did they go? I can't believe they're gone!" I blurted out loud.

I noticed that some of the other diners turned around after hearing me, so I lowered my eyes. Aggravated, I was ready to go home.

While standing on the sidewalk, I decided to hail a cab. I didn't want to spend the extra cash, but after thinking about the evening's events, it was the prudent thing to do. Usually, the streets are saturated with yellow cabs looking for a fare. I waited over 15 minutes until the first one appeared. I raised my hand to flag it down, but it passed me by, already occupied.

I began to feel restless. The entire evening did not go well for me. I didn't want to have a pity party for myself, but it was surely beginning to feel that way. Two more cabs passed by. The only thing I wanted was to simply get home and feel the comfort of my own apartment, my familiar and safe space. That wasn't asking too much I thought, but apparently, it was.

"This is bullshit!" I shouted out loud.

I turned to see if anyone walking by was staring at me.

"Nothing is going right for me tonight! How much bad luck can a girl have in one night?" I continued to bellow.

Feeling embarrassed, I realized that I needed to compose myself. My cheeks started to flush and I felt a little light-headed. Maybe a drink would help, just a glass of wine or maybe two.

I changed my mind about going home and walked the two blocks to Jerry's Bar & Grill. There weren't many people there yet. After a few minutes, a boisterous birthday crowd walked in. Getting lost in a large group with lots of noise was perfect. In that way, I would blend in with everyone and no one would notice me.

Anonymous me! Just the way I wanted it for the rest of the night.

I sat down on a wooden stool at the end of the bar. The bartender was busy slicing lemons. I always liked their fresh smell. There is something so pure about lemons.

"What'll you have?" the bartender asked.

"A white wine will do, thanks."

I finished about half of my drink when two young women entered the bar. One of them looked familiar but I couldn't place her. Sometimes faces blend together to form someone you know or would like to be closer to. It's a picture of familiarity you develop in your mind that doesn't really exist.

The women sat down at the bar and ordered their drinks. For whatever reason, they attracted my attention. I watched them and played a little game in my mind called "How long will it take before someone hits on them?" It wasn't as if I had anything else to do at that moment. Besides, it was a good distraction considering the day I had. My guess was that it would only take five minutes before someone would approach them.

They both looked as if they were in their early twenties. The taller of the two wasn't very attractive, yet she did have striking green eyes. Her nose was a little too large for her face. Mostly it was her large nostrils that seemed out of place. Her lips were pouty which made up for her nose. I changed my mind and decided that she was nice-looking. After all, her long, dirty blonde hair with one long red extension seemed to fit her overall look. She was dressed in black leggings with short red boots. Her tunic type top revealed some cleavage, just enough to get your attention.

Her friend was shorter and a little more rotund. She also had blonde hair, but hers was cut rather short with long bangs covering parts of her eyes. I never understood that. Why would you want to obstruct part of your vision? I guess style is more important than comfort to some people.

I finished my wine and was contemplating ordering another glass when I noticed two handsome guys approaching them. The conversation lasted only a few minutes and then the men went back to their respective tables. I was trying to figure out if the women were just not into these men or if they already had boyfriends. I didn't want to leave the bar since it was getting interesting, so I ordered another glass of wine. I gave each of them an identifying name; "Red" for the taller one and "Blondie" for the other.

The bartender also seemed interested in them. He was attentive and personable. Every chance he had, he would talk to them, especially "Red."

Watching people interact with each other has always been interesting to me. It's like being a fly on the wall. This scenario gave me a surge of power. Seeing it unfold made me feel as though I was part of it.

What a great feeling!

A few more customers came in. Some settled at the bar while others sat down at the rustic wooden tables. No one seemed very colorful or interesting, so I brought my attention back to "Red" and "Blondie."

The bartender seemed to be making some headway with "Red." Their body language suggested to me that there was definite interest on both their parts. Just as that thought entered my mind, I saw "Red" pass him a small business card. At least that was what it looked like. Score 1 for the bartender, zero for the two guys at the table.

The fun ended and I realized it was time to leave Jerry's Bar & Grill and head home. Tomorrow was a workday and it was already past 11:00 PM.

•

The cruise couldn't have gone any more downhill than it already had.

"Stop yelling at me, Daniel!" I screamed back.

"Are you kidding me? I was worried about you and came to see if you needed any help. Now everything is beginning to make sense. How many times have you cheated on me, Evie? Let me guess: ten, twenty, a hundred?" Daniel yelled.

"This is the first time, but I wanted to do it before," I said in a low matter of fact tone.

Then I began to cry so profusely that not only were tears streaming down my face, but my nose was running and it became difficult for me to breathe. I then started to become light-headed which frightened me.

"I don't feel good, Daniel! Please get me some water. I'm not sure but I think I'm getting an anxiety attack."

"You must think that I'm even stupider than I am. You got caught and now you want to play the, 'I'm not feeling good' card. Just get dressed and get out of my sight. I'll think of something to say to Troy and Ashira."

"Please, Daniel! I'm begging you! This is not a charade. I can't get out of bed. Please call the ship doctor."

My skin color became very pale and my entire body began to convulse. It was at that moment that Daniel realized I was not faking it.

"Okay, try to relax. I'll call the doctor."

Finally, Daniel's rage began to dissipate.

"Oh yeah, and pull the bedsheet over yourself since we've all already seen the goods," he added.

There was a knock on the door a few minutes later and Dr. Kinnemon entered the room. He did not need to ask who the patient was. It was quite clear.

"Can you lie down?" he asked me.

"No, I can't. Why?"

"I need to examine you, but it seems you're having an anxiety attack. Please relax as much as possible. This will pass in a few minutes."

Two aides came in with Dr. Kinnemon. One of them proceeded to take my blood pressure, while the other began to massage my arms. She then put a cold compress on my forehead.

I started to calm down just by the fact that someone else was in the room.

Dr. Kinnemon reached into his black bag and pulled out a small plastic vial.

"Place these two tablets under your tongue. You should begin to feel better in a few minutes."

Dr. Kinnemon was correct. The pills took effect almost immediately, and I began to feel more like myself again.

"Just relax and come to see me tomorrow morning. You should be fine for the rest of the evening. I'm going to leave two pills with you. Don't take them unless you get another anxiety attack. I'll see you in the morning."

"Thank you, Doctor," I said meekly.

With all this turmoil, I didn't realize that Daniel had left the room. He wasn't so nice after all!

The anxiety attack passed. If Daniel had truly cared about me, he would not have left the cabin until he saw that I was alright. So maybe this was meant to be. But then again, what was I expecting from him? After all, I was the one who cheated!

End of story!

Being by myself in the room was a comfort of sorts. It was a good time to take a shower. The warm water was soothing and just what I needed. Afterward, I got dressed and then grabbed my purse and room key. Now I was the angry one. It was time to confront the situation and get everything out into the open. I didn't care anymore as to what Troy and Ashira would think and definitely didn't give a damn as to what Daniel thought.

The first thing I did was to go downstairs to the spa. I walked over to the receptionist and asked if Fernando was still there.

"He's just about to finish with his last client for the day. Do you want to leave a message for him?" the receptionist asked.

"Thank you, but I need to speak to him in person. I'll just wait."

"No problem. He'll be out soon."

I reached into my purse and took out five $20.00 bills. I inserted them in one of the tip envelopes that were on the receptionist's desk. I wrote, "FOR A JOB WELL DONE!" on the envelope and sealed it.

Seven minutes later, I saw Fernando walking towards the reception room. The moment he saw me, he lowered his head. I knew that he was still angry but understood that he would contain his emotions as he didn't want to lose his job.

"Hello, Fernando. I forgot to give you a tip for the massage you gave me the other day."

I placed the envelope in his hands and promptly left, not giving him a chance to embarrass either one of us.

I left elated and hoped that this would make up for what had happened. It was a small token to show that I was sorry for being dishonest with him. My next stop was to find Daniel or Troy and Ashira. It didn't matter to me whom I saw first. I needed to cleanse myself of all this anger towards Daniel and begin a new chapter in my life.

CHAPTER 8

I awoke with sunlight staring me straight in the eye. I shouldn't have stayed out so late at Jerry's Bar & Grill the night before. I didn't want to begin the day with negative energy and give Bill a reason to be upset with me.

Having overslept, there was no chance of making it to the office on time. I wanted those extra few minutes to lie in bed with my eyes closed. Those are the best moments before the day starts.

A shower and breakfast were out of the question.

"This would have to happen to me today of all days," I said to myself.

I really wanted a long, calming shower to soothe me. However, it was my fault that I couldn't take one.

Scrambling around, I pulled out a sweater from one of my drawers and a gabardine pair of pants from my closet. I jumped into them and then grabbed my purse.

During the bus ride, I thought about not taking that shower. I had a packet of wet wipes in my pocketbook. My coffee break would be the perfect time to use them on my privates. I began to feel much better.

The workday was humdrum, but thankfully busy, so the time went by quickly.

"You did a lot of catching up so far, and your work has been excellent, Evie. We should be up to speed by tomorrow," Bill said.

I guess that was his way of making amends for his poor behavior from the day before.

"Thanks," I said in a semi-jovial voice. I didn't want to give away my hurt feelings.

It was 7:30 PM when Bill told me to wrap it up and call it a day. I was one of the few lucky ones who didn't have to work more overtime that night.

Again, I started my routine of going to Mom & Pop's to pick up some dinner that I could nuke at home. I remembered that an expensive bottle of Bordeaux was stashed in the back of my bottom kitchen cabinet. A glass of wine with dinner would work well for me. Maybe I would have another one later in front of the TV. I couldn't wait to get home.

❖

While opening the bottle of Bordeaux, thoughts of my mother came to me. One winter, she bought a duck to serve for dinner. It had to be a special occasion because duck was expensive. It was just the four of us, but money was tight. My father had been out of work for a while and this fine bird would be just the thing to lift his spirits.

But it was not meant to be. My mother wanted to wait a while before serving us that succulent duck. She couldn't bring herself to cook it. It felt too extravagant for her. She didn't feel worthy.

Time passed and she finally decided to roast the duck. It had been kept in the freezer part of an old refrigerator that stood in our unfinished basement.

Unbeknownst to my mom, or anyone else in the household, the refrigerator had stopped working. This probably happened about a month prior to this unexpected discovery. When she finally opened the refrigerator door, an awful stench wafted out.

The duck was completely spoiled and had to be thrown away. My mother was horrified. She didn't say anything, but the look on her face said it all.

I felt so bad for my mother. I didn't care about some silly old duck. It probably would have tasted like chicken anyway.

Why didn't I remind Mommy that she needed to check on the duck? Why didn't I try to help out?

"I'm sorry, Mommy," I said softly to myself, too many years later when it didn't count anymore.

I'm not worthy!

But Mommy, you were always worthy.

After thinking about my parents, I started to feel restless again, so I turned on the TV. I began channel surfing, but nothing

appealed to me. I was about to turn the TV off and call it a night when I spotted someone familiar on one of the local channels.

Oh my goodness! It was the woman I had seen with Ben! I only caught the end of the segment, but it was definitely her. It seemed that she was hawking a skin cream product on an infomercial I hadn't seen before.

I quickly turned off the TV and angrily threw down the remote. To add insult to injury, not only was she beautiful, but also successful and on TV to boot!

"I HATE HER!" I screamed at the top of my lungs.

●

As I ran around the top deck of the cruise ship, I finally spotted Ashira. She was sipping a cocktail and chatting with the couple next to her.

"Hi Ashira, where's Troy?" I asked her.

"Well hello to you too! I don't know exactly where he is, but he's somewhere with Daniel. Why? What's up?"

"I need to talk to you in private. Can we move to that table over there?"

"What's the rush? I'm speaking to these fine people over here. Evie, meet … sorry, I forgot your names, ha, ha."

"This is serious, Ashira! Take your drink with you and let's move over to the empty table."

Ashira looked at me rather quizzically.

"This must be important. Okay, let's go over there."

"I don't know how else to say this, so I'm just going to say it exactly as it happened. And I'm only going to say it once. Daniel and I are over, totally finished!"

I thought Ashira's eyes were going to come out of her head. Her shock was so evident that I almost laughed at how ludicrous her bulging eyes looked.

"What are you talking about?" Ashira asked.

"I cheated on Daniel and I'm not sorry for it! It had to happen sometime, and that sometime happened today! Oh yeah, and it happened yesterday too."

"I still don't understand what you're saying," Ashira remarked.

"I cheated with the masseuse and it was great! Daniel walked in on us and he became unhinged."

"Wow! What did you expect? Did you want him to join you?"

"That's very funny, Ashira. I knew that Daniel and I were not going to last and I seized the moment, so to speak. Opportunity came knocking, and I opened the door."

"That's not all you opened, ha, ha."

"This is not meant to be a comedy show. I'm telling you this because I need a big favor from you."

"What is it?" Ashira asked.

"Will you guys share your stateroom with me tonight? It's going to be impossible for me to be in the same room as Daniel. We leave tomorrow so it's just for one night," I begged.

"It's okay with me as long as it's okay with Troy."

I saw a waiter walking in our direction holding a tray of assorted drinks. It was just what I needed at that moment.

"There's a drink with my name on it. I'll be right back, Ashira."

As soon as the drink was handed to me, I swigged it down and then asked for another. The waiter hesitated, but then handed me a second one. I walked back to where Ashira was sitting and grabbed a lounge chair.

"Do you want to talk about it anymore?" she asked.

"There's no more to tell. Do you really love Troy?" I asked her in order to change the subject.

"Of course I do! What a ridiculous question to ask me!"

"I didn't mean to insult you. It's just that if you weren't that into him, you might have done just what I did."

"I would never do anything like that! Why didn't you just break it off with him and be done with it?" Ashira asked.

"It's not as easy as you may think. It was a good relationship at first, but it just got boring along the way. Daniel is a good guy, but we just aren't right for each other. You see …"

In the midst of me speaking, Ashira began waving her arms and I knew Troy and Daniel were in view. Hopefully, this was going to be quick and painless but somehow I doubted it.

•

My blanket is lying crumpled on the floor. As I pick it up to wrap around myself, I notice dust balls attached to the corners along with some of my hair that had fallen out. My hair used to be thick with a bounce to it when I walked. It was long and healthy hair; the opposite of what I have now. That thought depressed me, so I just waved it away.

I began to stare at the clutter strewn throughout the apartment. There was some mold on the top and bottom corner of the living room wall. That started me thinking about my bathroom. I walked towards it, stood there and stared. I had been meaning to clean the mold on the shower walls and ceiling for a while. The mold had spread into the grout that surrounded the white tiles. It cast a shadow on the tiles which in turn gave them a grayish look. I knew that this problem had to be attended to soon.

I'll get to it shortly, I thought. Who was I kidding? I knew I wouldn't.

I walked into the living room and lied down on the couch. I tossed and turned for most of the night and couldn't fall asleep for more than a few minutes at a time. Finally, I gave up and went to the kitchen, poured myself a glass of water and placed a slice of orange in it. It was still dark outside.

Apparently, I'm not the only one who can't sleep right now. My neighbor who lives across the way from me also has his lights on. I've never met him, but whenever I catch a glimpse of him walking by his window, it always reminds me of my first apartment in Manhattan.

At that time, I was in my early twenties and living in Alphabet City. Whenever I would stand at the kitchen sink, I could see everything that my then neighbor, Ray was doing. He didn't have any shades covering his windows, which gave me a perfect view into his bedroom. Well, it wasn't really Ray's bedroom, but his living room where he chose to put his bed and TV.

Each time Ray saw me looking at him through the window, he would quickly move away. I did the same thing, except when I didn't. It was embarrassing, but we did this dance constantly.

I would concoct this ritual every night by walking to the kitchen window at 11:00 PM, with the purpose of wanting to see what Ray was up to. His light would be on as usual. However, this one particular time, he must have had a dimmer on his lamp as the room was not as bright as usual. He was definitely in his bed because I could see the covers moving. I was never sure of what was going on beneath those covers. There was too much bouncing for me to continue to watch!

Sometimes I wondered how old Ray was. He looked to be around 65 or maybe older, but I wasn't sure. We've always had nice conversations in the entry hall of our building and sometimes we would chat by our mailboxes. Seeing him up close made me think he must have been very good-looking when he was younger. He seemed to be the type to have had his fair share of women. I always wondered if he had been married since he never spoke about his private life until …

One rainy day as I was walking into my building, barely holding on to three heavy bags of groceries, I saw Ray standing with a friend. They were laughing and having what seemed to be a merry time. As I got closer, Ray greeted me and introduced me to his buddy, Joe.

"Nice to meet you," I said and continued walking towards the elevator.

"Wait a second, Evie. Do you want help with the bags?" Ray asked.

"Sure, thanks."

Ray took two of the bags from me and held them in his arms. His friend was ready to leave and so they said their goodbyes.

"Something smells good. What's in the bag, Evie?"

"I bought some eggplant parmigiana and pasta from Mom & Pop's, along with other items to hold me for the rest of the week."

"You know, Evie, I just realized that I never invited you over for a cup of coffee. I've been meaning to ask you, but things always get in the way."

"Maybe another time since all these perishables need to be refrigerated," I responded.

"Do an old man and neighbor a favor. Let's just have a cup of coffee and some conversation."

At that point, I couldn't refuse Ray. It was quite a stretch from a few random conversations to asking me to his apartment for coffee.

"Okay, why not?" I said with some enthusiasm in my voice.

I would have preferred to go to my place, but he seemed so needy at that moment. Even needier than I was at the time!

Entering his apartment was surreal. It was devoid of all furniture except for a very small kitchen table with two chairs. The living room consisted of a recliner, his bed and a very large TV. There were no pictures on the walls and no knickknacks of any kind. The apartment was so sparse that it was almost eerie to be in there. Maybe that was why he seemed a little strange to me at times. Who knows?

"Do you want espresso or regular coffee, Evie?"

"Regular is good for me, thanks."

Ray placed a bowl on the kitchen table and filled it with a freshly opened box of chocolate chip cookies. He then put two mugs on the table and filled each with the best smelling coffee. He sat down on the chair opposite me and began to speak.

"I've wanted to talk to you for a long time, but I didn't want to impose myself on you. You seem like a caring person. When you mentioned the eggplant parmigiana, I knew it was a sign that we should share some coffee and have a nice conversation, like neighbors do."

I realized at that moment that Ray was lonely and all he was looking for was some company, and maybe someone to listen to him. But it was odd to me that he would use eggplant parmigiana as an excuse.

"What would you like to talk about, Ray?"

"You know that I was married once, right?"

"All I know is that you live alone, at least I think you do. I don't know anything else about you."

"Well, I got married a very long time ago. Let me tell you a little story. I grew up in Romania. When I was 22 years old, I realized how difficult it was for my parents to make ends meet. So, it was time to find full-time work. Wherever I went, the door was shut in my face. One day I met a group of young men who were in the same position as me. They were friendly to a point. All they talked about was going to America, the land of opportunity. I kept listening to them speak until I began to believe everything they said. We decided to go to California together. In that way, we would be able to pool all our money and live in one apartment until we got squared away. I was so naïve!"

"So, what happened?"

"Upon arriving in America, I immediately changed my name from Radu to Ray, thinking it would help me along the way. The rest of the guys did the same. We got a basement apartment that was filled with roaches and leftover cigar smoke. No one complained because we knew it was only temporary. The problem was that none of us knew English very well. We took on menial jobs which meant extremely low pay. It didn't take long for us to realize that we couldn't make it."

"What happened next?" I asked.

"We began to argue constantly, and it was clear that we had to part. It was at that time that my cousin Augusto contacted me. He was living in a large house in Sorrento, Italy. I told him my life story, and so he asked me to relocate to Sorrento and move into his home since he had a large house with many rooms. Augusto ran a large wine and cheese shop there, which was doing well. He said that if I wanted to, I could start working for him immediately. The best part was that I didn't have to pay any rent until I got on my feet."

"How could you refuse such a generous offer?" I asked Ray.

"Exactly! It was as though an angel had come down from heaven at the right time."

"Go on, this is very interesting."

"Everything was going great for about two months. Every day was the same as the one before until this young woman came in to buy some cheese and two bottles of wine. The minute I laid eyes on her it was clear that she was going to be my wife."

"What happened to her?"

"It's a complicated story, but this is basically how it played out. Her name was Angelina and she was truly a vision to me. She was a few inches taller and weighed a little more than I did. That didn't matter to me because she was the most beautiful woman I had ever seen. I couldn't wait until she would come into the store next. Before I knew it, she was visiting the store every other day. Soon after, it became a daily routine for her and so it was clear that she liked me too. I would always put a little extra cheese in her order but never charged her for it. I told Augusto to take it out of my pay, but he never did."

"How did you finally break the ice?"

"One day she came in wearing a white dress dotted with green and yellow flowers. Attached to the collar of her dress was a small red pin in the shape of a heart. I couldn't stop looking at the pin and took it as a sign to make my move. Luckily, there was no one else in the store at the time. I wrote my name on the same paper bag that I put her wine and cheese in along with, "Will you go out with me?"

"Why aren't you with her now? Um, is she still living in Italy?"

I knew that question shouldn't have been asked, but the words just came out of my mouth.

Ray paused and seemed to have drifted off into a time gone by. He placed his hands on his face and began to wail like a baby. I didn't know what to do, so I started munching on a cookie as I waited for him to compose himself.

"I'm so sorry! I didn't mean to break down in front of you like this. It's just that this story doesn't have a happy ending and I'm still so in love with Angelina!"

His crying made it impossible for me to continue to listen to his sob story. He's not the first person who loved and lost and he's not going to be the last. I didn't feel pity or empathy for him. I just wanted to get out of there and so I stood up and began to speak.

"Sorry Ray, I have to go now."

"Please, please, let me just finish the story. I'm almost done and then I won't bother you again," he pleaded.

"Okay, but I need to get to my apartment."

I knew that I was being a little curt but listening to Ray's problems was becoming exhausting. I had enough of my own to deal with.

"It will only take another few minutes."

He got up and grabbed a box of tissues, wiped his face and then blew his nose. This irritated me, and I did all I could to continue sitting on the chair. Ray then continued his saga.

"Angelina looked at the bag and gave me the most beautiful smile I had ever seen. We started to go out and everything was great. Whenever she would cook for me, it was usually eggplant parmigiana. She made it in such a special way, that I always looked forward to it. Each time I saw her, my heart would race. To my cousin Augusto, she was average looking. He said that she seemed nice, but that she had a few pockmarks on her face and that her hair was too short. He also felt that she would be good to bring home to your mother, but that I would have to have girlfriends on the side in order to be pleased the way a man should be. I never responded to him because I owed him so much."

•

The waters became a little turbulent, and the cruise ship began rocking back and forth. It wasn't scary, but it wasn't pleasant either.

Daniel saw me and immediately walked away. Troy cocked his head slightly so he wouldn't have to make eye contact with me. Daniel obviously told him what had transpired between us, so it must have made Troy nervous to be around me. Thankfully, Ashira broke the ice.

"Are you ready for dinner yet, Troy?"

"Yes, let's go right now so we won't be late for the show tonight," he responded.

I gathered up all my courage and spoke up for myself.

"I know that this must be awkward for you Troy, but I'm not asking you to choose sides. This has nothing to do with you.

We're both at the same dining table on this cruise, but if you prefer, I'll take the later seating."

"Daniel is my friend and he is really hurting right now. I don't want to be rude to you but it's going to be an unhappy situation for all of us to be at the dinner table together."

"I thought you just said that you didn't want to be rude, Troy. Well rude you are!"

Not waiting for a response, I walked away quickly and headed for the bar. Two red wines and a few handfuls of pretzels later, it was almost nine o'clock. I had to get to the dining room soon or else there would be no dinner for me. Although food was always available on the ship, it was my last night and I wanted it to be enjoyable with a sit-down meal. I grabbed my bag and headed in the direction of the dining hall. I sat at an open table with strangers. At first, it was uncomfortable, until the person across from me ordered champagne for the whole table. It turned out to be the most relaxing dinner of the vacation. To hell with Daniel and his friend Troy!

To hell with them all!

•

Today is Wednesday. I move toward the window of my apartment and peer through the pane of glass. It's raining lightly outside. Everything looks the same, except this time there is a sea of brightly colored umbrellas to view.

As usual, I wanted to go outside, but couldn't bring myself to do it.

Again, it was difficult for me to function. It's been like this almost every day for the last six months. I need to make changes and live my life.

•

I hurried back to the ship's bar area. The background music was lively and continued to elevate my good mood.

"A white wine, please."

The bartender placed a blue napkin in front of me and then poured the wine into a glass. I became lost in thought and played out the past year of my life. Everything was going relatively well for me. I was happy, my job seemed secure, and then I met Daniel. It was easy being with him, but I needed a guy with more of an edge. It may have seemed like I didn't appreciate the gem Daniel was, but truth be told, I was just not into him.

"Are you ok, Miss?" the bartender asked.

"Yes, I'm fine."

I began to sip my wine and tried to think of something else besides Daniel.

"Is this seat taken?" came a sexy voice out of nowhere.

Was I dreaming or was this real?

"Fernando! What are you doing here?"

"I can't leave the ship until it docks, ha, ha," he responded.

"I mean, why are you here right next to me? I thought you hated me."

"I have to apologize to you as I didn't handle the situation well. It made me very uncomfortable, mostly because you're engaged. I'm not that kind of guy."

"No worries now. I'm not engaged anymore. Not only that, I hope the ship has an available room for me tonight. I don't want to spend the last night in the cabin with my now ex and I'm sure the feeling is mutual. Actually, I should look into it now."

"Wait! This may sound like a line, but it isn't. You can spend the night in my room if you want to. It's very small with only one bed if that works for you. I promise I won't touch you!"

"That's awesome Fernando! By the way, please promise you will touch me!"

Fernando kissed me ever so gently on my lips. It made me so hot.

He was still the master!

•

Either Ray didn't realize that I wanted to leave, or he was just ignoring me. Regardless, I continued listening to him.

"To me, Angelina was beautiful in every way. Whenever I was near her, it was truly heaven on earth. We dated for about three

months when I decided to propose. She said yes, but Angelina was old fashioned, so I had to ask her father for permission to marry her. He was put off at first because I had nothing material to offer his daughter, so he refused to give us his blessing. However, Angelina did not give up. Every day she told her father how well I treated her, which convinced him to finally accept me. We got married four months later. Since I didn't have a lot of money, my cousin gave us the most generous offer. He said that we could live in his house and just pay a small sum for the utilities as long as Angelina would cook dinner every night. We both agreed and were overjoyed with the plan. Angelina and I were very happy together for three and a half years. One day when I came home from the store, I noticed that Angelina did not look right. Something was wrong but I couldn't put my finger on it."

Ray paused for a moment to clear his throat which apparently had become dry. He got up and poured himself a glass of water. His breathing seemed labored and he broke out in a sweat on his forehead.

"Are you okay?" I asked him.

Ray continued speaking as if he didn't hear my question.

"Since that day, her attitude towards me slowly changed until she didn't want anything to do with me at all. Every time I tried to give her a small kiss on the cheek, she would push me away. She wouldn't talk to me and when she did, it was always an argument. This went on for a good month or two until I finally saw what was in front of me all along. Angelina was having an

affair with my cousin, Augusto. At first, I didn't want to believe it, but unfortunately, it was true. He was able to give her what I couldn't, all that money could buy. This wasn't just an affair, because he also fell in love with her. I became very distraught and depressed over the situation. Shortly after, I also found out that Angelina was pregnant. This was too much for me to bear, and so I was hospitalized with severe depression. When I finally started to come out of it, I was never the same. To this day I still don't know if that child is mine or my cousin's."

Ray placed his hands over his face and continued sobbing. It was so sad to see him that way and it became extremely uncomfortable for me. I did not know how to console him, so I just sat there and waited for his story to end.

"The saddest part in all of this was that Angelina thought she had the perfect life. Augusto treated her well in the beginning but refused to marry her. Angelina had all the money she wanted from him until she started to gain weight. Unfortunately for her, she liked her own cooking way too much. The weight gain disgusted Augusto. On top of that, he was very flirtatious and had continuous affairs. One day, a very pretty young woman caught his eye and his heart. Augusto told Angelina that he no longer was in love with her. Angelina tried everything she could to keep him interested, but nothing worked."

"Would you have taken her back if she wanted you again?"

"I would have taken her back no matter what. I had no pride or self-respect. What I had was a deep love for Angelina, or maybe it was just loneliness at that point."

"Is there an end to this story?" I said, thinking it would go on forever.

"Angelina committed suicide!"

"What!" I yelled out in complete shock.

I couldn't believe the words that just came out of Ray's mouth! My feelings of discomfort and boredom immediately changed to those of sadness and empathy.

"She threatened it many times and Augusto laughed in her face. Then she finally did it!"

"That's so sad. I'm so sorry for what happened to you and Angelina."

Ray looked at me as if to say, "Now do you understand?"

"I have to ask you, how do you know all of this information, Ray?"

"Surprisingly, Angelina's father was on my side. He couldn't believe how his daughter was behaving and that she could do what she did. I won't even repeat the names he called her. Every month I would receive a letter from him with an update on Angelina. Out of nowhere, the letters stopped coming. I didn't hear from him for six months. I even tried to call him, but he never picked up the phone. Not long after that, I received that horrible call from him. Angelina had jumped in front of a train shortly after she miscarried in the early part of her second pregnancy. She died immediately! Angelina's father adopted their only child since Augusto didn't want anything to do with him. Unfortunately, I never had the courage to tell Angelina's father that the child might be mine."

We both sat there numb for a few minutes. I got up and took my grocery bags. Ray helped me bring them to my apartment, but neither one of us spoke. I was really shaken and was reminded that it's not always about me. Other people have problems too.

What a revelation!

As Ray was about to walk away from my doorway, he spoke again.

"I needed to tell this story to someone and felt you were the right person, Evie."

He was waiting for some sort of acknowledgment from me, but I couldn't speak at that moment. A tear ran down my cheek and hopefully Ray didn't see that. Regardless, I knew that our casual friendship would never be the same.

•

Hopefully soon, I will finally be able to get myself out of my apartment. Maybe I will treat myself and buy a brightly colored umbrella like the ones I saw outside my window. Small steps lead to big steps.

I washed my face and began to brush my hair. My hairbrush is filled with clumps of tangled hair from many uses. There are so many gray hairs there now, which I never noticed before. How long has it been since I really paid attention to myself?

I have an unhealthy diet and rarely go to the doctor, even for checkups. I cannot stand doctors with their stark white offices and snotty receptionists. Well, maybe it's not them. Maybe I'm scared to find out that something is wrong with me that cannot be cured.

There is something wrong with me!

I have to be totally honest. I did see a psychologist named Dr. Megan Hunter. I used to go once a week to pour my heart out, hoping she would rid me of my demons. Things went well for a long time, but the demons reappeared. They are still here partying in my head.

I haven't seen Dr. Hunter in some time, and it's not doing me well. Although she was nice and listened intently when I spoke, she was way too lax. I didn't always listen to her suggestions and overpowered her easily. She always caved in and it became a game for me in the past year. Sometimes, I attended the sessions just to see how much power I had over her. I don't know what my thought pattern was at the time, but apparently, I wasn't well.

So, I stopped going! Not a great decision.

I didn't pay for all of the sessions and that was a game also. How long would it take before I had to pay? This was another way of exerting power over Dr. Hunter.

Power is very intoxicating. It fools you into thinking that you are someone you are not, someone superior or G-D like. What I didn't realize at the time was that I was playing a game where I

would be the loser. I thought I was so smart and ended up outsmarting myself.

What a surprise, not!

My focus should have been on taking care of myself instead of playing games.

•

Sweet Ben, Complicated Ben, Handsome Ben, Sexy Ben, Good Ben, Bad Ben.

Romantic thoughts bring themselves into view. Sometimes they are unpleasant to digest, sometimes they fill a void. Why did he have to come into my life? Was Ben real or a figment of my imagination? I'm not sure now. I have to sit down and think this through. Sometimes I've had trouble distinguishing between events that have happened and those that have not.

I had talked to Dr. Hunter about this, and I'm not really sure what she said. Actually, she didn't say much. But then again, maybe I wasn't really listening.

No help there!

Upon entering the stateroom, I was so thankful that Daniel wasn't there. I hurriedly packed my few belongings. Then I wrote a short note to Daniel and left it on the bed.

Dear Daniel,

I know that I put you through hell. It wasn't my intent to hurt you. You are a great person in every way. I am not the right one for you and you will see that when all your anger dissipates. There is a very special lady waiting for you and hopefully, she will come into your life soon.

I will spend tonight in another stateroom. I will ride back in the car with all of you tomorrow and gather my stuff from your apartment. Let's just get through this with as little drama as possible. Please forgive me. – Evie

Even though Fernando's room was small, it felt right for me to be there. After I explained to him what had transpired once he left my cabin, he took my hand and kissed it. He touched my face ever so gently and then caressed it. I was definitely under his spell and he knew it. He kissed me again on my lips and then on my shoulders. It was so sensuous and mesmerizing that I was powerless to move. Fernando took off his shirt and exposed his six-pack. He sat back down on the bed and kissed me again and again. Each kiss made me feel more passionate until I couldn't control myself anymore. I cupped Fernando's face with my hands and kissed him hard and long on his mouth. He cradled me in his arms and began to touch and kiss every part of me. I returned the favor and it went on for hours, or at least that's what it seemed like. Every moment was filled with passion and I definitely didn't want it to end. But end it did, and we both fell asleep completely exhausted in the most pleasant way.

The last day of the cruise was short and very sweet. Fernando had unbelievable stamina, and we made love early in the morning and then again just before breakfast was served.

"I have no appointments today because the ship is docking since the cruise is over. We can stay in my room until the last minute. You are a beautiful woman and a great lover," Fernando said to me.

"You helped me through a very uncomfortable time on this ship. Mostly, you gave me the kind of comfort money can't buy. I'm going to miss you."

"I am going to miss you too, Mujer Bonita."

I didn't know what that meant but realized it was something good.

Fernando pulled me towards him, but I turned it around and took control of the game. I pushed him onto the bed, jumped on top of him and went down south … Both of us fell asleep soon after.

I woke up to Fernando kissing my thighs, and it was clear that he could give it another go. I only had seven minutes left before I had to leave the ship, and so seven minutes of ecstasy it was!

What a spectacular ending to a lousy vacation!

The three weeks I stayed in Daniel's apartment after we came back from the cruise were hell on earth. He wouldn't speak to me except when he told me I had until the end of the month to get out. Luckily, I found another apartment quickly.

•

It's late in the afternoon and the rain droplets are banging against the windows of my apartment building. Back in the day, if I was stuck in my apartment during a thunderstorm, I would order in. I can't open my door for a delivery person or anyone else, so that's not happening. I really need to eat something, but there's hardly any food in the apartment. I'll have to make do with whatever there is. Actually, eating whole wheat crackers topped with peanut butter and a cup of coffee sounds pretty good to me. It's not gourmet but it will work for now.

While lost in my thoughts, I heard a soft knock on my door. I chose to ignore it since it might not have been real. But then I heard it again, harder this time. Who could it possibly be? I was not expecting anyone and didn't want to answer the door.

I won't answer the door!

Whoever it is will just have to go away. But they didn't. Instead, the doorbell rang three or four times in rapid succession, as if the person knew someone was home. I stood as still as possible and tried to breathe quietly.

I heard something drop against the door. By the time I looked through the peephole, I could only hear footsteps walking away. What was left at my door? Maybe it was something dangerous? Would my door blow up, and me with it? Panic started to set in! My heart began to race and I knew I needed to calm down.

Willing myself to the couch and wrapping my comforter around me, was just what I needed. The warmth brought me peace. I closed my eyes.

CHAPTER 9

It was the morning after I heard something drop against my door. I opened my eyes to daylight staring me in the face, even though my living room drapes were closed. I started to make my way to the bathroom. As I proceeded towards it, something pulled me back. My energy and strength seemed to be sapped, but I persevered.

I turned on the shower and waited a moment for the hot water to start. I closed the shower door and allowed the water to run down my back and then all over me. As I soaped myself, feelings of happiness arose. The warmth of the water and the smell of gardenias from my soap brought me a sense of calm.

Entering my bedroom, I removed a clean pair of underwear from my dresser drawer and quickly put it on. My black jeans and white pullover sweater were lying on the floor. They looked wrinkled, but I picked them up anyway and put them on. Thank goodness they didn't smell. I couldn't remember the last time I did laundry.

I went to the kitchen and sat down with thoughts of yesterday, the hard knocking and the footsteps walking away. Was a package left by my door? There was only one way to find out.

"Please G-D, give me the strength, give me the courage to open the door," I whispered.

The hallways in my building were always dark, no matter what time of day it was. On top of that, the lights were often out, so I grabbed a flashlight from one of my kitchen drawers. I walked back to the door, flashlight in hand, with a definite determination to see this task through.

I got to the door and began to feel squeamish. Suddenly, I wasn't so confident anymore. I looked through the peephole but couldn't see if anything was placed on the hall floor. I had no choice but to open the door. No more excuses, fears or procrastinating. It was time to move forward.

I placed my hand on the safety catch of the lock and removed the chain. I became anxious and felt my heart beat faster. I then took slow breaths through my nose and slowly exhaled them through my mouth.

I heard the click of the tumblers in the lock moving as I turned the deadbolt.

"Keep going, you're almost there," I murmured to myself.

I worked my way down to the bottom lock. The door was finally unlocked! Could I turn the knob?

"I cannot stop now," I repeated to myself.

I finally turned the doorknob and peeked out. Instantly, I felt the difference in the hall temperature. It was colder than the inside of my apartment. My thoughts diverted my attention from the task at hand and I needed to focus. And there it was … the package, my package!

I bent down to pick it up. It was the size of a large box of chocolates like the ones given on Valentine's Day, but not wrapped as pretty. It was covered in dull brown paper, no frills to speak of. I checked the parcel for a return address but did not find one. This was puzzling. Who would have sent this to me?

I re-entered my apartment and placed the package on the counter. I wanted to rip it open but was afraid of the contents. Staring at it made me more and more curious. I had to be brave and open it.

The brown paper came off easily enough and revealed a white box with a popular store's name and logo on it. I used to shop there a lot.

Wondering who sent me a present perked up my curiosity. It was time to open it. I removed the tape on each side and opened the box.

I could not believe what I saw! Lying in the box were things that belonged to me. My personal possessions were in there!

I started to go through the items and took out a few pieces of costume jewelry, a scarf, one earring, a pair of panties, two bras, some papers and four unopened letters. I took the letters in my hand and began to study them. Each letter was from me addressed to Ben.

Four unopened letters to Ben! What the fuck!!!

I held the letters in my hand and began to cry. As much as I tried to stop the tears, it was not possible. My crying became more and more intense as tears were streaming down my face. Remembering when those letters were sent made things crystal

clear. It has been so many years, and I thought Ben was out of my life forever.

All those bad memories started flooding towards me like a tidal wave. I began to feel faint and light-headed. I held onto the counter and steadied myself. My throat felt dry and I needed to get a glass of water and then sit down.

I looked at the front of the envelopes again, checked their postmarks and then placed them in chronological order with the earliest date first. I stared at them for a long time and finally ripped open the first one.

My Dearest Ben,

I miss you so much. It is so difficult for me not to be able to see you, touch you, kiss you, etc. I hate that you are so far away. I know that you are abroad for work, but these are my feelings. It's been way too long for me. Yesterday was an easy workday. I was caught up on everything and actually had to look busy.

Did you receive the balloons I sent you for your birthday? I didn't hear from you. Maybe you were very busy with clients. Let me know when we can speak again. Last week's phone call was too short. I miss you so much more than you know. I love you so much!

Yours forever,

Evie   xoxoxoxoxoxoxo

It was so many years ago with so much wasted time and so much pain. Now I knew that Ben never opened my last four letters. It all made perfect sense. No return letters, random phone calls that kept getting shorter and further apart, and then nothing.

It has been so many years since I last heard from Ben. I think a part of me still loves him and I don't know why. The relationship started out great as most do. We were in love, at least I was, and everything was in sync.

I had hoped and dreamt about seeing Ben again after that first coincidental meeting in the lobby of my office building. It was the building where I used to work before becoming mentally comatose. Seeing him with his gorgeous girlfriend at the restaurant did not dim my hopes of meeting him at some time in the future. In my mind, he would look at me and realize that I was what he had been searching for all of his life. He would approach me and we would melt into each other's arms. We would be in love forever!

That fairytale didn't materialize, but the nightmare did!

When least expected, is usually when things happen. It never seems to fail. If you go to the supermarket with no makeup on and dressed sloppily, it's almost guaranteed that you will meet someone you know. That's how it happened to me so many years ago. I left my apartment wearing a bleach-stained jogging outfit. My hair was pulled back in a ponytail with a rubber band that I had taken off of a plastic grocery bag. I had no makeup on my face to speak of. I also had a slight cold, so my nose was red and somewhat crusty from me constantly blowing it. I won't even get into the description of the painful zit on my chin that was the size of a marble. I looked a sight.

The day was Saturday and I was taking part in my usual weekend routine, a stop at Barry's Bakery for my corn muffin and scone. It was a treat I reserved for the weekend. While on line, I was thinking of adding pumpernickel bread to my order when there was a light tapping on the bakery window. Instinctively, I turned around. It was Ben!

OMG, it was Ben!

He had a smirk type of smile on his face and was waving his hand. I looked at him, not sure if he was trying to get my attention or someone else's. He made direct eye contact with me and so I waved back. Then I stepped outside and walked up to him.

"Were you just waving to me?" I asked him.

"Yes. I think it's time for introductions. Hi, I'm Ben Robertson."

I started to blush. Hopefully, he didn't see that, but it was impossible to miss.

"My, my name is Evie, Evie Harris," I stammered.

"I know it seems a little bold, but I think you're following me," he said jokingly.

Of course, I became defensive, not understanding his sarcasm. That usually happens when you feel less than good about yourself.

"I'm not following you! You're the one who asked me for directions, and then showed up in the restaurant and ..."

He showed me that smile again with his gleaming white teeth. No spinach caught in there!

"No, you misunderstood me, Evie. I just said that as an icebreaker."

He laughed that nervous laugh when you don't know what else to say.

"I'm sorry I snapped at you. I was just caught off guard. Let's try this again. I'm Evie and I'm glad to meet you."

I gave him my best smile and extended my hand. He took it gently, but not in a limp fashion. He then bent down and kissed it. Electricity went through me. I was on fire and beyond hooked.

"Would you like to go for some coffee, I mean after you finish your bakery run?"

"It's okay, the bakery can wait. It will still be there later. Let's go to Café Allegra. It's just down the street," I said while quickly regaining my composure.

As we walked on, I became tongue-tied and didn't know what else to say to him. Ben, on the other hand, did not have this problem. We entered the coffee shop and sat in the middle of the room. The café was very busy as usual, filled with business people making deals, mothers with infants, retired people whiling away the hours and people like Ben and myself.

Ben ordered a regular coffee, nothing fancy. Mine was a latte, extra hot, in a glass mug. Before the coffee was ready for pickup, Ben moved closer towards my face. He almost whispered as he began speaking to me.

"Hopefully this doesn't sound too bold, but I wanted to see you again after the first time we met in the lobby of your office building. It was a meeting of chance when I saw you coming down those escalator steps. I wanted an excuse to talk to you, so I pretended that I needed directions. I didn't know how else to do it. Then, as fate would have it, I saw you again at Pompidou!"

"But you didn't even make eye contact with me when you walked into the restaurant," I responded.

"I know. It was kind of awkward trying to approach you. I was also with someone."

Yes, it was clear that he was with someone. He didn't have to point that out. The barista called out Ben's name because our coffees were ready. He didn't get up to get them, which made it awkward for me. So, I stood up and went to the counter. I paid for them as I wasn't about to go back to him and ask for the money. I placed the drinks on the table and sat back down. Ben began to drink his immediately.

"Thank you for the treat, it's delicious!" he said.

Normally, I would be very turned off by this, but something was pulling me towards him. Therefore, I continued with the conversation.

"I'm glad you had the courage to knock on the bakery window. So tell me, who is Ben Robertson?"

I began to relax. It was as though I was with my best friend. It felt so good sitting there with Ben. It was as if I didn't have a care in the world. But it turned out that Ben would not be my best friend. Ben would not be my friend at all!

"I have to get back to work," he said quietly, as though it were a secret.

"Oh, you work on Saturdays?"

He didn't respond to the question and instead asked one of his own.

"Would you like to go out for dinner sometime next week, Evie?" he asked nonchalantly.

"That sounds great. Which day is good?"

I thought I picked up on a moment's hesitation before he answered but disregarded it. I was too smitten by him and his charms.

"I'll have to give you a call early next week. Would that be okay?"

"That's great! Let me give you both my numbers. If I don't answer, just leave me a voice mail," I responded way too eagerly.

Ben stood up, stretched a little and picked up the piece of paper that I scribbled my number on. He then said goodbye and left.

Something wasn't right. I got an uneasy feeling at that moment but unfortunately decided to ignore my intuition.

Wrong move!

He had set the stage perfectly and I ignored all the red flags that were waving in front of my face. Innocent Ben wanted to meet me. How did he recognize me as I was in the bakery with my back turned towards him? We briefly met only once before in the lobby of my office building. I should have known that it didn't make any sense. And if it doesn't make any sense, it may not be steeped in truth. But I didn't understand that, and more importantly, didn't want to.

Maybe I still don't.

Only a half hour had passed when Ben left. I returned to the bakery, ran my other errands and then walked into an upscale women's boutique clothing store. A new dress for the upcoming date with Ben was in order. I surveyed the new arrivals when a beautiful black knee-length dress caught my

eye. The material was shimmery with scalloped three-quarter sleeves, but not too fancy. It was perfect!

Standing in front of the mirror, I held the dress up to my body. At that moment, I noticed a saleswoman eyeing me suspiciously. It was probably because of how I was dressed and all of my packages. Regardless, I bought that dress immediately and left the store.

What a stroke of luck! I never bought clothing that quickly. I was so excited to wear that fabulous black dress on my first real date with Ben.

I danced all the way home!

I arrived at my apartment elated. After warming up the corn muffin in my microwave, I took a big bite and then placed it back in the bag. I was about to make myself a cup of tea when my attention went back to my new black dress. I tried it on and was very pleased that it fit perfectly. I hung it in my closet and then made myself that cup of hot tea. I placed a cinnamon stick in the glass mug along with a tea bag.

As I slowly sipped my tea, Ben came into my thoughts. I still couldn't believe what had taken place earlier in the day and had to remind myself that it was not a dream. As I was deep in thought, the phone rang.

"Hello. Oh, hi, Briana, how are you?"

"Good, and you?" she responded.

"You will never guess who I met today and had coffee with," I said happily.

"Was it someone from work?" Briana asked.

"No. It was someone very special. You'll never guess who!"

"Don't tell me it was that guy you haven't stopped talking about!" she said.

"Yes, you guessed it! His name is Ben, and he is wonderful," I gushed.

I proceeded to tell Briana everything that happened, and ended with, "So what do you think?"

I never should have asked the question if I didn't want the answer.

Too late!

"There's just something not right about him. First, he's just this random guy you met in the lobby of your office building who asked you for directions. Soon after, you see him in a restaurant and didn't think he saw you in there, but apparently, now you know he did. So, let's say that the bakery meeting was pure coincidence, even though it happens to be the bakery you go to every Saturday. When he saw you through the window, you weren't facing forward, so how did he recognize you from the back? All of a sudden, he has coffee with you, asks you out for dinner, but then doesn't make specific plans for another date? It just seems extremely odd to me," Briana responded.

"You're just reading into things," I said defensively.

"Okay, whatever you say, Evie."

"He's a nice guy who spotted me at the bakery. We went for coffee, and he wants to see more of me. What's so strange about that?"

Briana did not want to hear any more about Ben. She switched the subject to an incident she had at work. We chatted for a few more minutes before hanging up the phone. I wasn't going to let her dampen my good mood. However, it was impossible to get what she said out of my mind.

So much for my good mood!

Why do people always have to spoil it for others? She could have just listened to me and passed judgment at a later date if necessary. She didn't even know Ben. As a matter of fact, I didn't know him either and it didn't concern me. After all, you don't get to know someone immediately. Besides, do you ever really know someone?

Truth be told, Briana had planted the seeds of doubt. If only I had watered the garden.

Time passes too slowly and time passes too quickly. Obviously, it all depends on the situation. I didn't expect Ben to call me immediately, but each passing day that I didn't hear from him became harder to get through. It was already Friday of the following week, and I was beginning to lose hope that he would call.

Later that day back in my apartment, I nuked a frozen dinner and added a glass of Chablis to make myself happy. Saturday night came and went with no call from Ben. I began to think negative thoughts about him, and just as quickly dismissed them. I wanted to believe he would still call. Actually, I prayed that he would.

Ben appeared and disappeared in one fell swoop.

•

Being at work the following Monday was nerve-wracking. From the moment I arrived, the frenzy began. Some of the files had errors that needed to be corrected immediately. Clients were constantly calling and had to be pacified, and so it went. It was so hectic that I was grateful for the office meeting scheduled for 2:00 PM. At least then I could relax to a degree and not have the insanity I was dealing with all day. I would be able to drink a cup of coffee and enjoy it instead of having to gulp it down.

At 4:00 PM I was given a 15 minute break. My thoughts floated towards Ben. Maybe he wasn't going to call after all. Did I do something wrong when we had coffee? Maybe my breath was bad or maybe he simply decided that he didn't like me. Not only

did I think of a million reasons why he wasn't calling but was certain it had to be my fault.

It seemed that it was always my fault. At least that was my distorted way of thinking.

Immediately after work, I went to Mom & Pop's and picked up some dinner. Once I was back in my apartment, I unpacked the foil-wrapped food and found that it was still warm. I sat down to eat while fumbling through a magazine. Even though it was still early, I decided to get ready for bed. I took a shower and then brushed my teeth.

I slid under the covers and closed my eyes. Instead of falling into a relaxed sleep, I sat up quickly realizing that I needed to check my phone. Maybe someone called me while I was in the shower.

Not really expecting anyone, I saw my answering machine was blinking. My heart started pounding, hoping it was a missed call from Ben. I checked the message.

It was from Ben!

"I knew he would call!" I shouted out loud several times.

My prayers were answered! I listened to the message:

"Hey Evie, it's me, Ben. I didn't get a chance to call you sooner. I'm very busy at work. Call me when you can. My number is ..."

I listened to it several times. He didn't say he was sorry, which was disappointing. I wanted to call him back so badly but didn't want him to think I was desperate. Who was I kidding? I called him back immediately.

"Hi, Ben! It's Evie. Sorry I missed your call. It's been over a week since we had coffee together, so I thought you had lost interest."

There I was, apologizing immediately and putting myself down for no reason.

"No problem, I've just been really busy. Do you want to grab some drinks right now?"

Does the sun set at night?

"Sure, that would be great. Where do you want to meet?"

"How about your place?"

It took me a moment to recover from that question. Meet at my place? What was he talking about? This must be a joke. It was probably his way of kidding around, I assumed. But it was no joke ... he was serious.

"Did you say at my place?"

"Sure, why not?"

I was embarrassed to ask him any more questions, fearing that he would change his mind.

"Okay. Let me give you my address. I have some wine, but it's not a full bottle."

"I'll gladly bring one with me and I should be there around 10:30 PM."

"Okay, see you soon."

I was thrilled that Ben was coming over that evening, but it didn't feel quite right. It was very presumptuous of him to think that I would allow him over so late at night and on such short notice. Yet I did allow it. So much for me not wanting to appear desperate. I looked around the apartment. It was neat and tidy for the most part. I dressed quickly and threw on some mascara and blush. I looked in the mirror and realized that some lipstick was needed. I then brushed my hair quickly and sprayed on a few drops of my favorite perfume.

I called down to the front desk and told them to expect Ben and allow him up. An hour and a half had passed since he had called. It was getting very late and I was starting to become a little irritated.

Finally, my buzzer rang from the front desk. I pressed the button for the intercom.

"Your man is here, Miss Harris."

"Thank you," I responded.

He's not my man, at least not yet. I stuck a piece of gum in my mouth, chewed it for a few seconds and then quickly spit it out.

The doorbell rang twice. I looked through the peephole. It was Ben of course, so I opened the door and let him in.

"Hi," was the only word I could think of at that moment.

He stretched out his arm and handed me a bottle of Opus One. That definitely made up for him not paying for the coffees at Café Allegra.

He gave me his coat in an abrupt manner and then hugged me tightly. It felt fantastic and made me forget that little bit of doubt I was feeling.

We sat down on the couch. Nervously, I started to twirl my hair with my left hand. I could sense that he was self-assured and very relaxed. I stood up and walked towards the counter in the kitchen, opened the bottle of wine that he brought, and poured a glass for each of us.

"I didn't think you were going to call me," I shouted out from the kitchen.

I regretted that statement as soon as it came out of my mouth. Once again, an insecurity of mine was on full display.

Ben responded immediately.

"You know how it goes. Time seems to get away from you."

No, I don't know how it goes; it's just a simple phone call. Instead of saying what was on my mind, I became meek and let it go. I walked back to the couch with both glasses of wine but did not sit down.

"I understand, so how are you doing?" I asked him.

"No complaints. I wanted to see you again earlier, but my schedule was so packed. My job is very intense and there is a lot of traveling involved. Spur of the moment works best for me. I'm glad you're open to it."

I handed Ben one of the glasses of wine and then sat back down on the couch. I took a sip   and placed the glass on my miniature coffee table.

"Well, you're a nice guy. Why shouldn't I make it easy?"

I wasn't even sure why I said that. Yes, I was. I was an idiot, an idiot with no confidence.

He chuckled at my remark and then took a few sips of wine. He put his glass on the coffee table and looked directly at me.

"So, what is Evie Harris all about?"

"There's not a whole lot to tell. I work for an advertising company in the office building that you are already familiar with. I think of myself as a good person and try to be as truthful as possible. I don't smoke or do drugs but do love a glass or two of wine. This apartment has been my home for the last few years. That's my story."

There was that awkward pause in the conversation, so I continued to speak.

"What about you? What's your story, Ben?"

"There's also not much to tell. What you see is what you get. I'm staying at the Warner Hotel downtown until I know if I will be working in NYC permanently. My company usually relocates me every five years."

I didn't get a good feeling when he said he gets relocated every five years. If there was a chance for us, moving every five years wouldn't work. I chose not to worry about that just yet but knew it would be in the back of my mind.

Ben gulped down the rest of the wine and I followed suit.

"Would you like to have another glass?" I asked.

"Only if you will join me," he responded.

I got up from the couch, grabbed our empty wine glasses and went back into the kitchen. I took out a small block of Gruyere cheese that I had in the fridge and placed it on a round tray. I removed the cheese knife from the drawer, picked up the tray, proceeded to the living room and placed the items on the coffee table. Bcforc I sat down, I went back into the kitchen, opened one of my top cabinets and removed a box of whole-grain crackers to add to the tray. I filled both wine glasses again and placed the box of crackers under my left arm. Then I picked up the glasses and carried everything very carefully back into the living room. It would have been nice if he had offered to help me.

Ben and I continued sipping our second glass of wine while munching on the cheese and crackers. The conversation was

flowing, and I didn't realize until later that I had learned nothing about him that entire evening.

I was having a great time and hoped he would want to stay the night. Just at that moment, Ben looked at his watch and said it was getting late. I was disappointed but understood perfectly. He had to go to work in the morning and so did I. What was I thinking? I barely knew the man.

He kissed my hand and gave me the same type of hug as when he first came in. I wanted so much more and had to restrain myself from jumping on him. We said goodnight and in an instant he was gone.

Briana did not need to know what had transpired with Ben on such short notice. She would be judgmental and negative, but for my own good of course. I was feeling too happy to have anyone rain on my parade even if it was in my best interest. I went to bed and fell asleep almost immediately.

•

The next morning brought rain, but I saw it as sunshine. My mood was so good that I stopped by the bakery before work and bought a dozen assorted doughnuts. My co-workers would love this treat, and it would buy me some brownie points with them.

Throughout my workday, thoughts of Ben floated in and out of my head. I wanted him in my life and believed that there were many good times ahead for us.

A few days went by since Ben came over to my place. Every morning thereafter I expected him to call me, and every night I was disappointed. I told myself that I was being silly by expecting too much too soon. After all, it was only Wednesday.

Two weeks passed and I still hadn't heard from Ben. It was becoming stressful to expect his call and not get it. I decided on another strategy; not to be so needy and desperate. If he liked me, he would call. We're not a couple and he didn't owe me anything, except maybe some good manners.

CHAPTER 10

It was Friday, and after three weeks of not hearing from Ben, I decided it was time for some rest and relaxation. So, I called my favorite travel agency.

"Hello, this is Gem Travel Agency. How may I help you?" was the voice on the other line.

"Hi, I know this is short notice, but do you have something available for this weekend?"

"Where would you like to go to?"

"I'm not sure, but I'm open for something fun that caters to singles for this Saturday and Sunday. No airplanes, please. Do you have something close to home since I live in NYC?"

"Just a moment, let me check my screen. Okay, I have the perfect trip for you. It's a bus trip to Atlantic City which includes vouchers and lunch. There's a great hotel offering a special for this weekend only which includes ..."

I wasn't fully paying attention to what she was saying but got the gist of it. I was so ready to get out of town that a vacation in a swamp would have worked. The travel agent took my information and credit card numbers.

After hanging up the phone, I flew around my apartment gathering together clothing and toiletries. I threw everything into a large tote bag.

What the hell! The Atlantic City bus was filled with all senior citizens! The travel agent told me that this trip would be perfect for my age group and single status. I was so pissed off that she lied! The bus was already moving, so I resigned myself to the situation and leaned back in my seat. Just as I was about to doze off, the woman sitting behind me tapped me on the shoulder. I rolled my eyes thinking that she was either going to ask me to push my seat back up or to do her a favor. Instead, she told me that I could lean back further to be more comfortable. I told her I was okay. Then, she offered me a piece of cake that she had wrapped in foil. It did look good, but I told her I was on a diet.

"Too bad that you're on a diet because when we get to the hotel, they are going to have a wine and cheese reception for the bus group," she said.

"Did you say wine and cheese?" I responded pleasantly surprised.

"I guess the diet is going out the window!" the woman said jokingly.

Her warmth and personality made me feel bad that I was so closed-minded about older people. Shame on me!

Staring out the window and checking my phone kept me from falling asleep. I should have brought a book to read to occupy my time. Looking at my phone again, there were some emails, most of them spam, and a message from my boss. I opened that one up and it said that there was going to be another office

meeting on Monday regarding sales. There was nothing else of any importance. I was so bored!

As more time passed, I started getting tense and then my anxiety kicked in. I started doing my breathing exercises to alleviate it and it made me feel better. A nurse told me about this a long time ago. I was, and still am so grateful to her.

I looked out the window again, and this time did a double take. I saw Ben walking down the street! I looked away for a second, and then looked back again but didn't see him anymore. The bus was moving too quickly at that point.

Damn! I'm not sure. Did I see him or didn't I? Was I starting to hallucinate?

The laughter and chatter on the bus got very loud and distracted me from my thoughts about Ben. I started to focus on the loudest and most animated people on the bus. I listened to the many conversations happening at the same time. It seemed as if I was hearing what Briana and I would probably sound like many years from now.

The bus finally reached its destination. The ride was approximately three hours because we encountered heavy traffic. I let everyone get off before me. It was just easier that way. As each person descended, the bus driver gave them a voucher for $10.00 towards a buffet lunch and $20.00 in free chips. The people who were staying overnight at the hotel, which included me, received an extra dinner voucher and an additional $5.00 in chips.

I'm not a big gambler but did find it relaxing to sit at the Blackjack table. Texas Hold'em and Roulette are fun, but regular Poker has always been my favorite game. I brought

$300.00 for gambling with me, expecting to lose it all, and I did. What a ridiculous way to have fun!

CHAPTER 11

Was I happy or sad that I brought this package inside my apartment? I looked at all the items   again, needing to touch each one and feel Ben through them. Why did I have the need to "feel" Ben? After all he put me through and the continuous therapy thereafter, I really thought I had become immune to him.

I took out each item and placed them in the palm of my hand. They filled me with conflicting emotions of love, hate, loneliness, and anger. I guess that sums up a large piece of the puzzle that is known as my life.

So many years have gone by, and I thought I was no longer bound by the chains of that which were Ben. However, he managed to come into my life once again through this package. I should have hated him, but hate is an emotion, and I would like to believe that I have no feelings for him anymore.

I find myself sitting in the dark again, which is very depressing. Yet, I won't get up to put the lights on. Maybe I want to suffer and punish myself. Who knows? The doubts are always there. I feel as if I will never know how to get out of this spider web in which I am trapped.

I'm beginning to get hunger pangs. Unfortunately, there is hardly any food left in my fridge. I need to go to the supermarket yet cannot bring myself to leave my apartment. Gathering all the emotional strength possible, I begin to look through my cabinets. A quick mental inventory makes me realize that my food supply will barely last a week, but I decide to put off shopping for now.

I cannot bear the thought of going outside since I feel mentally frozen. This fear is greater than anything else I have ever felt. It is even stronger than love.

Wow! Even stronger than love!

I am so messed up, that even I can't believe it.

Believe it, Evie!

"Poor Me, Predictable Me, Please Feel Sorry for Me." That's who I have become. I am aware that all I keep doing is having pity parties for myself, with myself, and by myself. They are no fun at all! It is almost like having a tea party where you invite all your friends, but no one shows up.

Is feeling sorry for yourself healthy, or is it a tactic used to shield your mind from experiencing pain that is too difficult to deal with in any other way?

I started to focus on the one earring in the box. I kept looking at it as if I was seeing it for the first time. It was not oval-shaped but rather more obelisk-like, with delicate gold scrollwork around the outside. The inside stone was turquoise with the post in gold. It was very fragile, beautiful and full of memories. How could I have forgotten about it?

That earring took me back to my childhood. It brought back wonderful memories of my mother. She was truly a remarkable person. As a mother, she was always kind, giving and always doing the right thing. She was a very quiet woman who never spoke much but was definitely wiser than anyone else in the room. She didn't like to call attention to herself, but instead gave it all to her children and my father. He was wonderful also.

I remember when she took me to get my ears pierced. I must have been four or five years old. She bought me these little heart-shaped gold earrings. I loved those earrings and still do. I still have them but haven't worn them in a long time.

For my sixteenth birthday, my parents presented me with turquoise earrings. They were beautiful. Actually, they were exquisite and too fancy to wear every day. I cherished them, yet I was careless at the same time. I wore them one day when I was in my last year of college. To this day, I cannot figure out how I lost one of them. It was devastating to me. I knew that I had to tell my parents. When I did, they understood and were so wonderful about it.

It took me awhile getting over being upset and feeling guilty about losing that earring. Then I came up with an idea. I would wear the one earring as a new fashion trend. Why not? It brought me the attention I craved.

Those were such fond memories.

There weren't such fond memories of my younger sister, Raquel. When we were very young, we had the typical sisterly fights about toys, borrowing clothes without permission, etc., but those were our good old days. From very early on, Raquel made it very clear that she did not like me and unfortunately, nothing has changed.

A sister is supposed to be your friend, not your adversary. In our teen years, she changed our relationship forever.

Raquel stole my boyfriend!

Raquel married my boyfriend!

Raquel never sent me an invitation to her wedding!

Raquel gloated over my pain!

Raquel told me she hated me!

Even though she was so mean to me, I still wanted her in my life. She will always be my sister!

Raquel used to always tell me that I was ugly and fat, even though she was not particularly pretty. She had a large brown mole on her left cheek which always seemed to have a hair or two growing out of it. Raquel always talked about having it removed, but every time my mother took her to the doctor's office to do it, she chickened out. That made no sense to me. Everyone in school used to tease her about it, but I never did and instead tried to protect her. Raquel also had a small scar on her other cheek, which happened when our next-door neighbor's dog got out from his fence and bit her. However, it was her eyes that always made you look at her twice. They were mesmerizing and drew you towards her.

Raquel had a very outgoing personality. She was friendly to everyone, everyone but me that is. I was never jealous of her, but rather admired her. It seemed to me that competition was the name of the game for Raquel. I didn't know why at the time, but maybe it was because I was the older sister. I was never competitive, at least not to the point of rivalry with her.

Maybe that's how sisters are? I'm not sure.

Could it be that Raquel wanted to be the older sister? She acted like she was since she controlled all aspects of our relationship.

When you're young, you want to be older!

When you're old, you want to be younger!

Family distancing from each other always seems to start with small things. Eventually, there is conflict of some sort, be it jealousy or animosity, maybe both or nothing at all. It gains momentum and seems to almost have a life of its own. It strangles the lifeblood out of what was once a family filled with unconditional love and compassion. Communication stops, everything stops. No one wants to give in, but hurt feelings last forever!

My parents tried for years to get us to be on an even keel. They knew we would never be close, but they did hope we could at least be civil to each other. Unfortunately, their efforts were in vain. That did not stop them from trying, until one day, they just gave up. They realized it was an effort in futility.

CHAPTER 12

A few months after Daniel and I broke up, I got on a plane to visit my Auntie Nina in Florida. She was my auntie through marriage, and I didn't know her very well. It was time for me to become closer to her since I was feeling very lonely and she had always been nice to me. I thought it would be a good idea to pay her a surprise visit. At first she was upset that I didn't tell her I was coming.

"Why didn't you tell me you were in Florida? I would have made you a nice dinner," she exclaimed.

I knew she was a little annoyed, but not with me. She wanted to be a good hostess and show me that she cared. But I already knew that she cared which was why I chose to visit her.

"Sorry, Auntie Nina, but I didn't want you to have to fuss over me. I thought it would be easier this way."

As I was munching on some homemade sugar cookies, Auntie Nina stood up and went over to a drawer in her kitchen. She came back with a folder which she placed on the table in front of me.

"I have some pictures I would like you to look at, Evie. I don't think you've ever seen them before."

I looked at the photos, which were mainly of her when she was around 25 years old. I could not believe how absolutely gorgeous she was.

"You were very striking! You had movie-star good looks," I said to her.

My auntie blushed because she loved the compliment. My statement was absolutely true.

I then focused on a single picture of my auntie with another woman whom I did not recognize. They were sitting together on a large blanket at some beach, holding ice cream cones and smiling. It looked like it could have been a postcard from the 1950s.

"Auntie Nina! Who is that young woman in the picture with you?"

 Her response floored me.

"That's my sister, Penny!"

I almost fell off my chair.

"Your sister!" I blurted out way too loudly.

I took a breath and continued speaking.

"I didn't know you had a sister! Why didn't you ever mention her to me or anyone else?"

It was out of character to speak to my auntie in that way. It took me a minute to absorb the news. I had known her for a long time and my auntie never mentioned that she had a sister. How could she have kept that secret for so long?

I looked at my Auntie Nina. She did not offer any further information. I surmised that her sister must have done something quite awful to her. What could Penny have done to make Auntie Nina completely erase her from her life, from all of our lives? My auntie kept this secret for so many years. Now that it was out, I had to know what happened.

"Is your sister still alive?" I asked in a quiet tone.

"Yes."

"Do you know where she lives?"

"Yes."

"Do you speak to her?"

"No."

Her one-word answers were not conducive to start a meaningful conversation. I was trying to figure out if Auntie Nina was upset or glad that she finally allowed this heavy weight to come off of her shoulders. I decided to question her one more time.

"Auntie Nina, I don't want to pry, but you just dropped a bombshell on me. Please tell me what happened between you and your sister."

She poured herself a cup of herbal tea and then sat down at the kitchen table across from me. She looked at me several times as she was dunking her tea bag in her mug. Then she began to speak.

What she said shocked me even more.

"The answer is very simple. I don't remember."

"You don't remember why you're not talking to your sister?"

She didn't seem to hear what I had just said. Instead, she just began speaking about Penny and the words flowed quickly out of her mouth.

"About five or six months ago I was walking down the street towards the Sawgrass Mall. From a short distance away, I saw my sister on the same side of the street, walking in my direction. I recognized her immediately, even though I hadn't seen her for many years. I was sure she recognized me as well."

"So, what happened then?" I asked eagerly.

Auntie Nina paused for a split-second and then continued walking.

"We walked past each other as if we were strangers. Neither of us gave any indication that we recognized each other," she said with a sad tone to her voice.

It was difficult to believe what I had just heard. It took some time to absorb this information and take it all in.

"How could you two pass each other like that? Why didn't you at least say hello?"

Auntie Nina took a sip of her tea and looked directly at me. She looked so sad.

"I don't know," was her only response.

I stared at my auntie. Could it be that she was also responsible for what had happened with Penny? There was one more thing left to say and therefore I said it.

"Divine intervention put you and your sister together at that moment, after so many years of not speaking to each other. I still don't understand why you didn't say hello to her?"

A little upset with my remark, she retorted quickly.

"She didn't say hello to me either!"

"You were given a wonderful opportunity, and both of you blew it. What a shame!"

My auntie did not respond. Instead, she took another sip of her tea and swallowed hard. At that moment, I realized that I was judging her without really knowing all the details. Unfortunately, it seemed that pride got in both their ways. Too much time had passed, and neither sister would give in. How sad! How typical!

It was time for me to be on my way. I gave my auntie a big hug and kiss, and then left. I knew she had lots of soul searching to do.

While standing outside my auntie's building, I began to reflect on my own sister while waiting for a cab. It wasn't clear to me why Raquel didn't speak to me. Even though she wronged me, I still wanted her in my life. How do you grow up in the same household with the same parents, and end up with personalities on the opposite end of the spectrum from each other? What is it that shapes you into either a good person or one that is selfish and destructive to others? I wish I knew the answers.

CHAPTER 13

I placed the earring back in the mysterious box and looked at the other items again. None of them had any sentimental value. I started to ask myself the most obvious questions. Who was this person who sent me this package? Did Ben send this to me? If so, why was it sent now, so many years later? All of this was very puzzling.

No matter how this came about, I was so glad to have the earring back, the remnant of my parent's gift to me.

Again, I kept asking myself questions about the package.

Was this Ben's way of trying to contact me? Maybe after all these years, he realized how wrong he was and that I was the right one for him after all. This could be his way of breaking the ice. Maybe he'll send me flowers anonymously as well. Evidently, my imagination was working overtime again.

My anxiety started to build again. I felt myself becoming disconnected as if my body and my brain were separate. I needed to sit down since I was beginning to feel light-headed.

Slowly, I walked over to the couch and plopped myself down. I grabbed my blanket and as usual, wrapped it around me for emotional comfort. It reassured me that everything was okay, even though I knew it was not. Sitting there rocking back and forth and humming was a ritual that usually relaxed me.

Why was Ben still in my head? It had been so many years, and yet he still mentally possessed me. I thought I had let go of him ages ago, but now I can't stop thinking about him again. He managed to make himself visible to me once again, thanks to this delivery. Like the snake Ben was, he slithered back into my thoughts.

Maybe I still love him? But how can I feel that way when he has put me through so much pain? He has shrouded me with a net of self-doubt.

Each day I fall a little further into oblivion. All the trials I have gone through have brought me to this state of mind. I wonder how many more are awaiting me.

Again my thoughts go back to the package. I sat there staring at the items for some clue as to who would have held onto them for this long. It's like looking into the refrigerator and hoping the food choices will change the longer you stare.

I heard clanging which snapped me back to the present and realized it was the phone. I listened to the rings and could not bring myself to answer it. The ringing finally stopped. A moment later, it began to ring again. No one calls me. Who could it be? And then the answer came to me. It's Ben! It had to be Ben! He definitely wanted me back. My excitement started to grow. I felt a little better about myself. It was momentary, but the feeling was real.

Was it a wrong number? The Caller ID was blocked and there was no message. The phone rang two separate times. There was no doubt it my mind that it was Ben calling to apologize. He was probably going to tell me that he is a changed man and that he wants to make it right, I just knew it!

I started to prepare myself on how to respond to Ben. Maybe just listening to what he had to say would be best. I went into the kitchen and sat on a chair waiting for the phone to ring again. Not being able to sit for long, I made myself a cup of coffee and something to eat. This diverted my attention for a while. It was the best thing I could have done for myself.

The phone did not ring again.

I continued to sit and wait.

An hour passed but it felt much longer. Pouring myself another cup of coffee was a great idea. It tasted so good, probably because of the added cinnamon. It was almost midnight, and the phone had not rung again. Ben will probably try again tomorrow, I thought. Hopefully he would!

How pathetic am I?

I couldn't sit on that kitchen chair any longer.

I went into the bedroom and lied down on the bed knowing that sleep would not come quickly.

CHAPTER 14

Life is what you make of it. Sometimes you have chains around you. Sometimes others put them there. Sometimes, you manage to crawl into them yourself. I think I belong to all of these groups.

I am a member of an unwanted club!

I look around my apartment and realize it's quite a disaster. It was never the neatest, but it has never been this bad. I don't care how it looks anymore and haven't cared for months, and it shows. Maybe I'll start to clean it up tomorrow.

Maybe I will, maybe I won't.

•

B - E - N!

How did three letters of the alphabet control so much of my life?

Life before Ben was not perfect, but it was good. What is perfect anyway? I was more or less a creature of habit. Weekdays I awoke at 6:30 AM, showered, dressed and ate breakfast. My hair primping lasted about 10 minutes before running out the door to work. Afterward, I would often stop at Mom & Pop's before going home. That was my mundane pattern.

The weekend consisted of errands, laundry, catching up on mail and paying bills. On Friday and Saturday nights I would usually go out for dinner with Briana or the occasional date. I didn't have a particular love interest at the time, but my dating life was fine.

All things come in due time. Unfortunately, my time came, but with the wrong man. If I would have worked later that day, I wouldn't have met him. A three minute delay would have made my life go in a completely different direction.

Maybe not!

Are things destined to be, or do we create our own destiny?

But I did go down the escalator that day, at the precise time Ben needed directions. There were so many people around and he had to choose me. Was it fate? Well, I don't believe in fate. I don't believe in anything anymore.

•

It was late in the afternoon. Again I drew my drapes back, looked out the window, and watched the same scenes play out, only with different actors. I then heard the phone ring. This time I was going to answer that phone. This time I was prepared for Mr. Ben Robertson!

"Hello," I said nonchalantly.

"Hi, Evie, it's Dr. Hunter."

"Dr. Hunter! I didn't expect you to call me. I can't talk right now because I'm waiting for a very important call," I said convincingly.

"I just need a moment of your time. I called you twice yesterday, but you didn't pick up the phone. I just wanted to check in with you and see if you're okay. When are you going to make your next appointment?"

So it wasn't Ben who tried to call me the day before. I was both sad and angry.

"I'm sorry, Dr. Hunter. I'll call you back."

I hung up the phone abruptly feeling dejected and worthless. It wasn't Ben after all.

It would never be Ben again. Ben is gone!

This package brought Ben back into my mind in such an unhealthy manner. I felt as though I was falling for him all over again.

So there I was, with Ben inside of my head. Why couldn't I just leave him in the past? Obviously, I didn't want to let him go. It was both comfort and pain.

Memories seem to last forever!

I remember how Ben called me two weeks after coming to my apartment for the first time. It always seemed to be two weeks until he would contact me again. It became rote, so I just expected it. Unfortunately, I also accepted it.

It's as if it happened yesterday. My phone rang and ...

"Hey Evie, I want to see that new rom-com that just came out. It got great reviews, and it has some big-time actors in it. Do you want to go Wednesday night?"

"Why only on Wednesdays? We rarely go out on weekends when there's no work the next day. Can't we go out on a Friday or Saturday night?"

"You know I don't have a set schedule the way you do. My hours are all over the place. We'll do a weekend soon, I promise."

He sounded so sincere and almost wounded that I would question him. I started to feel guilty that I was putting pressure on him when he was making an effort to be with me.

"Wednesday will be fine. I know you work hard, Ben and hope your boss realizes that, especially when it comes time for a raise."

"Actually, I'm glad you said that. My commissions haven't been coming in as quickly as I thought they would, and truthfully, it's time for me to get an apartment. This hotel stay is majorly tugging at my wallet," he said kind of sheepishly in a toying sort of way.

"Staying at the hotel makes no sense, Ben. Even the cheapest one comes out expensive after a while, and you've already been there for three months."

"The company was supposed to pick up the tab. That's what they inferred at my interview, or that's how I understood it at the time. But when I inquired about it, they said that was not included in my contract. I feel kind of embarrassed about it. It's kind of depleted my savings," he explained.

"So what's your plan for now?"

"To pinch my pennies until my commission checks start rolling in on a regular basis. In order to rent an apartment, I need to have the first and last month's rent, one month's security and the realtor's fee. I don't have it all right now. Staying at the hotel keeps me from being able to get all the money together. It's kind of like a dog trying to catch its own tail. It just doesn't work. Anyway, I don't want to bother you with my finances. Everything will work its way out. So I'll pick you up at eight and we'll catch the 8:45 PM show."

"Okay. That will be great. See you on Wednesday."

I hung up the phone feeling totally befuddled. I thought he was a successful businessman, but he just spoke to me as though he didn't have two nickels to rub together.

Maybe he was testing me to see if I was after his money? Could it have been that he was not as smart as I thought? All kinds of possibilities started racing through my mind. I started to realize that Ben knew almost everything about me down to the smallest detail, yet I still knew almost nothing about him. I was afraid to ask him too many personal questions even though I didn't have that problem with any of my other past relationships. But with

Ben, it was always in the back of my mind that he wouldn't like me anymore if I pried too much. I wanted this relationship to cement

first and then I would slowly learn to fill in the blanks. I figured that there was plenty of time for those types of conversations. I just wanted to enjoy that which was Ben.

Apparently, I was great at deluding myself!

•

Wednesday night came and we walked to the movie theater. The film was enjoyable, but I felt that Ben was distant. There was definitely something on his mind. Afterward, as we were walking towards the exit doors, I entwined my arm into his. We walked for a few minutes in silence. It was actually relaxing to me, but it was anything but relaxing for Ben. I could feel tenseness emanating from him.

"If you don't have to get back to the hotel right away, let's grab a cup of coffee and maybe a muffin, my treat," I said too hastily.

Ben looked at me with true pain in his eyes. I thought I saw a weeping child.

"I never should have told you about my finances. Now you feel sorry for me and probably think I'm a loser," he said rather upset, but not in an angry way.

"No, I don't think that at all. I'm so sorry. It's just a small thing, the coffee I mean."

"It's time for me to get back," he said as he walked away and left me standing on the sidewalk, totally embarrassed and feeling very small.

Wow, did I read him wrong! At that moment I realized what a proud man he was. There was no question in my mind that I truly loved him and had to find a way to have him return that love. First, I would have to give him back his pride and secondly, I needed to make his life easier. I needed to concoct a well-thought-out plan that would help him out. It couldn't be obvious. That lesson was learned. Not only did I have to figure it out, but I had to figure it out quickly.

I was so involved in thinking of how to please Ben that it never occurred to me how truly rude he was. He left me in the street all by myself, without turning around to look back. He didn't even call that evening to see if I made it home safely.

Ben left angry, but I surmised his anger was directed at himself, not at me. Unfortunately, my low self-esteem always seemed to make excuses for him.

Once back in my apartment that evening, I made myself a snack which consisted of three-day-old fruit salad. Not the greatest, but still okay. It gave me something to munch on as I tried to come up with an idea.

Thankfully, I had been frugal for most of my life. I had also inherited a nice sum from my parents. My savings and inheritance amounted to approximately $80,000 and I had a $15,000 CD. Not too bad for someone with an average income.

I had never been poor and considered myself comfortable. I could float Ben a loan of $5,000 with no interest, and he could pay me back once he got on his feet. I wouldn't have a problem with small increments on a monthly basis either. I was happy with my decision but then started to think of the downside of loaning someone money. That thought was dismissed almost as soon as it came to my mind because I was so crazy about Ben.

The hardest part was yet to come. I had to tell Ben in a way that he would not feel insulted, but was not sure of how to go about it. I decided to wait for his next phone call. Hopefully, I would be ready by then.

Two weeks passed and there was no word from Ben. I was missing him a lot, and decided to call him on Wednesday, "our date day every two weeks."

"Hey Evie," he said as he answered my call.

"Hey, I haven't heard from you and just wanted to make sure you're alright."

"I'm okay," he responded.

"Glad to hear it. I've missed you and was wondering if we could see each other this week," I asked timidly.

My heart was beating out of my chest. I didn't think this was a very bold move, but yet I was afraid he would say no.

"This week is good. How about some drinks at Salt & Brew after work tomorrow?" Ben asked.

"That sounds wonderful! I'll see you tomorrow at 6:00 PM."

"Sounds like a plan," he said, and then hung up the phone.

That worked out pretty well, I thought to myself. I went through the rest of the day happy as a lark. Something was actually going right for me.

Or so I thought.

❖

It was almost 10:00 AM the following morning. I was just getting ready for my coffee break when one of my not so favorite co-workers began to approach me. She immediately dropped a bunch of folders on my desk that made a loud thud as they landed. Surprisingly, none of their contents spilled out.

Her name was Bettye. The first day she met me, she emphasized the "e" at the end of her first name. This was to let me know to never, ever, misspell it. She was tall with a heavy body and very thin legs. I always wondered how those thin legs held up all that weight. While Bettye was boisterous with an acid tongue, she could be sweet and gentle when she wanted to be or needed to be.

I did not like her at all! Staying out of her way was impossible. I had to work with her and therefore had to get along with her. Unfortunately, there is always someone who has to ruin your day, and in my case, her name was "Bettye."

To be fair, it seemed every office had its share of know-it-alls, bossy people, gossip mongers, and so forth. Bettye was all of these. If you were lucky, you sat next to someone who was nice and did their job. I always thought of myself as that person.

Today was my day, or should I say night with Ben. Finally, it was not on a Wednesday. No one was going to ruin this for me. Tonight was going to be sheer pleasure, and I couldn't wait.

CHAPTER 15

I picked up the strange box and once again removed the cover. Nothing had changed. The box was the same, the contents were the same, and the tissue paper inside was also the same.

I flipped the box over and dumped all of the contents onto my bed. I began to examine each piece as closely as possible. It was time to give up this useless search. While placing my earring back in the box, it occurred to me that I hadn't taken the tissue paper out. I felt compelled to do that, almost as if an invisible hand was guiding mine. Removing the paper exposed a small envelope scotch taped to the bottom of the box. I removed it and placed it on top of my white, eyelet bedspread. Could that be the missing piece to this puzzle?

I ripped open the envelope and saw a piece of torn notebook paper inside. It was a handwritten note penned in green ink.

Dear Evie,

I was cleaning out my clothes from the closet I had shared with Ben many years ago. That's when I came across this box. I had never seen it before. I was curious and opened it up. I saw the letters with your name and return address on the envelopes. I had originally sent them to that address, but they were sent back to me. Luckily, I was able to track down your new address.

At first, I was really mad when I noticed your belongings, but then I was glad I found them. I kind of feel like a kindred spirit with you.

I'm the other woman, or should I say, one of the many "other" women from Ben's past. I should also add the adjective "foolish" to that sentence.

I thought you might want your stuff back, as I certainly have no plans to keep them. I do not know why Ben held onto them, but apparently, he had his reasons.

Samantha

I re-read that letter at least 20 times for some hint as to why she sent the package to me. I was trying to understand what really motivated her. It had to be more than trying to be nice or as she

said, "feeling like a kindred spirit with me." Maybe I was wrong and it was exactly as she wrote; Samantha was simply another one of Ben's victims.

I finally put the letter down. At least now it was clear who sent it. Did Ben ever mention me to her? Did he love her? This started to become an obsession.

The envelope which held her letter had a partial return address. The last name of Gordon and an apartment number were written on the upper left-hand corner of the envelope. There was no street address, city or state. I looked at the postmark on the brown wrapping paper. It showed New York, NY.

She lived in my area, but where? Somehow this letter gave me renewed energy. It invigorated me as if I just came in from a great run or biking experience. I had to figure out how to go about finding this woman. It didn't occur to me that she might not want to be found.

"That's it!" I said out loud.

I would call information and get her address and phone number. That plan petered out almost as soon as it began. The operator had no street address or phone number for a Samantha Gordon. I was disappointed, but not defeated and wasn't going to give up on this quest.

I felt exhausted and slouched down on my couch. I spent the next several hours trying to fall asleep but was not successful.

•

Date night at Salt & Brew with Ben finally came. I chose a table in the back of the bar and waited for Ben. He arrived within a few minutes. I was filled with excitement, as always when in his presence. He gave me a delicious kiss and a short hug. The evening started out great.

After a few glasses of wine and light conversation, it was time for me to bring up the loan. There was no point in delaying it any longer. Gathering up all my courage, I took a deep breath and led the conversation towards it.

"So how was work today?" I asked nonchalantly.

"Mostly like any other day. I'm working on a big deal. If that comes through, all my money worries will be over," he responded easily.

Bingo! He actually laid the groundwork for me. From here on in, it was going to be easy.

"I don't want to put a damper on it, but what if it doesn't come through?"

"I thought about that. I'll have to take out a loan. What else is there to do?" he responded.

Bingo! Bingo! There it was, easy as pie.

"Taking out a loan from the bank is a good idea, but the interest rates are usually high. If you can't make the payments or are late, there are penalties. It just puts you further in the hole," I said as business-like as possible.

"I'm hoping it doesn't get to that point, but that's my plan for now," he responded.

Ben seemed calm, and content, as he spoke. I didn't expect that from him given his last reaction on the subject. I actually felt a little off-center but decided to move forward with my plan anyway.

"A thought just came to me," I said.

I acted as though I was surprised by my own words. I took Ben's hand in mine and held it gently. He did not pull away, but instead surprised me by taking my hand and kissing it. What a

sublime moment; it was as if it was written in a movie script specifically for me.

"Do you want another round?" the waitress asked.

I didn't see or hear her approach the table. Why do they always show up at the worst moments? Oh, that's right, Murphy's Law.

The spell was broken.

"Okay," Ben said.

The waitress picked up our empty glasses and quickly hurried away. I had to get the momentum going again. I would wait until Ben drank some more wine. It would be better that way, fewer inhibitions on his part and mine.

"Maybe instead of getting a loan from the bank, you could get a loan from a friend that's willing to help you. What do you think?"

"I haven't been here long enough to have made friends who would float me a loan. Besides, I wouldn't want to impose on anyone."

"You do have a friend! She's looking at you right now."

Whew! I was so glad that this was now out in the open.

He reached over and kissed me on the lips. Then he leaned back and smiled for a moment before speaking.

"You are not only beautiful but also a very giving person. However, I could never accept such a generous offer from you."

What! I couldn't believe the words coming out of his mouth. He wasn't going to accept a loan from me? Wow, what an honest, upstanding and genuine guy!

Then an idea hit me.

"Okay, I understand and respect you for it. Wait, I just got a better idea that you may like. Instead of a loan, how about moving in with me? There would hardly be any noticeable difference in my expenses, so it would be perfect. In fact, there would be no need for you to pay any rent until you're a lot more comfortable with your finances. It's the perfect solution, don't you agree?"

Ben was still for a moment and then looked directly at me. He had that business-like demeanor, calm, cool and very collected.

"It sounds like a plan, a good plan actually. Let's seal the deal with a kiss."

Very corny I must say, but I ate it up anyway, especially the kiss part. Truthfully, his breath was not the greatest at that moment, but I didn't care because I was so thrilled that my plan worked.

Ben was moving in with me! How lucky can a girl get?

We talked for an hour or so about move-in dates and miscellaneous things. I wasn't really paying attention to any of the details. I was too filled with joy.

My mind was going in so many different directions. This was a dream come true. I was on such a high, that I didn't want to come down. However, Newton's Law of Gravity would eventually become applicable to this situation.

What goes up must come down …

•

Two weeks, three days, 11 hours and 12 minutes passed since Ben and I discussed moving in together. While sitting at my office desk, I couldn't wait for the day to end. I was finally going to see Ben again. This time dinner was going to be at one of the more upscale restaurants.

I must have been doing a lot of daydreaming. Each time one of my co-workers needed to speak to me, they had to repeat my name several times to get my attention.

"Something is very different about you today. Besides your great mood, you seem very distracted. Are you in love?" Bettye asked sarcastically.

I hated that bitch!

I just looked at her and smiled, which irritated her. It was not to be mean, just a little revenge for her constantly annoying me. In reality, I did kind of enjoy it.

"Okay, don't answer me, I'll find out anyway," she said and walked back to her desk.

The rest of the day flew by. I met with three of our top clients. The meetings went very well and I was proud of myself. Bill nodded in approval after each client was taken care of. He then called me over to the side.

"Evie, you did a very good job. I will note this on your record which will do you well when your review period comes up."

"Thank you so much, Bill."

Ten minutes before it was time to leave the office, I spritzed on some perfume. I didn't want the scent to be overwhelming when I met up with Ben.

I stood up from my desk ready to put my jacket on when Bettye got in my face. I was startled and backed away. She didn't retreat, but instead let out a loud, bellowing laugh and then walked away. The other people in the office looked our way for a moment and then just continued on with what they were doing. She got the better of me once again.

I will get her … eventually.

Maybe.

CHAPTER 16

That stupid box! Backward I go.

There I was, back to obsessing about Ben, hoping he would call me. How moronic of me! Ben wasn't going to call me! That was a fact I had to accept and make peace with. Besides, why would I want to have anything to do with that horrible person again? I really needed to see Dr. Hunter because my thoughts were out of control, not to mention the fact that I was hardly living for the past six months.

Dialing Dr. Hunter's number was an excruciating task for me. I felt as though I had no energy and was in limbo. If I wanted to get better and truly live my life again, that call needed to be made. But I just couldn't do it!

•

Ben and I were living together for almost five months when our relationship began to fall apart. It was very slow at first and then I was blindsided as to how quickly it deteriorated. It was as if a tidal wave slapped me directly in the face.

Was I the only one who didn't know what was happening?

Apparently, so it seemed.

There was constant whispering behind my back at work, not to mention strange looks and sometimes even snickering. It's easy to sense when it's about you.

They knew what was happening, but I didn't. Did they overhear my private phone conversations with Ben? Why was I so blind? How did my co-workers know anything? I never told them shit!

•

The first three months Ben and I lived together could not have been sweeter. He behaved like the ideal man, being attentive to all my needs and anticipated them before they even occurred. As a bonus, I got to see him every day instead of once every two weeks or so.

Money never seemed to be an issue for us, or should I say for Ben. Although he paid for all our evenings out and bought groceries from time to time, he never offered anything towards the rent or utilities. I hoped for at least a modicum of monetary help at some point.

I thought it over and decided that having Ben in my life was more important than a few extra dollars. It was not as though my bills doubled, but I was very concerned about Ben's job. I wasn't

exactly clear on what he did or how much he earned. Other than his name and cell phone number, there wasn't much else I knew about him.

Suddenly I had a bad feeling in the pit of my stomach. I moved a man into my apartment because I fell in love with him. Was my thinking straight? Trying to extricate the negative thoughts from my mind and delete them forever was an impossible task. Why was I having doubts about Ben? He had been good to me and good for me. Why was I allowing a few dollars to ruin a perfectly good relationship? It was a dichotomy of thoughts.

Money is the root of all evil, I thought to myself. Yes, it is, especially if you don't have any. I had to let these thoughts go if I wanted this relationship to continue.

Upon entering the fourth month of living together, I still didn't have any more details of Ben's personal or professional life. Every time I questioned his lack of sharing this information, he didn't answer. To avoid a fight, I excused it and moved on. There was one time, early on, that he told me the name of his company, but stopped short after giving me that information.

The person who would not excuse Ben was Briana. Whenever she would ask me questions about him, I could never answer them. I would usually dodge the questions or change the subject. Briana was nobody's fool. She never let me get away with it. She always came back to the subject at hand, which would make me squirm. Briana knew I was not hiding the answers; she knew I didn't have them. Even though I had suggested going on a double date, she refused. Briana felt that he wasn't right for me and it would be futile to meet him.

During one of our get-togethers, she finally confronted me directly with a stare that said, "It's time to be honest with me, Evie." I had to take a deep breath before letting it all out. At first, it was hard to tell her what was happening. As I continued speaking, the conversation got easier. I expressed all my fears and doubts to her. Briana was very clear with her advice.

"Put it to him straight. Tell him you don't know anything about him and that it's starting to bother you. Let him know that you were an open book from the beginning. There was no prodding necessary on his part to get detailed information from you, was there? Now it's time for him to fill you in," she emphasized clearly.

Even though her advice was sound and the way to go, it was difficult for me to follow it. I just couldn't do it. Again fear reared its ugly head. My fear of losing Ben superseded all of my instincts

that were telling me something was not right. I disregarded my intuition, Briana's advice, and any common sense that I had.

•

It was a bright and sunny Saturday morning when I woke up to the smell of my favorite dark roasted coffee. Ben was making breakfast, as he always did. I loved this part of the day with him.

I loved every part of the day with him!

"Honey," I called out from the bedroom.

"Just finishing, Baby. Stay relaxed and I'll let you know when breakfast is ready," he responded.

I was so happy! Those moments were so precious to me.

I closed my eyes and thought of our intimate time together from the night before. Ben was so loving, so gentle, and so passionate.

"Time to get up, Baby Doll," he called out.

His voice was music to my ears. I loved everything about him and believed he loved me too but wasn't 100% sure. He always kept me off kilter, just enough to make me doubt myself every so often. It was his way of controlling me and I didn't realize it. A lot of things he did to control me were subtle, yet some were very clear. If I had only chosen to pay attention …

I sat down at the table and looked at the goodies in front of me. Ben had made scrambled eggs mixed with scallions and bits of parsley. On a separate plate were two toasted whole-grain bagels and some mini cheese pastries. The array of foods looked delicious. Ben looked delicious! I was ready for a repeat of the previous night, but Ben wasn't in the mood.

After breakfast, we took our coffee mugs and sat on the couch to watch mindless TV. After a few quick kisses, Ben began to speak.

"I have to meet a client today, and then hit the gym, so I'll be back later," he said in a matter of fact way.

There it was! Ben was not taking my feelings into consideration. Once again, he let me know at the last possible moment that I was going to spend my Saturday alone. He constantly behaved this way, playing with my emotions, and I always accepted it. The morning started out on a high note and quickly dissipated by the early afternoon. I made up my mind that this Saturday would be different. This was the day that I would finally speak up.

"I really wanted to spend the day with you. The weather is nice outside. I thought we could go for a leisurely walk, have a nice lunch in the park, and just relax."

"I want to spend the day with you also, but you know that I'm trying to build up my business. I have to meet clients when they're available. Right now my time is their time. You need to understand that," he said a bit harshly.

I felt deflated! I did understand business, but he never informed me of the specifics of his situation. I didn't want it to become an argument and dropped the subject. So much for me standing up to him.

"I forgot to tell you that the eggs tasted really good. Thank you for making them," I said to diffuse the situation.

He smiled at me, but it wasn't one of love. Something was brewing beneath the surface. I just didn't know what it was.

When Ben came back later that day, he was in a foul mood and made it quite obvious. Although I had no clue what was bothering him, I went over and gave him a hug.

"What happened at your meeting?" I asked softly.

He looked at me with some surprise on his face before he responded.

"My clients didn't show up!"

That was all he said. It was definitely not a good time to continue the conversation. It seemed that it was never the right time for any serious conversations with Ben.

"I'm sorry that happened to you. Let's go out for dinner and relax. Don't worry, it'll be my treat."

"You always have a pat answer for everything. No, I don't want to go out for dinner! Just because I'm living at your place doesn't mean I'm a charity case or that you're better than me!"

Ben shocked me. It was the first time he lost his temper and raised his voice. Something was very wrong, and I had to find out what it was. He was so riled up, that I was too scared to ask him why he didn't just come back home since the clients didn't show up. He was gone an entire day. What did he do with all those hours? I was going to pursue this, or at least try to.

"Ben, where is all of this coming from? I never said that I was better than you. Let's forget about today and move forward."

There were a few moments of silence, and then Ben spoke again.

"Didn't you hear what I said? The clients never showed up! That makes me look bad to my boss, and it also means no money!" he shouted at me.

I stood there frozen, not knowing how to respond.

"I don't understand why you're acting this way. You're having a fight with me for no reason at all. And one more thing, I know absolutely nothing about you!"

"Oh, you want to know something about me! Okay, I'll tell you something, Evie! One day, when I was 15 years old, my father beat me so hard that one of my eyes closed. It was so swollen that I was in extreme pain for about a week. There was no reason for him to do that, except that he needed to take his rage out on someone. Since my mother had left us years before, I became his proverbial punching bag. And, that was when he wasn't drinking. Does that give you enough information or do you need to hear more?"

I had no response at that moment. I felt awful as to what Ben had been through. I finally understood why he kept so many things from me. I could only imagine how much he was hurting inside. I was about to apologize, but before I had the chance to do so, Ben stormed out.

He never came back to the apartment that night or the next.

Where was Ben?

I was extremely upset not knowing why he didn't return. My anger turned into fear that something might have happened to him. Maybe he was hurt or worse!

On the first night, I called his cell phone eight times and left numerous messages pleading with him to call or text me that he was okay. I didn't hear back from him and it made me even more frantic!

On the second night, I called all the local hospitals in the area to check if Ben had been admitted or was lying in the emergency room. "We have no patient by that name," was the response from all of them. Although relieved, I still had an uneasy feeling. If he wasn't in any of the hospitals, maybe he sacked out in his office. People did that all the time. If that's where he was, why didn't he return any of my calls? It would be cruel not to. Was Ben cruel? Of course not, I thought to myself. Something had to have happened to him.

Guilty feelings found their way into my head. Had I not questioned him, would he have left the apartment in such a bad mood? What if he got into a car accident because of the stress I caused him? This was all my fault since I suggested treating him to dinner. But then again, why would that

have bothered him? Maybe I should have suggested giving him a massage. Maybe I should have just given him a good old-fashioned blow job. He never would have left if I would have been kind to him. I couldn't help but blame myself.

•

It was Monday morning, and I didn't know whether to call Ben's workplace or the police. I really didn't want to involve them, especially if he wasn't truly missing.

I decided to call Ben's office at Universal & In Sync Properties LTD. I would be anonymous, and Ben would not be the wiser. It seemed like a good idea even though I was a little anxious about calling his job. He was always so secretive with me when

it came to anything involving his job. But I had to call because it was my last option. I needed to know for sure that he was okay.

I gathered up all my courage and called information for the number.

"Universal & In Sync Properties LTD, how may I help you?" answered the chirping voice on the other line.

"Yes, um hi, is Ben Robertson in?"

"Ben Robertson?" she repeated questioningly.

"Yes, is he in?"

"Sorry, but we don't have anyone here by that name."

"Maybe I wasn't clear. The Name is Ben Robertson, R- O- B- E- R- T- S- O- N."

"Sorry, we don't have anyone by that name in our directory," she responded.

"Thank you," I said and immediately hung up.

My body began to tremble. How could this be? Maybe I had the wrong company? No, that couldn't have been it. That was the name Ben gave me. It made no sense to me. My head started spinning and I had to sit down in order to digest the information just given to me. Something wasn't right … big time!

What was I supposed to do next?

I was toying with the idea of calling the police but decided to call Briana instead. Since I was late for work and didn't want to be fired, I had to put her off until lunchtime.

I rushed into the office and quickly landed on my chair. There were nine emails that needed to be answered, all from my boss, Bill, except for one. It read, "Meet me at Allegra at 6:00 PM tonight. Don't be mad at me. I can explain."

It was Ben! Thank G-D it was Ben! At least I finally knew he was safe.

I was still deep in thought when Bill approached my desk. I looked up at him and knew immediately that I was in trouble.

"Please step into my office for a few minutes," he said without any emotion in his voice.

The body language said it all. I followed him and sat down with my hands folded like a little school girl waiting to be scolded by the principal.

"If you're not going to be able to come in on time, at least call in and give us some notice. You have a lot of phone calls to return and there are still some outstanding files that need your attention."

Immediately after, he walked out of his office without giving me a chance to reply. I wasn't going to get angry with Bill. No sooner did that thought leave my head, when Bill reappeared in the doorway and added, "And you need to stay late today to make up the time you missed this morning."

Again he left quickly, so there was no opportunity for me to respond. Of all days, I couldn't stay late that evening. I needed to call Ben and let him know what was going on.

CHAPTER 17

I tried so hard to locate Samantha Gordon, but all my searching proved fruitless. Did she have an unlisted number? Maybe she used a fake name so that I couldn't track her down. It was as though she didn't exist, and maybe there was no Samantha Gordon after all.

I packed up the box exactly as I originally found it and placed it back in the same spot outside my door. By doing this, I felt that Samantha would come by and check to see if the package was brought in. It was a fantasy that I concocted in my mind which seemed to make sense to me. In reality, it was simply ridiculous.

•

I needed to know where Ben disappeared to for those nights and if he was truly okay. Since I was so behind with my work, I didn't take any breaks and skipped lunch so I could catch up. There would be no time to call Briana and I was good with that. I wanted to hear what Ben had to say before telling her anything.

At 2:35 PM, I emailed Bill with a status report so he would know that I was almost up to speed. Taking a deep breath, I dialed Ben's cell phone.

"Hey," he answered.

"Hi Ben, are you all right? I was so worried and tried to locate you, but nothing worked. I was driving myself crazy worrying about you so I called all the local hospitals …"

I continued babbling on until I realized Ben wasn't responding to anything I was saying.

"Did you get my message, Evie? I need you to meet me at Cafe Allegra tonight at 6:00 PM."

"I have to work late today. Can we meet around 7:30 PM instead?"

"I guess so," he said slightly annoyed.

"I'm not thrilled about it either, but I don't want to lose my job. I can't believe you're making a big deal about it after you disappeared for days."

Did I just stand up for myself? I couldn't believe it!

"You're right. I'm just stressed and we'll talk about it when we see each other. Then you'll understand and everything will be clear to you," he emphasized in a less agitated tone. I was pleasantly surprised by Ben's response.

"I'll see you at 7:30 PM," I said and then hung up.

I made a mental list of all the questions I was going to ask him. First and foremost was about his disappearing act. I needed to be strong and not pathetic, as I always seemed to be when we were together. I was so angry, but also couldn't wait to see him.

The workday finally ended.

•

As I walked towards Café Allegra, my stomach started churning. I was getting anxious. Ben should've been the nervous one, not me! I didn't do anything wrong. It wasn't me who walked out for days without a word.

But it was me who still cared.

I entered the café with a positive attitude. I didn't want Ben to see me behave in an immature way. He needed to know that he wasn't the only one in control. The showdown had begun.

He was sitting at the counter, which I found very strange. How are we going to have a conversation there?

"Hi Ben," I said in a semi-pissed off way.

"Do you want a latte?" he asked as though nothing had happened between us.

"Thanks, but let's move to a table so we can talk."

Ben shook his head no. I sat down next to him and kept my arms crossed, letting him know that I was upset about the stunt he pulled.

There was complete silence until the coffee was served. Ben barely looked at me, which made me feel very uncomfortable. He was still playing a game and wanted to keep me off balance.

As usual he wanted to dominate the situation, and as usual, he was doing a great job.

Finally, Ben turned towards me and looked me straight in the eye. I was surprised by that sudden move but went with the flow.

"There's a lot of explaining that I have to do, but first let me tell you that none of this is your fault."

Really! What a jerk! Looking at him stoically, it was obvious that he was really full of himself and a great con artist. I wasn't going to allow him to intimidate me at that moment and certainly didn't want to be made a fool of. My decision was to not answer him. I looked into his eyes and didn't utter a word.

When there was no response on my end, Ben saw a side of me that he had never seen before: control! His charm instantly disappeared, and his smile dissipated.

"Maybe sitting at a table instead of the counter would be better. Is that okay with you, Evie?" he asked in a pleasing tone.

"Sounds good to me," I responded.

Did he forget that I had already suggested the same thing a few minutes before? Needless to say, I followed his lead and we sat down at a wooden table with three chairs. I placed my brown leather pocketbook on the empty chair next to me and looked up at Ben, but did not speak. I was beginning to think that I was actually in control of the conversation at that point.

"Evie, I'm not a good man and haven't been honest with you. It's time for me to come clean. You're too good a person to be with someone like me."

Talk about a sucker punch! That was the last thing I expected to come out of his mouth. It took me several minutes to digest what he was telling me. Was I dreaming? No, it was real, very real. Ben must have seen the change in my facial expression as he began to speak again.

"I know that I just shocked you. You're very important to me, and I need you to know everything about me. More importantly, you have to trust me."

I still did not respond. It was as though I was moving in slow motion. Was he conning me or actually being sincere? Maybe he could vindicate himself, but I strongly doubted it. Even though I still loved him, I didn't want to be anybody's fool either. Hopefully, my heart would not interfere with common sense.

Finally, I looked at him and said, "I'm ready to listen."

Ben took my hand in his and leaned in very closely. Speaking in just above a whisper, he asked me to pay very close attention. Then he gave me explicit directions.

"It is very crucial right now that you do not respond to me verbally or with any extreme body movements."

Fear came over me very quickly and I did exactly the opposite of what he asked.

"I'm scared of what you are about to tell me, but I need to hear it," I said while nervously fanning my face with my shaking hands.

Why did he suggest a public place for such a private conversation? We should have met in my apartment. That would have made a lot more sense. The situation was getting weirder and weirder by the minute.

"I haven't been living a clean life. I'm in debt big time, and to some very unsavory people. I did it all; drugs, gambling, and things that shouldn't be talked about. My disappearance these last few nights was not by choice!"

I stood up, scared out of my wits, and ran into the bathroom. I became nauseous and felt as though I was going to pass out. After sitting down on the toilet seat, I closed my eyes and pictured what had just happened. Was he serious or was this some kind of a hoax? Why meet in a café to discuss this type of information?

I pulled some brown paper towels from the dispenser, ran lukewarm water over them and blotted my forehead. I started to feel better and knew it was time to go back to the table, assuming Ben and my pocketbook were still there.

I sat down once again. It didn't seem as though Ben had moved a muscle.

"Is this some sort of a sick game?" I asked him.

"It's the truth, I swear it," he whispered.

He seemed so serious at that very moment, that I became doubtful of my own intuition. Maybe he was being honest.

"Is there more to this story, Ben?"

"There's a lot more. Unfortunately, I can't share all of it with you. Do you believe me and do you trust me?"

"I believe and trust you," I answered quickly, going against my better judgment.

"Good. Let me tell you why I wanted to meet you here. I think they're watching your place to see if I'll show up."

"What!" I screamed out loud, forgetting that I was in a public place.

I then grinned out of nervousness.

"Shhh! Lower your voice. I can't risk calling attention to myself."

"What are you going to do? Maybe you should call the police?"

"I can't do that. With these people, you don't involve the police."

"I don't understand any of this. Are they trying to kill you?"

"No. They just want their money, with interest, and they want it now!"

My head was aching. There were too many questions that needed answers, and those I had were not making any sense at all.

"I can't think in this place and don't understand what's going on, Ben! You know what? I do not want to know anymore! I have to leave. Goodbye!"

I grabbed my bag and ran out the door. I flagged down a cab and gave the driver Briana's address. Going back to my place was not an option. I was too frightened by what Ben said and needed to talk to Briana right away. I should have called her earlier and told her what had happened with Ben in the last few nights. But as usual, I didn't want her to think any worse of him than she already did. Regardless, Briana was the type of friend who would understand me showing up on her doorstep unannounced and allow me to stay the night.

CHAPTER 18

Briana lived in a doorman building with a concierge. It used to be a fancy hotel back in the day. I gave the doorman my name and Briana's name. He rang her apartment and then told me to go upstairs.

Briana opened the door. She was already in her pajamas. I apologized profusely while walking into her entryway. She then closed the door and locked it. Briana looked at me quizzically but did not say a word. I went over and hugged her and then started to cry. All my emotions were pouring out of me. I could not stop weeping for at least 10 minutes before composing myself.

"I'm so grateful that you are my friend. I wouldn't know what to do without you right now. Thank you for letting me in. Can I stay the night?"

"Of course you can stay, Evie. You're always welcome. This has to do with Ben, doesn't it?"

"How did you know that, Briana?"

"Because my dear, it smacks of man trouble! What else would make you show up this late and ask to spend the night? You can't stop crying, you didn't call before you came here, and you also look like a big mess. I think that gives it away," she said in a sarcastic yet loving tone.

Briana had no clue as to the news about to be dropped on her. I felt bad about bringing her into the situation, but there was no other choice if I wanted to keep my sanity.

"I guess you were getting ready for bed," I said as if it wasn't obvious.

"No problem. Why don't you sit down and tell me what's going on."

Her voice was caring and welcoming.

"Evie, would you like a cup of tea or coffee first? I have some new herbal teas that I would like to try out."

"A cup of tea would be great, with milk, please. It's the English way."

Briana brought each of us a ceramic mug which she placed on a wooden tray. She set it down on her oval cocktail table and then handed one of the mugs to me. The tea was soothing and calming. After taking a sip, I described everything in detail pertaining to Ben, especially what he told me earlier at Cafe Allegra. I was cringing knowing Briana would most likely lecture me on how naïve and stupid I was. Thankfully, she chose a different path.

"I think you need to drop him and do it now! He's trouble, big-time! I don't know what he's involved in, but you need to get him out of your life. And I do mean now!"

"I know that everything you're saying is true and the right thing for me. Yet something is stopping me from doing anything."

"Evie, are you listening at all? This guy is dangerous and a liar. Who knows how many crimes he has committed? Don't you realize that you can't even stay in your own apartment tonight? You are afraid of him and his partners in crime, or whatever you want to call them."

"I am afraid of him," I said very meekly.

"Actually, I'm very afraid. But something keeps me drawn to him. I don't know what it is, Briana."

"You have a death wish! It's very late and time for me to go to bed. Please think about what I said. The alcove has a pull-out bed, and all the bedding is in the chest next to it. Make yourself another tea if you want to. Stay here tomorrow also. We'll talk more then."

Briana then walked into her bedroom and closed the door. I was very surprised at the abrupt way she ended the conversation. Then I realized that she had to get up for work in a few hours. It was quite selfish of me to impose on her late at night without any notice. I forgot that she was a human being too.

I sat there for a few more minutes trying to make sense of everything. There were only two things I figured out for sure. I needed to get to sleep because I had to work the next morning. The other was that I wasn't going to give up on Ben.

One of those decisions was definitely a bad one.

The next morning, Briana and I rushed to get ready. It was somewhat hectic for both of us. I didn't want to be a nuisance but told her that I was definitely going to spend another night at her apartment. She gave me her spare key and told me to come and go whenever I pleased.

What a fabulous friend!

•

Once I arrived at the office, it couldn't have been more obvious that my co-workers were talking about me. It must have been because they noticed that I was wearing the same clothes as the day before. I couldn't borrow any of Briana's clothing because I was a lot taller than her. I wasn't going to explain a thing to my co-workers and liked the fact that I didn't feel the need to justify myself.

As I sat down at my desk, my cell phone began to ring. It was Ben! I stared at the phone but did not answer. Was I being strong or just trying to control the situation? It was disappointing that he didn't leave a message. Was he was toying with me? He knew it and I knew it. It was a matter of who would cave in first. The answer was obvious, it would be me. What I didn't know at the time was that I was following a script all laid out for me by Ben, and unknowingly, I played my part perfectly.

I thought I was very strong by waiting until the end of the workday to call him back. I naively believed that he would regret not coming clean from the beginning, assuming everything he told me was even true.

It was finally 5:00 PM. I walked over to a vacant office and called Ben from my cell phone. He picked up on the first ring. I found that impressive. Apparently, it didn't take much to impress me at that time.

"I'm glad you called. We need to talk," he said.

"I only called to understand what is going on. I'm just not sure if this is a joke. If it is, it isn't funny, Ben."

"We need to meet and talk," he emphasized strongly, not giving me any additional information.

"I do want to see you, but I'm really afraid of you and whatever it is you're into," I stated bluntly.

"There's no reason to be afraid, Evie! I would never hurt you. I just want to finish explaining everything that is transpiring. Once you hear what I have to say, it will all be crystal clear. You'll see that you have nothing to worry about. Please meet me tonight. Now that you know the most crucial things that are going on in my life, the rest is just filler."

He wasn't really begging, but he was very convincing. I kept hearing Briana's voice in the back of my head telling me to cut all ties with Ben but ignored it.

It was at that moment that I made a decision. It was time to trust Ben. I was in love with him and had to give him the opportunity to explain himself. To be truly honest, the situation was scary, but also exciting to a point.

"Sure, I'll meet with you. You have to be fully upfront with me and you can't hide anything," I emphasized.

"I will tell you everything that I know, but we can't meet at your apartment."

"Why not?"

"Just trust me this once. Let's meet at Hotel Elite. How soon can you get there?"

"Are you talking about meeting in the lobby and talking there?"

"I think we should get a room. That way, it'll just be the two of us. We will have the opportunity to say whatever we want to each other without any interruptions. We could stay all night or leave at any time. I made a huge mistake having us meet in public last night. So, are we on, Evie?"

Why was he leaving the decision up to me? I didn't comprehend it at the time, but this was his way of leading me to say "yes" to his plan. He had thought it out very carefully, and I was very gullible. I was "ripe for the picking," as the saying goes.

"Fine, Ben. I'll meet you at 7:30 PM in the lobby of the hotel. See you then."

"Wait! I need you to make the room reservation and put it on your credit card. I can't use my name right now for the obvious reasons," he said a little anxiously.

"That makes sense. No problem! I'll get there a few minutes earlier and take care of it."

I hung up the phone and felt satisfied with my decision. I was going to be paying for the room, knowing full well that Ben would never offer to pay me back. I excused and rationalized it to myself; how could he have paid me back considering all of his money problems? There's nothing like an old fool, but in this case, also a young fool.

I took a few deep breaths and then called Briana.

"Hey, Briana! I'm going to stay in my apartment tonight. Please, don't worry. It's all good. Thanks so much again for letting me stay the night."

"Are you sure?" she asked me.

"Yes, but I have to hang up now. Talk to you later."

I hung up the phone quickly in order to remove myself from any interrogation. Lying to Briana was something that did not make me feel good.

My cell phone rang almost immediately afterward. The caller ID showed it was Briana. She knew something was not right and wanted the truth. She probably suspected that I wasn't following her advice about Ben. Briana wasn't going to let me get away with that and therefore I let it go to voice mail, determined that nothing would stop me from meeting with him.

Briana would surely forgive me once all of this was over … hopefully.

●

Hotel Elite was very inviting. The well-lit lobby, although small, was comfortable. There were four chairs aligned in a semicircle with a matching couch, all in the French provincial style. The furniture was elegant, not gaudy or flashy. There were 10 to 12 people mulling around, most of them were on their cell phones.

I didn't see Ben and decided to go to the front desk. The clerk was well-dressed in a dark blue suit, a white shirt and a navy tie. His head was shaved and he had the most beautiful brown eyes. His eyelashes were the thickest I had ever seen on a man. As I approached the counter, he turned to me with a wide smile.

"Good evening, may I help you?"

"Yes. I'd like a room."

"For how many days?" he asked.

"Just for tonight."

His demeanor seemed to change slightly. Maybe it was only my imagination. Doesn't anyone else ever take a hotel room for just one night?

"Do you have any luggage that needs to be taken to your room?" he asked.

"None, thank you."

"That will be $499.00 plus tax. How will you be paying?"

"By credit card."

I didn't expect the room cost to be that high, but then again, it wasn't expensive for New York City.

I placed my credit card on the counter and waited for the paperwork to be processed. The clerk handed me a little paper receipt to sign and then gave me the key card to room #475. I texted the room number to Ben, placed the card in my pocketbook, and then went to the elevator. I got off on

the fourth floor and located the room on the right side. I went in, took off my jacket, and sat on one of the oversized chairs.

After about 20 minutes, I became restless and started pacing back and forth in the room. Was Ben standing me up?

I walked over to the one window in the room and stared outside to bide my time. The view was of a large apartment building with a doorman standing in front. He was opening the door of a black stretch limo that had just pulled up. A few minutes later, I looked at my cell phone again and realized that 40 minutes had passed by. I walked away from the window and started to think that something bad might have happened to Ben. Soon after, my feelings changed from fear to anger. After all he said to me the other night, he had the nerve to not show up at the hotel room that I had just paid for! If Ben didn't arrive within the next ten minutes, it would be time for me to leave and show him that I had some modicum of self-respect. To hell with the money I just spent.

Two minutes later, there were three knocks on the door. I knew it was Ben and quickly let him in.

He looked at me and my heart melted. All I wanted was for him to hold me in his arms and kiss me sweetly.

It didn't go that way.

Ben sat down on the bed and leaned against the headboard. He hardly looked at me. I didn't want to sit on the bed with him because it would defeat the real purpose of this meeting.

I turned the chair around to face Ben and sat down. He emanated confidence and seemed very sure of himself. There is nothing more intoxicating than a man who knows who he is and doesn't apologize for it.

"You're so beautiful, Evie," he said in a low voice.

He then paused for a moment and cleared his throat.

"I owe you so much more than an explanation. I haven't been the easiest guy to get along with. I'm aware of that, but there have been circumstances beyond my control."

He almost got to me with the "beautiful" compliment which he used frequently. But, I reminded myself that this was not a time for confusion, but for answers. A half hour had passed by and he hadn't said anything of substance. I didn't know anything more than before he stepped into the room. It was time for me to show some backbone. I needed to approach him with some direct questions since he wasn't revealing anything new.

"Ben, we haven't known each other for a very long time, but long enough that we should be in a better place. I don't know much about you. You've managed to keep me in the dark and have been very deceptive about everything. It's like a "Cloak and Dagger" thing that's going on with you. Just be as honest with me as I have been with you this entire time. Just tell me what's going on!" I said pleadingly.

Ben sat there for a minute or two before he began to speak. It intimidated me and again he made me feel off-center.

"That's why I wanted to meet with you. I want to be honest and am being honest! Before we met, I was on the wrong path in life. All of my bad decisions were due to my father's abuse. I was doing some low-level drugs and gambling a lot. Unless you're constantly winning, your money dwindles down very quickly. You can never make enough, and the gambling gets worse."

"Wait a minute! Before I forget, I called Universal & In Sync Properties and was told by the receptionist that there was no Ben Robertson on the roster. Why did you tell me you work there when you obviously don't?"

"That receptionist was a temp for the day and she didn't know what she was doing. Don't worry about it, I absolutely do work there. So as I was saying, Evie, I kept betting, thinking I was going to hit it big and be able to pay off all my debts. It didn't work out that way. I never hit it big, but kept on gambling and using drugs. I then started selling them just to get by. When you came into my life, I knew immediately that I wanted to be with you, which meant that I would have to clean up my act. A lot easier said than done!"

As he continued to talk, I started to be taken in by his flowery words. Once again, I was beginning to feel empathy for him and allowed myself to be deluded by his sob story. My low self-esteem and desperate need for his love canceled out any common sense that I had.

"So where do we go from here, Ben?"

"I'm sure your apartment isn't being watched anymore, but to be sure, let's stay here for the next few days."

I foolishly agreed and booked the room for the next two nights as well.

CHAPTER 19

Before Ben came into my life, I would go grocery shopping on Mondays or Thursdays during work. I would skip lunch and use that time to buy staples for the week. They were light purchases, so I would store my perishables in the office fridge.

On one particular Thursday, I changed my routine and decided to shop in one of the local bodegas near my office. I had this recipe for chili con carne which needed some ethnic spices that were not always available at the regular supermarket.

Upon entering the bodega, wonderful aromas began wafting toward me. I then noticed all the open burlap bags sitting on the vinyl floor. There were many varieties of rice, spices, beans and other foods unfamiliar to me on display. The woman behind the counter explained their uses. She was gracious and answered all of my questions.

When I brought my selections to the counter, a very handsome man walked in. He stepped in front of me and greeted the woman behind the counter. She acknowledged him and they chatted happily for a few minutes. She was glad to see him and she wasn't the only one! He was hot! I didn't mind waiting.

He was around 5'11" or so and had a solid build. What blew me away was his face. He wasn't handsome in the conventional way. He had thick, jet-black hair which was pulled back in a ponytail. His eyes were dark, almost black, and his mouth was full. He had a chiseled jaw and sported a thin mustache with maybe a day's growth of beard. He was very sexy and exuded confidence, which attracted me the most. Everything about him appealed to me, so of course, I was going to do my best to meet him.

How do I go about getting his attention, I thought to myself. At that moment I devised a plan. I purposely dropped one of the glass jars onto the floor from the counter. I knew that he would turn towards the noise and then notice me. I let out a small scream and began to apologize to the proprietress. She immediately came around the counter and started cleaning up the mess. That handsome guy with the ponytail also came over. I looked at him and made an, "I'm so clumsy and helpless" type of face. He smiled at me and then began to laugh. I followed suit and also began to laugh. Just as I planned, he extended his hand and said, "Can I help you with your groceries?"

Life is going to be good in the bodega, I thought.

"I'm usually not this clumsy," I said in the sweetest voice possible at that moment.

He looked at me with those intense, dark eyes. I absolutely loved it!

"Hello, my name is Eduardo."

"My name is Evie. I feel so foolish for dropping the jar on the floor."

"You shouldn't be embarrassed. You did nothing wrong. Everybody breaks something sooner or later. It's not a big deal."

That is true, but not everybody does it on purpose to attract the attention of a big hunk of testosterone standing right in front of you, I thought to myself.

"Thank you. I appreciate you saying that," I stammered a little.

Once the mess was cleaned up, I was hoping Eduardo would continue to talk to me. At that moment, his cell phone rang. He became immersed in conversation and wasn't looking in my direction anymore. I knew that if I stayed any longer it would become awkward and obvious. I took my grocery bags and left disappointed by how it had ended.

All through dinner I couldn't stop thinking about Eduardo. While I was so physically attracted to him, it was mostly his confidence that drew me towards him. Finding a man with confidence is very enticing.

•

The next day I came up with another silly plan. I would visit the bodega every two to three days, purchasing little odds and ends, hoping to see Eduardo again.

Two weeks went by, and he didn't show up. I waited another week before my next visit to the bodega.

It seemed the grocery lady behind the counter knew exactly what was on my mind. Women always know when a man is involved in another woman's plans. That was okay with me. She was a nice lady, and I wasn't doing anything wrong. I was just trying to speed up the process of getting to know Eduardo.

"Hello, Miss, my name is Maria. It's nice to see you again. Is there anything in particular that I can help you with?" she asked me.

There it was. My cover was blown. She knew that I wasn't coming in to look at the hot peppers on display.

"Hi Maria, my name is Evie. I'm not sure what I want yet, so maybe I'll browse for a little while longer."

"Maybe what you want is not on the shelves," she said with a small smile on her face, which clearly indicated cooperation.

I began to giggle after her statement, and she let out a hearty laugh. I had just made an ally and maybe even a new friend.

"Eduardo's out of town right now. He's in the army reserves and should be back next week. He usually comes in on Wednesdays," Maria said as she winked at me.

"Thank you so much, Maria."

I placed a small jar of guacamole and a cellophane bag filled with rice on the counter. I included the cost of the jar I had broken a few weeks ago and paid for my purchases.

Life was good at that moment. I felt confident that I would not only see Eduardo again but that he would ask me out on a date.

Although I kept thinking about Eduardo every other minute, the week flew by. It was finally Wednesday! I had made sure to be in perfect form that day. I wore the new blue dress that I had purchased a few weeks before. It was sleek and fit my curves without revealing too much. I usually didn't wear jewelry to the office, but the thought of seeing Eduardo made me want to sparkle. I put on a gold bangle bracelet and small gold drop earrings. A little blush was added to my makeup and it was time to go to work.

As usual, Bettye sauntered over to my desk, trying to irritate me. It's sad how boring her life must have been.

"What's got you on cloud nine today?" she asked me jeeringly.

She had said it loud enough for everyone to hear. I couldn't be bothered by both her need for attention and desire to needle me. Well, it was not her lucky day, it was going to be mine.

I garnered the biggest smile possible and said, "Today is the first day of the rest of your life, Bettye!"

Of course, I emphasized her name in a sarcastic tone. It gave me a "feel good" moment. It was childish behavior on my part, but I couldn't help myself. She looked stunned, as though she was hoping to rattle me. Instead, Bettye got an answer that she didn't expect, even though it made no sense. She walked away defeated, but I knew she would be back for more.

Just before it was time to leave the office, I opened my compact mirror to check my makeup.

I took the escalator down to the lobby and off I went. I felt as though I was a rock star going on a world tour. Getting to the bodega couldn't come soon enough for me. Even if Eduardo wasn't there yet, I could hang around without raising suspicion because Maria knew exactly what was going on. She definitely could be counted on if necessary.

Two hours passed by with no sign of Eduardo. Yes, I spent a full two hours hanging around the bodega in hopes of seeing him. It was time to leave and go home. I was about to tell Maria goodbye when Eduardo walked in. I quickly grabbed a jar of pimientos off the shelf and began to read the ingredients. Then I proceeded to walk towards the back of the store. I was so happy that my heart started racing.

A few moments later, I turned around to walk towards the front of the store, not realizing Eduardo was in back of me at that very moment. We ended up face to face and I thought I was going to faint!

"You're the lady I saw in here a couple of weeks ago, Evelyn, right?"

"Almost right, it's Evie."

"Do you live in the neighborhood?" he asked.

"I work in the area but don't live too far away."

There was a slight pause and the conversation became a little awkward. I wanted to see him so much, and now that he was right in front of me, I became tongue-tied.

"I hope I'm not keeping you from your husband or children," he said in a jovial manner.

I don't have any children but wouldn't mind making a baby with you tonight, I thought.

"You're not keeping me. I'm not married and I don't have any children," I said in a matter of fact tone.

I didn't want him to think I was interested. Who was I kidding? He knew I was interested!

Very interested indeed!

"If I'm not being too bold, would you like to have dinner with me tonight?" Eduardo asked.

"I don't know you, but I do feel comfortable with you."

"Is that a yes?" he questioned.

"That's a yes! Where are we going to go?"

"I know a nice cozy restaurant on 85th Street. They serve gourmet pizza, pasta and the freshest salads," he offered.

"That sounds great! We can leave directly from here since it's getting late. Do you have a car, or should we take a taxi?"

"I have a car, but let's hail a cab. You can never get a parking spot there," he said.

I smiled, and he smiled. My plan had worked to perfection. Sometimes you just have to push the envelope.

The décor of the restaurant on 85th wasn't fancy, but it was filled with customers waiting to be seated. That was usually a sign that the food was good. We were seated at one of the last tables available. Unfortunately, it was near the bathroom. Oh well, you can't have everything.

The waiter came over almost immediately and gave us two menus. I wanted to say, "I'll have Eduardo on my plate," and didn't realize that I had giggled with that thought. However, Eduardo did.

"What's so funny? Can you let me in on the joke?"

I was flustered for a minute not knowing what to say and then regained my composure.

"It's just something silly that happened at work today, and it just came into my mind."

"What would you like to order?"

"I'll have what you're having," I responded.

Ugh! That was definitely a no-no. Why couldn't I choose something from the menu for myself and by myself? The waiter appeared at that moment, and Eduardo ordered two Caesar salads and two orders of pasta primavera.

"Very good, Sir, will there be anything else?" the waiter questioned.

Eduardo looked at me wondering if he should just go with it or ask me.

"Would you like some wine with dinner, Evie?"

That question was right up my alley.

"That would be great. I would love a glass of Cabernet."

"We'll have two glasses of Cabernet and we're good," he added.

The waiter left with our orders, and soon after a busboy appeared with our place settings and two glasses of water. Mine had a lot of ice in it and very cold beverages hurt my teeth. I didn't want to have to explain that to Eduardo but did so anyway. I began to discard the ice on my napkin when Eduardo signaled a waiter and asked for a glass of water with no ice. That was so gentlemanly and sensitive of him.

"Thank you for being so thoughtful," I remarked.

He smiled. What a beautiful smile and very kissable lips. I had to stop fantasizing while I was with him, but couldn't help myself. I was really in need of a night with some good loving by a strong and amorous man. Hopefully, that man would be Eduardo and hopefully, that night would be tonight!

The waiter brought over our wine and salads. Everything looked great. Eduardo picked up his glass, raised it a little and then took a sip. I did the same. The wine was smooth as it went down my throat. I took an extra sip and placed the glass back on the table.

"So, tell me something about yourself," he said as he started to eat his salad.

"There isn't much to tell. My life is rather simple. I'm an account executive and work mostly with clients, especially the difficult ones. I seem to handle them better than the other executives."

"Do you like working at your company?" he queried.

"It's alright. It's not a dream job, but it pays the bills and leaves something over."

I paused and then asked him, "What do you do?"

He didn't respond to my question. Instead, he continued asking me for more information.

"If it's not what you really want, then why don't you look for a job that is more fulfilling? Wouldn't you rather be spending all those hours a day doing something more meaningful?"

His advice to me was sound, but I didn't understand why he was asking me so many questions regarding my job. It was as though he was grilling me instead of having a conversation. It seemed that he was way too focused on something that wasn't his concern, especially on a first date. I was starting to feel uneasy.

"I hadn't thought about it that way. For right now, changing jobs is not a good option for me. There's always room for advancement at my company, but I must prove my worth first."

My answer didn't seem to satisfy him. His behavior changed, and suddenly he seemed distant. I didn't know what he was thinking but did know that this date was going south fast.

He took another sip of his wine.

"Eduardo, could you signal the waiter? I'd like another glass of wine."

Wine always seems to calm me down and clear my head.

"Do you have any brothers or sisters?" I asked him.

I changed the subject in order to make the meal more pleasant since this would probably be my first and last date with

Eduardo. After everything I went through to meet the guy, this is what he turns out to be like? What a huge disappointment!

"I'm sorry. I overstepped and didn't mean to get that passionate about you and your job. I just feel that people don't always reach their full potential. They usually give up or get used to a routine which makes them feel comfortable when they're really not," he explained.

What he said made sense, but it sounded more like a lecture than having a conversation. I was losing interest fast. I had such high expectations, but this date continued to spiral downward. I didn't find him interesting anymore.

"I'm not unhappy and like what I do, but thank you for your concern, Eduardo," I said sarcastically.

Just at that moment, our dinner was served. I gave the waiter my empty salad bowl. I lost my appetite and was contemplating ending the date right then and there but didn't. I don't know what made me stay. Maybe I just didn't have the guts to leave. Apparently, Eduardo was feeling the same way as he was sensing my discomfort.

"Why don't we finish our dinners and call it a night. I think we got off on the wrong foot. I would like to see you in a few weeks when you might like me again."

How presumptuous of him! He's assuming that I would want to go on another date with him! Why would I do that? He wasn't a good first date. What would make him any better the next time?

"I need to go," I mumbled.

I stood up and grabbed my purse, took out twenty dollars and dropped it on the table.

"I hope this covers my share," I said in a snarky tone.

Not waiting for a reply, I promptly left. Even though I was so turned off by him, I was hoping he would run after me like they do in the movies. He didn't.

Two weeks passed by and I couldn't stop thinking about Eduardo. Each time his face came into my head I tried to dismiss it, but was rarely successful. I would constantly ask myself, why was I still thinking of a man I had a terrible first date with? Why was I so fascinated with him? The more I thought about it, the less clear it became.

I then came up with another one of my brilliant plans. I would return to the bodega, speak to Maria and see what her thoughts were on this.

●

Back to the bodega I go!

There were two large windows on either side of the entry door to the bodega. Each window was plastered with multiple flyers advertising store hours, specials, and posters for many different entertainment venues. It was difficult to get a good look as to who was inside, so I gave up on the idea that I would be able to tell if Eduardo was in the store. I gathered up my courage and walked in.

Maria was filling a large glass bowl with stuffed jalapenos. She spotted me immediately and motioned for me to come over.

"Hello, Miss. I'm sorry but I don't remember your name," she said apologetically.

"It's Evie. Do you have a few minutes to talk?"

"Go to the back of the store. You will see a door by the side of the bathroom. That's my office. Wait for me in there and I'll see you in a few minutes," she told me.

"Thank you so much. Are you sure I'm not taking you away from your work?"

Obviously, I knew full well that I was.

"It's totally fine," Maria responded as she continued filling the bowl. Then she placed the remaining peppers on a plastic tray.

I walked towards the back room. It was a small space, filled with cans and jars of varied food items sitting on metal shelves. There was also a refrigerator, a small table with a computer on it, scattered papers, and three chairs. Two of the chairs had rusted metal legs, and the third one had black electrical tape on the vinyl seat cover. I chose that one to sit on.

There was nothing to do but wait. To pass the time, I started to look at all the glass jars. As I was trying to name the foods in each one, the door opened abruptly and Maria walked in. She closed the door quickly behind her and then locked it. I found that odd and a little creepy but ignored it.

"Eduardo just walked into the store. Do you want him to know you are here?" she asked me.

"No, I don't. Can I please stay in here until he leaves?" I asked in a begging manner.

"No problem this time, but you can't make a habit of it. Tell me what you wanted to talk about," she asked.

"Eduardo asked me out. We went for dinner and it didn't go so well."

"What happened?"

"He was very domineering and controlling. He wanted to know everything about me but gave nothing in return."

"I still don't understand what the problem is. If he didn't treat you right, why are you still interested in talking about him?"

Maria was straight to the point, so I knew it would be best to tell her the truth. She was one of those no-nonsense people who would see right through me if I didn't.

"Even though he wasn't what I expected, somehow I'm still attracted to him."

"Maybe you could tell me something more about the date that would help me out," Maria said.

"I left the date abruptly which wasn't right of me. Maybe I got a little too heated. I would like a second chance with him."

Before I could finish my story, there was a knock on the door.

"Maria, Miss Rosie needs you to help her out with the counter foods," a male voice said loudly.

"I'm coming, I'm coming," Maria called back.

"I have to go and service the customers. My advice is to follow your brain first, and then your heart."

I couldn't believe how simple and good her advice was. Unfortunately, I followed it in the reverse order.

I went back to the bodega exactly a week later, hoping that Eduardo would be there. I would say "hi," and try to start a conversation as if nothing ever happened. That was my grand plan, but he wasn't there that day. I continued going back on Wednesdays and still did not see him. Maria stopped paying attention to me and I couldn't blame her. Frustration was setting in due to my lack of success, so I thought it was best to forget about him.

Finally, a smart move on my part!

CHAPTER 20

Monday morning was a very relaxed day at work. There weren't too many fires to put out with any of my clients. The office was comfortably quiet, as most of my co-workers were out. Eduardo came into my thoughts once again, but I dismissed it quickly. I busied myself with some mundane filing work, but that didn't help.

I started to think about going to the bodega again, and then realized how ridiculous that would be. Instead, I chose to call Eduardo. It would be a risky and foolish move, but I had to do it.

I went outside for a short break from work. I took my cell phone out of my purse and started to dial Eduardo's number which Maria had given to me.

"Hello," he answered.

"Hi, Eduardo, it's Evie. Do you still remember me?"

What a dumb way to start a conversation! I was angry at myself, but what could I do? The words had already come out of my mouth.

"Of course I remember you. I'm surprised that you called me," he responded.

"Surprised in a good way or a bad way?"

"In a good way, of course! I would have called you myself but didn't think you wanted to talk to me again."

"I thought about what had happened. Maybe we were both at fault. I'm willing to try it again if you are," I said to him.

"I'm game. How about taking it a little slower? Would you like to go out for coffee tonight?"

"Coffee is good. Do you want to go to Café Allegra?"

"7:00 PM at Allegra it is," he responded.

Hooray for me! I couldn't believe I did it. How smart was I in pulling off that coup? Meeting with Eduardo at 7:00 PM seemed light-years away. I kept checking the clock at work every few minutes. The day dragged on. Finally, it was time to leave the office.

Walking towards the café, I reminded myself to be relaxed and to be a good listener as well. I saw Eduardo sitting at a table checking his cell phone. I took a deep breath and then walked over to him.

"Hey, how are you?" I asked.

"Good, good. I just got here a few minutes ago. Please, sit down. What would you like to drink?" he asked me very politely.

I sat down and realized that he was less hyper then the last date we had. He seemed more mellowed out and that made me happy. I had a good feeling about how the evening was going to go.

"A latte works for me, thank you," I said sweetly.

He got up and ordered for both of us. It gave me a chance to look in my compact mirror to make sure my eye makeup wasn't smudged and that no food was stuck in my teeth.

Eduardo returned to the table rather quickly.

"I hope you like cinnamon muffins with your coffee," he said.

I liked the surprise. It indicated that he was trying to please me. It was a very good sign!

"I love cinnamon muffins. Thank you for getting them."

We started munching on the muffins and drinking our coffees. In between bites, Eduardo spoke about his family and the many places he'd traveled to. The conversation was going well and I saw another side of Eduardo; a side I liked.

"Hola, Lover!"

A female voice called out of nowhere as a young woman approached our table. Where the hell did she come from?

She was young and very beautiful with sparkling eyes and a flawless complexion. A shimmery violet lipstick perfectly covered her full lips. Her jet black hair flowed over her beautiful white blouse with silver sequins. She wore tight black jeans with black velvet high-heeled boots to match. She was quite a vision, I had to admit. My jealousy meter went sky-high!

"Emilia!" he responded in surprise.

He immediately rose from his chair and greeted her with a hug and a kiss on each cheek.

"How nice it is to see you! Are you living in New York now?" Eduardo questioned.

I thought I was going to be sick. What were the odds that this would happen during my second chance with Eduardo?

"I rented an apartment about eight months ago and the city is where I want to live forever," Emilia replied.

Hello! Doesn't anyone see that I am sitting at this table? It was quite evident that they were in a world of their own. I was contemplating leaving when Eduardo came back down to earth and realized that I still existed.

"I'm so sorry," Eduardo said to me.

Not as sorry as I would like you to be, I thought.

"Emilia, this is my date, Evie."

She extended her hand to me and I reluctantly shook it. It was rather limp, not a businesslike handshake. She gave me a sneer-like smile, and then said, "Nice to meet you."

We both knew she didn't mean it.

"Nice to meet you also," I said.

I didn't mean it either. We immediately hated each other.

Game on!

I wasn't certain of the relationship between them. Was this an ex-girlfriend of his? Was he still interested in her? Did she dump him and now she wants him back?

She was way too sexy!

I was becoming exasperated and very anxious. I didn't want to give either of them the satisfaction of knowing that I was jealous. Emilia looked at Eduardo for a signal to let her know that it was okay to stay. I realized that immediately and decided to be bold. Two can play at this silly game. I took Eduardo's hand and placed it in mine, and then placed my other hand on top. Emilia looked at me and then at Eduardo. Receiving no invitation to sit down and join us seemingly annoyed her.

"Well, I have to get my coffee. I come in here most weeknights just to relax. See you," Emilia said nonchalantly directing her reply to Eduardo.

She left and went over to the counter to order. I was trying to figure out if I won or lost that round. She definitely let Eduardo know that he could find her there almost every night if he wanted to.

What a clever bitch!

I quickly pulled my hands out of Eduardo's. Without a doubt, he understood what had just happened. I should have just let things go in their natural order. If I had only allowed her little ploy to play itself out. After all, if he was interested in her romantically, he never would have introduced me as his date.

I began to feel a little self-conscious. Eduardo seemed to have a puzzled look on his face. He undoubtedly felt the tension.

"This muffin tastes so good," I said quickly, hoping to break the uneasiness in the room.

I didn't know what else to say at that point. I was unnerved by her and it showed.

We continued to make small talk, but it was obvious that there was a haze of discontent hanging over Eduardo. The date ended early, and again, not on a good note. It was time to let go of a dream. It was evident that I was better off without Eduardo, even though I was so attracted to him. It was a mature decision on my part, although the fact that he didn't call after the date only made me want to see him again.

•

After my two dates with Eduardo, my dating life dwindled down to nothing for a few months. For whatever reason, I continued to think about him. Maria had my phone number, so she would leave me messages letting me know when he was in the store. Maria was sharp; she knew that I still liked him. I wasn't completely sure if she was playing matchmaker or just being a savvy shop owner.

Even though I made a vow to mentally let go of him, I couldn't. The thought of Eduardo not being interested, drew me to him even more. I continued to come to the bodega on the days Eduardo shopped, yet he never seemed to be there which became frustrating.

I was taking a big chance trying to bump into him. Things didn't flow right with us the two times we went out. Why would anything change if I did see him again, especially in the bodega?

Finally, I made a decision to forget about him. I was hoping to keep to it this time. When the spark isn't there, it just won't work. He had my phone number. If Eduardo had any interest in seeing me again, all he had to do was pick up the phone and call me. But then I wondered if he was reluctant to get in touch because he thought I would reject him. So of course, acting on impulse, I called him.

"Hi, Eduardo, it's Evie. How are you?"

There was a momentary hesitation on his end. It seemed he didn't even remember who I was.

"Oh hi, I'm fine, how are you?" he finally responded.

He sounded surprised that I called, and maybe even a little bothered.

I knew immediately that this conversation was not going to go anywhere, but I still wanted to keep on trying. After all, the call was already made. What was there to lose besides more of my self-respect?

"I'm good. I just thought that maybe we could meet for a cup of coffee and clear the air. There was a misunderstanding between us and I would like to be friends."

"Well, I don't have any hard feelings towards you, but we should leave it where it is. I'm seeing someone, so I have to go now. Thanks for calling and good luck to you."

He then hung up the phone without giving me a chance to respond. He was short and quite blunt with me, but I deserved it. What was I thinking when I made that call? Undoubtedly, I wasn't thinking at all.

Was Maria messing with me? She must have known Eduardo had a girlfriend. Something here wasn't right, but I wasn't going to pursue it any further. This time I meant it! I felt so low at that moment. All I wanted to do was crawl under my covers and go to sleep, so I did.

●

A few days after my pitiful phone call to Eduardo, I became depressed. I started overeating, especially at night when I was alone in my apartment and no one could see me. It got to the point where I didn't even taste the food anymore. It simply became a bad habit. I certainly understood that eating large amounts of food wasn't good for me, but it seemed impossible to stop. The more food I ate, the more I wanted to continue eating, never feeling full, never feeling satisfied.

I had to get a new wardrobe as my clothes were getting too tight. Everyone at work was gossiping behind my back about my weight gain. Of course, Bettye would constantly come over to my desk to taunt me.

"Would you like this candy bar? I have an extra one," she asked me in a singsong voice.

Bettye never waited for an answer. She would constantly leave a candy bar on my desk and walk away laughing. I acted like I was ignoring her, but I was hurting inside. I'm sure she knew it. It's always been amazing to me how people can take pleasure in other people's pain. Truth be told, I always wanted to eat those candy bars … and sometimes I did.

Periodically, I would catch my boss, Bill, taking sneak peeks at me when he thought I wasn't looking. It was devastating to me that my weight gain was so obvious. What I couldn't understand was why it was so bothersome to other people.

I tried to control my eating by making salads and watching my portions, but it didn't help. The bulk of my eating started at night and continued for several hours until I went to bed. The binge eating was only satisfying at the time I was doing it. I would always feel guilty afterward, but that never stopped my addiction.

My overeating had spiraled out of control. It was time to be good to myself and to stop having pity parties. After all, I was the only one attending them. It was obvious that I needed professional help. It took a lot of therapy for me to understand

my problems at that time. It turned out that it was not what I was eating, but what was eating at me. I was so lonely and alone.

I had to work on gaining self-confidence and stop being so pathetic. Maybe if I wasn't so desperate and needy, life would turn around for me. Was I the captain who was always steering her ship into turbulent waters? I realized that I was. If I kept acting the same way with these men, the end results would keep repeating themselves. You didn't need to be a genius to figure that one out.

●

For the most part, Dr. Hunter was a compassionate and understanding psychologist. Looking back, while she was often passive, she usually knew the right moment to interject a comment or offer advice. I always felt both good and bad after leaving her office. Certain revelations were difficult to accept, and those were the ones that hurt the most. It's hard to be made aware of your failings in life, especially when they are a direct result of your weaknesses.

Although I had been seeing Dr. Hunter regularly for my general anxiety, we spent a considerable amount of time delving into my unhealthy eating habits and weight gain. It was getting very costly to see her once a week, as my insurance barely covered it. However, I made the decision to stick it out as long as possible since she was definitely helping me.

Four months went by and I lost 25 pounds, with 20 more to go. Back at the office most of the staring had stopped, and the gossip seemed to have petered out.

Another two months passed with a continued weight loss and no thoughts of men or dating. The latter wasn't thrilling, but in an odd way, it was quite refreshing. It was similar to a spiritual cleansing. I felt as though my life was just beginning. It was becoming easier to breathe. The slate had been wiped clean and from that moment on, everything would be brand new.

As I was checking my calendar at work, I noticed that my vacation time was coming up and decided to take it. I needed the change of scenery and had always wanted to go to Hawaii. It would be costly, but so was my psychologist. I booked the trip and didn't let any doubts form in my mind. It was going to be an enjoyable vacation for me no matter what.

I made a quick call to Briana during my coffee break.

"Hello."

"Hi, Briana!"

"What's up, Evie?"

"I have a two-week vacation coming up next month. I finally decided that this is the time to go to Hawaii. Would you like to come with me?"

"I would love to, but I won't be able to leave by then. My vacation time doesn't begin until two weeks later."

"Bummer, I was really looking forward to us going there together. It would have been so much fun!"

"I know, but I can't ask my boss to switch my vacation time. It would create too many problems. Sorry."

"We must coordinate our schedules for next year. I guess I'll have to go alone," I said sadly.

"You don't have to be alone. You can join one of those organized group tours. They even have singles tours."

"That's perfect! It never occurred to me to do that. Actually, that will be an experience in itself. It's time I tried something different."

"I have to run. Speak to you later," Briana said.

I was so excited and couldn't wait to start checking out the different tours online.

I finished my day at work looking forward to being in my apartment with a glass of red wine in front of my computer. It was going to be a productive night.

After two hours of searching the internet, my eyes became very dry and I was beginning to feel worn out. There were so many tours and tour companies, that it was difficult to narrow them down. Just as I was about to log off, an ad caught my eye. It was colorful and showed people having fun at a bar on the beach. What caught my attention was the headline: "FUN IN THE SUN WITH SINGLES FROM 25 - 40." I surmised that

since the trip was expensive, most of the people would be closer to 40. That would work for me since I preferred older men.

It was getting late. I typed the number into my cell phone and intended to call Sea & Air Travel Co. during my lunch break the following day.

I went to sleep happy as a lark.

•

"Sea and Air Travel Company, how may I help you?" the operator's voice answered predictably.

"I'd like to book a reservation."

"What's the ID number of the trip you are booking and for which dates?"

Her voice was so low and monotone, that my patience waned. I let her know that I would book it online instead. She immediately hung up on me. She was so rude and inefficient, yet she had this job.

Interesting, isn't it?

I located the site online and booked the trip from April 1st through April 11th in sunny and beautiful Hawaii. This was truly going to be a fun vacation.

CHAPTER 21

The Haleakala Hotel on the Big Island was absolutely beautiful. The coral facade of the huge hotel was draped by palm trees and the most gorgeous flowers I had ever seen. It was breathtaking. The visual effects of this picture-perfect postcard made me feel as though I had arrived on an enchanted island. That was not far from the truth.

My group was meeting in the Kamalani Room at four in the afternoon. I had just enough time to unpack my suitcase and a small travel bag. The young woman with whom I was sharing the room had also just arrived.

"Hi, my name is Evie Harris. Isn't it great! We have 10 glorious days to bunk together."

"My name is Jaycee Elmore. I usually go on these trips with my cousin or sister, but neither of them could make it this year," she responded.

"My best friend couldn't make it either, but that doesn't mean we're not going to have fun. I plan to enjoy every moment," I said excitedly.

"I agree! Let's go down to the meeting room. I read in the brochure that we are going to get champagne and hors d'oeuvres," she responded.

"I'm good with that, but what I'm really looking forward to is meeting some hot guys."

"That would be great if it happens, but I hate to burst your bubble. I've been on a few of these trips, and most of the hot ones are either too old or a little bit weird."

"So, you've never met anyone on any of your trips?"

"I've met plenty of people, but not boyfriend material," Jaycee said.

"Then why do you keep coming back?"

"I'm still positive about meeting someone, but I'm not counting on it. I'm here to have fun. That much I can be sure of. We should go downstairs now or we'll miss the party, Evie."

"Then let's go!"

We walked into the Kamalani Room which was decorated in typical Hawaiian fashion. There were beautiful floral arrangements everywhere. Most of the vases were filled with hibiscus, pikake, and

heliconia flowers which were interspersed with birds of paradise blooms. They were truly spectacular to look at.

Each of us received a lei made of purple and white orchids. We were told by the hotel guide to feel free to take a glass of champagne. He did not have to tell me twice!

I looked around the room and saw about 25 people mingling around a long buffet table. Placed on it were pre-filled champagne glasses, bottled water, hors d'oeuvres, and bowls laden with pineapples, mangoes, bananas and lychee nuts.

"Let's go get some champagne," I said to Jaycee.

"Sounds like a plan to me," she agreed.

I took a sip of the champagne and it was dry. I preferred sweeter champagne but wasn't going to complain. My goal was to be happy, and I wasn't going to sweat the small stuff.

Jaycee seemed to like it and finished her first glass in record time and then picked up another.

"Yummylicious," Jaycee said as she reached for a second glass.

We started walking towards the area of the buffet table where the hors d'oeuvres were laid out. I took one that looked exotic but had no idea what it was. Jaycee also reached over and accidentally spilled part of her drink on them. She didn't seem embarrassed when a few men laughed at what had just happened. I gave them a dirty look for being so childish and trying to embarrass my newfound friend. It was at that precise moment that I saw the face of an Adonis.

I totally forgot about the spilled champagne.

I never saw a man who was as handsome and classy looking as he was. I was frozen in place and could not move. He was very tall, at least 6'2" and trim. He had intense hazel eyes that made him look like he had eyeliner on his lower lids. His close shaved dark brown beard fit his face perfectly.

I was captivated and absolutely fell under his spell. How was that possible? We didn't even speak yet.

He looked in my direction without expression for a few seconds. He then sealed the deal by giving me a fantastic smile. He started walking towards me, and I could feel my heart pounding. He was almost next to me when the most unbelievable thing happened. He walked right past me and went over to Jaycee! What the f …! I seriously thought I was going to faint from the disappointment.

I immediately returned to the area where the champagne glasses were displayed. I grabbed a glass and gulped it down to calm myself. I had to burp and tried to do it as quietly as possible. It was hard for me to digest what had just happened. How did I misread the signs? Then I realized that Jaycee was also looking at him at the same time. Since she was standing so close to me, it seemed as though the smile was meant for me.

Those are the breaks. So be it!

I was trying to decide whether to eat something or possibly skip the rest of the "Meet & Greet," when a representative of the hotel came over to me.

"Hello, my name is Kaiholo. I am one of the goodwill ambassadors of the hotel. How are you enjoying your trip so far?"

Did he come over to me because he picked up on what had just happened and wanted to make me feel good? I was toying with what to say to him and then just blurted out my true feelings.

"I came here to have a good time, and it seems that it is not going to be that way for me!"

I must have sounded immature or a little off to Kaiholo, not realizing that part of his job was to mingle with the guests. He ignored my answer and instead continued to speak.

"The Meet & Greet is almost over. You will have an hour to yourself before dinner. If you like, you can view our beautiful gardens outside. It is very relaxing and good for the soul."

Then in an instant, he was gone. It happened so fast that I wasn't sure if I was imagining the conversation with Kaiholo or not. Regardless, I decided to take a walk outside and check out the scenery.

It was actually very invigorating to walk the grounds by myself. I felt the delicious balmy breezes on my skin. I sat down on a wooden bench and took in the beauty of my surroundings. It was as though I was looking through a kaleidoscope, viewing a multitude of colors and shapes. I was mesmerized by it all.

The hour flew by quickly and it was time to walk back inside the hotel. I wanted to eat dinner and then relax with a glass of wine during the "Island Show" that was scheduled for 10:00 PM. That would be enough activity for me for one day, considering it was only the first day of my vacation.

The dining room was huge with dimmed lighting that gave it an ambiance of romance. There was a separate section roped off for our group. The tables were set up with place cards and centerpieces of anthurium and tuberose flowers. Very classy!

I was very grateful that I wasn't seated with or near any men. I was flanked by a woman on each side of me, and that was fine. It made dinner much more enjoyable. I was starting to think that every man sucked, only some were better looking.

When I got back to my room several hours later, Jaycee was already asleep. I was glad and didn't want it to be uncomfortable between us. What happened was nobody's fault. It was just … I'm not even sure what to call it. There was no point dwelling on it and spoiling my vacation.

How mature of me! At least that time I was.

The following day was going to be very busy. We were scheduled for a tour of the island, some free time to shop, and a luau in the evening. I was excited for all of those activities.

CHAPTER 22

My apartment felt warmer today. As usual, I didn't feel like getting out of bed yet, but knew that it would have to happen at some point. I was hungry and had to go to the bathroom; two things that were constant in my life besides sleeping.

Slowly I pulled myself out of bed, making sure that my feet went into my slippers instead of on the cold floor. I was not as sleepy as usual and felt a surge of energy within myself. That was quite puzzling to me.

There was hardly any food left in my cabinets and refrigerator. I needed to go shopping but it was so hard for me to leave my apartment, the safety of my walls and my locked front door. Yet, if I wanted to live, I had to eat. That was quite obvious, even to me.

I put on a pair of jeans and a cotton sweater. Not realizing that I had lost weight, my jeans were loose on me. I should have been overjoyed at this discovery, but it did not have that effect on me. I walked back to the kitchen and sat down on the chair.

The door was physically easy to open, but mentally, it was difficult. I was afraid to have to face people but mostly terrified of meeting someone from my past. It would crush me to see people who hurt me years ago living happy lives. Not only did I not want to see anyone, but I didn't want anyone to see me. I had changed dramatically, and not for the better. I had that depressed look that I used to see on other people whom I had always pitied. Now that pitiful person was me. My skin was overly dry and my hair was unkempt with too much gray. I didn't care about myself and it clearly showed.

"Snap out of it, Evie! It's a big city. There are so many people out there. What are the chances you'll see someone you know?" I asked myself out loud.

"Okay Evie, time to stop talking to yourself," I continued.

I walked over to the living room window and drew back the drapes. Looking out, I saw the same familiar scenes. There was nothing new, different or unusual.

What did I expect to see out there? I needed some kind of sign to let me know that it was okay to open the door and leave. At least that would have made it easier for me.

My nerves began to get the better of me and so I started to pace back and forth. Finally, the decision was made. I couldn't delay this any longer.

I remembered Dr. Hunter's words from one of our sessions, "Fear is conquered by action."

Needing to act and determined to do so, I grabbed my purse and keys. I walked to the door, unlocked the metal chain and then the deadbolt. I placed my hand on the doorknob and started to turn it. The door wouldn't open even though I pulled at it several times. I forgot that the bottom lock needed to be opened as well. I placed my key in it and turned it two times to the right.

Finally, the door was fully unlocked!

I stepped out into the hallway, locked the door and quickly darted towards the elevator. Again, this was not easy for me. It had been too long time since I had stepped outside my apartment.

I rang the down elevator button. What were the chances that no one would be there when the doors opened? It didn't matter. I kept telling myself that I am a human being, just as valued as anyone else, struggling to come back into the world.

I became more and more anxious waiting for the elevator. Finally, the bell dinged, and the doors opened. I could not believe my good fortune. It was empty! I stepped inside and pressed the button marked "L" for the lobby. A few seconds later, the doors closed and the car started to descend. I was both fearful and happy. I didn't know that it was possible to feel those emotions at the same time.

The doors reopened and it was time to step out into the lobby. I froze and couldn't do it, so I stood there motionless until the doors closed again. There was no movement by me for at least 20 seconds, which seemed like an eternity. The button for the eighth floor lit up and the elevator began to ascend.

Once inside, there was nowhere to go and nowhere to hide. I prayed that when the doors opened again, no one would recognize me. I lowered my head and turned to the side. It would be a clear message to anyone entering that I did not want to be friendly.

The doors opened and two teenage girls were standing there. They were wearing heavy backpacks and hiking boots. As they entered the elevator, they continued their conversation and did not take any particular notice of me. That was a lucky break!

The elevator automatically descended to the lobby, and again the doors opened. The girls quickly exited but I didn't. However, this time I wasn't so fortunate. Mrs. Tilden from the fourth floor and Mr. Emory from the third floor entered. I recognized both of them and unfortunately, they also recognized me. Mr. Emory was more reserved and greeted me with a nod and then turned his face towards the doors. I wasn't so lucky with Mrs. Tilden.

"Well hello there, Evie! I haven't seen you in a long time. How are you?" she asked in a very jovial voice.

I did not want to have to speak to anyone, let alone her. She was a very strange sort of person. Sometimes she greeted you and was extremely friendly, and other times she acted as though you didn't exist. I never knew her to be on an even keel and did not want to respond. However, I knew I had to or she would continue to ask questions.

"I'm fine," I said in a low tone.

I did not continue the conversation, which caused her to stop paying attention to me. As the doors opened to her floor, she waved goodbye and walked out. Mr. Emory had gotten off on the prior floor. Thankfully, I was by myself again.

I had started to feel queasy going up and down so many times. Eventually, someone would catch on that I wasn't getting off the elevator. This could have opened the gates to gossip by nosy neighbors. I was also making myself nauseous and started to feel like I was going to throw up.

Again the elevator descended to the lobby. The doors opened, and without thinking, I flew out as quickly as I could and left the building. After a few minutes of fast walking, I found myself somewhat out of breath, so I slowed down to almost a standstill. I then continued walking at a normal pace while passing a bunch of familiar neighborhood kids. They were doing what teenage kids do: talking, laughing, play punching and so forth. I always used to wave to them, but this time hoped that they would not notice me. As I passed by, there was nothing about me that caught their attention.

Looking up at the sky was indeed fascinating. I had forgotten what it was like to be in the real world.

☐

Never having been truly appreciated in most of my past romantic relationships was very damaging to me. Part of the problem was that I was a magnet for immature, selfish men. Why did I always excuse their bad behavior toward me? Why did I involve myself with men who would hurt me?

Dr. Hunter said it was a form of punishment that I was inflicting upon myself. She thought I felt guilty for being insensitive to people from my past. According to Dr. Hunter, by entering into these bad relationships, I thought that I was not deserving of kindness and true love from another human being. She had a point, but other than Daniel, I never really hurt anyone. I was always kind to people, whether they were my boyfriends, friends or family members. Although she hit the nail on the head with many things, Dr. Hunter didn't know it all. I guess there are some things that we need to figure out for ourselves.

Instead of letting it go, I started to obsess about what Dr. Hunter said. Wanting to punish myself? How absurd! This got me very angry with her. What was she trying to say? Did she think it was my fault why all of my past relationships didn't work out? I've been avoiding therapy with her for a while only because I haven't been able to leave my apartment. However, thinking about what Dr. Hunter had said made me very angry. Maybe I won't go back to her for therapy any more at all!

Let's see how she likes that!

My Hawaiian vacation continued.

The tour of the island was interesting, but it lasted a little too long. Afterward, we were dropped off at the local shopping area which was geared to the tourist trade. It was apparent to me that the locals don't shop there. On display were the usual must-have trinkets that are never looked at again once you arrive home. I bought a few bangle bracelets and continued to look around. After about an hour of browsing, I became thirsty and decided to get a cold drink.

The Hualani Juice Bar was packed with tourists and a few locals. The "all natural" sign attracted me, so I went in. I ordered one of the special fruit drinks decorated with umbrellas. Sipping it was very refreshing.

I looked around the bar and immersed myself in people watching. Most of the patrons seemed to be having fun. It was obvious by their happy conversations and laughter. However, there was a little girl crying and a very upset mother trying to console her.

I was kind of happy to be alone at that point. Jaycee was in one of the clothing stores. Hopefully "Mr. Adonis" would not be around. It would have been too embarrassing to see him again. Of course, no sooner did that fleeting thought leave my mind when he walked into the juice bar. I was praying that he wouldn't notice me. It's amazing how things work out; whenever you don't want something to happen, it usually does. I couldn't believe it, but he began to approach me.

"Hi, you're Jaycee's roommate, right? I meant to introduce myself to you earlier. How are things going for you on this vacation?"

"So far, so good," I answered dryly.

"I can't wait for the luau tonight. I've always wanted to experience one. What about you?" he asked.

"I'm looking forward to it also. I've had enough of shopping. I'm ready to go back to the hotel."

As the conversation continued, I realized that I didn't know his name and he didn't know mine either. He was very nice and not the jerk I originally thought him to be. Just as my feelings of anger towards him began to dissipate, he began to flirt with me.

"Did you just buy those bracelets? They look really good on your thin wrists. You have well-defined arms. Do you work out a lot?" he asked.

"Um, thank you. No, I don't work out."

"I hope I'm not making you uncomfortable," he continued.

He then winked. That seemed weird to me. Just at that moment, Jaycee appeared in the juice bar and walked over to us. Apparently, this was where they planned to meet up. Now I felt uncomfortable around Jaycee, thanks to "Mr. Adonis" and his flirtatious remarks toward me.

"Hi, Evie, I was wondering where you were. I didn't see you in any of the stores," she said.

Jaycee did not give me a chance to respond and continued talking.

"Evie, this is Boyd Fleming. Boyd, this is my roomie, Evie."

She then grabbed his hand and gave him a quick kiss on the lips.

The message was loud and clear!

I left the juice bar feeling a little disheartened. Boyd Fleming left me totally confused. I needed to be very careful when speaking to Jaycee. It wasn't like Boyd was her property or even her boyfriend, but clearly, this guy was bad news. Maybe she should've been paying more attention as to where his eyes were roaming, or maybe he should've been more careful with what came out of his mouth to me.

The shuttle bus brought our group back to the hotel.

The luau was about to begin. I loved that the night air was warm and pleasant. The grounds set aside for this festive occasion were filled with bright lights and colorful decorations. The never-ending tables were set with small glass vases filled with white orchids. There were purple orchid petals strewn on the white tablecloths throughout. It was meant to look very haphazard, but it was clear to me that it was very well planned out.

There were circular tables filled with so much food that I thought they might collapse. Everyone had a drink in their hand. Most of them were Mai Tais, Pina Coladas and Blue Hawaiians. All the guests were happy and that included me. I was taking part in the laughter, and definitely in the drinking.

Kaiholo appeared out of nowhere and blew a loud whistle. Everyone stopped what they were doing and looked at him for direction. He smiled easily and began to speak.

"Ladies and gentlemen, tonight we celebrate Hawaiian style. Let the fun begin!"

Within moments we were surrounded by beautiful young women wearing the traditional grass skirts and head ornaments. They were shaking their hips vigorously to the most powerful drum music I had ever heard. After them came male dancers and other performers such as fire-eaters. Entertainers were coming at us from every direction. The show was spectacular! We were truly in paradise!

I couldn't help but notice that Boyd, who was standing with Jaycee, kept looking at me from time to time. At first, I thought it was my imagination, but it happened too many times for me to think it wasn't real. What was he trying to do? Was he flirting with me again? Was he testing me? Maybe he was having a little sadistic fun because he knew I had checked him out before he made his way over to Jaycee. Whatever his reasons, he was definitely playing some sort of game. What a jerk I thought, but inwardly I kind of liked it, both the attention and the flirting.

Maybe I was the jerk!

CHAPTER 23

Did I actually step out of my elevator? Am I really outside of my apartment building? No sooner did that thought cross my mind, when the stench of horse poop drifted towards me. Yup, that definitely made it clear that this was real.

The city streets had a pungent smell that permeated the warm air with a vengeance. I didn't mind it. I was overdue for a dose of reality, bad smells and all.

I neared Mom & Pop's. It was very difficult for me to just walk in. The young guy who worked the slicing machine cutting cold cuts and various cheeses knew who I was, as did the owners and the stock boy. There was a drastic change in my appearance, and I knew it would be impossible for them not to notice it. I dreaded the thought of them asking me what happened, or worse, making believe that they didn't recognize me.

As I stood outside the store, I began to feel light-headed and started to perspire. An indescribable feeling came over my entire body. I knew immediately that an anxiety attack was coming on. I've always hated all the feelings that happen to me during an attack. It produces so much mental anguish which translates into physical pain. Yet there was nothing I could do. Well, that was not true. I had pills that would help me through it but didn't have them with me at that moment. Did I forget to bring them because I didn't care enough about myself? Was I punishing myself? Why was I agonizing over this? Maybe, just maybe, I simply forgot to bring them.

I leaned against the doorway and started to cry softly to myself. I held my pocketbook up to my face shielding it from view, not realizing that this would bring more attention to me. I held on to the iron stabilizers that were attached to the awning on the store windows in case I would start to feel as though I was falling.

After about three minutes, I finally stopped whimpering and slowly started to feel better. I started to think back to how nice everyone had always been to me whenever I came into Mom & Pop's. Why would they change now? I was being ridiculous! Slowly, I gathered control of myself and entered the store.

Once in the store, everything was the same as I had remembered it, except that there was a different bag boy. No one looked at me in amazement, shock or otherwise. It was just business as usual.

What a relief! The fear of entering the store was just that - fear.

I bought enough food to last me the month, or maybe a little longer. I gathered up my large grocery bags and left the store.

I took the bus and arrived at my avenue within a few minutes. I walked the few blocks to my apartment building and headed for the elevator. When the doors opened, it was packed with people. Thankfully, there were no familiar faces and I arrived at my floor without incident.

The grocery bags were heavy, and I was happy to put them down on my kitchen counter. I walked over to my couch and plopped down on it. I was exhausted from the "experience of experiencing life," even though it was for a mere few hours of one day.

I had to admit to myself that it felt good to be in the fresh air. It was almost as though I had never been outside before, never feeling the warmth of the sun or the wind against my face and hair. Everything was foreign to me. It was as if I had just been born and placed inside a magical wonderland. It was so freeing and I finally felt alive for the first time in many months. This reminded me of something Dr. Hunter once said. In fact, I remember her exact words, "Evie, healing takes time, effort, energy and most of all, the will to want to be free, free from invisible chains that are only alive in your mind."

An invisible door opened for me today. It was not planned, it just happened. Maybe it was a path that was laid out for me or maybe I laid this path out for myself. It doesn't matter why or how, because without a doubt, I made a huge breakthrough.

I left my emotional safe space and experienced the real world!

Those feelings of joy comforted me to the point where I felt so mellowed out, that I changed into a pair of silk pajamas that I had never worn before. I pulled the covers over me and quickly fell asleep. There were no nightmares this time.

I awoke at 3:00 AM because I had to pee. I didn't put on my slippers and enjoyed the cool feeling of the floor on the base of my feet. I took a glance at my living room curtain and then continued to head to the bathroom. There was no hesitation and no fear. I just did what was considered normal, in a normal way. I went back to my bed with a smile. This was something I hadn't been able to do in a very long time. I wasn't able to fall back asleep until many hours later, but things had changed for the better. The pendulum never stands still and it was finally starting to swing in my favor.

Six and a half hours later, it was 9:30 AM and I immediately thought of Briana. It was time for me to call her and apologize for shutting her out during this tough time in my life. It would release me from my feelings of guilt and bring my friend back. Even though she didn't expect more from me than what I had to offer, it was time to take responsibility.

The phone kept ringing, but she did not pick it up. Was she purposely not answering my call or was she simply not at home? I could call her on her cell but didn't want to. I was afraid to make a second attempt. I'm always afraid of being rejected, even if it's from a good friend. These feelings are so hard to shake no matter how much I have tried to do so.

I can't seem to get away from fear. I'm always afraid to do the right thing for myself. Yet, I have been perpetually eager to please all of the awful men I have chosen to involve myself with. I would constantly lose my sense of self and get fully invested in whatever was important to them. I had a pattern of choosing men who would use me and then soon reject me. Why did I do that? When the answer finally revealed itself, it all made sense to me. Simply put, they did not value me because I did not value myself.

My phone started ringing. Since I was so deep in thought, it startled me. I looked at the phone with some hesitation before answering it.

"Hello," I said in as normal a voice as possible.

"Evie, it's me, Briana," was the reply on the other end.

It took my brain a moment to understand that my best friend was on the line.

"Briana! Oh, how wonderful it is to hear your voice! I was going to call you again, but you know me, I can't follow through on anything."

"Don't put yourself down. I saw that I missed your call. Why didn't you call my cell?" she asked.

"I didn't know if you wanted to talk to me. I'm so flaky," I responded defensively.

"Don't be silly. I know you're going through a hard time and I'm so glad you called. Do you want to talk?"

"There is so much to tell you. I took a very big step yesterday by going outside."

"That's wonderful! Would you like to get together?" Briana asked.

"I still can't leave my apartment at will. I need time to adjust to following a normal routine. I'm still afraid."

Briana understood. She constantly gave great advice and never pushed for additional information. Instead, she always gave me an opening to continue the conversation whenever I was ready.

"Evie, I care about you and hope you will call your psychologist and start some sessions again. You know that those have always been helpful to you. You took a big step in the right direction. Just continue the process. Please, please make that call and continue to move forward," she urged, almost pleading with me.

Briana was correct. She was spot-on about my need to see Dr. Hunter. It was urgent for me to go back to her. But saying it and doing it are two very different things. Although Briana knew everything about me and my problems, she was still on the outside of the situation, so she could never fully understand what I was going through.

It is very difficult to have empathy for someone's pain unless you have experienced it yourself. However, no one's situation is exactly the same. This is why it is up to me to move forward. I cannot put that responsibility on anyone else, including Dr. Hunter.

There were so many demons within me that needed to be exorcised. How does one do that? Every time I thought I had rid myself of them, they resurrected themselves and took hold of my mind. This, in turn, produced a complete mental shutdown for me.

Briana's advice was great. If only I would have just followed it immediately.

CHAPTER 24

I didn't get together with Briana that week, nor did I make that appointment as soon as I should have with Dr. Hunter. How foolish of me! I so desperately needed these two people in my life. Was my avoidance another form of self-sabotage? If I didn't attempt to get help when it was necessary, then I probably didn't want it. But I did want it. I just couldn't get myself to do it!

Another day passed and it was drizzling outside. I stood at the window, but this time it was different. I was looking out but did not see what was directly in front of me. Instead, my mind went back to a few days ago, when I left my apartment for the first time in a while. I was able to smell the aromatic air, hear the sounds of laughter and eavesdrop on varied conversations. It was a wonderful few hours spent outside in complete satisfaction. I had accomplished a task that was left undone for too long.

I walked towards the kitchen and opened the drawer where I kept my package from Samantha Gordon. Receiving that box triggered my anxiety related to Ben. All of the mental and emotional anguish caused by him started to come back to me. To think I hadn't thought about that fucker for so long until I opened that box!

It was time to let go of Samantha and the package. She was just another woman used by Ben and was trying to be nice by returning my items. This fruitless search for Samantha Gordon was now over.

End of story!

But there was more … and it had nothing to do with Ben.

•

It was finally time to give in and make that appointment with Dr. Hunter, but first I needed to make myself a cup of coffee. Before I could do so, my phone rang and reluctantly I answered it.

"Hello."

"Hi, Evie! It's Briana. Did I just wake you up?"

"Oh, hi, Briana. No, I was just deep in thought. I'm glad you called."

"Why is that?"

"Because I feel so down."

"Did you make an appointment with your psychologist?"

"No."

"Evie, you have to get a grip. If you want help you have to make that call. Only you can start the process of getting better. No one else can do it for you!"

"You're right. You're always right."

"I called to check on you and I'm glad I did. Please make that call. Make it after you hang up with me."

"I'll do it. I was really planning to in a few minutes anyway. I need to go. Thanks for thinking of me."

Hanging up the phone was a bit rude. Briana was trying her best to help me and I wasn't truly appreciative. I just couldn't deal at the moment for whatever reason.

Before I knew it, night had fallen, but I wasn't tired.

I opened the refrigerator and took out the box of chocolate covered cupcakes that I had bought from Mom & Pop's. They looked decadent and were the perfect fix for the emotional voids in my life.

I ate one, and it tasted really good. I then poured myself a glass of milk and took half of another cupcake. I devoured it in seconds and felt the need to eat just one more. I took the other half and popped it into my mouth while adding more milk to my glass. The continuous eating fest brought instant gratification, so another one found its way into my mouth, and then another. I ate them so quickly that I stopped tasting their sweetness.

I finally stopped after having eaten four of the eight cupcakes. I sat there for a moment or two and thought about what had just happened. As usual, feelings of guilt and remorse came over me. Binge eating satisfied my anger and pain, but unfortunately, that satisfaction only lasted for the few minutes it took to overeat in one sitting. The feelings of anger and pain returned almost immediately. My binging was in vain and I knew that well; as I had been there before.

There will never be enough food to fill the void that is within me. Although binging was a feel-good medicine for me, it was only a temporary fix. Nevertheless, I grabbed a fifth cupcake.

I walked over to my couch and sat down. Have I given up on life? No! I have just given up, period.

•

It was 4:43 AM. I awoke with a start and realized that I had fallen asleep on my couch with half a cupcake in my hand. I felt very tired and wanted to go to my bed but had to pee first.

I didn't put the light on in the bathroom because it would bother my eyes. While starting to sit on the toilet, I lost my balance and fell into the open shower stall. My head scraped against the uneven tile as my shoulder hit the stationary soap dish which jutted out from the wall. I cried out in excruciating pain, most of it emanating from my right shoulder and upper back. Sobbing from both the pain and fear of not being found, I understood for the first time how truly alone I was in this world.

While lying on the bathroom floor in complete darkness, I lost control of my bodily functions and began to urinate uncontrollably. Even though no one else was present, I felt embarrassed by what was happening.

I tried several times to sit up but just couldn't do it. The pain was extreme and I was sure that I was paralyzed. I became very fearful that I would be in here for days, maybe weeks before being found. That fear led me to a state of panic so extreme, that I forgot my pain for a moment, and reached for the towel bar attached to the shower door. I was able to grab ahold of it with my left hand and pull myself up. Thank goodness I had long arms. I started to scream for help.

"Help, help, someone, help me! Please, someone help me. Please!"

Each time I called out, I felt weaker, as though all my energy had been sucked out of me. Didn't anyone hear me? Where were my neighbors?

I had to get out of the bathroom and find the phone. My landline was on the kitchen table, but that was way too far for me. My cell phone was a better choice as it was in my purse and closer to the bathroom, but it was rarely charged. I started to pray that it had some battery life left.

I held on to the towel bar as tightly as possible, when a lightning bolt of pain shot through me. There wasn't much time to get help before losing that tiny bit of strength I still had and possibly falling again. I didn't know if anything was broken. All I knew was that the pain was truly unbearable.

Enough time had passed when some streaks of sunlight entered from the small window near the ceiling. Looking around the bathroom, I saw my dust mop leaning against the wall by the door. If I could get to the mop, it could be used as a crutch. I edged to it very slowly, cringing in pain with each movement. Finally, I reached it. The dust mop was a lifesaver because I knew it would help me reach the landline and not worry about whether my cell phone was charged or not. I inched toward the kitchen table, hunched over while writhing in pain. My hands were shaking, but I was able to grab my phone and dial 911. The shivering was so severe that I was barely able to give any details to the operator, but she knew my address and that it was a serious situation.

It seemed like an eternity until the police and ambulance arrived. In actuality, it was only six minutes. When I heard the knock at the door, I was leaning against the wall in my kitchen while holding the mop, but I was unable to walk to the door and unlock it. The police managed to unlock my door without breaking it down. I was thrilled to see them walk in, but it was also highly embarrassing as I was completely naked. So there I was, standing against my kitchen wall, completely naked, with a mop in my hand. On top of it, I hadn't shaved my legs or bikini area in forever. The hair on my body looked like it could've done a better cleaning job than the mop in my hand.

Did it really matter what I looked like? These people were first responders and here to save me, not to judge me. The EMTs draped my blanket over my body and administered painkillers.

As I was taken away on a stretcher, several neighbors were watching the action from the lobby. Where were they when I needed them?

I started to feel grateful, very grateful. I thought about how lucky I was that my life was saved, hairy legs and all. With that thought in my head, the pain medication kicked in and I fell asleep on the stretcher.

I could not have been asleep for more than a minute when the medic riding in the ambulance with me woke me up. It took me a moment to realize where I was.

"Why did you wake me up?" I asked in an agitated and unappreciative tone.

I started to become angry at that moment because not only did I want to go back to sleep but noticed that they left my comforter in my apartment. Instead, they placed this white blanket type sheet over me.

"You might have a concussion, Miss. You can't sleep until the doctor checks you out." he said in a very consoling manner.

Of course, he was right. I instantly began to blush while placing my head back on the pillow.

"I'm so sorry about that."

He smiled at me and told me it was no problem.

"Also, we need to know your age."

"I'm 45."

I fell asleep once more, and again the medic woke me up. This time he was holding my hand very gently, almost as though he was not touching me.

"It's going to be ok. We're almost at the hospital. The painkillers that you were given are putting you to sleep, but we need to keep you awake," he said.

It was totally inappropriate to feel this way, but I got a chill as he was holding my hand, and it wasn't because I was still cold. It was very sensuous to me. No sooner did that thought enter my brain, when he let go and placed my hand under the sheet that covered me on the stretcher. This might have been routine for him, but it was exciting to me. So there I was, on a stretcher in an ambulance after a bad fall, doped up with pain medication and thinking about sex.

•

I was wheeled into the hospital and placed onto a mobile ER bed. One of the emergency aides helped the hospital staff place me in a curtained off area.

"The doctor will be with you shortly," the aide said and then left quickly.

I was beginning to feel woozy as the temporary pain killers began wearing off. The doctor finally came into the room. He held a chart in his hand which he glanced at on and off as he was looking at me. He was great of stature, thin and very handsome. He was young and couldn't have been more than 35 years old.

"I'm Dr. Justin Levy. I see that you had a fall. How are you feeling? Are you in pain?" he asked.

Duh, you think I thought to myself.

"Yes," I responded meekly.

"I'm going to examine you and then we'll take some tests to see if you need to be admitted."

His examination was painful, but thankfully not lengthy.

"Nothing seems to be broken, but to be sure I'm going to order some x-rays and other tests. I'll see you after I get the results," he said and promptly left.

I had been placed on a temporary gurney near the nurses' station until the decision to admit or release me was made. It was around lunchtime before Dr. Levy came back in to see me.

"I have good news for you. There are no broken bones, but you have multiple contusions, abrasions, and a slight laceration on your liver due to your fall. Your wounds must be kept clean. Do you have someone at home to take care of you?" he asked me.

"I live alone."

"Do you know anyone who can come to your home to help you?"

"I'm kind of all alone right now, Dr. Levy."

"That will be a problem. You are in no condition to take care of yourself. I am going to admit you for two days. You can speak to the social worker and see what your options are. I will check in on you tomorrow."

"Thank you for your help, Dr. Levy."

Those words barely left my mouth when I fell asleep. Within what seemed to have been only a few minutes, an aide awakened me and wheeled me into a room that had two other patients in it. One was fast asleep and the other was moaning in pain. Moments later, another aide and a nurse came into the room. They lifted me up and placed me onto the empty bed. The aide took the mobile bed and left immediately, but the nurse stayed.

"You've had quite a day, or should I say early morning. I'm your nurse, Rosa."

Rosa covered me with the typical hospital sheet and then placed a thin blanket on top of it. She explained how to use the emergency button and the sedative button. It was all matter of fact to her and very routine. She could have been more personable, but then again, what was I expecting from this nurse? Hoping for affection in the form of friendship was ridiculous! I had forgotten what I was there for.

Why do I always attach such strong emotions to people I don't even know?

I pressed the button for more pain medication and fell asleep shortly thereafter. I must have been sleeping for a few hours when I was awakened by an aide. She took away my filled urine bag that hung over the side of the bed and replaced it with a fresh one. It amazed me how many times the aides and nurses came in and out of the room. It really annoyed me, but what bothered me the most was the constant loud chatter and the intercom calling doctors' names. How was a patient supposed to rest?

I tried to turn over to my right side, but the excruciating pain stopped me. I decided to lie still and hoped that sleep would come quickly. It did, but it did not last.

At 6:00 AM Rosa woke me up. She proceeded to take my temperature and checked the drip on the intravenous tube that was flowing into my vein. She then changed the almost empty bottle that the tube was attached to and also checked my bandages.

"Rosa, I'm in agony. Can't you increase the pain dosage?" I pleaded.

She looked at me and responded quickly.

"All medicines are prescribed by the doctor. I will leave a note for him in your chart," she stated and then walked out.

No real help there!

Breakfast arrived at 7:00 AM. I was hungry but couldn't eat. Chewing food seemed like a difficult chore at the moment, so I was happy that no one came in to see if I was eating. All I wanted was for the pain to go away and to be back in my apartment while wrapped in my comforter.

Wishing didn't make it so.

Dr. Levy came in to see me in the late afternoon with a small entourage of young, eager looking people. It was easy to surmise that they were either interns or residents. I began to pray that they would not touch me.

"How are you feeling today?" he asked me.

"I'm in a lot of pain. Can you please up the meds?"

Dr. Levy did not respond right away. He checked my vitals, and then took my blood pressure. He proceeded to check my bandages. Lastly, he listened to my heart and lungs.

The interns and residents followed every move Dr. Levy made. They were evidently sopping up every little thing that was being done. It was obvious that they respected Dr. Levy. I liked him too, but at that moment, all I wanted was more pain medicine.

"The social worker will be in shortly. You need to get someone to take care of you when you get released tomorrow," he said.

"Released tomorrow? I can't walk or do anything right now. How can they release me when I'm in so much pain? I don't feel comfortable reaching out to anyone and I can't afford to hire someone. Please let me stay another few days until I can work something out," I begged.

"It's not up to me, it's the insurance companies. I don't have enough reasons to keep you here any longer. I'll see you tomorrow morning," he said and then left the room to see his other patients.

I felt distraught and didn't know what to do. There was no one I could think of to call except for Briana. I couldn't burden her with this when she had her own issues for years. Thinking about this brought on some of my anxiety. On top of it, the pain medicine had started to lose most of its effectiveness. It was almost unbearable to wait until the next dosage, but there weren't any other choices available to me, so I had to suck it up.

No sooner did that thought begin to leave my head, when a flutter of activity began to take place in my room. The emergency bell attached to the patient that was moaning went off. An array of doctors and nurses ran into the room, as well as an orderly wheeling in an oxygen tank. A nurse immediately pulled the drape around the bed so that the patient's privacy would not be disturbed.

A shiver went through me. I began to tremble at the thought that this woman might not make it. It was a dreadful thought, but also the reality of the unfolding situation. Thoughts of my own mortality surfaced.

I began to realize how much time I wasted being unhappy, depressed and needy. I finally understood that life is short. Once again, my mother's words came into my mind … "the days go by slowly and the years fly by quickly."

Just at that moment, the monitors surrounding the moaning woman's bed began to sound an eerie alarm. I knew this meant that things were not going well. I pushed my pain button, but nothing came out. It was too soon, but I had to try. I became very anxious and my entire body felt as though I was going to lose consciousness.

It's hard to describe the feelings I was experiencing. Fear took over and I felt an extreme loss of control. I then realized that an anxiety attack was coming on, and although I knew it would pass, I was still scared. Having forgotten to push the emergency button, I began screaming uncontrollably for help and started to shake. One of the nurses came over and quickly pushed it for me.

"It's going to be alright. Just try to relax. You're fine," she kept repeating in a very reassuring, low tone.

The voice from the emergency intercom responded quickly.

"What's the problem?" asked the nurse on duty.

By this time my body had started to calm down. The nurse that was with me explained the issue to the nurse on the intercom. Less than four minutes later, an aide entered the room with a small round fan. She plugged it into the wall behind my bed and placed it on the table next to me. The circulating air from the fan made me feel better. She poured water into a plastic cup and asked me to take small sips.

"I can't get up," I told her.

"I know you have pain, but you must sit up because you also need to start walking," she said in a stern voice.

"You don't understand! I am having an anxiety attack! It is the most horrible feeling and the most helpless feeling! I can't sit up! It takes a while for me to be able to do that after I've had an attack."

The aide left the room without answering me. It was apparent that she had no idea what happens to a person experiencing an anxiety attack. Luckily, the nurse who was helping me understood the situation.

"I'm going to let you rest for a little while. I'll leave a note for the nurse on duty that you need to sit up and start walking, even if it's only a few steps."

Why didn't they just raise the bed automatically? Wouldn't that have helped me? I didn't understand why that wasn't done but lacked the energy to question it. The nurse was kind and I knew that what the aide said about walking was true, but being able to do so was another story altogether.

The ongoing flurry of activity in the next bed had stopped. The woman they had been trying to resuscitate was being wheeled out with an oxygen tank attached to her bed. I assumed that they were taking her to intensive care. At that moment I didn't feel sad for her. In fact, I didn't feel anything at all. I could only think about my own problems. I pushed the button for the pain medication and this time, it was available to me.

 A little later on, Nurse Rosa came into my room.

"I heard that you had an anxiety attack. How are you feeling right now?"

"It passed, but I still can't get up."

"Let me see what I can do to help you."

Nurse Rosa came over to the bed and tried to lift me up by holding onto my arms. She wasn't able to do it. As the pain medicine kicked in, my pain lightened substantially, yet it was still impossible for me to stand up.

She was frustrated but didn't voice it.

"I'm going to send in someone who is a specialist in these types of cases. He always knows how to get people to sit up and walk."

I was skeptical at best. A few minutes later, a man walked into the room and came over to my bed. He drew the curtain around me and removed the top sheet and blanket.

"My name is Curtis. I'm here to help you get out of this bed and walk."

I stared at him intently and held back laughter.

"What magic powers do you possess?" I asked him in a sarcastic tone.

He ignored my snide remark and elevated the bed. I was so stunned that he did this without letting me know first. I was speechless. I guess he took me by surprise.

"I'm going to put my arm behind your back for support and you are going to put your legs over the bed slowly as I am lifting you up."

Curtis was direct and took full control. He was behaving like the professional he was, and I was acting like a bratty child. As he began to lift me up, my legs automatically started to move over the edge of the bed.

"Now I want you to move slowly and stand on the floor with both legs. Hold on to my arm with one hand and to the metal pole that is attached to your intravenous bottle with the other. Walk slowly."

I was thrilled that he was able to get me to sit up and walk. I didn't think he could do it. I began to feel ashamed as to how disrespectful I was to him.

"I owe you a big apology, Curtis. I'm very sorry for how I acted towards you before."

I waited for the typical response of "no problem," but instead he just nodded. I guess he was used to people being rude to him even though he was helping them.

I walked through the hallway, paused at the nurses' station and then went back to the room. During my short walk, I saw other patients in wheelchairs, including a young man who was missing a limb.

It took the fall and the panic attack for me to appreciate that I was able to walk. In an instant, my whole world could have changed for the worse. I couldn't believe how lucky I was.

After getting back into bed, an unfamiliar woman came into the room. She walked over to me and began to speak.

"Good afternoon. Are you Evie Harris?"

She looked so young as if she had just graduated high school. I was a little apprehensive but responded to her question.

"Yes, I'm Evie."

"I'm Elie, from Social Services. How are you feeling?"

That was a ridiculous question for her to ask me. My body was completely bruised and in pain. How did she think I was feeling? I was becoming more agitated with her in the room.

Again, I became ungrateful!

"When the pain meds kick in, I feel better. When they start to wear off, I'm in pain. I would appreciate a higher dose!" I answered her testily.

"You need to discuss this with your doctor when he comes in later. I'm not allowed to dispense medicine. We need to figure out how to get you the proper help at home. The hospital will not allow you to stay past tomorrow morning."

"There's no one to help me and I don't have any money for a private aide."

"I'll see what I can work out for you."

And with that, she walked out. Her abruptness was very disconcerting to me. Hasn't she ever met anyone else who was alone like me? I couldn't have possibly been the only one.

Why do people have to be so mean? Because they can, is the answer. But it was me who was being mean this time; once again biting the hand that was trying to feed me. I don't know why I responded in that manner. Was I turning into a hateful person? That thought terrified me. I definitely needed to talk to Dr. Hunter about this.

Elie returned shortly after and stood in the middle of the room.

"I have some good news for you. You will be getting an aide to help you at no cost. She will come to your apartment for three hours every other day, for a total of two weeks. You should be as good as new by then."

Elie seemed very pleased with herself, as though she accomplished a major feat, which she did. She looked at me waiting for some type of approval or acknowledgement. However, I just sat there expressionless and resigned myself to the news. I should have been so thankful but wasn't. There was a major mean streak in me, and it was undoubtedly showing.

"Will she be here to take me home?" I asked in a monotone voice, devoid of emotion.

"I'm sure I can arrange that. I'll have all your paperwork ready for you to sign tomorrow morning. You have to leave after breakfast as per the hospital's orders."

That was the last time I saw or spoke to Elie. She performed a miracle for me, yet I behaved like such a bitch and didn't even feel guilty about it.

The idea of having an aide, a perfect stranger living in my apartment, was distasteful to me. It would also be embarrassing because she was going to see how messy my place was. I knew I had no choice in the matter, so I pressed the pain relief button and fell off to sleep.

Morning came and I was served a small breakfast. A hospital aide came into the room and began to speak.

"I will help you get dressed. It's time for you to be discharged," she said.

I was ticked off at her because I was not ready to leave the hospital. It wasn't her fault, but I had no one else at that moment to be angry at.

 Dr. Levy came in for a final check and remarked that I was getting better.

"You're healing very well even though you have pain. It will subside more and more every day. You'll be good as new before you know it. Good luck to you."

And that was that. "The die was cast," as it is said. I had to leave the hospital. My going away package consisted of two pain pills with a prescription for 16 more and a cane. The nurse who handed me the cane commented on how lucky I was to receive a free one from the hospital. I responded by rolling my eyes at her. So there it was, once again I should have been grateful, but I seemed to have forgotten what that word meant.

CHAPTER 25

Exiting the elevator of the hospital with my aide, Mitali, was difficult. Using the cane relieved some of the pressure I was placing on my right side and it also helped me with my balance. I guess that nurse was right; I was lucky to have that cane.

We reached my apartment and I gave Mitali my keys to unlock the door. I was so glad to be back that I immediately went over to my couch and sat down. As much as I wanted to remain there with my comforter wrapped around me, it was too uncomfortable. The support of a chair with a hard back was what I needed, and so there was no choice but to go into the kitchen.

"Do you want some tea to drink, Miss Evie?" Mitali asked.

What I wanted to say was that I could use a stiff drink but acquiesced to a cup of tea.

I was not comfortable with Mitali. She seemed nice enough but didn't come across as the warm and fuzzy type. Then again, her only job was to take care of my physical needs. She wasn't there to tend to my emotional ones. I had to tread lightly and not make too many demands or it would quickly become very uncomfortable for the both of us.

Two weeks went by and I was starting to feel a lot better. I hated having Mitali in my apartment and couldn't wait for her to leave. It wasn't Mitali herself that bothered me. I just didn't like having a stranger in my home, even if it was for only a few hours. It made me so uncomfortable knowing that I needed help because it reminded me of how alone I was.

"I'm going to the grocery store to buy some vegetables and will be making soup later. Do you want me to put some chicken in it?" Mitali asked.

"Just vegetables and maybe some quinoa mixed in. Thank you."

That was a great opportunity for me to call the social worker and tell her that Mitali wasn't needed anymore. Then the realization came to me that this was her last day anyway.

•

After eating Mitali's soup (which I had to admit was extremely delicious), I started to think of the stories I heard about aides and the patients they were entrusted to. One that especially came to mind involved a sweet woman named Cara, who worked at Café Allegra for a short while. I would generally come in during her shift for coffee and a blueberry scone, so I became a familiar face to her. When it wasn't busy at the cash register, we would chat about general things. On one of those occasions, she mentioned her father. She told me that he was an elderly man in his 90's who was very frail and had the beginnings of dementia.

"I'm very worried about my father. I want him to live with us, but my husband is against it. I think I'm going to have to put him in a facility," she said in an emotional voice.

"I'm not familiar with these things. Maybe you need to call the government and ask if there is an agency that helps with these matters," I said to her.

She thanked me and took the next person who was waiting in line. I was glad to be finished with that uncomfortable conversation.

Two or three weeks had passed, and I noticed that Cara was not working her usual shift. After about a month and a half of not seeing her, I inquired as to why she was not working there anymore. No one seemed to know. I figured that she must have changed jobs, so I didn't look into it any further.

A few days later, as I was sipping my coffee in Café Allegra, one of the servers approached me.

"I overheard you asking about Cara," he said.

"Oh, where did she go?"

"She didn't go anywhere else. Her dad was in trouble and she left to help him out full-time."

"I knew that he needed help, but I thought she was going to put him in a facility."

"At first she was going to put him in a nursing home, but then she changed her mind," he remarked.

"What made her change her mind?"

"She heard too many horror stories, so she decided to hire someone to take care of him in his home."

"So, if she did that, why is she also taking care of him?"

"That's the rub. The woman she hired didn't treat her father well. She was always yelling at him, didn't feed him properly and even hit him! Who knows what else she did to him that Cara wasn't aware of?"

I sat there in shock after hearing that information. He then continued to speak.

"He's a helpless man, and this woman was torturing him. Cara fired her and decided to take care of him herself."

"That's awful, but how did she know for sure that she hit him?"

"Well, her father didn't say anything to her because he was afraid and a little confused. One day, when Cara went to her father's house, she heard the aide yelling at him in his bedroom. She stood in the living room and listened as the aide berated him. Then worst of all, Cara could hear the aide smack him several times before she even had a chance to enter his room."

"What happened after that?" I asked breathlessly as my heart started racing.

"Cara said that she quickly ran over to her father to protect him by standing in front of him. She then screamed at the aide to get out and told her she was going to call the police."

"That was a horrible thing to do to a defenseless old man who couldn't protect himself. I feel so badly for him and Cara. What happened to the aide?"

"I don't know. I haven't heard from Cara since then. I have to go back to work now but that's what went down," he responded.

"Thanks for letting me know. I really appreciate it."

I had a hard time processing all the information that had been given to me that day. How awful and sad it was. At least Cara was able to catch this woman's criminal and disgraceful behavior before she had a chance to hurt her father any further. I had watched many TV documentaries about elder abuse but never gave it much thought. I guess it's difficult to understand this unless it has happened to you or a family member.

Truly shaken by this information, I knew that I had to do something, but just didn't know what. Then the thought came to me. I had to see Cara. Somehow, I had to make a difference.

I took out a pen but didn't have anything to write on. I pulled out a paper napkin from the dispenser and asked the barista for Cara's phone number. He said he wasn't allowed to do that. I then wrote down my name and number on the napkin and handed it to him.

"Please call Cara and give her my info because I'd love to help her," I asked politely.

"Alright, I'll get in touch with her," he replied as he put the napkin in the front pocket of his apron.

I didn't bother to finish my coffee because I was too upset. I needed to get home.

When I arrived at my apartment, I couldn't shake the thought of Cara's fragile, old and defenseless father being so mistreated. What could make someone so mean and hateful to the point of exerting physical pain on a helpless man? This woman was violent, so maybe she was also mentally ill herself. What if Cara had not visited her father at that moment? Would he ever have spoken up? I needed to see Cara and have a conversation with her. This subject could not be swept under the rug.

Why was I so deeply concerned about Cara's father? I had never met him and didn't even know Cara that well. Why did I care so much?

Then it hit me.

I was alone. What if I end up in the same situation when I'm older? Who is going to be there to save me?

•

After high school, I attended a local junior college since my grades were not the greatest. I made a few acquaintances there but no real friendships. I didn't have any high expectations in the friend zone so, it didn't bother me.

After graduation, I was able to get a part-time job as a teacher's aide in an elementary school. At that time, I was still living at home so my expenses were kept to a minimum. I tried to make the job fun, but it wasn't. It just didn't do it for me. I didn't particularly like grading test papers or helping kids take off their boots on rainy days. Working with young children wasn't my forte. About eight months into my work as a teacher's aide, I felt it was time to become independent by moving out and getting a full-time job. That brought me to the News 'N Print Stationery Store in Bayonne, NJ.

At News 'N Print, every day was the same as the one before until my boss hired George. He was a slight man with gray hair and always wore huge glasses. He would constantly blow his nose with a checkered handkerchief that he kept in his pants pocket. I judged him to be about 65 years old. He was basically in charge of the newspapers and magazines. I didn't pay much attention to him, but he was most definitely paying attention to me. He constantly made nasty remarks attempting to get a rise out of me. I never responded to him, yet he continued the insults on a daily basis. I figured he was probably a wimp at home and took it out on me. That didn't make me feel any better about it. After a while, I couldn't stand it any longer and complained to Grant, my boss.

"Do you have a minute, Grant? I need to talk to you about something."

"Sure. Let's step outside of the store," he said.

"This is difficult for me to say, but George is giving me a very hard time. He always insults me and revels in it. Could you please talk to him?"

"I can't believe that about George. He's a good guy," Grant replied.

I was stunned by that response! There was nothing further left for me to say to my boss after that statement.

After working at the stationery store for about six months, I received a call on the public phone located in the back of the store. The phone was near the bathroom, and everyone had access to it, be it customers or staff. One of my co-workers, a woman of about 40 named Patty, answered that random call.

"Evie, it's for you."

I was sitting at the register and there were no customers in the store at that moment.

"Who is it?" I asked her.

"I don't know. It's some guy and he asked for you."

I left the counter and answered the phone.

"Hello."

"Is this Evie, the girl who works at the cash register?"

"Yes," I responded.

"Well, I want to fuck you."

I was so shocked at the response that I immediately hung up the phone.

"Patty, you are not going to believe what this guy just said to me!"

"What did he say?" she questioned.

"He said he wanted to F-U-C-K me."

"What!"

"That's what he said."

"Who is he?"

"I don't know, and don't want to know."

"It's probably some lunatic who just keeps making prank calls. Don't worry about it," she said.

"I don't think it's a prank call because he knew to ask for me by name. It's very disconcerting and scary. Maybe he knows me. What should I do?" I asked her.

Just at that moment, a few customers came in, so we had to end the conversation.

From that point on, I began to scrutinize every male who walked into the store, trying to figure out who made that call. It was an impossible task. The only clue I had was that it was a man with a young-sounding voice, probably in his twenties or maybe early thirties. That wasn't much to go on. It probably described a third of the population in the town.

I put the incident in the back of my mind. I chalked it up to a sick individual with nothing else to do. Unfortunately, my peace of mind was short-lived.

A month or so went by and the store was very busy on that particular day. I was ringing up mostly newspapers, magazines and cigarettes at a steady pace when the back phone rang again. None of us could get to it and eventually, it stopped ringing. My attention was directed at the customers, and therefore I didn't think about the phone. Shortly thereafter, the phone began to ring once more.

"I can't stand that damn phone," George said in an agitated tone.

"It always rings when we're busy," he added.

He threw down a newly arrived stack of magazines on the floor, which caused a loud thud. He cursed under his breath and then answered the phone. George was not told of the previous phone call I received and the conversation that had occurred. Therefore, he did not have the opportunity to delight in it. He dropped the receiver which was attached to a long cord and let it dangle by the wall.

"It's for you, Evie," he said in a disgusted tone.

"Who is it?"

"I don't know!" he said angrily.

I could have sworn I heard him murmur "bitch" at the end of that sentence.

"I'll get it in a minute."

I wrapped up the purchases for the last person in line and then went over to answer the phone.

"Hello."

"I want to fuck you."

I was stunned for a brief moment, having forgotten about this disgusting man. Then I began to speak.

"Not you again," I said in an irritated tone.

"Yes, it's me."

"What do you want?"

"What do you think I just said?" he responded.

"What's your name?" I asked.

"I'm not telling you that."

"Why not, Mr. Big Shot?"

There was no further reply so I just kept on talking. Why didn't I just hang up on him? What was I thinking by talking to this man? He knew where I worked, my hours and clearly who I was. How difficult would it have been for him to have followed me home?

"Do you come into the store?" I asked him.

"Yes."

"What makes you think that you know who you are talking to now?" I asked.

He must have gotten frightened or embarrassed because he hung up immediately. I guess the thrill of a prank call goes away if the victim doesn't seem offended.

The next day, a young man came into the store and bought only a pack of gum. I found that odd because no one had ever come in just for that. Gum was an item customers usually added to their newspaper, magazine or greeting card purchases. I also found it strange that the rim of his baseball cap was pulled down to the point where it practically covered his eyes. I tried not to stare or make it obvious that I was checking him out. As he approached the register, he seemed slightly uncomfortable. He didn't look directly at me, and instead placed the exact change on the counter with his head tilted downward.

I realized at that moment that this had to be my stalker.

He was about 5'6" with sandy brown hair and a light complexion. I considered him average looking; he wasn't the type that would stand out in a crowd. He looked like a shy little boy who saved up his allowance in order to buy a candy bar for the very first time. But in this case, it was gum.

He must have realized that I was on to him because he almost ran out of the store. I never saw him again and the phone calls stopped right after that.

Soon after, I gave my two weeks' notice to News 'N Print. That was when Grant apologized for not taking my complaint about George seriously. He finally witnessed his nasty behavior toward me a few days later.

"So now you know I was being truthful," I said.

"Yes. I'm sorry you had to deal with him the whole time that you worked here. You've been a great employee and I think you are a genuine person. George has a lot of issues and I feel terrible now knowing that he has been taking them out on you. Since you're only going to be working here for a few more weeks, there is no reason for me to confront him. It's best to let it go."

I had accepted Grant's apology, even though I shouldn't have since he was such a coward. Why didn't I tell Grant that it didn't matter that I was leaving? He still should have reprimanded George for his behavior!

What I finally realized years later, was that I gave George power over me to exert at his whim. I should have responded to his statements as soon as he said them. While Grant was a nice guy, I also gave him power over me, because I allowed him to disrespect me.

CHAPTER 26

And so a new day began.

It was the day after Mitali left and also the day that I was finally free of pain since falling in the shower.

"Dr. Hunter's office, is this an emergency?" came the cheerful voice on the other end of the phone.

"No, but I need to make an appointment with her as soon as possible."

"Let me see what we have available …"

I finally began the process of moving forward by calling my psychologist. Thinking I could get better on my own proved to be impossible. That fall was a real wake-up call for me. With Dr. Hunter's help, and my will to move forward, the road to recovery was probable.

The appointment was set for 7:00 AM the next day. It took everything within me to get out of the apartment that morning. I went through the same rituals, fears and emotions as I did a few weeks before, when I finally made it to the outside world. It was difficult to open my front door again, but I was determined to get to that appointment. I knew that if I didn't see Dr. Hunter that morning, I would never have the motivation to try again.

•

The office looked the same as it did the last time I was there. Dr. Hunter's name was embossed on a gold rectangular plaque on the outside entry wall. Opening the door gave way to a comfortable waiting room. From there, a door opened to the area that I referred to as "the couch room," where I sat and poured my heart out to her. Behind Dr. Hunter's desk was a door that was always kept closed. I presumed that led to her private office where she kept all her files.

"Good morning, Evie, I'm so glad you are here," were Dr. Hunter's soothing and kind words.

I sat down on the comfy chair by her desk. I did not like sitting on her billowy couch because I envisioned other people plopping down on it which grossed me out. More importantly, if I sat on it, it would be like cheating on my own couch in my apartment. I knew that was such a silly and ridiculous thought, but I believed it and held onto it.

How can one cheat on a couch?

Dr. Hunter's voice interrupted my thoughts.

"What would you like to talk about today, Evie? We haven't spoken in a while."

It took me a moment to clear my head and stop indulging in my intrusive thoughts.

"I wasn't able to walk out of my apartment for many months. Finally, I mustered up the courage and went outside a few weeks ago. Since then, I couldn't go out again until today," I blurted out.

I waited for Dr. Hunter to compliment me in some way for my achievement. However, there was only silence. I looked at her for guidance and did not get any reaction. It's always good to hear those five words, "I'm so proud of you," no matter how old you get.

"I don't know what else to say. No, that's not true. I have so much to say. I want to get myself straightened out and desperately need your help."

Dr. Hunter put her pad and pen down and clasped her hands on her lap. She then looked directly at me with no apparent emotion. The only thing I was sure of was that she was listening to me. At that moment, that was all I needed.

"What kept you from leaving your apartment?" she asked me.

"I'm not exactly sure how it started or when it started. One day I just couldn't bring myself to go outside. I felt the need to close myself off from the whole world, including those who meant everything to me. Maybe because I'm going to be 45 soon and I'm afraid of getting old, but I think it's something else."

"Go back further. What was going on in your life a month before that time?"

"I can't remember and don't want to remember!" I shouted.

I didn't realize that I had stood up and was flailing my arms and stomping my feet at the same time. This must have been very scary looking to Dr. Hunter. It took me a moment to realize how strange my behavior was. My cheeks flushed and I could not look directly at her, so I lowered my eyes and quickly sat down.

"What just happened, Evie?" she asked me in a very soft-toned voice.

"I don't know, I just don't know."

The session ended shortly thereafter, and I wasn't sure whether it was fruitful or not. What I was sure of, was that another appointment was absolutely necessary.

•

Nine days later, I came back to see Dr. Hunter. I opened the door and sat down on the soft chair. Dr. Hunter was sitting there with her pad and pen.

"You look happier today, Evie."

"I'm starting to feel better about myself. It's an uphill battle, but I know that I'm going to win."

"You've won before and you'll do it again, so let's get started. What would you like to talk about today?"

"There are a lot of things I haven't been able to say to you. I've kept a lot of secrets."

"Tell me why it's been difficult for you, Evie."

"I'm too afraid, and to be honest with you, I'm a little embarrassed. It's so complicated and so ugly."

Dr. Hunter was listening very intensely to me. She looked extremely serious. For the first time, I saw her as a real person. I never thought of her as someone with feelings or emotions. Through her tinted glasses, I saw her kind eyes.

"Evie, you've been through hell and beyond. What could there possibly be that you feel you can't tell me?"

"I can't talk about it just yet."

Dr. Hunter stood up from her chair and asked me to stand as well. I was taken aback by this request but obliged.

We stood face to face, and I wasn't sure what was going to happen. I then noticed that her teeth were perfectly spaced, but I wasn't sure if they were real or not.

"Evie! I want you to focus and just look at my eyes. Think whatever thoughts you want to, but don't look away until I tell you to."

I did as she commanded and stared at her eyes. All sorts of emotions stirred within me, and I realized that Dr. Hunter was not only my psychologist but also my friend. It wasn't the same way Briana was my friend. This was a special type of bond that existed between patient and doctor in a professional setting. We stood there, face to face, for about three full minutes. It doesn't sound like a long time, but it surely felt that way.

"You can go back to your chair, Evie. How do you feel now?"

"I'm beginning to understand. You're really trying to help me. I feel so much better and trust you, Dr. Hunter."

I never thought I would utter those words. It was because I never felt that way about her before. Trust is not an easy thing for me, especially since I have been disappointed so many times by so many people.

Shortly thereafter, the session was over, but my new life had just begun. One of the chains that held me down had finally been broken.

•

I'll never forget that meeting with Dr. Hunter two years after Ben destroyed my life but wish I could. I was still in my early thirties.

It was a Thursday afternoon in the middle of the summer. Dr. Hunter was very impressed with my progress in getting over Ben. Not only did I stop thinking about him day and night, but I also stopped blaming myself for his actions. She knew that he was a terrible boyfriend and dishonest, but I never told her what really happened with him. I was too ashamed and couldn't bring myself to do it. Before I left the session, Dr. Hunter told me that I had made great strides. It was so good to hear those words. I left her office feeling better than I had in a long time.

Instead of rushing back home, my decision was to be very good to myself. I hailed a cab and went over to Café Allegra. Once inside, I placed my yellow jacket on the back of a chair next to a small table. Then I went over to the counter and ordered a cappuccino in a glass mug. Back then, nothing made me happier than to sit in Cafe Allegra with Briana or just by myself, with a hot drink in hand.

While I was waiting for my coffee to cool down, I began scanning the room. No one looked familiar to me and I was very glad of that. I wasn't in a social mood and simply wanted a nice moment to myself.

Slowly, I began to sip my cappuccino. I thought about my session with Dr. Hunter and how proud she seemed to be of me. I really felt amazing.

I looked into my mug and saw that it was nearly empty. I left my table and ordered another cappuccino, only this time I asked for skim milk. I also decided to treat myself to a brownie with a side of vanilla ice cream. I brought both items back to my seat.

As I was sitting at the table with my cappuccino in hand, thoughts of my life continued to swim around in my head. It was almost as though my entire existence was being played out on a movie screen and I was sitting in the audience watching it unfold. If only I had been a better director and changed the outcome thus far, but that was just a fantasy. However, I could stop dwelling on my past and just move on.

And then I saw Ben standing in front of ...

CHAPTER 27

I thought my heart would stop! There was Ben standing right in front of me! Was that an apparition? Unfortunately, it wasn't. After blinking my eyes several times, the bastard was still there!

He was stoic, with that sweet, innocent boyish look on his face. That was the same look I always fell for, no matter how badly he had treated me. I would forgive and forget, and Ben knew that all too well. He was aware of all my weaknesses and always used them against me. Then again, Ben could only do that with my permission. Unfortunately for me, I always gave it to him.

"You must be drinking your favorite cappuccino," he said in his usual charismatic way.

I was so startled by his presence, that I became tongue-tied. All I could do was continue to stare at him as if he were a figment of my imagination. I finally got control of myself and began to speak.

"What are you doing here?"

"Same thing as you are. I came in for something to drink and relax. I saw you sitting alone and thought I'd come over."

He was so nonchalant that I wanted to slap his face. It was the first time I truly wanted to hurt him physically. Well, maybe not the first time.

"You have some nerve trying to talk to me after everything you put me through," I replied while looking straight into his eyes.

It seemed as though he followed me there, waited until I had a serene moment, and then decided to walk over and take away my small slice of happiness.

"It's been a while and I just thought we could talk."

No emotions came forth from him, just verbiage.

"I cannot believe the crap you have put me through! How dare you have audacity to walk over to me, and expect us to have a conversation like nothing ever happened? You are a sicko, a thief, a liar and very evil!"

I became so riled after that statement, that I grabbed my pocketbook and ran out the door. Even though my jacket was still on the chair, I wasn't going back in there to get it. I grabbed a taxi and headed home.

It was outrageous that Ben made it seem as though nothing had happened between us. He hurt me in every possible way and scammed me out of my money. Yet, he still had the absolute chutzpah to approach me as if we were the best of friends. This proved to me that he had no conscience, no shame, and certainly no soul. I gave everything to him, and in return, he used and abused me.

How could I have loved that man so much?

The taxi dropped me off in front of my building and I quickly ran into the lobby. The elevator doors were just beginning to close. Normally, I would've been hesitant to enter with so many people already crowded in there. However, this time, I didn't think twice about sticking my arm in to stop the doors from closing.

Back in the safety of my apartment, I lied down on my couch curled up in a fetal position. My eyes began to close as I started to relive my past life with Ben. A chill coursed throughout my entire body, and I felt a headache coming on. I sat up and walked into the kitchen and poured myself a glass of water. I then went to the bathroom, opened the medicine chest and took out a bottle of aspirin. I swallowed two pills and drank the entire glass of water. Assuring myself that my front door was locked, I returned to my couch to relax.

I took a moment to re-evaluate my surprise encounter with Ben. I should've realized how easy it was for him to find me. He knew where I loved to eat, where I shopped for clothing, etc. Ben was very well aware of all of my daily routines. After all, that's how he found me in the first place.

After piecing everything together, it became evident to me how Ben snaked his way into my life. This good-looking man, who approached me for directions, wasn't lost at all. It was I who was lost. He had marked me as his pigeon weeks before and knew exactly what to do and how to do it. From Ben's first attempt to meet me, to showing up during my Saturday bakery run and the "coincidental" sightings in between, I should have realized something was amiss. Being desperate and naive clouded my ability to grasp the severity of the situation.

While sitting in my bed, I started to dial Briana's number.

"Hello."

"Hey Briana, it's me, Evie. I hope you have some time to speak."

"I know this is going to be a man story, right? What happened now?"

"It's more than a man story, it's a Ben story."

"Don't tell me it's about Ben again! When are you going to stop thinking about that monster? He nearly destroyed you and you still want him back. There's something majorly wrong with that!"

Briana stopped short of saying the problem lies with me. She was trying to spare my feelings and be truthful at the same time.

"I don't want him back and that's not what I wanted to tell you ..."

Briana interrupted me.

"I don't know if I can listen to another Evie self-destructing story."

"Briana, just let me talk. Please! I was at Café Allegra tonight minding my own business, drinking my cappuccino and then I looked up. Out of nowhere, Ben appeared right in front of me! He spoke to me as if nothing had ever happened between us!"

I waited for Briana to respond to my statement, but instead, there was silence on the phone.

"Briana! Briana, are you still there?" I began to shout.

"I'm here, Evie. I think I'm in shock."

"If you're in shock, how do you think I feel?"

"Are you telling me that Ben came over to your table and started a conversation, just like that?"

"Yes! That man has ice water running through his veins. I still can't believe it happened."

"You're telling me you had a dialogue with him?"

"I wouldn't call it that. He said a few words and I responded with a few words and flew out of there as quickly as possible leaving my jacket on the chair. It was as if a mob of angry villagers were after me with burning torches and pitchforks! I couldn't wait to get away from him."

"So what did he say to you?"

"He said that he wanted to talk."

"He wanted to talk! Is he for real?"

"I guess he thinks I'm still under his spell and that he can manipulate me into doing whatever he wants. You have to help me! I didn't know that he was already out of jail. The warden was supposed to inform me when he was getting released."

"You should call the police and see what they have to say. Regardless, you need to get another restraining order immediately. There is nothing else for me to tell you, Evie."

"I can't believe he invaded my personal space like that. I hate him so much! I need to find a way to get him out of my life permanently. Ben seems to be capable of anything. What if he comes to my apartment building?"

"Just inform the doormen and the security team not to let him in. They should also call the police if they see him loitering around outside."

"To think he's free and already roaming the streets is so scary! As far as I'm concerned, he should have been put in jail forever instead of getting a second chance to do this to someone else!"

"Do you want to come here tonight? You are more than welcome."

"Thanks, but now that I'm home, the last thing I want to do is go out again."

"Go and get that restraining order first thing tomorrow, Evie!"

"You gave me such great advice, and no one cares about me the way that you do. You're the best!"

With that, I hung up the phone and decided to have a small glass of wine to calm myself down.

Why did Ben have to come back into my life? I was finally moving on from him and didn't want the Café Allegra incident to set me back.

I drank my glass of wine and then crawled into bed. I drew the covers over me and closed my eyes hoping to fall asleep quickly, but that didn't happen. I kept tossing and turning while thinking about the short but powerful incident earlier with Ben. All sorts of visions conjured up in my head, but mostly I saw a monster that I might've still been in love with.

How sick was that?

CHAPTER 28

Nearing my mid-thirties, I was still single while Briana was enjoying married life with Paul, her high school sweetheart. I didn't like him at first but then he grew on me. Paul always gave us our own space when I would come over to their apartment, which I appreciated. He would either find a book to read or work on his computer. There wasn't much conversation between us. Paul probably just tolerated me because I was his wife's friend. I suppose I shouldn't have begrudged that.

Briana rarely mentioned him in our conversations. It wasn't as if he was off-limits, yet she was reluctant to include him in them. I figured that she just wanted to keep her married life private.

I was getting ready for work one morning and had some time to spare. It was about six months since Ben showed up unexpectedly at Cafe Allegra. I had a new restraining order in place and hoped that he would adhere to it.

My cell phone rang and it was Briana. I answered it immediately.

"Hi, Briana."

"Evie, I have to talk to you. When can we get together?"

She sounded anxious, which was not like her. Briana was always in control of herself. I started to feel uneasy as she was speaking. I was getting an ominous feeling that something was wrong. I held my breath until she continued.

"Evie! Did you hear me?"

"Yes, I'm sorry. Can you just tell me what's going on? You're making me nervous."

"I don't want to discuss it over the phone. It's very important. When can we meet?"

"Tonight, right after work if that suits you. It just can't be at Café Allegra for the obvious reasons."

"No problem. Can I come to your apartment?"

"It's not a good idea since it's not that clean and there isn't much food to offer you."

I felt a little guilty having to say no, but my place wasn't very tidy as I kept forgetting to do my laundry. But there was another thing I was forgetting which was more important; Briana was

always there for me. She was my friend and I wasn't doing a very good job of being hers. Besides, there was no way she would care about the way my apartment looked.

"Never mind!" and then she hung up the phone.

I couldn't believe I just turned down my best friend's request, which was nothing more than a few minutes of my time. How could I have been so insensitive? I had to call her back immediately.

The phone kept ringing and went into voice mail. I didn't leave a message. A few minutes passed before I called Briana again.

"Hello, Evie. I shouldn't have picked up the phone knowing it was you."

"I'm truly sorry. I reacted badly. You've always been there for me. Now I'm going to be there for you. If you can deal with an apartment that's upside-down, then you're welcome to come over tonight."

"Are you sure?"

"Yes. I was feeling kind of embarrassed but realized that you would understand and not judge me."

"I would never judge you, Evie. We've been friends for too long. Is 7:30 PM good for you?"

"Yes. See you then."

I hung up the phone and knew I would have to make a run to Mom & Pop's during my lunch hour. I figured that I could pick up two prepared meals and dessert. A bottle of wine would make the meal complete, and I already had that taken care of since there was a case sitting in my apartment.

A few weeks prior to Briana's call, I did make a promise to myself to begin the tedious process of cleaning. That meant discarding excesses, especially clothing that wasn't worn in a long time and opening the countless pieces of mail that I had sitting around my kitchen counter. On top of it, I had accumulated way too many items throughout the year, or should I say junk. It was emotionally difficult for me to part with them. I didn't consider myself a hoarder but seemed to be veering in that direction. Maybe Briana could help me with this problem. She would see it firsthand for herself and help me get organized. With that in mind, I was forgetting that she was coming over to get advice from me to solve her own problems. Instead, I made it all about me.

Why?

•

It was 7:30 PM on the dot when Briana arrived. I let her in and immediately began apologizing for the appearance of my messy place.

"Evie, I'm not here to judge you or your apartment. I just want to talk to my friend and unload some of what's been bothering me."

"I'm sorry and don't know why I'm acting so fidgety around you. I'm just nervous because I can't be a good hostess."

Briana looked at me and seemed irritated. It was obvious that she wanted to leave right at that moment, but something stopped her. She looked so sad and despondent.

"Briana, please sit down on the couch. I'll be with you in a second."

I went into the kitchen and took out a bottle of Shiraz. I poured the wine into two glasses and brought them over to her. As I handed Briana the glass, she immediately waved it away and shook her head.

"That's strange. I never saw you refuse wine before. It's really good."

"Well, it's not that I don't want it, it's that I can't have it. Maybe I should say that I shouldn't have it."

"What are you talking about?"

"That's the reason I came here."

"You came here to talk about why you shouldn't have wine?"

Briana breathed in and out quickly and appeared to be exasperated with me. I couldn't grasp the importance of why she came over. Maybe I wasn't paying attention, or I didn't want to know. After all, Briana wanting any advice from me was truly absurd. I should've been the last person anyone would come to for help.

Briana stood up and looked directly at me. At that moment, it was clear that she knew it was a mistake coming over. Regardless, I didn't want her to leave.

"I don't understand what is going on, Briana. I know that I upset you but truly don't know why. Let's sit back down and talk."

Finally, something lucid came out of my mouth. She sat down and continued to speak.

"I came here because I trust you. There is a problem that I have been dealing with for several months. Actually, it's been almost a year. I just want to relieve myself of a great burden."

"I still don't understand what this has to do with the wine. Did you become an alcoholic?"

"Evie, please! Let me speak, just let me speak!" Briana yelled at the top of her lungs.

I guess that was my cue to stop talking.

"Evie, please listen to me. I have a big problem and came here as one friend to another to discuss it. You need to hear me out. It has nothing to do with the wine."

Instinctively, I placed my hands under my thighs. This would always help me concentrate on the situation at hand and prevent me from interrupting people, something I seemed to do often. I looked directly at Briana and she knew that I was ready to listen to her.

"I've been trying to get pregnant and it hasn't happened so far. I've had two miscarriages. One happened when I didn't even know that I was pregnant. The other took place just shy of being two months along. Paul is so disappointed. He really wants children and so do I. I don't know what to do."

I was so stunned by this revelation. It would never have occurred to me that something could go wrong in Briana's life. I had always been so bogged down with my own problems. I never took into account that she had issues too.

I was still hesitant to speak, so I just stared at her. She had this distant look in her eyes, as if she was reliving a past episode. It was momentary, and then she began to speak again.

"We've been to a few specialists but all of them tell us the same thing. What I came here to say is that I am very afraid Paul will leave me if I can't have children. I just don't know what to do!"

I was so moved by what Briana just revealed and so sad for her at the same time.

"Maybe you should just continue trying until it happens," I offered.

"How many more times should that be? Would one more time be enough, or would two more times be better? How about ten more times? I'm sorry, Evie. I'm behaving like a fool and my problem has nothing to do with you."

Briana began to cry and I immediately hugged her.

"I'm so sorry for what you're going through, but I'm sure Paul understands that this is not your fault."

"That's just it. It seems that he does think it's my fault. He's been distant lately and doesn't even want to have sex anymore unless I assure him that I'm ovulating."

I was surprised by that information and didn't know what else to say. I had no choice other than to find the words that would put my best friend at ease.

"The best thing to do right now is for you to go home. Sit down with Paul and tell him exactly what you're feeling. Let him know that you're afraid he will leave if you can't conceive."

"He's never going to listen to me."

"Make him listen! If it's truly important to him, he can't just ignore you. If he does that, then he's behaving like a little boy. You married a man!"

"I just don't know. I feel uncomfortable with my own husband. It's as though he's moved away from me emotionally and physically as well. I can't get him to see me in the same way anymore. When he looks at me, it's as though I'm not a woman."

"Talk to him, Briana. Let him know that these things don't always go smoothly. It's not the end of the road. There are so many things you can do to have a baby."

I couldn't go on any longer after I uttered that last sentence. It became too overwhelming for me and Briana sensed it.

"Thanks for everything, Evie. I have to go now."

She stood up and began to look for her pocketbook.

"You can't go just yet. I have dinner for us. I went to Mom & Pop's and bought two delicious lamb chops with string beans and mashed potatoes. All I have to do is nuke them."

"Thanks so much for thinking of me in that way, but I'm not hungry. I'm so sorry, but I have to get back to Paul. You gave me great advice, and I need to take it before I lose my nerve."

With that, she picked up her purse and headed for the door. Each of us said a quick goodbye and then Briana was gone.

I had lost my appetite, so I went to the refrigerator, removed the two dinners and placed them in the freezer. However, I did go over to the table in the living room, picked up my glass of wine and drank it down in 3 gulps. Then I picked up the one I poured for Briana and proceeded to my bedroom. I sat on my bed and drank it slowly. Shortly thereafter, I fell into a deep sleep.

CHAPTER 29

It was 9:00 AM the morning after Briana confided in me about her problems with Paul. I had overslept, so I scrambled around my bedroom trying to find my navy-blue suit. There was no time for a shower or to brush my teeth. I grabbed my purse and ran out of my apartment to the elevator. I knew that I was going to catch hell from my boss. It was clear that the wine had given me a great night's sleep, but it also acted like a sedative which was not a good thing. I promised myself that I would never have more than one glass of wine late at night unless it was the weekend. Yeah, like I would keep that promise.

Entering my office, I looked around to see if my boss, Bill was there. Luckily he wasn't. I sat down at my desk, opened my computer and checked for messages. Nothing jumped out at me that seemed problematic. A moment later, Bettye appeared at my desk. She stared directly at me and then began to speak.

"You're in big trouble with Bill. He's going to fire you today. When he called in earlier, I asked him if you were taking the day off, just in case he wasn't aware that you weren't at your desk."

As soon as she finished her last words, she began to laugh and quickly walked away. She sounded like a cackling witch. I was furious and wanted to wring her neck. Actually, at that moment I could've choked the life out of her. As usual, Bettye relished in needling me and making me as miserable as possible, whenever possible. But this time she had gone too far by putting Bill in the picture. I didn't think Bill was going to fire me, but he certainly was going to talk to me about coming in so late. That stress hung over me for the rest of the day.

The hours dragged by. One of my co-workers said that Bill was at a meeting outside of the office and would return later. Every time the office door opened, I would instinctively turn around to see if it was him. It was impossible for me to stop thinking about what Bill might say to me. I built it up so much in my head, that if he did fire me, I would have felt it was justified. It was amazing the head games Bettye played with me. I had to put a stop to them but didn't quite know how.

It was nearly 5:00 PM when I began to breathe a sigh of relief thinking that Bill was not coming back to the office. Of course, at that very moment, the door opened and he appeared. He didn't greet anyone as he usually did, but instead hurried off to his private enclave and closed the door.

The workday ended a few minutes later. I wasn't sure whether to stay and take my medicine or just leave. From the corner of my eye, I saw Bettye staring at me but ignored her. It was time to leave the office. If Bill wanted to talk to me, he would probably do so in the morning.

Walking in the brisk air made me feel better as it always did. I was toying with the idea of having a glass of wine at Tootsie's Bar & Grill. It was a local bar where I liked to go to once in a while to relax and not think about anyone or anything. It was early enough to spend some time there. I liked the idea of being anonymous and surrounded by people. I guess I was a people watcher.

Upon entering Tootsie's, I was surprised to see how crowded it was. I wanted to sit at the bar, but there weren't any seats left. I ordered a glass of red wine and stood behind a small counter that had a plastic wash basin filled with dirty glasses and silverware. This area was perfect because it wasn't well lit, yet I could see everything. I was so busy watching the interactions of the patrons, that I didn't take notice that someone was watching me.

"Hey, haven't we met somewhere before?" A man said with the deepest and sexiest voice I had ever heard.

I was taken aback for a split-second and then focused on this average looking guy. He was slim in build, possibly 5'4" and bearded. There wasn't enough light in the bar for me to get a better look at him, but I knew immediately that he was not my type. I didn't respond and turned my head in a different direction. It appeared that he wasn't going to give up easily.

"I guess you must not have heard me. I think we know each other," he said in a louder tone.

His voice was difficult to ignore. He drew you in with that, and so I turned towards him and gave him one of those fake smiles. Again, he spoke.

"We met at a party on E. 67th Street a few years ago. Don't you remember?"

"So, you weren't using that old pick up line on me! Yes, now I remember you. We actually did meet. You had a girlfriend that you brought to the party. I can't remember her name right now. Are you still with her?"

"No, we broke up a few months ago. I was thinking of marrying her, but she wanted to explore life on her own. She wasn't ready to settle down. What are you doing here?"

"Just having a drink to unwind from the workday. I really need to get going soon, since I have to be at the office early tomorrow morning."

"Too bad, I thought we could share a table and have a drink together, if one opens up, that is."

His voice was mesmerizing. Even though I was not attracted to him physically, I wanted to continue listening to him speak. I thought about his offer for a minute and decided that I had nothing to lose. This was not a difficult decision to make, and so I made it.

"Why not! Hopefully, a table will open up shortly," I said.

He smiled, and it was a great smile. His teeth were straight and very white. He must have been using that packaged stuff. I was beginning to like him a little bit more. He seemed nice and not arrogant or full of himself. As that thought fleeted away, a table became available. We immediately sat down. He let out a small laugh, and then cleared his throat.

"I just realized that I never introduced myself to you. My name is Henley, Henley Lewis. I have to admit that I don't remember yours."

"My name is Evie, Evie Harris," I responded as I finished my drink.

"How about getting another glass of wine, Evie?"

How about if you just talk for the next hour and I'll just listen? I nixed that thought and responded to him instead.

"Thanks for the offer, but it's time for me to leave. I have to get up early for work tomorrow and wine puts me to sleep."

I didn't want to come across as that fascinated by him. He might get the wrong idea that I was into him. It was fine to sit at a table with him for a short period of time, but that was about it. Listening to him speak was definitely titillating to me. There was no way to deny that truth.

Expecting him to leave, Henley surprised me by not standing up. He acted as though I never responded to his question.

"C'mon. It's just another glass of wine. I'll be happy to drive you home since my car is parked right outside. If you're concerned don't be, I've only been drinking soda," he argued lightly.

"No thanks. I have to go in about five minutes."

I didn't like the way he was pressuring me. I was sorry at that point that I agreed to sit down with him at all. Clearly, he didn't understand the word "no." I loved his voice but didn't care much for him. I stood up and grabbed my pocketbook that was hung around the back of my chair. Henley began to apologize profusely.

"I didn't mean to upset you. It's just that I was enjoying your company and thought that we could get to know each other; that's all. Maybe another time then, take care."

With that last statement, he stood up and abruptly left the bar. I stood there dumbfounded with my mouth open in sheer surprise. I was the one who was supposed to have walked out on him! Instead, he turned the tables on me and left first! What a jerk! In any case, I was glad to be rid of him. I changed my mind and decided to stay and order a meal. I didn't see any waiters around so I walked over to the bar.

"I'd like to order something to eat. Could I get a menu?" I asked the bartender.

The bartender pointed towards a rectangular wooden box that held a stack of thin paper menus. I took one out and went back to my table. As I neared the chair, I let out a loud scream. My pocketbook was not on the back of the chair anymore! Absentmindedly, I had placed it back on the chair right after Henley walked out on me. For the few seconds that I left the table, someone managed to steal my bag! I couldn't believe it. What was I going to do? All my cash and credit cards were in there.

Hearing me scream, all the people in the bar looked in my direction trying to figure out what was going on.

"Someone stole my pocketbook! It's not on the chair anymore!" I yelled out.

With that, I began to sob profusely. The manager of the bar came over and asked me to step into his office. He offered me a tissue and then asked me to sit down.

"Would you like me to call the police?"

"What good would that do? I'm not getting my bag back. I also don't have any money to take the bus home."

He quickly pulled out a twenty dollar bill from his pocket and handed it to me.

"My pocketbook cost a lot more than that," I said in an angry tone.

It wasn't the manager's fault, but I couldn't help but act like such a bitch to him. He looked annoyed and it was clear that he just wanted to get me out of his establishment.

"Unfortunately these things happen. Next time try to be more careful with your belongings. This is not Mayberry," he said in a matter of fact tone.

Luckily, I had put the keys to my apartment in my jacket pocket. Otherwise, I would have been beyond scared since my ID was in my pocketbook.

He pulled out another twenty and handed it to me. I took it and didn't thank him. I was unappreciative and inwardly blamed him for what had happened. I left his office, walked into the main part of the bar and exited. My third shock of the evening was about to unfold.

A large food truck honked its horn just as I stepped outside which diverted my attention. When I turned my head back towards the street, I saw Henley standing there smoking a cigarette. He looked directly at me but did not walk over or acknowledge me in any way. I wasn't sure if I was more surprised or annoyed that he had been hanging around outside the bar that whole time. I should have been cautious and more suspicious as to why he was still there. Instead, I let my anger get the best of me and therefore didn't use good judgment.

I walked over to him and said, "Is the offer for a ride home still good?"

He nodded and we began to walk towards his car.

While sitting in the passenger seat, I glanced over at Henley. He didn't feel like a stranger to me. I didn't quite understand why. Maybe it was the familiarity of having met him a few years ago, although it was nothing more than a quick introduction and the exchange of a few words. I didn't know who he really was or anything about him. I should've known better considering what I went through with Ben. Yet there I was, in his car, on the way back to my apartment. Regardless, he was a good diversion to the evening's events.

How stupid can I be?

Very!

Ouch!

Henley pulled up in front of my building but did not speak. I began to feel uncomfortable and somewhat guilty. I thanked him profusely for taking me back to my place, but it was clear by his body language that he was hoping for more.

"Would you like to come up for a sandwich? I don't have anything else and you must be hungry."

"I don't want to put you to any bother. You said you had to get up early in the morning," Henley responded.

"What I had said was true. However, you went out of your way for me, so I don't mind. We'll make it a short night though."

"Sounds like a plan to me," he answered.

Why didn't I just leave well enough alone? Since he drove me home, I felt that I had to do something nice for him. Big deal! A simple thank you from me would have sufficed, yet in my mind, it was as if I owed him the world.

Once inside my apartment, things moved along rather quickly, but not in the way I had intended.

"I can make us a cheese sandwich if you like."

"Good idea, I'm kind of hungry."

I reached for two glasses that were standing in my kitchen cabinet, along with the opened bottle of wine from the night before when Briana came over. As I was doing that, Henley placed his arms on my shoulders. I turned around quickly and almost hit him in the face with the bottle of wine.

"What are you doing?"

"You look so sexy that I just wanted to touch you," Henley said.

There was no smile on his face. I was too weak to say anything else, and I wanted nothing more than for him to leave. There was no doubt that Henley realized this, yet he wasn't embarrassed in any way.

"Why don't I pour the wine, Evie?"

He then brushed up against me and took the bottle from my hands. This made me hot and made me consider making out with him. However, the only thing I found attractive about his mouth was the sound that came out of it. After pouring the wine into both glasses, he spoke again.

"I love the sound of wine falling into long-stemmed glasses."

That voice somehow drew me in more and more. He took both glasses and then walked with them towards the living room. I followed him like he was the Pied Piper and I was one of the mesmerized children. He handed me one of the glasses, and then we both sat down on the couch. He continued talking, and again I became lost in the sexuality of his voice. I drank my wine too quickly and my head began to spin.

"I'm feeling dizzy, Henley!"

"Don't worry. Let me help you lie down. It'll pass in a few minutes. Maybe you need to eat something."

He proceeded to the kitchen and checked the contents of the refrigerator. He removed some sourdough bread and a package of Swiss cheese. He made a sandwich for each of us. Then he went to my cabinet and removed a glass and filled it with water. He brought the sandwiches and water back to the living room and placed them on the table in front of the couch.

"I'm going to help you sit up. We're going to do it slowly."

Henley was very strong for such a thin man. He pulled me up gently and propped up my body against the back of the couch.

"Even if you don't feel like it, start eating the sandwich. It will make you feel better," he said in a caring manner.

Henley took a few bites of his sandwich as he was watching me eat mine. He then told me to drink my water, which I did. He stayed with me a few more minutes and then said he had to go. That was a surprise. I was beginning to enjoy his company and didn't want him to leave just yet.

"Make sure you lock up. Get a good night's sleep."

He turned to leave and then stopped short.

"By the way, what's your number?"

As soon as I responded, he left. I could not finish the sandwich and placed it back on the table. I stood up slowly and went to bed. As I wrapped my comforter around me, I began to replay Henley's voice in my head. I was so preoccupied with my thoughts that I completely forgot to lock my door.

•

I awoke the following morning feeling happy and relaxed. I had about a half hour to get ready before work, but instead, I spent that time lying in bed and thinking about Henley. Once again, that cost me the inability to take a shower and eat breakfast. I dressed quickly, threw my hair in a ponytail, grabbed an apple from the fridge and ran out the door. I couldn't afford to be late to the office again, at least not this soon.

The workday was almost pleasant. Bettye didn't try to upset me, and my boss was occupied with his supervisor for most of the day. I spent a lot of time daydreaming about Henley. I wasn't sure if he would call me, but I wanted him to. The more I thought about him, the more I seemed to like him. The sound that came from his lips was so sensual that I felt spellbound. It was almost as if a net was cast over me, pulling me towards Henley's mouth for orgasmic kisses.

•

I made a decision!

Although it was only two months since I fell in the shower, all of the pain was gone and I was walking perfectly well. Considering that I hadn't taken good care of myself for quite some time, I was very surprised at how quickly my body healed.

It was again time for me to make another appointment with Dr. Hunter, the third once since my fall. After being so physically broken, all I wanted was to repair myself mentally. Therefore, asking for a double session was necessary as it was time for me to let my secret out. It had devoured all that was good within me for too many years.

At this point in my life, I was no good to anyone, but in particular to myself. If I were to value myself as a person, I would have to come to terms with my demons of long ago and eliminate them from my life.

I picked up the phone and dialed Dr. Hunter's number without any hesitation.

"I'd like to make an appointment for a double session."

"Is next Thursday at 2:00 PM good?" was the response on the other line.

"I'll take it, thank you."

It was as easy as that. The appointment had been made, and there was no turning back. It was finally time to free myself of all my burdens!

•

It was Saturday morning, a few days after Bettye claimed that my boss was going to fire me. I had slept in since there were no pressing matters to attend to. Although there were some errands to take care of, none of them were urgent. I had started to think about what I was going to do for the day when my phone rang.

"Hello," I answered in a groggy voice.

"Sounds to me like someone's still in bed," was the familiar voice on the other end of the line.

"Henley! It's so good to hear from you. How are you?"

I wasn't interested in how he was. I just wanted him to keep on talking.

"I'm good, how about you?"

"I'm good also."

There was a small awkward pause and then he continued to speak.

"I'm in your neighborhood. Would you like to go out for some breakfast?"

"What time is it?"

"It's 10:35 AM."

"I need some more time to get ready. How about I meet you around 11:30 and we can make it brunch?"

I had been somewhat fearful that he would say, "Let's make it another time." Regardless, I needed to take a shower, get dressed and apply some makeup.

"No problem! This gives me some time to run a few errands. I'll be in front of your building around 11:30 waiting for you."

With that, he hung up the phone. I couldn't believe that Henley called. That phone call raised my interests in getting to know him better. Somehow I had a change of heart. Hopefully, he would be more than just a sexy voice.

I rushed out of bed and headed for the shower. I got myself ready in record time, then grabbed my purse and went downstairs to meet him.

As I walked out of my apartment building, I began to look around for Henley. He was nowhere in sight. I stood there and waited for him because I believed he would arrive at any minute. I repeatedly kept checking my makeup in my compact mirror and looking at my cell phone. It was 11:40 and I was beginning to get upset at that point. Was Henley standing me up, or was he upset that I made him wait an hour since his call? All I knew was that he was nowhere in sight. I decided to call him and let him know that the date was off.

His phone went straight into voice mail. I toyed with leaving him a message and decided that I wouldn't. I was too pissed at him and did not want to give him the satisfaction of hearing my voice. I hung up the phone and began the ten-minute walk towards the avenue. There were a few small cafes there that I liked. Having brunch by myself seemed like a good thing right at that moment. After all, I looked good and had to be seen, even if not by Henley.

As I continued to walk, several police vehicles with flashing lights and blaring sirens were passing in front of me. An ambulance was trying to make it through the usual heavy traffic. It wasn't out of the ordinary in NYC so I didn't think too much of it. Once I neared the avenue, I was horrified by the scene I saw. I let out a loud shriek and ran over to the bloodied body lying in the street.

It was Henley!

The police immediately yelled at me to move away.

"You don't understand. This is my date!" I said to the police officer.

"You can't help him now. Stay on the sidewalk and out of the way!" he said gruffly.

I couldn't believe my eyes and began to cry. The tears were streaming down my face. I wanted to help him but knew there was nothing for me to do. I wasn't sure if he was alive or dead. He wasn't moving and that was not a good sign.

The ambulance finally arrived. The medics ran out to Henley and placed an oxygen mask on his face. They continued administering CPR, which the police had initiated. A large crowd was gathering and began to obstruct my view. I pushed through them and was at the edge of the sidewalk again. I saw

Henley's head and neck being secured, and then he was placed on a stretcher. I was so glad that he was still alive.

I couldn't see what was going on in the ambulance, but it made sense that he was either getting an IV or they were administering additional first aid. I just wanted them to get him to the hospital as soon as possible. A minute later the ambulance started to leave and the crowd began to disperse. I took that opportunity to run back to the same police officer. He was not glad to see me.

"Can you tell me anything about his condition?" I pleaded with him.

"Were you a witness to what happened?"

"No, I wasn't. I just want to know if he's okay."

"Are you family?" he questioned.

"No, I was supposed to meet him . . ."

The officer cut me off mid-sentence.

"We're very busy here trying to collect evidence. Step back, Miss!"

I was so taken aback by his brusque manner, that I stopped persisting and did what he told me. It was evident that I wasn't going to get any information from him. It never occurred to me that he was just doing his job and I was in the way. I turned around and hurried back to my apartment.

Once inside, I kicked off my shoes and ran into my bedroom. I grabbed my comforter and brought it over to my living room couch. I wrapped it tightly around my body and began to cry. I was not crying for Henley, but instead was crying for myself, feeling cheated once again. How come this had to happen? It would have been a great date. This wasn't fair! I began to rock back and forth on my couch continuing to make sobbing noises, which only made sense to me.

Months passed by since that incident. I never took it further. I had thought about calling all the hospitals in the area to find which one Henley was in, but I didn't. Part of me was fearful that he died. I would not have done well with that information as my psyche could not have been able to handle it. What if he was alive? Was he back to himself, or wrought with all kinds of physical and mental problems? I simply could not bring myself to check on Henley. I was not only a coward but selfish as well.

Looking back, I am surprised at how insensitive I was. I now realize that I was using this apathy as a protective shield to surround myself with. In that way, I didn't have to face the reality of what might've been a very tough situation.

•

The events that took place with Henley reminded me of how short life is and that you never know what the next day will bring. This brought me to thoughts about my sister. They were mostly negative, but there were also some positive ones. I had a hard time remembering those. While we had the typical sisterly conflicts, there was always that additional tension involved because Raquel did not like me as a person.

As we grew older, there was constant fighting over boys. We also didn't do well being respectful to each other's possessions.

Raquel would always take my clothing and costume jewelry without permission. She could never understand why it bothered me, yet she behaved exactly the same way when it came to her things. Taking all this into consideration, our behavior would have been considered fairly normal had she not maintained such extreme, unjustifiable hatred towards me.

Our parents always treated us equally, so I could never tell if they had a favorite child. They tried their best to keep us close or at least on civil terms, but that proved to be a failure. Once we hit adulthood, my sister and I were as far apart as possible. There had been no relationship for years between us. Raquel did not want to have anything to do with me. She made that crystal clear when she didn't invite me to her wedding, not to mention the fact that she married my first love. It truly broke my heart, mostly because I was not sure how we had reached this impasse. This devastated my parents, who couldn't understand why their children did not get along with each other.

These feelings of rejection from my sister impacted my behavior toward other women, with the exception of Briana. I didn't dislike women, but it was easier for me to get along with men. If the relationship with a man became intimate, it never worked out for me either. This was just another layer that weighed me down along with all my other disappointments and failures.

There have been many instances when I had the urge to call Raquel and confront her in the hopes for dialogue. Each time I thought to do it, I chickened out. I usually got as far as dialing part of her number and then would hang up. I wasn't able to get up the courage to just ask her why. I was too fearful that she would reject me without an explanation. I couldn't have dealt with her throwing me away. Therefore, I left it alone.

Well, at least I tried to leave it alone.

Thinking back through the years, my thoughts roam towards when I was nine years old and Raquel was seven. My father loved to go fishing. He would often go out on a party boat with his friend, Norman. One day, they decided to go fishing from the pier in New Rochelle. On this particular occasion, Dad invited me and my sister along.

"It's time you girls learned how to fish. You'll love it!" he said with so much enthusiasm.

Neither of us responded to that statement. We just went along not knowing what to expect. It would never have occurred to either of us to say "no." That would have been unheard of in our household.

Dad first stopped off at The Bait & Tackle Store and bought a box of live worms. I was so surprised when I opened the lid and saw the worms crawling about in some sort of thick greenery. It didn't scare me to see them wriggling around inside that white box, but it certainly scared Raquel. She began to scream and ran out of the store.

"Go get your sister. Bring her back in here. This isn't the time to be squeamish," he said sternly.

I immediately ran out of the store to find Raquel. I saw her sitting on the rustic wooden chair that was beside the entry door.

"Raquel!" I yelled.

"Dad wants you back in right away."

"I'm not coming," she yelled back.

Her head was down and I wasn't sure if she was crying or not.

"You have to come now or you'll be in trouble."

Raquel didn't respond and instead removed some soil from the flower pot that was near the chair. She then got up and threw the soil in my face. I began to cry immediately. Some of it had landed directly in my eye. Raquel began to laugh as she was looking at me. Dad came out of the store at exactly that moment.

"What's going on here?" he asked Raquel.

She shrugged her shoulders and cocked her head, feigning ignorance. Dad didn't fall for her act and instead decided to ask me.

"Raquel threw dirt in my eye! I didn't do anything to her! I just told her she had to come back into the store."

"She's lying! She called me names and made fun of me," Raquel said.

I was so stunned that she lied so easily, that I didn't continue to defend myself. Dad took that as a sign that maybe I wasn't so innocent after all. He told both of us that he would never take us fishing again. That was the beginning of the end of the innocence of sisterhood. Raquel realized at that moment that it wasn't that hard to put one over on the old man. But mostly, she realized that she could get the better of me if she wanted to.

And she always wanted to!

Dad baited the hook for each of us and helped us cast the rod into the water. Raquel and I stood there holding on to our rods, not knowing what to expect. It didn't take long for us to realize that we were bored with this "whole fishing thing," until I felt my rod being pulled down toward the water.

"Dad, Dad, come quickly. I think I have a fish."

Angling his rod against the wooden boards, Dad came running over to me. He grabbed my rod and tried to reel in the fish. After a few minutes, Dad gave the rod back to me.

"It must have been a really big fish to have gotten away. You did real good, Evie!"

He rebaited my hook, patted me on the head and went back to his section of the wharf where Norman was fishing. I was so excited that I almost caught a fish, a big fish that is. I glanced over at Raquel who was still holding her rod. She looked deflated, as though this should have been her moment. I didn't understand why she couldn't be happy for me. I ignored her and instead concentrated on trying to catch another fish.

It was time to break for lunch and Dad wanted our rods out of the water. As I was rewinding the reel, I saw something attached to the end of my fishing line. It was a starfish. It was tiny and very beautiful. I immediately showed it to Dad who removed it from the hook for me.

"You got a starfish, Evie. That's good luck! You should keep it in a safe place," Dad said.

I couldn't stop looking at it and smiling to myself. I also believed Dad when he said that the starfish was good luck, but obviously, not for the starfish. Shortly after lunch, we went back home. Raquel hadn't caught anything that day except for a bad attitude. She didn't show it outwardly when Dad was looking, but she made sure to let me know. Raquel ignored me the rest of the day and was snippy towards me the next day as well. I was hurt by her behavior and thought maybe she was just jealous.

"Raquel, can't you just be happy for me? If you would have caught the starfish, I would have been happy for you. Why are you mad at me?"

"I don't like you! I never liked you and I will never like you!"

I was stunned when she said that to me. It was awful to hear those words.

"I'll share it with you," I pleaded.

I so wanted her to like me.

Raquel did not say anything more. What else was there for me to say at that moment? She took great pleasure in making me feel bad. I didn't fully grasp the gravity of the situation at that point. I was only nine years old and it never occurred to me that this jealousy would continue into our adult lives.

I held on to that starfish for many years, and then one day when I went to look for it, the starfish was gone. I searched the entire house, but to no avail. I had always thought that if I could find that starfish, it would be my present to Raquel. Maybe somehow that would have made peace between us. But the truth was that Raquel wanted nothing to do with me and for all I know, she might've been the one who took it.

The years went by without any changes in either of our behaviors. Raquel kept pushing me away and I kept on trying to please her. This tug-of-war between us shaped my personality.

•

At 37, I was getting to a point wherein my biological clock was starting to tick quite loudly. I had always wanted to have children, but since I wasn't married, the opportunity did not present itself. Understandably, I didn't need to be married to have a child, but I wanted the traditional family setting. There weren't any real prospects out there for me since I wasn't dating anyone at the time. One night, while feeling lonely because of these thoughts, I started flipping through the cable channels. I was hoping to find a comedic movie. I realized that adding a glass of wine to this activity would lift my spirits even more. Before reaching the kitchen, my cell phone rang. I couldn't believe who it was.

"Hello."

"Hi, Evie, it's Henley."

"Oh, hi, Henley, how are you?"

"Long time no speak, huh?"

"Yes, it has been a very long time."

"How are you?" he asked.

"I'm good, thank you."

The conversation was quite awkward. I didn't know what to say to him since I was riddled with guilt. I had completely erased him out of my mind and therefore out of my life as well. If I had been a decent person, I would have at the very least found out which hospital he was in and visited him there. But it wasn't that I was a bad person or didn't care, it was more self-preservation. If I didn't know the particulars, it would prevent me from inviting more worry and intrusive thoughts into my mind. In that case, I wouldn't have to face reality. It was much easier to go through life that way.

"What happened that I haven't heard from you for the past year? We had a date and you stood me up and never even called to apologize!"

I couldn't believe the words that came out of my mouth. I just told him the biggest lie and tried to make him feel guilty at the same time. I was so ashamed of myself.

"I didn't stand you up. I was running a few minutes late, but then I had a very bad accident. I was crossing the street on the way to meet you when a car hit me. That put me in the hospital for a very long time."

"Oh, I'm sorry. Are you okay?"

"I'm as good as I'm going to get. I got very lucky, just a few scars and a slight limp."

"I'm so glad for you."

He wasn't handsome prior to his accident and I hated to think of what he might look like now. There was little else for me to say to him. But I did want to continue to hear his sexy voice. It had always made me swoon. How disgustingly selfish of me!

"I'd like to make another date with you if you still want to meet up. I feel awful knowing that you thought I chose not to show up that day. Please give me another chance," he pleaded.

I was beginning to feel remorseful for lying to him and acting like I wasn't aware of what had happened. At the same time, I did like that he was begging me for another date. How pathetic that I needed such attention.

"Sure. I'd be okay with getting together again."

"Does Saturday night at six o'clock work for you?" Henley asked.

"That's good. What do you want to do?"

"We can go for a drink or two at Tootsie's and then dinner at The Half Shell. What do you think?"

"That sounds great. See you at Tootsie's."

I had another date with Henley. Was I stroking my ego, being selfish, or just being more open? I didn't want to use him, yet I had to meet him at least one more time. Either this would go somewhere or we would part as friends. I expected the latter.

CHAPTER 30

Mom and Dad always worked hard. There was never enough money for "extras." In fact, extras were frowned upon because my parents always had to pinch pennies to make ends meet. If you bought something just because you wanted it and didn't really need it, it was considered wasteful.

I can remember when white leather skirts were in fashion. No matter where I walked, I would always see girls wearing them. I was jealous because I didn't have one. There was no reason to ask for this skirt since I knew the answer. Months after the skirts went out of fashion and no one wore them anymore, I was finally given one. It was a hand-me-down from one of the girls in our neighborhood. The skirt had a small yellow stain and was too big on me. I hated it but wore it anyway to please my parents.

I'm still angry about that.

•

One day I was on my way to elementary school. As I walked along the sidewalk, two boys who were a few years younger than me were playing with a pink rubber ball. This was another popular item I did not get. The ball bounced past me, hit a big rock and then ricocheted toward me. I caught the ball and continued walking with it in my hand. I did not turn around to throw it back to the boys. The thrill of me holding on to that ball was short-lived. The two boys ran up behind me and started yelling for their ball. I had no choice but to turn around.

One of them asked me very politely, "Is that your ball?"

"Yes, it's mine," I lied.

They had disappointed looks on their faces. They expected me to own up to the truth, but I didn't. I was happy that I had a pink ball. The boys didn't pursue it any further and I continued to walk to school with it.

Everyone in school wanted to play with me during recess since I had my own pink ball. I was having such a great day.

When I got home, I hid the ball in the garage underneath a box filled with my old baby clothes. Whenever I had the chance, I would take it outside and play with it by myself. One day, as I bounced it around on our driveway, Raquel came outside and saw me playing with it. She asked me where I got the ball from. Before I could even think of a lie, she ran into the house crying to our parents.

"You guys love Evie more than me! You bought her a pink ball, but not one for me!" She yelled in the most dramatic way.

My parents came outside and questioned me about the ball. I told them the truth. They didn't respond with any words. Instead, my mom took the ball from me, brought me inside the house and told me to wait in my room. A few minutes later, my mom came back into my room holding the ball. She then grabbed my hand and took me outside. She told me to take her to the block where I saw the boys playing with it. When we got there, my mom held my hand tightly as we went from house to house, ringing every doorbell. My mother was determined to find out who the owner of that ball was. Most of the people weren't home as they didn't answer their doors, and the ones who were home had no idea whose ball it was. Finally, my mom spoke.

"Evie, show me exactly where the boys were playing with their ball," she said in a very soft voice.

"Right here, Mommy," I answered meekly.

She then took the ball, put it on that exact spot, took my hand and walked me back home. That was it. No words spoken; no punishment given.

I never stole anything again.

•

I slept in since it was Saturday and although I had a few odds and ends to take care of, it was mostly going to be a relaxing day. My date with Henley was set for 6:00 PM. I had all kinds of visions as to what he would look like now. Would his face be difficult to look at? That was a terrible thought, but it did enter my mind.

As I was daydreaming while still lying in bed, the buzzer in my apartment rang from the front desk downstairs. I wasn't expecting anyone or anything. I pressed the talk button and spoke into the speaker.

"Yes."

"There are flowers here for you. They were just delivered. Do you want to come down and get them?"

That was odd! I wasn't expecting any flowers and assumed they were from Henley.

"Thanks, I'll be down in a few minutes."

Getting flowers was nice, but I wasn't thrilled. We hadn't even gone out yet. Henley was being presumptuous. I never gave him the idea that we were anything more than a date; a date which hadn't even happened yet.

Since I slept in a t-shirt the night before, all I had to do was throw on a pair of jeans and head downstairs. I didn't have a bra on but figured that the doorman wasn't going to notice. As I approached the front desk, I saw the flowers. They were magnificent. Multi-colored flowers with green ferns interspersed throughout were sitting in a large, etched glass vase. I loved the surprise!

I placed the vase on my coffee table. As I continued to look at the flowers, my heart softened. Henley was really trying to be sweet. Maybe it was best not to brush him off so quickly.

It was almost 2:30 PM and I didn't want to be late for my date with Henley. I took a leisurely shower and made sure to shampoo my hair, which usually gets very oily if not washed every two days. After applying some mascara and a light lipstick, I walked over to my bedroom closet and selected a blue cotton blouse with small flowers embroidered on the cuffs and around the collar. It was pretty and very feminine. Then I selected a pair of black slacks that came with a gold metal belt. The combo was classy and made me feel good. I was all ready for my date with Henley, but I had at least another hour before meeting him at Tootsie's. I lied down on my couch for a quick power nap.

•

It was dark and very crowded at Tootsie's. I saw Henley standing at the bar and went over to join him. It was difficult to see his face and notice any differences as the lighting wasn't very bright. Each of us had a glass of wine and the conversation between us was very limited due to the noise level.

"Let's get going. I'm really hungry. What about you?" Henley asked.

"What did you say?"

It was very loud and almost impossible to hear anything. This worked to my advantage since I didn't have much to say anyway. Henley had to shout in order to be heard. It was very irritating for both of us.

"Let's go to the Half Shell, okay?"

"Works for me," I responded at the top of my lungs.

The Half Shell Restaurant wasn't as packed as Tootsie's, nor as noisy. We were promptly led to an open table close to the restaurant's famous fish tank. I looked around and saw mostly couples who were dining on seafood. I began to get very hungry watching other people eat. I distracted myself by looking at Henley and was blown away as to how good he looked. He had let his hair grow longer, and it seemed as if it was shaped by a celebrity hairstylist. He was sporting a day's growth of beard, which definitely enhanced his looks. I couldn't see scars anywhere on his face. He wore an exquisite Italian silk shirt with a matching tie and had a classy gold bracelet on his left wrist. He looked fantastic!

Instinctively, I touched his hand. Henley moved his chair next to mine and placed his arm around my shoulder. He then gave me a small peck on my cheek. A waitress came over almost immediately.

"We're not ready yet," I said automatically.

The waitress hesitated for a few seconds and then left. This was going to be my moment with Henley and I wasn't going to let anyone interrupt us.

"It's good to see you after all this time, Henley."

"It's great seeing you too. You look more beautiful than I remember."

"Flattery will get you everywhere," I said coyly.

"I'm not just handing you a line. I mean everything I say. You also smell so good."

I did feel a little flustered at all of this praise coming from him so quickly. It had been a while since I had received such a genuine compliment from a man. I didn't quite know how to handle it. Changing the subject was my best option.

"This is a nice place. I've never been here before, have you?"

"This is my second or third time and the food is good. Would you like to look at a menu?" Henley asked.

"Please order for me. I'm good with whatever you like."

My insecurities were creeping in again and I couldn't make that simple decision. Ordering food is not a huge task that takes great effort. I shouldn't have left the decision up to him. I've done this so many times on dates before.

Henley realized that there was a prolonged silence between us and so he picked up the pace.

"Are you still at the same company?"

"Yes. I got a small promotion and a raise in pay so there is nothing for me to complain about. Are you also with the same company?"

That was a stupid question. He had been out of work for almost a year. How could any employer hold a position for that long?

"I met with my former boss two weeks ago. He gave me an excellent reference letter and also referred me to a colleague of his. He has a job opening for a junior executive with a six month review. If it all works out, the head account position will be mine. It comes with a good salary and some nice perks."

The waitress appeared again, but Henley hadn't opened his menu yet. He looked up at her and ordered two red wines.

The more Henley spoke, the more I liked him. He was respectful, complimentary and intelligent. I never would have thought to look beyond his nerdy exterior a year ago. I liked that he took charge, but not in an obvious manner. Henley was a man, not a boy, and that was what was missing in my life.

It was nearly 11:00 PM when we finished dinner. Henley offered to take me back to my apartment. I told him it wasn't necessary and that I could take a taxi.

"I insist! It's too late for a lady to go home alone. I'll accompany you in the cab and walk you to your door just to make sure you get in okay. Then I'll leave promptly. Is that alright with you?"

He didn't have to ask me twice. I was feeling on top of the world. I was with a real gentleman who liked me and respected me. I finally got lucky!

"That's fine, but you will have to leave right after that. I have to get up early since I have a lot of things to do tomorrow."

That wasn't true. I only said that to play hard to get. I definitely wanted a make-out session with Henley that evening, but I knew that if we had sex that night, it might ruin the chance for a good relationship. He was too good a guy for me to jump into bed with so quickly.

Henley gave me another soft peck on my cheek and off we went to hail a cab.

Standing at my door, I looked into Henley's eyes. They were gray with small brown flecks in them. How striking and mesmerizing they were to me!

As I began looking for my keys, Henley pulled me close to him and began to kiss me. His breath was sweet and his kisses were very sensual. He placed his hands on my face and drew me in for deeper and more passionate kisses. I kissed him back as though I had never been kissed before.

"I need to find my keys," I said breathlessly.

Henley began licking my neck with his tongue as I was trying to get my keys from my purse. I finally located them and opened my door. Henley had not stopped kissing me in all that time. He followed me into my apartment and quickly took off his clothes and started to unbutton my top. I immediately pushed his hands away and unbuttoned it myself. I then unsnapped my bra and began to take off my pants.

So much for me playing hard to get!

Henley continued kissing me and then his hands softly caressed my breasts. I never felt as content as I did at that moment. We did not let go of each other as we proceeded towards my bedroom. In our haste, I almost tripped over his leg. He then walked in front of me and I saw his limp. It was obvious, but it only made him sexier. I was quite fine with everything "Henley" that night!

Lying on my bed with Henley was an adventure in amorous passion. His hands were gentle and kind. He knew when to be playful and when to stop. My entire body tingled with each touch. It was as though we were the only two people in the world entangled in each other as one. It was truly heaven on earth. In my wildest dreams, I could not have asked for a better lover.

Basking in the glow of our lovemaking, I turned to give Henley a final kiss when I saw that he wasn't there. I looked around and realized to my great dismay that I might have just awakened from a very powerful dream. Could this have been possible? I sat up and began rubbing my eyes.

I got off the couch and went to check the bathroom for Henley. It was very disappointing that he wasn't in there. I then went into the kitchen and sat down on one of the chairs. I needed a moment to pull myself together. Making such passionate love to Henley felt so real, that it was hard for me to believe it never happened.

That was some power nap!

I took a look at the clock and realized that I had about 15 minutes to get myself together before meeting Henley. I brushed my teeth and fixed my makeup. I looked in the mirror and did a "practice smile," so that I would know what I would look like to Henley when he first saw me. I was excited and hoping that the evening would turn out exactly like my dream.

Before closing my door, I looked at the vase of flowers again. They were truly beautiful. I couldn't wait to thank Henley for them later that evening.

•

I arrived at Tootsie's a few minutes after 6:00 PM and looked around for Henley. He wasn't anywhere in sight. A moment of angst went through me.

"Please don't let this be a repeat of last year," I said to myself softly.

"Do you have a reservation, Miss?" the hostess asked me.

"I'm meeting a friend here. The reservation must be under his name. It's Henley Lewis."

She looked at her appointment book and said, "Right this way."

The hostess led me to one of the small tables which Henley had reserved for us. Since he wasn't there yet, I had my choice of where to sit. I chose the chair facing the front of the restaurant because it allowed me to see everyone coming and going. I hate it when I have to sit in a seat that keeps me from being aware of my surroundings.

A waiter appeared within seconds.

"Would you like to order a drink while you're waiting?"

"Sure, I'll have a white wine spritzer, thank you."

The waiter left and within a moment or two Henley walked in. He definitely limped and unlike the rugged look in my dream, his face was clean-shaven. His hair was longer than I remembered and appeared disheveled. As he neared the table, his scars were obvious. They weren't extreme, but they were noticeably there. However, I realized that it wouldn't be that difficult to get used to them.

"Hi, Henley," I said with a big smile.

"Hi, Evie! It's so good to see you after all this time. Glad I made it!"

Both of us giggled at that last statement. It actually was great to see him! He sat down and was about to continue with our conversation when my drink was brought over.

"Glad you ordered. I'll have a beer," he said to the waiter.

There was his sexy voice again!

I began to sip my drink when Henley took my hand, placed it near his mouth and kissed it softly. I knew that my dream of a romantic evening was going to come true. I wanted to suggest skipping dinner but knew better. Rushing it would scare him off, so I sat back and relaxed.

After two drinks and some less than stimulating conversation, we headed towards The Half Shell Restaurant.

Dinner was dinner. The food was good but not great. The conversation flowed with a lot of laughs. There was a change in Henley's demeanor from what I saw in the previous year. He seemed more mature and confident. As the date progressed, he became more attractive.

"I really enjoy your company. There's so much I still want to learn about you," Henley said.

"There's not that much that you don't already know. What you see is what you get."

"Then I like what I see," he responded.

He said all the right things and I began pondering with the idea of suggesting my place for a nightcap. It was at that moment that the flowers came to mind.

"By the way Henley, I loved the flowers you sent me. They are just beautiful. I put them on my living room coffee table. If you want to, you can come up to see them."

He began to shift in his chair, and his face seemed to have a look of surprise. He had become a bit flushed, and I noticed that his forehead showed a few beads of sweat.

"What just happened? Are you okay?"

"I'm fine. It's just that I'm a little embarrassed because it wasn't me who sent you the flowers."

I couldn't believe it! I never looked at the enclosed card because I automatically thought it was from Henley.

"Oh, now I'm a little embarrassed!"

"No problem. Sounds like you have another admirer. I'm not surprised, you're a beautiful woman!"

It was good that he thought he wasn't the only one, but he was the only one. I didn't want to upset the apple cart at that moment.

"Thanks for the compliment. Let's forget the flowers. Would you like to get out of here and come up to my apartment for a few minutes? We could have a drink."

"Are you asking because you think I feel bad about the flowers?"

"No, I'd really like you to come up, that is if you want to."

Henley smiled again. I was so glad that he felt at ease.

"Sure, I would love to, no flowers and all."

We left the restaurant and took a cab to my building. I must have looked really happy because the doorman winked at me.

Upon entering my apartment, I immediately took the vase of flowers and placed them behind my curio cabinet where they would be out of sight. I made a mental note to read the card after Henley left.

"You didn't have to remove the flowers, I'm not that sensitive," he remarked.

I smiled and let the subject drop.

"Would you like some red wine?"

"Sure, that sounds good."

I took out two glasses and began pouring the wine. Before I was able to finish doing that, Henley was behind me. He placed his hands around my waist and began to kiss my neck. I resisted playfully.

"Henley! What are you doing?" I asked in a sing-song voice.

It was clear to him that I was willing to be caressed.

I turned towards him and we began to smooch in earnest. His kisses were not like those in my fantasy. They were sloppy and wet. Either he did not have a lot of experience or simply sucked in that department, no pun intended.

"Let's sit on the couch and enjoy the wine," I said quickly.

I wanted to slow down the action. Unfortunately, Henley was not going to be anything like the lover he was in my dream.

Time to let go of the fantasy, Evie!

The rest of the evening was mundane, bordering on boring. I was sorry that I asked him to come up. He was a nice guy, but as much as I tried, I couldn't force myself to like him romantically. Henley, however, did not give up easily.

"Let's have some more wine. Neither one of us has to go to work tomorrow," he said nonchalantly.

The wine I drank at The Half Shell and the additional drinking at my apartment made me lose my inhibitions. Henley began to kiss me again and tried to remove my blouse at the same time. His hands were awkward, so I just took it off by myself. He removed his shirt and pants so quickly that there was nothing left to the imagination.

We went into the bedroom and I completed removing my clothes. He kissed me a few more times, fondled my breasts for a minute or two and then went for it. I would've preferred to be making love rather than simply having sex, but sex it was going to be. It all was over in a few minutes and I was not even close to being satisfied. Henley was a terrible lover and sex with him could never happen again.

I got up to go to the bathroom. When I came back to my bed, Henley was already sleeping. All I wanted was for him to leave my apartment at that point.

"Henley, Henley! It's very late. You should go," I said in a loud voice.

He didn't respond, so I shook his arm to wake him.

"Can't I stay the night? It's almost 1:30 AM," he said in a groggy voice.

"Okay, but we're not doing a repeat."

Both of us knew that this was not going any further. Henley rolled over on his side and pulled the covers over his shoulders.

•

It was a beautiful, sunny morning and I was glad Henley had left early. Since the sex wasn't even remotely satisfying, I had to finish the job myself. It was undoubtedly more gratifying than he was. I had let my imagination run away with me. I wasn't angry with him, just disillusioned, all because of some stupid dream.

It was time to hop in the shower and get the day started. Since it was Sunday, my plans were to go about the rest of the day in slo-mo. While walking back to my bedroom, I saw the tops of the flowers peeking out from the back of my curio cabinet. I had completely forgotten about them. I picked up the vase and brought it to the kitchen table. Most of the flowers had already wilted which didn't bother me. I took the card from the wire clip it was attached to and read it. It was from James to Valerie. What the hell! The flowers were given to me by mistake. Damn it!

I called Briana hoping we could meet up later in the day.

"Hello."

"Hi, Briana! How are you?"

"I'm good. Can we talk later, Evie? I'm busy with something right now."

"That's fine."

I hung up the phone feeling very lonely and a little depressed. I had wanted to complain to her about Henley, although her opinion of him wasn't important to me. We always had different mindsets when it came to men, but that didn't matter at the moment because I needed to vent.

Since Briana couldn't talk, I decided to go to the library and check out the action. It was a good place to be, since people usually congregated there. Maybe I would meet someone. I put on a pair of light blue jeans and a thin striped cotton blouse. I slipped into a pair of sneakers, grabbed my purse and left my building. It was a sunny day and that gave me a boost.

Arriving within view of the library, I stopped for a moment and glimpsed at the statues on the exterior of the building. I marveled at how intricately they were carved and how beautiful they were. I continued walking and saw many people congregating about. Some were sitting on the concrete steps eating lunch, some were socializing, and others were just people watching. There were even those who actually had books in their arms. Once inside, I was still amazed at how large the library was and the numerous people there. It was a world in a world by itself.

I selected a book on romantic poetry. It would be a good eye-catcher if some guy actually bothered to look at me. I went outside and sat down on the steps and began thumbing through the book. After a few minutes, I lost interest and thought of returning it. I glanced up and saw a young woman that looked familiar. She was too far away for me to recognize her, but I continued to stare. She was getting closer and then began walking up the steps.

OMG! It was my sister, Raquel! Instinctively, I turned away, and then just as quickly looked back at her. She was carrying a large canvas bag that looked heavy. It was probably filled with books as Raquel was an avid reader. She didn't see me, or at least that's what it seemed like. I only had a split-second to make a decision. Do I approach her or not? The moment passed as she had already walked into the library.

I thought back to my Auntie Nina. Was this similar in opportunity to the one she missed out on with her sister? I took this as a sign from above and waited for Raquel to come back out. I wasn't sure what to say but knew that this was my chance to approach her. Maybe she had time to mature and maybe, just maybe, she wanted me back in her life.

I stood by the steps, waiting for Raquel to come back outside. About twenty minutes later, she came out of the library and quickly skipped down the stairs and passed right by me.

"Raquel, Raquel," I yelled out while waving my hand in the air.

She turned around. At first, it seemed as though she didn't recognize me. Then Raquel stopped and made a peculiar face; it was one of disdain. I wasn't sure what to do at that point. Do I just turn around and forget about the whole thing, or see it through? As I stood there motionless, Raquel made the decision for both of us and began walking toward me. I was happy to see that I had misread her demeanor. After all, she was standing far away.

"What are you doing here?" Raquel asked in an annoyed tone.

"I had some time so I decided to relax and people watch."

"At least you weren't following me!"

I was both surprised and not surprised by what she said. She never liked me as a person or as a sister. Apparently, nothing had changed.

"That is a strange statement to make, Raquel. I thought maybe we could be on speaking terms and slowly try to mend fences. I don't even know what went wrong between us."

"You are not part of my life anymore, so stay the hell away from me!" she said angrily.

Raquel then turned around and left me standing there dumbfounded.

Those words really stung, so I stood there in shock for a good 30 seconds. There was no opportunity to respond before she hurriedly walked away. Maybe that was a good thing. Confrontation never resolves anything and usually deepens the wounds that already exist. I truly hated her at that moment and was glad that she was gone. I returned the book and went back to my apartment.

What a waste of a Sunday!

I thought about calling Briana again. She had told me earlier that she was busy. It was possible that she and Paul were having a fight at that moment. I was better off not interjecting myself into her situation at the moment, even though I really wanted to talk to her. It was important for me to let her know that I had just seen Raquel. I needed to be patient and eventually she would call me back.

•

The day after running into Raquel, I found myself extremely bored at work. When it was time to go home, I didn't feel like stopping off to get dinner as usual. There were some leftovers in the fridge and they would have to suffice.

I heard the phone ring as I was unlocking my door and quickly ran in to answer it.

"Hello."

"Hi, Evie, it's Briana. Sorry I couldn't talk yesterday. What is going on with you?"

"Maybe I should ask you the same question?"

"You know the answer," she said.

I dropped the subject and instead began to tell her about Henley. She listened attentively to what I had to say and commented only once.

"He sounds like a good catch. Don't discard him so fast. Give him a chance. Maybe he'll grow on you."

"I don't think you were listening to me, Briana. The sex was beyond boring. He's a nice guy and his voice is beyond sexy, but I just don't have any feelings for him in that way."

"I understand, Evie. I won't push you."

I went into detail regarding my encounter with Raquel. When I finished talking about her, I felt so much better.

"Do you have a night this week to get together, Briana?"

"It will have to be spur-of-the-moment. I'll call you when I know," she answered.

And with that, the conversation ended. We never did get together that week. I let it go and decided to try again another time.

CHAPTER 31

Falling in the shower was probably the best thing that had ever happened to me. Between the initial feelings of immobility to the dependency on another human being, I began to realize how lucky I was just to be alive.

It was almost two and a half months since that fall. I was about to have my third consecutive appointment with Dr. Hunter, and the therapy was definitely helping me. I used to see her quite often back in the day and was hoping to get back in the groove. It was 11:00 AM and I was scheduled to meet with her in a few hours. I was still lying in bed but was wide awake.

Out of nowhere, I sat up and for the first time decided to be in charge of me. It was long overdue and if I wanted to be happy, I had to do it by myself and for myself. I finally came to the realization that I was in control of my own happiness. All I had to do was believe it.

"Today is my day! I am going to go out and live in the real world. No one is going to hurt me anymore!" I said defiantly to myself.

I didn't know where this burst of energy had come from, but I was going with it. I literally jumped out of bed to start my day. In my excitement, I didn't see the clothing that I had left lying on the floor. I tripped over them but got up quickly and held on to the dresser to steady myself. I started to laugh at what had just happened. Maybe it was nervous laughter, maybe not. It didn't matter either way because I was happy to be laughing.

•

I told Dr. Hunter that I had a secret … a secret that had recently come back to haunt me. Although it had nothing to do with my current state, keeping it bottled in would only work against me.

It was my fourth consecutive appointment with Dr. Hunter and this time, I was ready!

"Hello, Dr. Hunter."

"Hello, Evie. Please, sit down."

I sat down on her couch this time. It was less difficult than I had imagined it would be.

"Dr. Hunter, I am so happy to be here today. Before I go into my story, I want you to know that today is my birthday and I'm 43 years old. I can't believe that I'm so old already. Anyway, it's time to cleanse myself, and 'let it all out,' as they say."

How do I continue? It was difficult to let the words out. I became very emotional and began to cry. The tears were running down my face and weren't stopping. It was very embarrassing to cry so profusely in front of Dr. Hunter even though I did it so many times before. She handed me some tissues and sat back down on her chair. She didn't try to console me or offer any words of comfort. At first, I was angry thinking Dr. Hunter should be more compassionate, but then I remembered this was her way of giving me therapy. I began to speak in between sobs.

"My painful past can be divulged to you because I know it will stay our secret."

Dr. Hunter acknowledged that she heard me by nodding her head. There were no facial expressions to let me know if she was interested in what I had to say. I let that thought go and continued speaking.

"About six years ago, I went on a date with a guy named Henley ..."

I spoke about Henley because I didn't have the courage to speak about what I needed to. My throat became dry and ordinary swallowing was difficult.

"I need a drink of water."

Dr. Hunter stood up, poured tepid sink water into a small paper cup and handed it to me. I drank it quickly and asked for more. At that point, I became somewhat agitated. She could have offered me a bottle of water but didn't. I began to feel uneasy and decided to leave.

"Can't talk anymore right now, gotta go," I said hurriedly.

"Before you leave, Happy Birthday, Evie."

"Thanks."

I ran out of her office and caught the elevator to the lobby. It was apparent Dr. Hunter didn't like me and only pretended that she cared. She knew that I was choking, well almost anyway. She could have asked me if I was okay. On top of it, tap water? She could well have afforded to spare one of her bottled waters that she kept in her drawer. This doctor was made of stone, no feelings and no empathy. It was clear that I was just another patient who was no more than a dollar sign to her.

As these thoughts whirled around in my head, I called her service to schedule an emergency appointment for the next day. I wanted her to feel bad that I left so suddenly.

Why was I looking for sympathy from my psychologist? My thought pattern made no sense.

My last conversation with Briana was all about her attempts to get pregnant, my stale sex with Henley, and bumping into my sister, Raquel. I hadn't expected to hear from Briana again for at least a few weeks. Surprisingly, she called me a few days later.

"Hi, Evie, do you have time to talk?"

"Sure. How are things going with Paul? Is he still hell-bent on getting you pregnant?"

Hearing silence on the line, I realized that I was too blunt, especially with such a sensitive subject. Those words just happened to have come out of my mouth without any consideration for Briana. She knew that I wasn't perfect, but she accepted me anyway.

"I had another miscarriage! It's not happening for us. I can't hold them, and Paul is more devastated than I am."

I didn't know how to respond since I had never been in her situation.

"So what are you going to do, Briana?"

"There's nothing to do. I can either keep trying, which is heartbreaking every time it fails, or just stop trying. I'm so scared because if we don't have children soon, I'm afraid that Paul will divorce me!"

"Why isn't Paul afraid that he's going to lose you? Your marriage has to be about more than just babies."

Briana broke out into large sobs. I hated listening to her cry. She stopped after a few minutes and then spoke.

"You are not my friend! How could you say that to me? How could you be so insensitive? Don't you realize that I am a person too?"

And with that last statement, she hung up the phone. I must admit I was in shock, not at what she said, but that she hung up on me. I never expected that, so I went into the kitchen to pour myself a glass of wine, my constant form of self-medication. My lifeline was just cut. Briana hated me and wasn't my friend anymore. I took several sips of the wine and set the glass down on the counter. I immediately picked it up again and finished the wine. I went over to my couch, picked up my blanket and began crying.

I had no other friends to turn to for advice or conversation. Reflecting on Briana's words made me realize that she was correct. I should have called her back, but my pride wouldn't let me. Again, I was a fool and very selfish. The realization came to me that no one had to accept my bad behavior, especially Briana. I decided that I would call her later in the day. At that point, cooler heads would prevail, especially on my part.

But I never followed through.

That evening, my thoughts turned to Henley. He was a nice guy, but there was no spark. Perhaps what Briana said was true; maybe Henley would grow on me. Sometimes when a relationship starts out hot it cools down quickly. However, it could be that the opposite was also true.

I considered reaching out to Henley to give it another shot, but then my ego came into play. What if he rejected me? I didn't know what to do, so I did what I do best; absolutely nothing!

The following evening, I found myself in my bedroom staring at my phone, hoping Briana would call. She knew that I wasn't the best at confronting a situation, especially when I was at fault. But in this case, it was me who had to make the first move. I was the one who screwed up.

My laundry was piling up, which meant that a trip downstairs to the basement level of my building was necessary. That's where the coin-operated machines and dryers were. I emptied my hamper and placed the clothes into a cloth laundry bag, grabbed a magazine and a bunch of quarters, and headed for the basement. I figured that since there were only two loads, I would wait there until they were finished.

Once in the laundry room, I began reading my magazine. A tenant I did not recognize walked in with her laundry cart. She took the last available machine and proceeded to unload her wash. It was annoying because I didn't realize that machine was available. After staring at her for a few seconds, I continued reading my magazine.

My first load was done and I placed it into the dryer. As I went to put the rest of my clothing into the washing machine, I saw a young man bring in his belongings. He was holding them in two plastic supermarket bags. Continuing to place my clothes into the washer, I watched him from the corner of my eye. He appeared unfamiliar with the laundry room setup. When he realized that there were no machines available, he started to walk out. I had not seen him in the building before, and by his uncertainty, he obviously was a new tenant.

"Excuse me," I said loudly enough to catch his attention.

He turned around and looked at me, not sure if I was addressing him.

"Most of the machines will be available within a few minutes if you want to wait, that is."

"Thank you. What happens if the people don't come for their laundry right away?" he replied.

"They usually do, but you can take their laundry out and leave it on the folding table."

"That's not a nice thing to do, is it?" he asked.

I wasn't sure if he was just making a statement or chastising me. I decided it was the former.

"I haven't done it, but there are people who do it when they're in a hurry."

"All right, I'll wait a little while longer. By the way, my name is Sean, Sean Graham."

"Hi, I'm Evie Harris."

"I guess you can tell that I'm new here."

"When did you move in?"

"Last week."

Two women walked in and went over to remove their items from their respective washers. They unloaded their clothing and freed up the machines.

"Excuse me. I have to take care of this," Sean said.

He placed the contents of both bags into one machine. I tried to see if any of them were female clothing, and happily, there were none. After he threw in the detergent, Sean sat down next to me.

"How long have you lived here?" he asked.

"I've been here for about three years."

Before we were able to continue our conversation, Sean's phone rang. He answered it immediately and walked to the exit door. I couldn't hear what he was saying since his back was toward me. Was he speaking with his girlfriend?

My wash had finished, so I removed my items and placed them in the dryer. Then I removed my clothing from the first dryer and began to fold them. Usually, I just throw them back into the bag. In this instance, however, my interest in Sean gave me a reason to prolong my stay.

Sean concluded his conversation and walked back toward the washing machine. He opened the top of the machine and looked at its contents. His facial appearance indicated that he was rattled by that call.

"If you open the lid, the machine just stops working."

I shouldn't have said anything but wanted him to continue talking to me.

"I don't know why I did it. Maybe it's out of habit," Sean responded.

"It's probably because something is upsetting you."

Would he reveal what was bothering him? If he was going to talk about a girl issue, I didn't want to hear it. He closed the lid and looked at me.

"You're very perceptive. Are you a problem solver?"

"No, it's just very obvious from the way you're behaving that you're new to doing laundry and that you're bothered about something. Do you want to talk about it? I'm a very good listener."

He was apprehensive at first, but then walked over to the folding table.

"Things are going on in my life that I'm not prepared to share with a stranger or anyone else at this time. I don't mean to sound callous, but it's rather personal."

"I didn't mean to pry. I just thought you might want someone to talk to."

I felt very embarrassed and wished that I could have taken my words back. I went over to the second dryer, removed my clothing and started folding as quickly as possible. Everything was damp because I had opened the dryer before the timer went off. I felt extremely uncomfortable and couldn't wait to get back upstairs to my apartment.

"I'm sorry about the tone I used. I tend to do that when I become defensive. It's clear that you were trying to be nice. Please don't take it personally, but I don't want to discuss what's irritating me, at least not at this time," he stated.

"No problem," I answered in a lackadaisical manner.

I placed everything in my bag and started to walk towards the door.

"Evie, please stay. I want …"

I didn't give Sean a chance to finish his sentence. He was disrespectful and I wasn't in the mood to continue the conversation. Maybe I overstepped my boundaries by inviting him to discuss his personal information with me, but he didn't have to speak so rudely. His apology meant nothing as far as I was concerned.

Once upstairs, I unlocked my door, threw the bag of laundry on the kitchen floor, and went directly over to my couch. I wrapped my blanket around me and turned on the TV. Sean had really upset me. I had been way too forward with him and his response bruised my ego. Hopefully, this would be a lesson learned. After all, I had often made bad choices by being too meek or too outgoing. It was time to find a middle ground and not fall for every guy the moment I laid eyes on him. When will I ever learn this lesson?

Will I ever learn this lesson?

•

The morning after my brief encounter with Sean, I awoke early so I could get my box of detergent from the laundry room. When I got there, it was nowhere to be found. Disappointed, I went back upstairs and ate a small breakfast, topping it off with a delicious cup of hazelnut flavored coffee.

It had been a few days since I had slept with Henley. Visions of our two-minute sex session kept entering my thoughts, and I tried my best to disregard them. This kind of repulsed me, yet for whatever reason, it kept jumping into my mind. I would never try to contact him again, but I did start to think about Sean. He was very different from most men I had met before. Physically, he was quite nice to look at. He was trim, about 5'10'' with light brown hair, some of it thinning at the top. He was clean-shaven, and his eyes were dark brown. His features weren't outstanding, but yet he was still very cute.

The more I thought about him, the more I realized how childish my behavior was. He apologized like a gentleman, but I stormed out like a drama queen. How could I have expected this complete stranger to share his problems with me? I wondered if I would ever see him again. If I did, a sincere apology from me was definitely in order. I stopped thinking about him and headed out the door to the office.

Work was very pleasant that day; probably because Bettye was on vacation. I left the office and went to Mom & Pop's and picked up some chicken cutlets and mixed vegetables to bring home for dinner.

I walked into my building carrying my shopping bag. It was irritating to wait at the elevator with other people who were unfamiliar to me. The doors opened and everyone entered. As they were closing, I heard a voice shout out, "Please hold the door!" Someone held out their hand and the elevator reopened. A man wearing a baseball cap and sunglasses entered. Since the elevator was crowded, I only saw his profile for a split-second before he turned to face the doors. I thought it was Sean but wasn't sure. It was hard to tell since a good portion of his face was hidden. Deciding to be bold, I remained in the elevator until he got off. After the first few people exited the elevator, the guy with the baseball cap glanced around. It was definitely Sean. He made eye contact with me for a second and then looked away. As I was wondering why he did not recognize me, the doors opened again and he got out. The elevator ascended and I got out on my floor.

I hung my work clothes on the back of my kitchen chair and changed into an old pair of shorts and a t-shirt. I ate my dinner and then watched TV. It was after 9:00 PM and I wasn't tired enough to go to bed. Briana came into my head. She had been such a good friend and I had been such a shit.

Briana needed support and I wasn't there. It was time to call her and ask to meet up. There were so many things to talk about; things much more important than Paul! Oh yeah, and I had to apologize to her. Really apologize! Doing so in person would be the most genuine way to show her that I truly meant it. Meeting at her place was out of bounds since Paul would be there. A public setting would be best.

I called Briana's cell phone several times and she did not pick it up. She was obviously very angry with me and rightfully so. Our relationship was frayed, and I desperately wanted to repair it. It was my job to be there in her time of need. I called again and this time left a message pleading for Briana to call me back. She did not. For once I wasn't going to give up. Briana needed my help and I was going to give it to her! Sending a note to her work address via the messenger service from my office would be the best choice. I would only write "Briana" on the envelope and she would most probably open it. Curiosity usually wins out. I wanted to make us right. Our friendship needed to be as strong as it used to be before I became selfish and self-absorbed.

Instead of brooding about my immaturity and bad behavior, I figured it would make more sense to clean my apartment that evening. In this way, I would always be ready for company and not be embarrassed by my messy place.

•

The following week I received a call from Briana.

"Hello."

"Evie, I got your note. Say what you have to!"

Briana's voice was curt with undertones of anger. This wasn't going to be an easy conversation.

"Briana, I want to apologize to you. You've been such a good friend to me and now it's time for me to be one to you. Let's get together and talk. It's long overdue. How about meeting at Tootsie's Bar?"

"I don't know if it'll do any good, but it might be a start. When do you want to meet?"

"What about tomorrow after work?"

"That's actually a good time. Paul won't be back until after 10:00 PM. See you then around seven."

"See you."

I was so glad that Briana was willing to see me after the way I acted towards her. If the tables were turned, who knows if I would have been so generous?

•

Surprisingly, there were plenty of tables available at Tootsie's, so I sat down at the one closest to the bar. Seconds later, Briana walked in. The timing was perfect.

"Do you want to have some drinks before we order dinner? They have a lot of non-alcoholic beverages here."

"I don't want to drink. I just want to talk and maybe have a bite to eat," Briana said.

She was very agitated. It was probably a combination of her frustrations with Paul, not being able to get pregnant, and of course, me.

"I don't blame you for being angry with me. I don't always know how to behave properly, like you do. I am very sorry for being so unfeeling towards what you are going through. Can we just wipe the slate clean and forget about the bad stuff?"

"No, we can't! I don't know whether to stop our friendship permanently or to just shake you until all your demons fly out of your head!" Briana responded.

"I deserved that. I wasn't sensitive to you at all. You have to forgive me! Please, forgive me!" I pleaded.

"Why? So you can do it again?"

"I deserved that also, but I'm starting to change and I am your friend! Please believe me. I love you like a sister! Sorry, those were obviously the wrong choice of words. I mean that I love you like the sister I wish I had!"

Briana stared at me for a long time. At least it seemed that way to me.

"I know what you meant," she said in an irritable tone.

The waitress came over and asked for our orders.

"What'll be tonight, Ladies?"

I looked over at Briana and saw that she put her face back down towards the menu. She told me to order first.

"I'll have the fish special and a glass of club soda with no ice."

"And you?"

"I'll have a burger and a Coke," Briana said.

"Is there anything else?" the waitress asked.

"Yes. A large order of curly fries sounds good," I added.

Hopefully, the food would make Briana less hostile. It was obvious that she wasn't going to make it easy for me, at least not this time.

Briana grabbed both of my hands. She placed them on top of the table with hers over mine and said, "Paul is my husband!"

She hesitated for a second and then continued speaking.

"You don't have to like him, but you have to respect him. He's married to me, not to you. You don't get a vote in this matter. All I wanted from you was support and maybe some good advice. You weren't there for me when I needed a good friend. I am going through a real life crisis. Do you hear me?"

Briana chastised me with those words. She made me feel like a child who deserved to be punished. I had never heard her speak in that tone of voice before. I was truly dumbfounded and afraid to respond.

"Don't you have something to say to me, Evie?" Briana continued.

Our drinks arrived in the nick of time. The waitress set our plates in front of us and began to speak.

"Your food will be ready shortly, Ladies. Will there be anything else?"

"No, we're good for now, thank you," Briana answered.

It was clear that an uneasy conversation was going on by our demeanor and raised voices, so the waitress left rather quickly.

"Evie, I'm not letting you get away with this. I'll ask you one more time. Don't you have anything to say to me?"

"What else is there to say? I'm afraid that whatever comes out of my mouth won't be right. You've made up your mind to cut me out of your life, haven't you?"

Briana took a sip of her soda and then placed the glass down.

"I am in so much pain. I constantly miscarry and don't get to full term, my marriage is on the rocks and my best friend doesn't have a clue as how to help me."

I couldn't believe what Briana just said. She considered me her best friend! Wow! What a revelation! At that moment, everything changed for me and I felt reborn. I had a best friend who also saw me as her best friend. This feeling of joy overwhelmed me. I got up, went over to Briana, and gave her a hug and kiss on the cheek. I then went back to my seat.

"What was that about?" Briana asked.

"I just realized how lucky I am. I can't believe it, I'm your best friend!"

Briana let her guard down and began to giggle. Her anger seemed to have disappeared. Our food arrived at that very moment. The timing couldn't have been better. Briana took a big bite of her burger and I started pouring ketchup on my fries.

"I promise to be respectful to Paul and do my best to be the same friend to you as you have always been to me. Now please, help me eat these fries as I really ordered them for you so that maybe you would like me again!"

Briana broke out into laughter. She couldn't stop, and neither could I. My friend was back in my life!

I was so lucky!

CHAPTER 32

The day after making amends with Briana, I ended up having to stay late at work. It was almost 7:30 PM when Bill told me to take a 15 minute break, so I made myself a cup of coffee and brought it back to my desk. I sat back down and hoped to think about nothing for the rest of my break, but that didn't happen. My thoughts turned to Sean. Checking him out any further would be futile. There couldn't be any romantic relationship with him since I had acted so childishly and stormed off when we first met. He probably had a girlfriend anyway. So I let things remain as they were and allow nature to take its course.

AT 9:00 PM, Bill told me that I stayed late enough. Since I was very tired and extremely hungry, it was prudent to go straight home and eat whatever leftovers were in the fridge.

I walked into the lobby of my apartment building and greeted Al at the front desk. He waved back and then continued with what he was doing. As I headed towards the elevator, Al called out my name.

"Miss Evie, Miss Evie, I almost forgot. I have a little something for you."

Puzzled, I walked back over to the front desk.

"A new tenant left an envelope with this box of detergent for someone by the name of Evie. You're the only Evie I know in the building. He said I should mention 'laundry room' and you would know who he was. Does this make any sense to you?"

My heart started to beat faster.

"Was his name Sean?"

"Yes, that was his name."

Al handed me the box of detergent with an envelope taped to the top. I couldn't wait to get into my apartment to open it.

Evie,

I met you in the laundry room a few days ago. You seemed nice and I acted like a jerk. I'd like to make it up to you. Would you like to have a drink sometime soon?

Sean   646-222-...

I couldn't stop laughing. I didn't act nice, and instead of Sean being angry, he sent me an apology note. After reading it, I felt good about myself and made the call to him right away.

"Hello."

"Hi, Sean, it's the laundry girl."

"Ha, ha. Thanks for calling. I wasn't sure you would."

"Why's that?"

"I was a little upset and took it out on you. Hopefully, we can get past that."

"Absolutely! I also felt bad about my behavior and was very happy to get your note."

"So, does that mean you would also be happy to get a drink with me?"

"Yes I would! Usually, Friday night works best …"

Before I could finish my sentence, I heard what sounded like a child crying in the background.

"Is that a baby crying or is it your TV?" I asked Sean.

"No, that's my son, Charlie. He often gets nightmares when he stays over because he's very attached to his mother. I have to check on him. Can you hold on?"

"Sure. No problem."

Of course the bubble burst. Sean was a divorced man with a child. What happened in his marriage? Did he cheat on his wife? Maybe she cheated on him. Regardless of the reason, he had baggage. I wasn't ready to deal with another woman's child or children. No matter what, his ex would be involved in Sean's life forever. That seemed like too much trouble for me.

"Sorry about that. He had trouble going back to sleep. So what were we talking about?"

"You asked me to go out for a drink. I guess it will have to wait a while," I said, hoping he would agree.

"Oh, you mean because of, Charlie? There's no problem. I have him once a week and every other weekend. We can get together almost anytime. That is, if you want to."

I felt apprehensive and didn't want to brush him off at that moment. If I did, he would realize that my interest in him had waned because he had a son. I wasn't sure what to do.

"Can I call you back? It's getting kind of late," I said to him.

"No problem. We'll talk another time. Take care."

And then he hung up.

I was surprised that he had given up so easily, since I was hoping he would beg a little. I didn't know why I wanted him to do that. Who was I kidding? I definitely knew why! It would have given me a feeling of superiority and control. So what happened next? I became even more interested in him than I was before the phone call! I was so upset with myself for acting in such haste. What harm would it have been if we spent an hour or two having a drink and some conversation?

Reality was a pill I didn't always want to swallow. I never paid attention to how my life was going. I made decisions based upon physical attributes or other things that were not important. Here, a good man came into my life who seemed to be the whole package, yet I threw an obstacle in the way because he had a child. Sean was very nice and had done nothing wrong.

I went to the refrigerator, took out a bottle of white wine and poured myself a glass. After rethinking my priorities, I made a decision to call Sean the next day to apologize.

•

I woke up very early the next morning and could not get back to sleep. I stayed in my bed and began to think of Sean. If I called him and he brushed me off like I did to him, I would feel very low. So, in my cowardly manner, I placed a note under his door that morning before going to work. He couldn't reject a note, could he?

My phone rang around 9:00 PM that evening.

"Hi, Evie, it's Sean. I got your note and I'm not mad at you. It's just that you seemed conflicted. You were interested in me at one moment and then seconds later you weren't. I don't get the hot and cold behavior."

He was completely on target and hit the nail on the head. I was often indecisive and had made it very obvious to him during that phone conversation. It sounded like I was being given a second chance, so I made up my mind to act mature and kind. Hopefully, I could pull it off.

"Everything you just said is true. I don't like to admit it, but I'm a little scatterbrained. If the invitation is still open, I'd like to have that drink with you."

"So, what time can I pick you up tomorrow night?" Sean asked.

He took me by surprise. I thought he would take at least a couple of days before being ready to go out with me. It was refreshing to talk to a man who was self-assured and decisive.

"It might be easier for me to meet you out since I'll be working until 5:30ish. How does Tootsie's Bar and Grill around 6:00 PM sound?"

"That's great. I'll see you tomorrow at 6:00 PM. Please don't change your mind again!" he said jokingly.

Conflicted was a good word to describe my way of life, questioning every decision and changing my mind often. I guess Sean read me perfectly, hot one minute, then cold, then hot again. I was impulsive, but also passionate, and those feelings can make one implode. I was somewhat apprehensive about meeting Sean, yet at the same time looking forward to it. I hoped that I made the right choice this time.

•

As I was approaching Tootsie's, I saw Sean standing outside. I started to feel excited and hurried to cross the street.

"Hi, Sean," I said with a huge smile.

"Hi, Evie," he responded.

We went inside and as usual, the place was crowded and noisy. We had to stand in line for a few minutes before we were able to get in. There were no tables available and every seat at the bar was taken. It was irritating, but not enough to make us leave.

"Would you like a drink while we're waiting?" Sean asked.

"It looks like we're going to be here for a while, so why not. I'll have a glass of red wine, thank you."

I was able to determine that Sean was a real gentleman. We could have just stood there and talked, but instead, he took the initiative and ordered us drinks. Obviously, he wasn't cheap. Nothing spoils a date more than a guy who literally counts his pennies in front of you. The wine arrived and we automatically clinked our glasses.

"To our first date," Sean said.

"Let's go outside where it's less noisy," he added.

"Good idea."

We sat on one of the available wrought iron benches located on the small patio. It was chilly outside, which was probably why we had the bench all to ourselves. We sipped the wine and our conversation flowed naturally, as if we had known each other for years.

"I feel there are things that you want to know about me, so go ahead and ask away," Sean said.

Okay, here goes!

"I know I seemed somewhat distressed during our phone conversation and I am sorry for that. I love it that you're so down to earth and easy to talk to. I want to be honest about something. When I first saw you, I was immediately attracted. I was so happy that the washing machines were all full because that gave me an excuse to talk to you. I don't know what it is, but I find you so sexy. Maybe I shouldn't have said that. I hope I'm not embarrassing you."

Apparently, I did because he blushed and then turned to the side for a moment before facing me again.

"Then what was distressing you? Is it that I have a son?"

"It's not your son directly. It's that I've never been a mother and I don't know much about children."

"You don't have to be a mother to accept someone else's child. He's with his mother most of the time. I wish he spent more time with me, but it is what it is."

"That's another thing that concerns me. You have an ex-wife and that scares me a lot."

Sean took a long sip of his wine as his face began to tense up. I must have hit a nerve by mentioning his ex.

"I was never married to Charlie's mother. I wanted to be, but she didn't. End of story."

"I'm sorry, as I didn't mean to pry. I was just being honest. We don't have to say anything more on the subject."

Sean didn't respond and instead motioned for us to go back into the bar. I felt ill at ease and it was clear that he did also. The hostess called out Sean's name as soon as we re-entered the restaurant. We were seated at a table and handed menus. The conversation dulled down to non-existent. I ordered pasta salad and Sean ordered the same.

As I rested my arms on the table, it began to wobble. I hate it when that happens. Sean got up and grabbed some paper napkins from the bar and put them under the leg of the table to balance it out. I liked the fact that I didn't have to ask him to do that.

"The food is always good here," I said awkwardly.

There was nothing else I could think of to say at that moment.

"Do you want another glass of wine?" Sean asked.

Actually, at that point, the whole bottle would have worked. I didn't want the date to end, but it could not go on much longer with all this tension.

"I have wine in my apartment. Let's finish eating and get back. We can relax and maybe talk a little more. What do you think?" I asked.

"I'm not really up for any intense conversations tonight. Maybe we should call it a n…"

I interrupted Sean before he could finish his sentence. Not wanting our time together ending on a negative note, I continued talking.

"Don't do this to yourself. It's obvious to me that something is on your mind. I'm not looking for gossip, but sometimes it's better to talk to someone who is removed from the situation. Maybe it will make you feel better to unload your troubles."

There was a long pause. He was ready to leave, possibly without me, when he said, "I'm acting like a jerk. Let's go back to your place. It will be much quieter."

I was so relieved and pleased. We ate quickly and then caught a cab back to our building. Once inside the lobby, we waited for the elevator. Sean turned and looked directly at me.

"You are a very smart woman and so mature. I'm so glad you made the suggestion to come back here and talk."

I was stunned and very happy. No one had ever told me that I was smart. Two compliments in one sentence, and in one night! How much more could I ask for?

Once inside my apartment, I poured each of us a glass of wine and placed the glasses on the cocktail table in the living room. After quickly removing the blanket and magazines from the couch, Sean and I sat down. Holding the glass in my hand, I waited for Sean to speak. A moment or two passed with no conversation, so I began to sip some of the wine.

Finally, Sean started to unwind.

"I'm really glad I met you. You brought something to light for me tonight. I do need to unload what's bothering me. I just didn't want to bother you with it."

"Why not?" I asked without hesitation.

Sean paused for a moment as if trying to decide which words to use, and then continued.

"Because you're my date and I didn't want to spoil it by discussing my problems."

"That's very kind of you, but I'm willing to listen. It's up to you. If you like, we can just drink the wine. I'm good with that also."

I actually wanted him to kiss me at that moment. I did all I could to restrain myself from jumping on him.

Sean continued to speak.

"At first Gita was going to have an abortion, but I talked her out of it. She is so happy that she has Charlie and always thanks me for that. I thought we could be a real family, but Gita's not ready for marriage, at least not with me. I've accepted this and moved on. What frustrates me most is when important decisions regarding Charlie's well-being need to be made. We can't come to a mutual agreement," Sean lamented.

"How old is Charlie?"

"He's two and a half and he's a great kid!"

The conversation went on for about another half hour and then we both realized it was time to call it a night. Sean gave me a kiss on the cheek, not the friendship type, but not the relationship type either. I opened the door and wished him a good night. I locked the door and then held my back against it. I took a deep breath in and exhaled slowly. It was the first time in my life that I acted, in what I thought, was a mature manner.

And it felt good!

•

I woke up early the morning after my date with Sean. It was so nice to take a long, hot shower and prepare a nutritious breakfast. I even had a few minutes to watch the news before I had to leave for work.

During my lunch break, Briana texted me that she wanted to talk again. She beat me to the punch, so to speak. I called her right away since we had the same lunch hour.

"Hi, Evie, I'm so glad you called. It's time we had some real girl talk like we used to. When can you meet?"

"I was thinking the same thing, how about Friday night?"

"Sounds good. Let's meet at Cafe Allegra around 8:00 PM."

"I'm afraid to go there in case Ben shows up again."

"Didn't you get a restraining order against him?"

"Yes, but with him, you never know. What about Tootsie's instead?"

"No, but how about Camilla's Place on 39th?"

"Great. I'll meet you there at 8:00 PM on Friday. Bye!"

I was so happy. My life was getting back on track. Briana and I were close again and I had a real love interest. A little pang of fear did creep into my thoughts regarding Ben. He was for sure the bane of my existence. I had to keep excising him from my psyche or I would be tortured by memories of his actions for the rest of my life.

☐

"Thank you, Dr. Hunter for seeing me again on such short notice."

"Come in, Evie. Please sit down."

It was the day after I stormed out of Dr. Hunter's office in tears. When I originally scheduled this emergency appointment, I did so to make her feel bad about our previous session. Since I had a good 24 hours to calm down, I showed up at her office for the right reason, in search of therapy rather than pity.

I found myself staring at Dr. Hunter. She looked tired, and for the first time, I noticed all the lines on her forehead. Did she use Botox in the past or was this the first time I paid attention to her face?

"Evie! Do you hear me?" Dr. Hunter asked.

"I'm sorry, I just spaced out. There's so much to tell you."

"During your last visit, you said that you had a secret. You were very upset and didn't want to talk about it. Why don't we start with that?"

I was surprised that Dr. Hunter was so blunt. She would usually let me control the sessions. This change in tactics was good for me and definitely for the better.

"I have a secret and it's very upsetting. There are only two people who know the whole story."

I became emotional again, but not as severe as during my last session.

"Dr. Hunter, there is no other way to say this but the way it is. I am a big fool."

Her eyes widened as if seeing me for the first time.

"All these years, I sat here telling you about my childhood, my longing for my sister, work and my stupid ex-boyfriends. I never told you the real story about Ben and what he did to me. I was too embarrassed and so I simply painted you a picture of another guy who broke my heart."

"What did happen with Ben?" Dr. Hunter asked.

"For many years, I was practically broke. Every penny that I got from work and disability was spent on bills, which included my visits to you. I just made it at the end of each month. I know I've told you all about my friend, Briana. Well, she loaned me

$2,000 in the very beginning so I could get back on my feet. It was a real struggle."

As usual, Dr. Hunter did not show any emotion. She nodded her head a few times and took notes.

"Go on, Evie," she said.

"As you know, I fell in love with Ben. He was the total package, or so I thought until everything imploded. Once he moved in with me, unless he had a meeting or was on one of his so-called business trips, my mornings began and my days ended with him. He was everything I wanted until I finally realized that he was nothing more than a con artist. Ben was a wolf in sheep's clothing preying on dumb and lonely women. Unfortunately, I was the dumbest!"

"What did he do to you?"

Here I go …

"He stole all my money, my self-respect and my peace of mind! And I let him do it! Even when I knew that he was a scammer, I still let him get away with using me. It was so easy for him. No matter how much he lied, I would always forgive him."

"What was so special about him?"

"He was different. No, that's not true. He actually wasn't much different than anyone else I had ever met. It was just that he was so charismatic and handsome. He always kept me on my toes which was very challenging and kept me interested. Most importantly, he made me feel good about myself."

"How did he make you feel good about yourself?"

"In the beginning, Ben was kind and nurturing. We had the greatest sex and he was always exciting to be with."

"What was exciting about him?"

"At first everything revolved around me, and then it became all about him. He lied over and over to me, but I always felt he would change as soon as his job would get better."

"I didn't hear the exciting part yet. Did I miss something?"

"You sound sarcastic, Dr. Hunter. I know I was young back then, but I loved him!" I screamed and then stood up.

My behavior was getting out of hand, and so I sat back down.

"Take a moment and relax. I'll be right back."

Dr. Hunter walked out of the room, probably to clear her head. I couldn't blame her. She returned a few minutes later.

"This is a CD with very soothing music. It will help you to talk to me. It will be very low toned, but you will hear it."

I took a deep breath and with an exaggerated sigh, I began to speak.

"Ben had chosen me as his victim. I don't know why I appealed to him in that fashion, but I did. From the very first day that I met him, he marked me as his pigeon. However, throughout the relationship, he always played the victim. And I fell for it hook, line and sinker. He always made me feel off-balance which in turn made me want to please him even more, yet I never could.

It was as though I created an image of the perfect man in my mind, and I believed that it was Ben. The one constant in our relationship was that I falsely believed he was ambitious and proud. He always spoke about his need for money but never asked me for any. Even when I offered, he refused it. He played the game quite well. I wanted to protect him and so I asked him to move in, thinking he would refuse the offer."

"Did he accept the invitation?"

"Yes he did, and at first, living together was great. Every day was happy and exciting. Soon it turned sour. I realized that I didn't know anything about him at all, including where he grew up or if he had any siblings. He was constantly lying and would dodge my questions every time I tried to get personal. I always accepted this, even though it was upsetting to me. When I finally began to get concerned with how he treated me, I was already way too deep into the relationship. I had always thought things would change and they did change, but not for the better. As time went by, he moved in for the kill. He gave me a sob story about owing the IRS money and that he was going to be arrested if he didn't pay up. He also talked about some shady people he owed gambling money to. That was a whole bunch of additional malarkey. Each time he spoke to me about his financial situation, he made sure to be extra nice and encouraged extra "lovemaking." I was so obsessed with him that I had no will or mind of my own."

Dr. Hunter handed me a bottle of water. I was shocked and also appreciative that she didn't give me tap water like the day before. I drank about a quarter of the bottle and then looked at her. She was taking notes the entire time.

"How do you feel right now?"

"I am so happy that all of this is out in the open. I feel so much better."

"Our session is over for today. You've accomplished so much in less than an hour. Keep focused and I'll see you next week."

I left her office feeling better than I had in a long time. I didn't finish my entire story but was finally able to alleviate myself of some of what was burdening me. A treat was in order, so I went to Cookie's Coffee & Bakery on 42nd Street. The scones were especially delicious there, and so were the lattes.

•

There were about two hours left until I could leave work, and I couldn't stop fantasizing about Sean. Not wanting to appear as if I was goofing off, I busied myself with deleting old files from my PC. While doing that, my cell phone rang. It was Sean.

"I'm not allowed to get personal calls at work," I whispered, and then quickly hung up the phone.

It was rude, but I didn't want Bettye to have something on me. She would have loved nothing better.

I stepped out of the office into the hallway and then called Sean back.

"Hello."

"Sean, it's me, Evie."

"Yes, I know."

"I didn't mean to hang up on you like that. There's someone in my office who would love nothing more than to get me into trouble with my boss. She's always watching me and I can't let her see me on a personal call."

"No problem. Next time I'll just text you."

"That works best, I'm glad you understand."

That seemed to have broken some of the ice.

"Would you like to come to my apartment for dinner tonight? I like to cook and you can critique it. What do you say?" Sean asked.

"I would love to. Is sixish good?"

"Sounds great, see you then."

I went back to my desk elated. I noticed Bettye looking at me out of the corner of her eye. I could only hope that she would get fired or move away. Unfortunately, hoping never makes it so.

The rest of the day was routine. I skipped my 4:00 PM snack in anticipation of eating dinner at Sean's. I had all different visions of what his apartment would look like. At first, I thought it might be white glove clean, and then I envisioned his son's clothes and toys everywhere.

The end of the workday had finally arrived. When I got home, there was just enough time to freshen up and reapply my makeup. I had a bottle of white wine in the kitchen cabinet that would be a perfect addition to the dinner. I locked my door and headed downstairs to Sean's apartment.

Ding Dong!

Sean opened his door and greeted me with a big, tight hug. It was a good start to the evening.

"Hi. I brought some wine from my stash. That's why it's not wrapped."

I wanted to bite my tongue as soon as those words came out of my mouth. Why was I apologizing for doing something nice? It made no difference if the wine was sitting in my kitchen or the liquor store. Again, I was feeling inadequate and literally wanted to run away.

"Ha, ha, I love unwrapped wine. It's my favorite brand!"

What a great guy! He eliminated my feelings of embarrassment in a split-second.

"Thank you for bringing that," he added.

Sean took the wine into the kitchen and opened it. His place was tidy but not "neat freak" clean. There were no toys strewn around. His couch was made of black leather and so was the matching love seat. He had a dark blue area rug lying over the wood floors. There was also a small table with four chairs near the wall. Everything was well-thought-out and put together.

"Here's to a tasty dinner," Sean said as he handed me a glass of wine.

He pointed to the couch and we sat down next to each other. Both of us began sipping our wine slowly.

"How was your day at the office?" I asked him.

"Since this is our slow season, I left early. Usually, I work from home. What about you?"

"More or less same old. So tell me, what do you do?"

"I'm an energy consultant and also work for a sports magazine part-time."

"What makes it seasonal?"

"Advertisers know when people pay attention to their ads. If it's a company that specializes in fishing equipment, they're more likely to advertise in the spring and summer."

"That makes sense. I never thought about it that way."

"What do you do?" Sean asked.

"I'm an account executive and for whatever reason, they always give me the difficult clients."

We finished our wine and Sean refilled both of our glasses. There was a slight pause in our conversation and then I asked him another question.

"If I may ask, what are your plans for the future?"

"I don't see much change right now. I'm saving whatever money I can, and maybe I'll buy a co-op. That will give my son a more stable environment and in turn, I will also be settled.

Besides, it's a great investment. I'm sure you know how the prices just keep going up here."

I didn't know about that, as I didn't know much about anything. I was kind of living in a vacuum cleaner bag. Listening to Sean made me want to learn more about the world and improve myself. However, I didn't want him to know how ignorant I was, so I nodded instead of speaking. In that way, at least in my mind, I was only telling half a lie.

Sean continued to speak.

"What are your plans for the future, Evie?"

To get married to you and live happily ever after, was my immediate thought.

"I honestly haven't thought that much in advance. It's something I need to consider sooner rather than later."

"Have you ever been married?" Sean inquired.

I was agitated by that question. Why would he ask me that? I figured he already knew the answer. I stayed composed and responded to what I thought was an inconsiderate question.

"No."

Sean changed the subject immediately, realizing that he had hit a sore spot.

"This is a really good wine you brought. Would you like a little more?" he asked.

"I'm good for now. Sorry I was so short with my answer. I don't even know why it frazzled me. I just didn't expect the question. Anyway, let's forget it."

I smiled and Sean smiled back letting me know that he wasn't upset. Luckily the timer went off in the kitchen at that moment.

"That sound means dinner is ready!" Sean said.

"What can I help you with?"

"Everything is under control. Just make yourself comfortable and sit down at the table over there."

"Okay, I'm good at following directions."

I was happy that there was nothing for me to do. Yes, I offered, but it was only to be polite. Being pampered for the evening was going to be fun.

Sean set out the plates, silverware, and napkins. He brought in a large towel folded over several times and placed it on the table. He then put a pot containing the most delicious smelling chicken on it. He also brought in a soup tureen and then a serving platter filled with rice and cauliflower.

"I need one more item to complete this."

Sean went back into the kitchen and brought out a basket filled with French bread and a small circular bowl filled with chive butter. He set them on the table and then sat down.

"Wow! You made all this for me?"

"No, this is how I normally eat each night. Ha, ha."

I loved the sarcasm in his voice. We both broke out into laughter and began to eat. The food was beyond delicious. The orange soup was seasoned perfectly, and the chicken was moist and very tasty. I was embarrassed to take a second helping of the chicken, so instead, I took a small portion of rice and placed it on my plate.

"You're an excellent cook and I so enjoyed this dinner."

I made a real effort to clean up, but Sean told me to leave it. This time I genuinely wanted to help but listened to what he said. We sat down on the couch and continued drinking our wine. Sean immediately poured us another glassful and both of us drank it quickly. He filled our glasses one more time and I knew exactly where this was going and was happy about it. I felt "footloose and fancy-free." I had lost all my inhibitions and wasn't going to worry about anything. Sean was a nice guy and had prepared a delectable dinner for me. A little sex afterward would make the evening complete. Hopefully, he would be better than Henley.

"How are you feeling?" Sean asked me.

"Good and you?"

"Better than good!"

He moved closer to me and reached for my chin. He kissed me gently on my lips. I kissed him back a little too eagerly and then the passion began. We ran into the bedroom and ripped our clothes off. His body was hard and I loved his broad shoulders. They were not as noticeable when he was clothed, but when he was naked, wow! Sean was definitely experienced or just a natural. Wherever he touched me, it felt like heaven. Sean knew when to be gentle and when to pump up the action. He was sensual and passionate. Most importantly, he wasn't selfish or fast. He was perfect!

What a pleasant surprise!

•

I met with Dr. Hunter the day after my incredible night of dinner and sex with Sean. I felt better than I had in years. It was the result of mending fences with Briana, but mostly due to my new love interest.

"Hi, Dr. Hunter!" I said in a cheerful voice.

"Hi, Evie."

I sat down on her couch eager to talk.

"You seem happy today."

"I am. My friend Briana and I are back on track. Also, I'm dating this guy who is so nice and respectful. It's such a breath of fresh air."

Dr. Hunter's interest seemed to have piqued by the expression on her face, but she did not say anything. I was glad to continue talking.

"I feel so much better with them in my life. Things are finally moving forward for me."

"Let's talk about Ben," Dr. Hunter said.

"I don't want to talk about him. I hate him!"

"Last time you said that you were obsessed with him. You had very strong feelings, and those have to be addressed."

I knew she was right. Dr. Hunter didn't even know half of the Ben story, as she simply thought he was just another crappy ex-boyfriend of mine. I knew I was only doing damage to myself by keeping it all inside. I couldn't bring myself to tell her what really happened, at least not just yet. So, I kept it simple.

"I haven't thought about Ben for a while now. I did love him and it grew into an obsession. I must have seemed pathetic to him. How could he have cared for me when I made everything so simple for him? No one likes a pitiful person, not even me."

"You still seem to have strong feelings for him."

"I hate him, but I don't. I'm not sure why that is. Maybe I'm still obsessed with him? That's it! I'm still obsessed with him. I don't love him, but love the person that I created in my mind. Wow! Thank you, Dr. Hunter. Thank you for urging me to continue to talk about him."

An hour had never flown by so fast.

"Our session is over for today. I'll see you next week."

Although I didn't tell Dr. Hunter what I should have told her, I did come to terms with the fact that my love for Ben wasn't real. Distinguishing between who Ben really was and who I built him up to be was major progress in itself.

What a breakthrough! Life was starting to go in a very positive direction!

•

It was already Friday, and I had plans to see Briana at Camilla's Place that evening. We had completely reconciled our friendship, but I still felt a little apprehensive about meeting up with her. It was probably my underlying fear of messing up again. I dismissed that thought, as I dismiss most of my bad thoughts, and went about the rest of my day.

It was time to see Briana. I arrived on time and entered the bar. Briana was already sitting on one of the stools and so I walked over to her.

"Hey, Girlfriend!" I said in an upbeat voice.

"Evie, I saved this seat for you," she responded.

The butterflies in my stomach disappeared immediately. I sat down and ordered a glass of red wine while Briana ordered soda water. Our drinks were served quickly and we took them over to a table closer to the kitchen. It was more comfortable than sitting at the bar and gave us more privacy.

We sat down, but then I quickly stood up. I took my glass of wine and raised it high in the air.

"I want to toast my best friend in the whole world!"

"What happened to Evie? You look like her, but you don't sound like her," Briana responded.

"I'm just happy and want to stay that way."

"Just give me whatever it is that you're smoking," she added.

I sat down and continued the conversation.

"How are you feeling? Do you want to talk about trying to get pregnant?" I asked her.

"I'm fine and yes, I do want to talk about it. I have tried everything possible except in vitro. I want to try that, but Paul doesn't like the idea."

"Why not?"

"He thinks it's unnatural."

"Let me get this straight. He wants to have a child, but you have a very hard time getting pregnant. When you do get pregnant, you miscarry. The solution might very well be in vitro, yet he doesn't want to do it. I am not against Paul, but you have a possible way out. Why is he being so stubborn?"

"He isn't being stubborn. He's upset that it's a baby being conceived in a test tube. That bothers him a lot. He doesn't seem to be able to deal with it. I would love for us to talk to a specialist to answer all of his concerns."

"So where does that leave you?"

"It has been very trying on our marriage. The stress is getting to us and we're constantly at each other's throats. We never stop arguing. I don't know how much longer either one of us can take it."

Briana was very upset and wasn't able to talk about it anymore. She finished her soda water and then sat there looking emotionally exhausted. I couldn't think of the right words to say that would soothe her. I wanted to tell her that she had a jerk for a husband, but then our friendship would fall apart again.

"Did you ever think of going on a short vacation with Paul? A change of scenery might take some of the stress off. Besides, it wouldn't hurt to get a little pampered with side by side massages and stuff like that. That could make all the difference."

What I really wanted to say was, "Why don't you dump that pompous ass of a husband and find yourself a better guy?"

"You know what, Evie? That's a great idea! I'll bring it up to Paul. Both of us could use some quality time together in a relaxed atmosphere. Hopefully, that will chill him out, and then he will hear what I have to say."

"You have to make him listen to you! It can't be just his way all the time. Let the first night pass with no discussions at all. Then tell him that you love him unconditionally and how much you want a child with him."

"I do love him, but he isn't being realistic about having a baby. It's obvious that I can't carry one to fruition."

"You have to give him options. There are so many out there. He also has to realize that you are as anxious as he is to be a parent."

"Maybe Paul doesn't love me anymore and he is using the baby issue as an excuse."

"Anything is possible, but I don't think so. How about getting counseling? Don't get mad at me, but I think Paul is being selfish and immature."

"I'm not going to get upset with you. Actually, I agree with you, Evie."

I was both surprised and pleased with that last statement from Briana. She knew that Paul had failings, but she loved him anyway. That's Briana. Taking in all the stray cats, including me.

"I don't know what to do anymore. He definitely won't go for therapy," she continued.

"Briana, please listen to me! I have your best interests at heart. I may not be the smartest person, but I know this; if you want to save your marriage, Paul has to know that there are many options available. I'm not only talking about in vitro. You can always adopt. There are so many wonderful children out there waiting for someone like you and Paul."

"He'll never go for adoption, but maybe he'll be willing to go away for a few days. That should relax him and give us a chance to talk."

Briana reached over and gave me a kiss on the cheek and a quick hug. She then continued to speak.

"Thanks, Friend. You gave me some sound advice. I just got hungry. Let's order some dinner."

•

I got home late that night and to my surprise, there was a note under my door from Sean. He liked to do that, and so did I.

"Would you like dinner tomorrow night at Chez Sean?"

I called him immediately.

"Hi, Evie."

"Hi, Sean! You knew that I would call tonight, didn't you?"

"I was hoping you would. So, are we on for dinner tomorrow?"

"Absolutely!"

Sean was so easy going. He knew how to speak like a gentleman, and act like one too. I was warming up to the idea that he had a child and an ex. I thought about the words I used with Briana regarding Paul. I then came to the realization that I was also closed-minded. Why wasn't I open to someone with a child? Who cares about his ex-girlfriend? That's exactly who she was to him, an ex. I was his present and she was his past. Briana's problems had opened my mind to new possibilities.

•

I couldn't believe how fast the days were flying by. Sean was wonderful, and we saw each other at least once a week and almost every weekend that he didn't have Charlie. He was still somewhat hesitant to bring me into his son's life, and that was understandable. We weren't very serious about each other yet. We were having fun, and slowly getting to know each other. Sean didn't want to confuse his son, and I respected him for that. It's funny how life throws you constant curveballs. Prior to meeting Sean, I never would have even considered going out with a man who had children. Now I was looking forward to meeting his son.

As for Briana, I was afraid to "jinx it" by telling her about Sean at this time. Since I didn't want to lie to her, I only told her that there was someone new and very special in my life. I assured her that if it goes somewhere, she will hear all about it. Briana and I both had our little quirks and superstitions when it came to men.

It had been a little over a week since I turned 43 and confessed mostly everything about Ben to Dr. Hunter. It was time for another appointment, so I scheduled it.

"How are you, Evie?"

"I feel good, Dr. Hunter."

"What would you like to talk about today?"

"I don't really have anything to say. Well, I mean I have been able to leave my apartment to come to these sessions. That must mean I'm doing better."

"You never finished your story about Ben."

I let out a big sigh mainly for attention purposes and then closed my eyes. I didn't want to talk about Ben anymore, but knew that it was time to finish my story …

"I was very needy and desperate for attention, the perfect pigeon! I craved being with a man. When Ben came into the picture, it was easy for him to manipulate me, maybe because on some level I wanted to be."

"Why do you think you wanted to be manipulated?" Dr. Hunter asked.

"Since I lacked self-confidence and self-respect, I made the perfect patsy. Even though I made the offer many times, he always shied away from accepting any money from me. That's how he got me. He led me to believe that the last thing he wanted from me was my money. I let my guard down and trusted him. He was able to gather all of my financial information and take me for every penny I had. The only thing I still haven't figured out is how he knew about my savings."

"Did you report him to the police?"

"Not right away. I was so shocked and so ashamed that I let it go for many months. I couldn't bring myself to let anyone know how easily I was taken. Look at how long it has taken for me to tell you!"

"Go on."

"He took all of my hard-earned money and the inheritance from my parents. I only recently opened a new bank account. For many years, I mostly lived off of a charitable fund for people who have been scammed."

"What about your job at the time?"

"I was too ashamed to tell my boss, so I muddled through as best as I could."

I began to cry as thoughts were whirling around in my mind of the con Ben played on me. Dr. Hunter handed me a tissue and then she sat back down. I composed myself quickly and continued speaking.

"He stole $75,000 from me! It all started on a Saturday when he disappeared for two nights. When he called me on the third day, I was so glad he wasn't hurt, that I lost any common sense I might have had. I agreed to meet him at Hotel Elite where Ben easily completed his con on me. After eating a light dinner in the hotel dining room, we immediately went back to our room. Ben became very amorous and all he wanted that night was to drink wine and have sex. I was more than willing with both. As he was kissing me, he whispered in my ear that he knew I was the one. Then he placed his hands over his face as if he was going to cry. He deserved the academy award for that performance."

"What's wrong?" I asked him.

"Baby, I owe a shitload of money!"

"What are you talking about?"

"I owe money to the IRS but that's not what I'm really worried about. I have only two days left to pay back some very seedy people or I will definitely be killed. These are the people I used to get my drugs from. This is what I was trying to tell you the other night before you ran out on me at Café Allegra."

I took a 10 second break from talking to Dr. Hunter so that I could stretch my arms and crank my neck. I then commenced with my story.

"Dr. Hunter, you can't even imagine the pangs of fear that struck me as I listened to Ben's tale of woe. I asked Ben how much he needed, and he said $100,000. He then quickly added that he would be able to raise that amount in about two or three months, but not in two days. I told Ben that I would loan him the money, but that I didn't have the full $100,000. He then said that even $75,000 would do, but nothing less. I didn't even take a second to think it through. I immediately offered him $75,000 from my savings and told him he could pay me back in three months. Not once did I question why he came up with almost the exact amount of money that I had in my savings account. Instead, I apologized for not having the full amount and asked him how he was going to get the rest of it. He told me that since it was close enough, it would work. Ben promised that he would pay me back with interest and wouldn't take no for an answer. He said that this will solve all of his problems and that everything will finally be perfect for us. I was so taken in by his words, that it never occurred to me to ask him to sign anything."

Dr. Hunter sat there completely dumbfounded.

"We're at the end of our session, but I need you to finish. Please go on."

"I withdrew the money the next day. I told the bank that I was moving and was going to change banks, which was what Ben told me to say. In that way, removing such a large sum wouldn't raise any red flags. They still asked a lot of questions, but I held my ground. I couldn't tell them it was to repay my boyfriend's gambling debts and the IRS. I then gave Ben the money and within a few days, everything went back to normal. Ben was all lovey-dovey again, and I felt so much better about us."

"When did he pay you back?" Dr. Hunter asked.

"Well, that's where the story begins and ends. About three weeks after us getting back on track, so to speak, Ben told me that he had the greatest news. His boss was sending him to California to work on a multi-million, dollar commercial deal. Ben told me that if all goes according to plan, not only would he be able to pay me back, but he would be raking in the money hand over fist. That night, he took me out to one of the most expensive NYC restaurants to celebrate his good fortune. Believe it or not, he actually paid for the meal. Two days later, he left for his business trip. Ben told me it was going to be a three month project. To keep me in his thoughts, I wrote him sweet love letters and sprayed my perfume on them. He never wrote back and whenever I would call him, it would go straight to voice mail. He would only call me once every week or two and kept the conversation short. He always used the same line, 'I'm out in the field and really busy, so know that I love you and can't wait to see you when I come back.' We never had any real conversations during the time he was in California and it stressed me out."

"Why did you accept this behavior from him?" Dr. Hunter asked.

"I so desperately wanted to believe that all was okay with us. Besides, I chalked it up to things are not always perfect in any relationship. If I started to question him, it would surely have led to a fight, and that was the last thing that I wanted."

"What finally happened?"

"The last two weeks were excruciatingly painful. He stopped calling! I didn't know what to do as I was beyond devastated, so I called Briana. She set me straight and that's when I realized that Ben had pulled a huge con on me! What a fool I was! All the signs were there and I just chose to ignore them. When I finally got the courage to call the police, Ben was long gone. There was no evidence other than the fact that I had withdrawn everything from my bank account. Then to add insult to injury, I had to tell the police that I lied to the bank."

"Is there anything else that you want to add?"

"I learned a very costly lesson, both emotionally and financially. But I got through it and came out even stronger than I was before. Maybe this had to happen in order for me to become a smarter person. But it wasn't totally over."

"What do you mean by that?" Dr. Hunter asked.

"Eventually the police caught up with him. Ben did some jail time, but the money was never recovered. He must have lived near me for years after afterward, because he had stalked me for a while, even though I had a restraining order against him. I'm sorry that it took me all these years to talk about this."

"You've been through a lot, but there's something else from your past that's bigger than what you just revealed to me. We need to address it. It might be the reason why you haven't been able to leave your apartment for the past six months. Please schedule another session this week. We need to speak about …"

<u>CHAPTER 33</u>

I had just turned 38 years old.

Briana and I continued to get together on a regular basis. I still didn't tell her anything about Sean, other than the fact that I was dating an incredible man and couldn't be happier. She didn't even know that he lived in my building. Briana was happy for me and didn't need "gossipy details." Being so secure in my relationship with Sean made me a better friend to her. The friendship stopped being about "Needy Evie" and instead, took a shift and began to focus more on Briana's obstacles. Her situation with Paul was status quo. She was still willing to do anything to have a child, but Paul's ideas of right and wrong were cemented in his mind. Therefore, there was no going forward in their relationship. I think it was Abraham Lincoln who said, "A house divided against itself cannot stand." And their house was definitely divided.

On the other hand, Sean and I were getting along really well. We had been dating for almost four months. Each date was better than the last and we truly got to know each other. He didn't press me for details but was interested in what I had to say. We were forging a friendship, and that always forms a good foundation for an intimate and long-lasting relationship. I felt more relaxed with him than I had with any other man in my life. Clearly, the operative word was "man."

I thought that I was truly falling in love for the first time.

•

It was Sunday and Sean had asked me to meet him in the park near the swings.

"I love the idea! I'll run down to the corner deli and get some sandwiches and two small salads. What time do you want to meet?" I asked.

"The food is already taken care of. I need to run a few errands first. How about we make it around 1:30?"

"That's so thoughtful of you, Sean. I'll see you at the park."

There was enough time for me to shower, change and then get to the park. It was such a sweet idea that Sean had.

I arrived at the park a little early, so I sat down on one of the benches directly across from the playground. I watched the children playing and laughing. Some were on the swings, some were going down the slides, and one child was swinging on the monkey bars. It was interesting to watch the interaction between the children and their parents. Suddenly a new child entered the playground with a parent running after him. It was Sean! I went over to greet him.

"Hi! Is that your son?"

"Yes, that's Charlie!"

"Is this a surprise for me or did you have to take care of him last minute?"

"It's a surprise. I wanted you to meet Charlie, and I wanted Charlie to meet you."

My heart melted and a feeling of jubilation came over me. I was so happy that I hugged Sean as hard as I could. I then turned to Charlie.

"Well, hello! What an honor it is to meet you.!"

Charlie stood there almost frozen. He looked at me but did not move.

"Charlie doesn't know you yet and he's very shy. He needs some time to warm up to people when he's not familiar with them. I'm just going to bring him over to his usual playmates. Don't worry, Evie. He's going to like you."

Sean took Charlie's hand and we began walking towards the swings. Charlie pulled loose and ran over to the big Weeping Willow tree where two little girls were playing. There was a woman leaning against the tree who called out to Sean. He engaged in conversation with her as Charlie and the girls began to run towards the stone animals.

"Hi Kelly, how are you?"

"Good, Sean and how are you?"

"Everything is great. I'm glad your daughters' Jordana and Jolie are here so they can play with Charlie. We're going to sit on the bench near the Willow Tree. I'll be able to watch Charlie from there," Sean said.

"Don't worry about it. I'll watch him also. He's such a sweet boy."

"Thanks. Oh, I almost forgot to introduce you both. Kelly, this is my girlfriend, Evie. Evie, this is Kelly. Her twin daughters always play with Charlie when we're at the park."

Could this day get any better? Not only did Sean introduce me to his son, but he also referred to me as his girlfriend. We never had "the talk," so I wasn't 100% sure if he was truly committed to me. At that moment, two things were certain; I had a boyfriend who was not only a great catch but was serious about me as well.

What a winning combination!

I sat back down on the bench with Sean. Everything was coming together in my life. I was finally on the road to happiness and was so thankful for it.

•

Sean and I continued to get closer and life couldn't have been better. I was up for a promotion at work and was sure to get it. I had visions of us getting married and living a wonderful life together. I loved Charlie, and he was a joy to be around. I was so lucky that Sean and Charlie were in my life.

One Sunday afternoon, Sean and I went bowling together. We had gone out for pizza afterward and I told him that it would be my treat. When I realized that I didn't have enough money with me, I began to get very anxious and upset. I didn't want to have a panic attack in front of Sean, let alone in a pizza place, but I did. As I felt it coming on, I told Sean what was happening. He immediately stood up and told me to stretch my legs out and rest them on his chair. He then asked the worker behind the counter for ice wrapped in a paper towel. Sean came back over to me and started rubbing my neck and shoulders. The worker then came with the ice and Sean held it to my forehead. He kept telling me to relax and not worry about a thing. The panic attack only lasted about two minutes and when it was finished, I kept apologizing to Sean for what had happened.

"What are you apologizing for, Evie? Are you telling me you are sorry for being a human being? My mom used to get panic attacks, so I have seen this many times before. I'm just glad that I was able to help you through it."

I was so relieved that he not only responded so genuinely but that he could relate to it as well. It was at that moment that I decided to tell him about Ben. I had kept it from him until then for many reasons. I was ashamed for being so easily fooled and was afraid that Sean would question my judgment. On top of it, since I was living paycheck to paycheck, I didn't want him to think that I was with him for his money. So, that evening while at Sean's apartment for dinner, I told him everything about Ben. Everything! Sean responded by saying one thing.

"Evie, I know how hard this must have been for you to tell me all of this. The fact that you trust me enough to do so only makes me like you more. In fact, love you more. I love you, Evie."

"You love me? Oh, you love me!"

And with that, I reached over and kissed him in the most passionate way and then …

•

Sean never treated me any differently after learning about Ben, nor did he ever ask me about him. If I brought Ben up, which was rare, Sean would listen and comfort me. I couldn't have felt more confident with our relationship. More importantly, I couldn't have felt better about myself.

It was really sad that my parents weren't still alive to see how life had turned around for me. I think of them often and wish that they were still here. I have so many wonderful memories, which thankfully, I can choose to relive whenever I want to.

CHAPTER 34

Sean and I were about seven and a half months into our relationship. Things were fabulous between us. My self-esteem escalated and Bettye from work had found someone new to harass. Everything was coming together!

It was almost time to leave the office for the day. There were still a few hours left before my date with Sean. I had brought a pair of comfy sneakers with me to work in anticipation of taking a long walk before seeing him. This would invigorate me since I was not a gym person, and the exercise would do me good.

I left the office building and began to walk outside at a leisurely pace. Looking through different store windows and the comings and goings of people on the street helped pass the time. Sean was all I could think about and in the most pleasant way.

In all my years of dating, I never thought of expanding my parameters by being open to men with children. The more I thought about it, the more I believed that men who had already experienced fatherhood would make excellent husbands. They were savvy in dealing with children, which had to be a daunting task. This would probably make them more patient and sensitive. Sean was that and a whole lot more. I was starting to realize that Sean was the ideal guy.

As I continued walking, I pulled out my phone to call Briana. I was so sure of Sean and was finally ready to tell Briana all about him. It was time to stop with my stupid irrational belief that I would ruin things by talking about the relationship. Sean and I had been together long enough, and it was not only time that Briana learned all the details, but that she met him as well. Just as I was about to make that call, I realized that this was something too good to share with Briana via a phone conversation. I decided that I would call her the next day, set an actual time to get together, and then give her all the details in person.

I was so lost in thought that I wasn't aware of how far I had walked. It was an area devoid of stores and only a few people were on the street. It took me a minute to realize that I was near the apartment building that I had previously lived in. Even though I had only lived there for a year, my curiosity was aroused as to what changes had been made to the interior. I wanted to walk into the lobby for a brief moment, and so I did. Upon entering, it was just the same as when I had lived there. Since it was not a doorman building, there was no desk clerk present. The entry was just as drab as I remembered. Apparently, no renovations were ever done there.

On impulse, I took the elevator down to the basement level to see the laundry room. As I entered, a young girl was there closing the top of one of the washing machines and an older man was folding his laundry. They didn't seem to take notice of me. Soon after, the girl left and within minutes the older man completed folding his laundry and also walked out. Being in the laundry room by myself was eerie. I closed my eyes and began to imagine what my life might have been like had I not moved out of this building. I most definitely never would have met Sean.

A minute or two must have passed when I felt a very powerful hand cover my mouth and an equally strong arm press against my chest. My eyes opened immediately as I struggled to get free, but it was to no avail. He was stronger than me and he spoke in a most disgusting way.

"If you keep quiet and cooperate, you won't get hurt. If you don't, I'll kill you."

The words he uttered made my body go limp.

He then turned me around to face him. His breath was vile, and his nose and cheekbones were contorted. He had an intimidating look on his face that was difficult to describe. He lowered me to the floor. I was frozen with fear and tried to speak, but his hand was now around my throat. I felt as if I was going to die and prayed that it would be quick. He pulled down my skirt and ripped off my underwear. Then, he inserted his penis as hard as he could. I could not stop crying, which angered him. He punched me in the face several times and I started to bleed profusely from my nose. My right eye closed from the repeated blows which seemed to excite him even more. His last punch knocked out one of my front teeth and then it was over.

"I hoped you enjoyed that, Bitch!"

And with that, he left.

I was curled up in a fetal position on the floor, writhing in excruciating pain. I couldn't stop crying. I placed my hand to my nose to try to stop it from bleeding any further. I was only able to open my left eye. It took all of my strength to roll onto my back. Just as I was about to scream for help, I blacked out.

Not remembering anything after that, I awoke in the emergency room with a multitude of doctors and nurses standing over me. I tried to move but couldn't, so I moaned out in excruciating pain.

"Do you know your name?" one of the doctors asked me.

"It's Evie."

"It sounds like she said Ebbie. It's probably because of her missing tooth. Too bad she doesn't have any identification on her," he said to one of the other doctors.

"Now that you're awake, we need to get some information and take a few tests. The police are waiting to talk to you. We'll administer additional pain medication after they see you. They don't want you drowsy. Please lie still."

The police came in immediately after. It was a policeman and a policewoman.

"You must be in a lot of pain and shock. We want to help you. Any information you can give us on the assailant, no matter how insignificant will be helpful."

The policewoman spoke to me like a mother would speak to her daughter. Her speech was low toned and it showed that she genuinely cared. She gently took my hand and placed it in hers. I felt relieved and at the same time could not wait for her to leave. I desperately wanted the additional pain medication.

"Tonight was a nightmare for you. Unfortunately, you were raped and brutally attacked."

She stopped talking to see my reaction. I knew what had happened but didn't respond. Obviously I was in shock and I just wanted her to finish the interrogation.

"Do you remember anything? Can you give us a description of the man and have you seen him before?"

I started to shake my head and stopped immediately. A sharp pain shot through my neck. I yelled out in agony and thankfully one of the doctors stepped in.

"She has been through enough! I need to give her more pain medication immediately. You'll have to come back in the morning," he told the police officer.

"We can't wait that long. Every second we wait, that rapist disappears further into the night. He gets a chance to rape and beat another woman, maybe even kill her. We're trying to stop that!" the policewoman responded.

The doctor was conflicted. He wanted to stop my suffering as quickly as possible, but he knew what he had just heard was true.

"You have no more than five minutes," he said.

"Please help us help you. Anything you can tell us will be advantageous," the policeman said to me.

"Don't know him, white guy, very ugly."

My words were a bit slurred but the police realized that I didn't know anything further and so they left. However, I knew that they would be back the next day.

The doctor came over to me while holding my chart.

"The nurse is going to take specimens to place in the rape kit. The ice pack will be placed on your eye throughout most of the night. A dentist will assess you in the morning."

I didn't even try to respond.

"I checked your other wounds. You have abrasions, contusions, and a broken nose. The nurse will prep you to receive pain medication through an IV. You will also be checked continuously during the night for a concussion. Also, a psychologist and psychiatrist will be seeing you in the morning. Try to relax as best as you can. The pain medication will work faster that way."

I couldn't even say thank you. I felt every possible human emotion at that moment. I wanted to scream and keep screaming until there was no breath left inside of me.

How could this have happened to me? How could this happen to anyone?

A guard was placed outside the door to my room. I was very grateful for that. I didn't care about the pain or how horrid I must have looked. There was only one thing on my mind, and that was for the police to find this rapist, even though the chances were slim. I couldn't even identify him. That horrible man! Within a few minutes he took my whole life away from me. He destroyed everything that I worked so hard to overcome. I had finally met a kind man who treated me with respect. We had a real chance of becoming a family. Now everything was lost. I knew that the scars of this rape would be with me forever.

I would carry them in my psyche every moment and would never feel safe again.

That evening, I was further tormented in my sleep. My dreams were filled with visions of the violent rape, but unfortunately not with the face of the rapist. I woke up many times during the night from these nightmares. Although I would fall back asleep, I would also go right back into the same dreams. Unfortunately, they would be recurring for many years. This was truly adding insult to injury.

Morning finally came. A psychologist by the name of Dr. Elias Brown walked into the room. He tried to talk to me, but I couldn't face him. The last thing I wanted to do was talk about what had just happened. He sat with me for a short time and then began to speak.

"It was a cowardly and violent act that was done to you last night. This was by someone who was exerting power over an unsuspecting woman in the most heinous way. This was not an act of sex. It was an act of extreme violence and control. In no way are you responsible for it. You had every right to be in that laundry room by yourself, the same way you have every right to walk outside at 2:00 AM. But unfortunately, we don't live in a perfect society where everyone obeys the rules."

I didn't respond because it was impossible. My body was in so much pain, and my mind had completely shut down. I was trying to erase the entire night. If I could do that, then maybe it would be possible to go on.

"As difficult as it is for you right now, can you give me the name of any relatives or friends for me to contact? You will need their support."

I began to wail uncontrollably. There was no one to help me out. My parents were dead and my sister didn't want anything to do with me. I couldn't laden Briana with any of this. She had her own troubles with Paul. And Sean … I couldn't even begin to put this on him. It would be too much for him to handle. He's the type of guy who would stick by my side and try to help me through this, but what if I couldn't get through it? Then what? I would then live with constant guilt, knowing that he would be wasting his life away while trying to make mine better. I couldn't do that to him. He was too good of a guy.

"I have no one, no family and no friends," I finally responded.

Dr. Brown began to speak to me in a softer tone. This brought my attention to his accent, which I hadn't noticed before. I couldn't place it at the moment but found it to be very soothing. However, he still wasn't able to fully calm me down. He left and returned a few minutes later with a nurse. She took my hand and began to talk to me.

"Don't worry, Miss. Everything will be alright. It will just take some time."

As soon as she finished her sentence, I blurted out, "Nothing will ever be alright again!"

The nurse left and came back with a vial of liquid and a syringe. She injected the syringe into the vial and then into an IV which was attached to my wrist. I understood that it was a sedative or some type of anti-anxiety solution. Dr. Brown began to speak to me again.

"Please try to relax as much as possible. A surgeon will see you tomorrow to double check your nose. The swelling on your right eye is calming down. Starting today, there will be a bevy of other doctors and nurses attending to you, including me. There will be an aide to sit with you for the night. She will not leave your side and will take care of your needs. I'm sure the police will be back soon to question you again. You are going to need every bit of strength to get through this."

"I don't care! I don't care about anything! I want to die!"

"I understand how you're feeling right now. You did nothing wrong and you will get better. You must try to relax. Your body and your mind have had a great shock. You have to help them heal."

Dr. Brown went over to the nurse in the room and gave her instructions for the night shift.

"I have to see my other patients and will return later to check on you."

As Dr. Brown turned to leave the room, he abruptly stopped and turned back towards me.

"Don't let that bastard take anymore from you than he already has!"

And then he walked out.

Nothing seemed to matter to me at that moment, as I felt worthless and dejected. I just wanted the physical pain to stop. Unfortunately, the mental and emotional anguish would always be with me.

Even though I was given a sedative, falling asleep for more than a few minutes at a time proved impossible. I was well protected in the hospital room but could not stop feeling afraid. Each time I fell asleep, I would wake up a few minutes later feeling frightened. I kept having nightmares to the point where I would yell out almost every time I awoke. These dreams were so real and happened so frequently, that I became a nuisance to the other patients in the room. The doctor's decision was to move me into a private room. That only made things worse as my strong reactions from the rape intensified. I became so upset that I refused to eat and even defecated in the bed.

Since I had no next of kin, excluding my sister, the doctors decided to move me to a psychiatric clinic where I would have the best care and a better chance for recovery. Thankfully, the state was picking up the tab, as I was in financial straits.

•

The decision to transport me to Heaton Psychiatric Hospital was made. After a few days into my stay, I started to think beyond the rape. Sean immediately came to mind. Up until that moment, I was too traumatized to remember that we were supposed to meet up that fateful night. Was he aware of what had happened to me, or did he think I wasn't interested in him anymore? Hopefully, it wasn't the latter. And what about Briana? She must have been worried sick wondering where I disappeared to. Briana and Sean were the only people in my life and they didn't even know each other. All Briana knew was that I was dating a guy named Sean who I was happy with. That was it. She didn't know his last name nor that he lived in my building. There was no way for her to contact him regarding my whereabouts. Sean knew all about Briana, but not her last name or where she lived either. I cannot even imagine what must have been going through both of their minds at the time. I cared so much about both of them, but I didn't have the mental capacity to get in touch with either one just yet.

The staff at Heaton Psych tried so hard to be patient with me, but I couldn't have been more difficult with them. I was given therapy every day but wouldn't allow it to work. I tuned out most of what was said to me and rarely answered any questions. I falsely believed that the more I withdrew from life, the quicker this nightmare would be obliterated.

•

Three weeks had passed since I entered the psychiatric hospital, and my period was overdue by two weeks. I knew that I was pregnant and couldn't wait to abort the baby. I would not allow a child to grow inside of me that was fathered by a rapist.

My daily routine consisted of watching TV while sitting in my wheelchair, as I refused to walk most of the time. I had gotten so used to being sedentary, that I needed assistance when standing up. One afternoon, while waiting for my physical therapist to come, I began to feel queasy and needed to get to the bathroom. The physical therapist was late, but luckily a nurse came by.

"I feel nauseous and need to get to the bathroom."

The nurse came over quickly and helped me out of the wheelchair. Unfortunately, it was too late. I stood up and immediately threw up all over her. I didn't apologize. I wanted her to hate me because if she began to like me, she would try to talk to me. I didn't want to talk to anyone but the psychologist that day. Truth be told, I didn't want to speak to him either, but he was the only person I could deal with.

The nurse sat me back down in the wheelchair and immediately went into the bathroom to clean herself up. After she removed the vomit from her clothes, she came over to me.

"Are you feeling better now?"

I nodded and could sense that she was frustrated with me. I didn't care about her or anyone else. Nothing made sense to me anymore. Thankfully, Dr. Brown, who briefly treated me at the ER in the previous hospital, also worked at Heaton Psych. Therefore, he became my assigned psychologist. He walked into my room a few minutes after I vomited on the nurse. She motioned for Dr. Brown to follow her to the doorway.

"Dr. Brown, I think either she has the flu or she's pregnant. I have to change my clothes. Maybe you can get something out of her. Good luck!"

Dr. Brown pulled a chair over to me and sat there for a moment before speaking.

"How are you feeling today?"

"I think I'm pregnant and I want an abortion immediately!"

"What makes you think you're pregnant?"

Didn't he just hear me? He had the necessary information. All he had to do was act on it.

"You have to talk to me, Evie. If indeed you are pregnant, you will need to be tested and you will need some additional specialized counseling."

"I don't need anything! I want an abortion!" I screamed at the top of my lungs as I smacked the palms of my hands onto my face.

Dr. Brown seemed taken aback. I couldn't understand what was so surprising to him. Has he never had a patient that wanted an abortion before?

"Try to calm down, Evie. I will speak with your doctor and make arrangements for a conference with a therapist who specializes in family planning and an OB/GYN. Your physical therapist will be in this afternoon. Please try to cooperate with him. I will see you tomorrow."

"I won't cooperate with him or anyone else that you send. All I want is this abortion and to be left alone."

Just as I was ending that thought, I had to vomit again.

•

A full month had passed since I arrived at Heaton, and I was receding into a dark and desolate world. I did not want to speak with anyone and refused to eat. Most of all, I did not want this baby. I barely existed and most of my days were spent in my hospital bed.

On Thursday, Dr. Brown came in to see me.

"Good afternoon, Evie. How are you feeling today?"

He always started each visit with that ridiculous question. I didn't understand why he always asked it because I never answered him.

"Evie, I'm going to tell you something. I want you to try very hard to listen to what I have to say."

I immediately closed my eyes and put my hands over my ears. I wanted to shut him out of my world. We played this game each time he came in to see me. He would talk and I made sure he knew that I wasn't listening.

"You can close your eyes and put your hands over your ears all you like, but I know that you can still hear me. What I have to say is important. Even if you tune me out, this course of action will still be in play. It's your choice. You can be part of the decision making, or decisions are going to be made for you. Which would you like?"

"I hate you!" I shouted.

Dr. Brown had the upper hand this time. He wasn't going to listen to my rantings anymore. Instead, he took control and continued to speak.

"A meeting took place with all of your doctors and some of your nurses. A decision has been made to insert a feeding tube into you. You have decided to starve yourself to death and we are not going to allow that to happen."

I was surprised at how cold and measured his words sounded. I would show him!

"I'll pull it out!" I said adamantly.

"Then we'll have to tie your hands to the bed."

Dr. Brown stopped talking. I became frightened that I would be totally incapacitated and fed as though I was a body devoid of a head, no brain with which to make decisions and no free will. I didn't respond and waited to see who would give in first.

"Everyone in this hospital cares about you, Evie. The gravity of what happened to you is severe. All we're trying to do is help you move towards the road to recovery. You need to help us in order for us to help you. Life is worth it!"

I began to cry uncontrollably.

"None of you have a clue as to what I went through! You talk about it as if it was a made for TV movie with a happy ending. There will never be a happy ending! Every ounce of happiness has been sucked out of me! Why don't any of you understand that?"

"I need you to take a step forward. If you begin to eat, then we can have a conversation without you screaming. You'll feel better after eating," Dr. Brown said.

"I don't want to feel better. How many times do I have to say that to you before you hear me?"

"I hear you, Evie, and care about you very much. You are a human being that has been extremely traumatized. It's not an easy road ahead, but it's doable. You must try. Please try! Everyone is here to help you."

I sat up in the bed, pulled my knees up to my chest and then placed my head down. I was so broken and so emotionally wounded, that I couldn't get the two most important words out at that moment, "thank you." I looked up at Dr. Brown and hoped he understood what I was thinking.

"I am going to order a light lunch for you, maybe a yogurt and a slice of toast. If you eat most of it, you'll have the same for dinner. If we see any improvement at all, the feeding tube will be off the table. If not, it will be inserted in two days. You're much stronger than you think. I will be back tomorrow."

I didn't quite understand it at the moment, but I had just made a decision to live. I didn't want to die. I just didn't know how to go on.

The sounds of metal clanging interrupted my thoughts. The trays were being taken off the lunch cart. The aide brought in my tray and set it on the portable table. He didn't speak or even look at me. His job was rote and automatic, yet I envied him. It was a ridiculous emotion for me to feel about someone who I had no familiarity with. How could I possibly know what his life was like? Maybe I was transferring my inability to cope with my own circumstances to the ease I perceived his job and life to be.

I looked at the tray. It was the usual metal dome covering a large plate, a paper cup, plastic utensils, and a small carafe filled with tea. In the corner of the tray was a small chocolate chip cookie. My attention was drawn to it. I picked up the cookie and unwrapped it. The wonderful smell of chocolate wafted towards me. I took a bite and swallowed it quickly. Having forgotten how delicious chocolate was, I popped the rest of it in my mouth and enjoyed the taste immensely.

The yogurt and toast were not at all appealing to me. I kept hearing Dr. Brown's words in my head about the feeding tube. It was imperative for me to eat something else besides the cookie. There was a small plastic container of butter and another one of strawberry jelly. I chose the jelly and spread it on the toast. I took a bite and then ate half of one slice. It made me feel full, so I got back into the bed. This was a modicum of success and Dr. Brown would just have to be satisfied with it.

●

After spending close to two months at Heaton, my life was starting to slowly come together. I was experiencing a lot of morning sickness, but I was eating enough so no one needed to be concerned. Most of the time, I would take my meals into the lunchroom with the other patients. The staff didn't monitor me as closely as before and I began to be a lot nicer to them. Obviously, the intense therapy was working.

On one drab and dreary day, I sat in the solarium watching the branches of the trees sway in tune with the wind. It was almost like watching a symphony, especially when I would see birds flying and settling there for short visits. While in my own dreamworld, an aide came over and handed me a letter. I was quite surprised to be given a piece of mail and didn't think anyone was aware of where I was. I opened the letter.

Dear Evie,

It took me a long time to find you. I was frantic when you didn't show up for our date. I tried calling you on your phone, went to your apartment, talked to your neighbors and even went to your office. No one seemed to know what had happened to you. I finally called the police. After a lot of perseverance, I found out where you were. I realize that you need your space and time to heal. I just want to tell you that I care and am here for you. Please let me know how I can help and if I can visit you.

Love,

Sean

I read the letter over and over and clutched it to my heart. Sean truly cared but I couldn't allow him to visit me. Although my nose had healed and was only slightly off-center, my tooth had not been replaced yet and most of all, I was still pregnant. I wasn't ready to see anyone or even talk to anyone, especially Sean. I was not the same person as I was before the rape. There was no doubt that Sean was a good man, but I didn't want to saddle him with a needy person such as myself. I couldn't make him happy anymore. The relationship was over and there was nothing I could do to get it back. This was the lowest point of my life.

I placed the letter back in its envelope and put it into my pocket.

"Miss Evie, you must be happy about something. This is the first time I have seen you smile," said Tanya, one of the aides.

"I was thinking about a very good friend."

"Keep thinking about that friend. It seems to make you happy."

"It makes me happy and it makes me sad."

"It's almost time for lunch. Let's go to the dining room," Tanya said.

Later that afternoon I kept re-reading Sean's letter. I was contemplating whether or not to answer him. I loved the notes we used to place under each other's doors. I considered them little packages of love and couldn't wait to read them. At the very least, Sean deserved an answer.

As I was pondering what to do, Dr. Brown walked into my room with a man I did not recognize.

"Good afternoon, Evie. This is Dr. Stephens. He is doing his residency here and will be assisting me."

I looked up at Dr. Stephens. He was not the "doctor picture" I would visualize. He looked more like he should be riding a motorcycle. His hair was long and braided. He had a mustache and a short beard. His glasses were tinted to give the appearance of sunglasses.

"Hi, Evie, I'm Dr. Joshua Stephens. I'll be sitting in on your sessions with Dr. Brown."

He had a nice manner about him. However, I wasn't happy about the intrusion since I was just getting used to Dr. Brown. I didn't respond when he greeted me so that the message would be clear.

"I'm very proud of you," Dr. Brown said.

I just looked at him and nodded.

"You've made a lot of progress in a very short period of time. If you keep moving forward, you'll be released soon. What do you have to say to that?"

Dr. Brown's words scared me because there was no place for me to go. Not knowing if I still had my apartment worried me. I didn't want to stay at Heaton, but my options were extremely limited. My stress level started to rise and I felt an anxiety attack coming on.

"I'm going into an anxiety attack!" I yelled.

Dr. Brown quickly placed a pillow under my head and began gently massaging my hands and forearms. He was only able to do so for a few seconds because it caused me to scream at the top of my lungs.

"Don't touch me!"

Dr. Brown let go of my hands and began fumbling through his coat pocket. Dr. Stephens stood up and went over to the other side of my bed.

"Try to relax and think of good things. Think of songs you know and try to recite the words or think of colors that you like," Dr. Stephens said in a very low and comforting tone.

"This will pass as they all do. Don't worry, we're here with you," Dr. Brown explained.

Dr. Brown then used his cell phone to call Dr. Witsky, the head psychiatrist.

"This is Dr. Brown. Evie Harris is having an anxiety attack. What do you suggest, Dr. Witsky?"

"I'm going to prescribe a fast acting SSRI. A nurse will be in there shortly," he responded.

Within a few minutes, a nurse came in with a pill that she told me to place under my tongue. Before I knew it, my anxiety started to decline and I began to feel better. However, I wasn't able to sit up on my own or get off the bed yet.

"This is what always happens to me after an attack. I can't get up."

"Let's give it a few minutes and then we will get you up and about," Dr. Brown said.

Dr. Brown, the nurse, and Dr. Stephens were having a conference in the corner of the room. I couldn't hear the conversation and didn't care at that point. Tanya walked into the room just as they were getting ready to leave.

"Dr. Stephens and I will stop in again tomorrow. You're in good hands with Tanya," Dr. Brown said.

I watched as both doctors and the nurse exited the room. Tanya walked over towards me and spoke as though she was the teacher and I was the student.

"Evie, I am going to sit you up right now and I need you to help me."

The tone of Tanya's voice clearly indicated that she was not going to stand for anything but total cooperation from me. If only it was that easy. She placed two additional pillows behind my back, pushed the button to lift the top of the bed into an upright position, and then placed my legs over the side of the bed. She did it so fast that I didn't have time to process what she was doing. She then placed her arm around my waist and began to slowly bring my legs to the floor. I stood up with her arm for support. I was so appreciative of Tanya at that moment.

"You did it, Tanya. I feel so much better. Thank you so much."

It was the first time since the rape that I showed genuine appreciation to anyone.

"We're going to walk in the hall for a few minutes and then you can go to the bathroom to splash some cold water on your face. Afterward, we'll walk for a few more minutes. Then, you can sit in the activity room or in the solarium."

"Thank you, Tanya. I don't know what else to say."

"You're welcome. That's enough talk for now. Concentrate on your recovery."

With that, we continued walking.

"Tanya, I'd like to sit in the solarium and I want you to join me."

"I can sit with you for 15 minutes and then I have to go to my other patients."

I couldn't believe it. I hardly knew Tanya, but I was getting used to her and already thought of her as a friend. I felt a little pang of jealousy that she was going to see other patients.

"Okay. I'll be able to keep myself busy," I responded.

We sat down on two chairs facing each other.

"Is there anything you would like to talk about, Evie?"

"I have so many things to say and yet I have nothing."

"Well you know, if you keep making progress, they will let you out soon."

"Believe it or not, I'm not ready to leave. I don't even know if I have a place to go to. I have to find out what happened to my apartment. Also, I'm sure you know that I'm pregnant."

"I know," she responded.

"I was told that I needed to fill out paperwork from the state before they would approve funding for the abortion. I can't help but think that this is another stall tactic being used by Dr. Brown, but I'm trying to cooperate. I cannot wait to get this abortion and the sooner the better!"

Tanya didn't respond immediately and instead stared directly at me. I felt somewhat bothered by that since our conversation had been flowing so nicely. After about ten seconds of silence, she spoke again.

"Do you want to talk about it?"

"I'm not sure. If you're going to try to talk me out of the abortion, the answer is no."

"I'm not a therapist. If I can help in any way, I would be happy to," Tanya stated.

Thinking about what she said, I gathered all my courage and yelled out to her.

"I was raped!"

There! The words were out of my mouth to a virtual stranger. Someone who did not know me, but wanted to listen to what I had to say.

"I'm so sorry, Evie. Now I understand why you don't want the baby."

"So you agree with me?"

"You have to do what is right for you. If it was my decision, I would have the baby."

It's not your decision I thought. After hearing what she had to say, all I wanted was for her to leave. It was as though Tanya heard me thinking because she stood up and said that she would see me tomorrow. I was done talking to her anyway! Who did she think she was? She wasn't raped! She had no idea what that does to a person. It demeans you and sucks all the joy out of your life. It brings in fear, doubt, and suffering. It's easy to talk about it so nonchalantly when you're not in that position and haven't experienced the ultimate insult in such a brutal way. Hearing Tanya's response only made me more persistent.

My plan for the following day was to tell Dr. Brown to bring the paperwork and no more excuses! I was ready to go forward!

I tossed and turned all night long and barely got any sleep. It was 5:00 AM and I couldn't stay in bed any longer. While sitting in the chair, with a cover wrapped around me, I began to reflect on all the memories I had made with Sean. Dear sweet Sean, a prince of a man who came into my life for a brief moment and lit up the dark with his goodness. Sean could no longer be in my life. He meant well, but he hadn't seen me in about two months or so. I was not the same person anymore. I had become like a cold stone that existed but did not matter. I was here but was truly nowhere. Sean was deserving of much more than I could give him. I felt emotionally dead, but his note had to be answered. I planned to do it after signing the abortion papers.

•

The dining room at Heaton was not my favorite place. The only reason I went there was to appease Dr. Brown. Therefore, he would have no reason to bring up the feeding tube again. It was the only ammunition he had in his arsenal to deal with me. Although I was eating, I was not eating enough. I had lost so much weight, that my skin was sagging. I looked gaunt and had dark circles under my eyes which made me appear a good 10 years older than I was. The last thing anyone would've thought was that I was pregnant.

I sat down next to an anorexic young girl. She couldn't have been more than 14 or 15 years old. I immediately felt sorry for her. Had she already given up on life at this tender age? She must have suffered tremendous trauma to end up in a place like this. I tried my best not to stare at her, as I'm sure she tried the same with me. It was almost impossible to stop looking at her beautiful, yet lonely eyes. They spoke volumes about her unhappiness. I gave her a slight smile and hoped she would understand that she could talk to me if she wanted to. But she never said a word.

Dr. Brown and Dr. Stephens came to see me that afternoon in the hospital library. I was staring out the window behind the columns of stacked books that needed filing.

"Hi, Evie. Let's take a seat in the solarium and talk for a while," Dr. Brown said as he pointed to the door.

"Do you have my papers?" I asked.

"Yes I do," he answered.

I never expected him to finally say those words. I was ecstatic and followed him like a little puppy dog. We sat down and faced each other. I didn't want to speak in case I said the wrong thing, and he would refuse to give me the paperwork.

"These are the documents that you have been waiting for. They're all in order. Take your time and read them thoroughly and sign each page by the X. The page marked copy is for your records. I will pick them up tomorrow afternoon."

I eagerly took the papers from him.

"I don't need any extra time. I want to sign them right now," I said anxiously.

"These papers are too important for you to sign now. Tomorrow will be soon enough. This is one of the most significant decisions you will be making in your life. I repeat, read them thoroughly. So, Evie, how are you feeling today?"

"I'm relieved that you finally gave me the paperwork."

"I want you to know that if you go through with this …"

"I am going through with this!" I interrupted in a rather loud voice.

There was silence for a few seconds before I spoke again.

"I'm sorry for the outburst, Dr. Brown. It's so difficult for me, and I just want it to be over with. I am trying to forget what happened to me. The ugly memory will never disappear until I have this abortion. I do not want anyone getting in the way of this."

"No one is standing in your way, but you are going to need continued therapy regardless of your decision. In any case, please read through those papers slowly and be thorough. If you have any questions or don't understand something, please come to me and I will help you with it."

"It's time for me to lie down. I'm tired and want to take a nap."

"See you tomorrow, Evie. Please think about what I said."

Dr. Brown did not wait for an answer. He knew I would not give him one. A few minutes later, Tanya came over and sat down opposite me.

"I would have come over earlier, but you were with your doctors. I need to apologize to you. I was rude to you yesterday and never should have said what I did. I'm truly sorry."

I looked at her. What was her game, her angle? I didn't need or want Tanya's apology. I just wanted her to leave me alone. As I was about to tell her that she began to speak.

"I want to reveal something that very few people know about me. My mother was only 14 when she went to borrow sugar from a neighbor three floors below her. She got in the elevator and there was a young boy in there. He couldn't have been more than 16. He started a conversation with my mom and smiled at her. She let her guard down and smiled back at him. He took that as a signal that he could do whatever he wanted to my mom. He told her that she could borrow the sugar from him. My mother followed him into what she thought was his apartment. He raped her repeatedly and beat her so severely that she became blind in one eye. It turned out that he was visiting his

cousin in the same building as her. He fled immediately afterward and was never found to this day. I am the result of that rape!"

My mouth dropped and I became nauseous. I began to heave, but nothing came up. I wanted to put my arms around Tanya and hug her. Tears began to trickle down my face. It was the first true sign of a positive emotion that I had exhibited in months. Tanya hugged me and then continued to talk.

"I'm glad that I'm here in this world. I would have preferred to have been conceived differently, but here I am. My mother loves me in spite of what happened to her. She always says that she was blessed the day I was born. Think about it. This baby is innocent! You have a choice and it's yours to make."

Life is all about choices, good ones and bad ones!

Tanya gave me another hug and walked away. I ran to my room, pulled the covers over my head and began to whimper. Tanya's words truly touched me.

CHAPTER 35

Briana was constantly on my mind since entering Heaton Psych. She must have been wondering what happened to me, or maybe she knew and didn't want to contact me until she thought I was ready. If the latter was the case, it didn't matter because I would never be fully ready. I had to make an effort to let her know what happened, but the thought of telling her made me sick to my stomach. Nevertheless, I needed Briana more than ever.

I chose to put off the abortion. Tanya had made a definite impact on my thinking. I finally understood that this baby was also mine. Even though this child would not come out of a loving union, the baby had a right to exist.

The new problem I was facing was complex. It was impossible for me to raise an infant for

many reasons. The financial obligations would be challenging, but the emotional and mental stresses were my biggest concern. I was not in the right state of mind to care for a child as I couldn't even take care of myself. What was also very concerning to me was that visions of the rapist would constantly fleet through my mind, and I would end up hating the baby. Nonetheless, I had to make sure that this baby would be properly cared for and loved. There were so many things that I did not know about, such as adoption agencies, private adoptions, etc. I had to step up to the plate and absorb as much information as possible on the many alternatives available.

•

"Good afternoon, Evie! How are you feeling today?" asked Dr. Brown.

"I think I'm getting better. I feel more relaxed and less anxious."

"That's good to hear. Have you made a decision yet?"

He didn't have to say the words. I knew clearly what he was referring to.

"Not 100%, but I think I'm going to keep the baby after all."

Dr. Brown did not indicate whether he was pleased or not. I understood that he wasn't supposed to show his emotions to any of the patients he was working with.

"You've been here two and a half months. It's time for you to leave and make a life for yourself and your baby. You cannot make this hospital your permanent residence. There's a whole world out there, a good world."

"I don't know what the status of my apartment is. It might have been rented out to someone else. I never notified my boss of what happened to me and I can't even begin to go back to work right now. On top of it, I have no savings or income to sustain me."

"We're going to take everything one step at a time. The social worker will see you tomorrow. You can discuss everything with her and then we'll talk further. See you tomorrow afternoon, Evie."

"Thank you, Dr. Brown."

The words finally came out of my mouth to a man who had been so wonderful to me. I should have already thanked him 100 times for helping me make all this progress. Better late than never, I guess.

The thought of leaving the hospital brought on new fears. I didn't realize how easy it was to get used to a new lifestyle and how quickly time passes. This made me think of Briana again. I would call her the next day … hopefully.

CHAPTER 36

I am now 62 years old. Dr. Hunter retired and a new psychologist, Dr. Chava Pennington has taken over her practice. To this point, I have been under a psychologist's care for over 35 years. Dr. Pennington had all my records and probably familiarized herself with my entire case history. I have an appointment with her this afternoon to which I am somewhat uneasy about. After all, I have not met her yet.

"Come in and have a seat," Dr. Pennington said.

I sat down and waited for further instructions. The change in psychologists after such a long time was problematic. It was difficult for me to be at ease with someone new. I had to build up trust all over again. Hopefully, this new psychologist would be as good as Dr. Hunter was.

"I have all your records and read them thoroughly. I also had an in-depth consultation with Dr. Hunter. You've made great strides."

I looked at her and tried to decide if this was going to be a good fit. It was impossible to know anything from a first meeting. I needed to give her a fair chance. Maybe I was a little put off because she looked so young. She was better dressed and perkier than Dr. Hunter. I decided to give her a break and be open-minded.

"I understand that you know everything about me Dr. Pennington, but there are some things I need to tell you myself."

"This would be a good time to start," she responded.

Her demeanor was not the same as Dr. Hunter's. She was quicker to speak and less reserved. I actually liked that but was not ready to trust her just yet. I needed to feel that comfort level that comes with familiarity and time.

"I'm not sure where to start."

"Start where you left off with Dr. Hunter, or where you feel most comfortable."

"I just don't think I can talk right now."

"What is stopping you?"

"I feel uneasy right now. I don't want to make you feel bad, but it would have been simpler if Dr. Hunter was still here."

"As you know, Dr. Hunter has retired. You need to move on with your life. Try to relax and take your time. I'm going to play a very calming CD which is different from the one Dr. Hunter used to play for you. It's all music and it has a mesmerizing tone to it."

She popped in the CD before I could protest. I didn't want to hear music. All that I wanted to do was just leave. As the music began, my body started to relax. It seemed as if the notes were hypnotizing me. Surprisingly, this actually calmed me down.

"What is the name of this song, Dr. Pennington?"

"It's called 'Fur Elise,' by Beethoven. Isn't it wonderful?"

"It is. I've never heard it before. It's very relaxing and soothing. Thank you for playing it."

"I'm glad that it's helping you to relax. We can speak about whatever you want to, or not speak at all. It's up to you, Evie."

I didn't say much and before I knew it, the appointment was over.

"Evie, our session is over for today. It will take both of us some time to get to know each other. Please realize that I have your best interests at heart. See you next week."

I didn't respond to Dr. Pennington and withdrew from exposing my inner self to her. I had to accept and adjust to the simple fact that she was going to be my new therapist. I wanted Dr. Hunter back, but there are a lot of things in life that I will never get. Part of moving forward is to accept life as it is, not as you want it to be.

I made an appointment with Dr. Pennington for Wednesday of the following week. I was warming up to the fact that this new doctor might be very helpful to me. I didn't have a lot of choices. Searching for another psychologist was not palatable to me. I could only hope that this doctor-patient relationship would work out.

•

Wednesday came and I was mentally ready for my second appointment with Dr. Pennington. I arrived at her office on time and she ushered me inside. I looked around the room expecting to see some changes in décor or knick-knacks, but there weren't any from last week. I was hoping to find an object that I could associate just with Dr. Pennington, but there were none. Had there been, it would have made it easier for me to adjust to someone new. Maybe it was better this way. I needed to live in the real world, not in Evie's make-believe world.

"You're right on time, Evie. Please have a seat. How has your week been so far?"

She didn't waste any time getting started.

"I'm all right, sort of. I'll feel a lot better when I tell you more."

"Let me help you. Everything you say in this office is strictly confidential. This is a safe zone for you. When you succeed, I succeed. Talk about anything that will unburden you."

"Since you read my records and had discussions with Dr. Hunter, I'm sure you know everything about me."

Dr. Pennington didn't answer my question and instead posed one of her own.

"Is Ben still a factor in your life?" Dr. Pennington asked me.

"Ben no longer exists for me. I attached myself to the man I thought he was and wanted him to be. This made me lose sight of who he really was. Being lonely and sad made me think that no other man would ever love me. What I didn't take into account at the time was that Ben never loved me. Until I finally got over him, it was as if he was living inside of me, still pulling the strings. Now it's clear that it was me who made him very important, and that I had control over those strings."

I stopped speaking at that point and took a drink of bottled water that I had brought with me. Talking about Ben always drained me, but at least now, all the feelings I had for him were gone. There was no space available for him to occupy in my mind anymore.

"Are you sure he no longer exists for you?"

That was an odd question, but I answered it anyway.

"There's no more room at the inn for him. All the rooms are filled and the gate is locked. There is no key or combination to get in. Ben doesn't exist anymore. Ben is dead!"

I cleared my voice and then concluded with an assured tone.

"Ben is dead to me."

Dr. Pennington smiled without parting her lips. Something told me at that moment that I was in good hands.

"Everything in my life was going great at one point. I had a misunderstanding with my best friend, Briana. It took a bit of doing on my part, but we became best friends again. Then I met this super amazing guy named Sean. He was everything that every man should be: respectful, sensitive, and caring. Besides, he was mature, intelligent and good-looking. He had it all, and I almost had him. But fate intervened, or maybe just bad luck. I'm not sure which."

Talking to Dr. Pennington about Sean was bittersweet. It was a reminder of what could have been but wasn't. I became nostalgic. It was hard for me to continue speaking, but I did.

"Instead of living in a fairytale, Dr. Pennington, I ended up in a nightmare."

Tears started to well up in my eyes and I began to feel a lump in my throat.

"I can't talk anymore, Dr. Pennington."

"Take your time. You don't have to say anything else if you don't want to. But we do have a few minutes left before it's time to leave. We can just sit here and I'll put in the CD you like."

The music calmed me once again. Dr. Pennington knew what would work. I truly began to trust and like her.

"I have something else that needs to be said," I blurted out.

"I'm here for you. Go ahead, Evie."

I stood up and began to pace for a few minutes. Then I stood still and the words flew out of my mouth.

"I was raped!" I shouted.

"I was raped, got pregnant, and was taken to a psych ward. Everything that was dear to me was lost! I wanted to die!"

I began to sob and pulled out a crumpled tissue from my purse. I wiped my eyes and blew my nose. Looking up at Dr. Pennington, I couldn't believe what I saw. She was teary-eyed. Never expecting any emotions from her, I realized that she was not only a psychologist but a person as well. She was a woman who understood and saw me as more than just a patient. At that point, no words needed to be spoken. Everything was understood.

Not needing to be told, I knew my session had ended minutes before.

"Thank you, Dr. Pennington."

She knew that I would be back the next week.

•

I was given notice to leave Heaton in two weeks. My social worker had made arrangements for a new apartment for me to live in, but I was responsible for furniture and the like.

Before being released from the psych hospital, several decisions had to be made. The first one was already taken care of, which was not to have the abortion. Secondly, the baby needed to be placed in a safe and secure home where he or she would be properly nurtured and loved. This was a priority, and I couldn't have thought of a better place and with more deserving people than Briana and Paul. I hadn't spoken to Briana since the rape and I needed to call her. The time had come. However, there were some doubts in my mind regarding Paul. Would he accept someone else's baby, especially under these circumstances? I didn't know, but I had to at least try. Briana and Paul wanted a child. I was pregnant but couldn't properly care for a child. This was the perfect solution for everyone.

And so the time came …

"Hello."

"Briana, it's Evie."

"Evie!" Briana yelled in a shrill voice.

"Are you okay? I haven't heard from you in ages! The caller ID says Heaton Psychiatric Hospital. What's going on?"

I never heard Briana so flustered, and rightfully so. It's quite shocking to have your friend call you from a psych hospital.

"I'm getting better. There's so much to tell you, but it can't be done over the phone. Can you come and see me?"

"I was going nuts trying to find you! I went to your building and spoke to your doorman. He said he hadn't seen you in a while, so I went to your office and spoke to Bill. Even Bettye was concerned about you. So what happened? You have to tell me something!"

"Please come and see me. I was raped ..."

"Oh my G-D! Oh my G-D! Evie, I'm so sorry." And with that, both of us cried to the point of almost wailing.

"I have to go," I said abruptly and then hung up.

I went back to my room and continued to cry. I started to relive the entire nightmare once again. I began to scream and started to throw whatever I could get my hands on in the room. A few orderlies came running in and disarmed me. They called for a nurse who rushed in and gave me a light sedative. She then took a wet towel and placed it on my forehead. I grabbed the towel and threw it across the room. I didn't have a headache or a fever. This nurse was truly not getting it!

•

I awoke the next morning feeling good because now Briana knew where I was and what had happened to me. I was hoping for Tanya to be on duty, so I could tell her what my decision was. I respected her as a person. I also thought that she could guide me in the right direction on how to approach Briana with my idea.

I went to the activity room. Sometimes I would play cards or a board game, but mostly I watched the other patients. It was people watching at its worst. That day, there were two women present who were always there and one man whom I had never seen before. He was about 25 years old. He seemed like any other young man except obviously he wasn't, psychologically that is. He stood by the window and kept pulling his hair. Every time he did it, I cringed. It was as though I was feeling the pain. I had to look away and immediately left to go to the solarium. On my way there, a voice called out.

"Evie!"

I turned, and it was one of the aides whom I didn't recognize.

"You have a visitor. Please come to the guest room."

I began to get butterflies in my stomach. I was both excited and frightened. Hopefully, it was Briana and not Sean. The aide led me to the guest room and there she was, waiting for me. I barely walked into the room when Briana jumped up to greet me. She hugged me and kissed me on the cheek. A few tears were streaming down her face, but they were tears of happiness.

"Briana! I'm so glad you came!"

"Of course I was going to come! You're my best friend and I love you."

"I love you too."

Both of us sat down and stared at each other. Briana had no idea of the next bombshell I was going to throw at her.

"Evie, I know this might sound like a stupid question, but how are you doing?"

"I'm getting better, but there is still a long way to go. It's very hard for me to talk about it. That's all I do in this place, is talk. But I must admit that it has helped me. At least I'm functional now. My nose was broken, but a surgeon was able to reconstruct it properly. As you can see, my tooth was knocked out. I'm getting it fixed in a few days. Tell me about yourself. How are things going with Paul?"

"Paul is Paul. I finally get it. He's very set in his ways and he's not going to change. We're both very frustrated. Oh, I'm sorry. You don't need to hear about that after what has happened to you."

"Talking about anything else is good. It takes my mind off of it."

Briana put a white gift bag on the table and gave it to me. I was pleasantly surprised.

"This is for you. I picked it up in the gift shop. It's just a little trinket," Briana said.

I pulled out the few pieces of white tissue paper and saw the cutest little brown bear. It instantly made me smile.

"Oh, Briana, thank you so much. This makes me feel so good."

We looked at each other in silence for a moment or two. I let a small smile escape from my lips before speaking again.

"Briana, I have something very important to tell you and also ask you."

"Go ahead. You can say anything you want to."

"I'm getting out of here in two weeks. I have a small apartment to go to, so I won't be homeless."

I hesitated again, but Briana did not speak. She knew that what I was going to say was both serious and difficult.

"I'm pregnant," I said in a low tone.

I could tell that either Briana wasn't sure if she heard correctly or it didn't register completely, so I repeated myself.

"I'm almost three months pregnant. It's from the rape."

The shock on Briana's face was instant. She stood up and then sat down. It was clear that she didn't know if she should hug me, speak or just sit there and wait for me to continue talking.

"I know that you're shocked, especially since you have been trying to get pregnant for so long. Are you pregnant now?"

"No, I'm not and we decided to stop trying. It doesn't make sense to either one of us anymore."

"To keep trying you mean?"

"Yes," Briana said.

"That's why I wanted to see you in person. I thought about this solution that would work for all of us. I can't raise a child. I can't even raise myself and I'm not a child anymore. If you and Paul are willing, you can adopt my baby."

"Adopt your baby!"

Briana hesitated for a moment and then continued to speak.

"I'm having a hard time processing all of this. I know I should be grateful and exhilarated, but Paul will never go for it. I am so sorry to have to say this, but the truth is that he would never accept how this baby was conceived."

"I'm not insulted. I know that I gave you news that needs to be digested before making a decision. Think about it and please try to discuss it with Paul. I know he and I don't see eye to eye. I truly believe that he would be a great father who could give this child a loving home. Paul would be paid back tenfold in what this baby would give to him."

"I love you for wanting to do this. I just don't want to get my hopes up and then be disappointed."

"Briana, just try. If he truly wants a baby, let him open his heart to this possibility. Please, just try."

Briana stood up. This was a lot of information for her to deal with in such a short period of time.

"Evie, before I leave, I have to say that you have lost a lot of weight. I don't want to be judgmental, but is that good for the baby?"

I immediately became defensive even though she was speaking the truth.

"I've gained back five pounds and things are going back to normal, slowly but surely. I'm under an OB/GYN's care. I'm in good hands. Don't worry, this will be a healthy baby."

Briana seemed conflicted. I started to think that she wasn't going to talk to Paul about this but hoped I was wrong.

"I have to go. I took a half day off from work and need to get back to the office now."

"Please, please promise me that you'll call me with an answer," I begged.

"I'll call you. Just give me a few days. I have to think of how to bring the subject up to Paul."

We hugged each other and then Briana left. I felt a lump in my throat and had to go lie down. I was spent!

•

Several days went by and there was no word from Briana about the adoption. That was not a good sign. It was too important for me to leave this to chance. I had to take the bull by the horns, so to speak. Phoning her at home was not an option. If she wasn't there, Paul could intercept the message. So instead, I left a message for Briana on her cell.

"Hi, Briana, it's Evie. I haven't heard from you. It's a big decision, but I need to know if you told Paul yet. Please call me."

It was a lot to ask from Briana, but I was also giving a lot. I understood that she had to choose her words carefully and find the right moment to approach Paul. Regardless, I couldn't wait for weeks or months to get an answer. I needed to have finality on this. I was carrying a human being inside of me that would soon be in this world, and the decision could not be left to chance. If Briana didn't call me by the weekend, I would put the baby up for adoption. There are plenty of childless couples out there praying for this kind of miracle. I started to think that maybe they deserved it more than Briana and Paul. Maybe that's the route I should have chosen originally and then it would have been a "fait accompli."

•

It was Saturday and I had just over one week left at Heaton Psych. I was happy to leave, but also somewhat scared. At the hospital, everything was done for me. Once that stay was over, I would be on my own.

The day went by very slowly. There was no therapy on the weekends because the staff was cut in half. As I was sitting in my chair, an aide came in and told me I had a visitor. It had to be Briana, and it was. Hopefully, she was bringing me good news.

Briana was sitting at the table in the same spot as when she first came to see me. She didn't get up to hug me and began to speak immediately.

"Paul won't go for it. I'm sorry," she blurted out.

I was stunned. How could he be so cruel and unfeeling? Everything was his way or the highway.

"What did he say?"

"You don't want to know. It's too terrible. I tried so hard, but he just wouldn't go for it."

"Do you still love him?"

Briana looked at me as if I was asking a ridiculous question.

"Of course I do! We're just not on the same page when it comes to this subject. I married him for better or worse. I have to respect his decision."

"What is there to respect? He's not considering your feelings or the big picture. Briana, you can't conceive, and I have a baby to give to both of you. You and Paul can enrich this child's life and this child will enrich yours. Why is he being so stubborn?"

"I agree with you, but Paul wants it to be biologically his. It's not worth arguing with him anymore. Maybe sometime in the future things will change, but right now I'm sorry for both of us. I have to go."

Briana left the room. She was just as upset as I was, maybe even a little bit more. It was very obvious to me that she wasn't in love with Paul anymore and was only putting up with him to save face. Briana didn't want to admit it to anyone, including herself, that she made a mistake by marrying him. I felt for my friend. We were both in miserable situations, but I would have traded mine for hers in an instant.

The next opportunity for me to speak to the social worker would be on Monday. There was no other choice. My baby was going to be put up for adoption.

Later that day, I walked into the non-denominational prayer room that the hospital had. I knelt down on my knees and prayed for this child to be taken care of by loving people. I had never prayed before and hoped my words would make a difference.

•

Another letter arrived from Sean three days before I had to leave the psych hospital.

Hi Evie,

I haven't heard from you and hope you are getting better. I tried calling several times, but you haven't returned my phone calls. I would love to come and visit you. It doesn't have to be for long, just a few minutes.

I miss you,

Sean

I read the letter quickly and then put it in the wastepaper basket. I did not want Sean to see me. My front tooth had been fixed, but all of the stress took a toll on my personality and looks. I definitely wasn't the same person anymore and didn't want him to see that. I preferred for him to think of me as how I was, instead of seeing what became of me. It was sad that I had to reject a good man, but it could never work at this point. There was way too much baggage on my end for anyone to deal with. Not answering his letter made the most sense. He would probably be curious for a while, and then let it go. That would be the natural order of things. I went into bed and pulled the blanket over my head but could not fall asleep.

•

Monday came and it was almost time for breakfast. I was told that a social worker would be coming to my room within the hour. She was a middle-aged woman of about 50 years old who had light blue eyes and a nice smile. Her hair was graying, and she didn't wear any makeup. Her suit looked expensive and so did her shoes.

"Evie Harris, I'm Ariella Payne, your social worker. How are you?"

I'm ducky! I'm in a psych ward and couldn't be happier, was what I wanted to say.

"I'm alright. I need to talk to you about putting my baby up for adoption."

Her facial expression showed disdain by my request.

"I see. How far along are you?"

"Didn't they inform you? I'm just about three months pregnant and I need you to find a good home for my baby when it's born."

"Have you had any counseling regarding this matter?"

She spoke so matter of fact, so rote, as if she was reciting lines from a script. Maybe it was how she was trained since she probably had many similar cases. Ignoring her aloofness was best at this point.

"Yes. I've had more counseling than ten people put together. My decision has been made. Can you help me?"

"Yes, Evie, I can and will help you. There's going to be a myriad of paperwork to fill out and other decisions you will have to make."

"What other decisions are there? My decision has already been made."

"It's not as simple as that. There are questions that need to be answered. I'll be back in an hour to go over what you need to know and what information is needed from you."

"I still don't understand, but whatever."

"It will all be clear to you when I return."

I started to gather my belongings, including the teddy bear Briana had given me. I placed them in a plastic bag near the only chair in the room. There wouldn't be anyone to say goodbye to, except maybe Tanya. If we had met under different circumstances, we definitely could have been friends.

Ariella came back in carrying a brown briefcase. She sat down on the chair and took out a thick folder. She then stood up and placed a variety of pamphlets on the bed.

"Please familiarize yourself with all this literature. I'm going to leave this pad for you. Jot down all your questions and they will be answered. In the meantime, I want to go over some very important things that you need to think about."

"Go ahead. Knock yourself out!" I responded.

Ariella didn't like my reply or my tone, and I wasn't too keen on her attitude. That made us even.

"One of the most important decisions that you will have to make is if you want an open or closed adoption."

"What does that mean?"

"Do you want an opportunity to be in the baby's life or do you want to be out of it? Before you answer, if you choose the latter, then you will know nothing about him or her. All information will be sealed. Think about it carefully. You may want to be a part of the baby's life later on when you are stronger, both mentally and emotionally. It will be the most important decision that you will make about this adoption. You don't have to answer any of these questions in haste. Take your time so you will not regret any of the decisions you make."

She gave me sound advice, but my mind was already made up. I wasn't stable enough to be in a child's life, even though this baby was mine. I didn't want to take the chance of being involved in the child's formative years or responsible for bringing insecurity into that life. My decision was clear and I would let Ariella know that the following day.

CHAPTER 37

"Hi, Dr. Pennington."

"Hi, Evie, please sit down."

This was my third consecutive appointment with Dr. Pennington. She started the session by placing "Fur Elise" into the CD player and turned the dial to low.

"Last week you spoke about being raped. You also said you had gotten pregnant."

I took a very deep breath and swallowed what seemed to have been a lump in my throat.

"I was mentally and emotionally unstable, and I didn't want to leave the psych hospital. That alone should tell you how low I had sunk in the world. Who wants to stay in a hospital when they have the opportunity to leave?"

"What made you want to stay there?"

"I didn't have any responsibilities. Almost everything was done for me. It was the perfect place to escape all of my pain. I learned how to function without actually functioning."

"What about now? Are you operating on an adult level?"

"I'm improving every day. It has been a very slow process, but now each day is a day illuminated with sunshine instead of darkness, for the most part."

"It seems that you have more to say, Evie."

I couldn't believe how perceptive Dr. Pennington was. It seemed that she could read me like a book!

"I had a very strong need to forget about this horrid and heinous crime that was committed against me. My thinking was that if I gave up the baby, everything would be erased from my mind. Then I could live the rest of my days without any reminders of that horrible night. What I didn't realize at the time was that there was no way to eliminate any of it. Instead, I had to learn to make peace with it."

After finishing my last sentence, it was difficult for me to breathe. Dr. Pennington became aware that I was uncomfortable.

"You're a very brave woman! What you revealed today denotes your strength, courage, and determination. I'm very proud of you. I'll see you next week."

I felt fabulous walking out of her office.

CHAPTER 38

It was Tuesday and my last day at the psych center. Briana wanted to pick me up and take me to my new living quarters, but it would have been too emotional for me. I had to do this on my own.

There was no fanfare and no one was crying because they were going to miss me. It was just business as usual. I vacated a room and now there was someone else out there, emotionally broken, and waiting to occupy it. Everything was set for my departure. My instructions, medication, keys, and personal belongings were placed in a plastic bag. A box containing essentials such as soap, toothpaste and the like were also given to me. The road ahead was going to be a steep climb, but I was going to tackle it. I was all packed and in the midst of signing off on my release papers when Tanya walked over to me. She gave me a big smile and then a hug.

"So, you're breaking out today! Ha, ha!"

"Yes, it's time. I've been here for three months and need to get on with my life."

"Lots of good luck to you, Evie. You made the right decision for yourself."

"Thank you. Once the baby is born, they will give me an option to see him or her for a few minutes. Ariella said that there are thousands of lovely people out there who would give anything to adopt a newborn. She said they do a background check on everyone and make the best choice possible."

"I know they take every precaution. Good luck and take care."

I hugged Tanya once more and then she walked away. It was highly unlikely that I would ever see her again. She was a good person and a friend to me during my stay.

I wished for a lot of things. As I've said before, wishing doesn't make it so!

I left the hospital and entered the eight-passenger van that was waiting for me. There were a few other ex-patients also being transported to their new homes, families, etc. I looked down, not wanting to make eye contact with any of them. I did not want to pity them, nor did I want their pity in return.

•

Arriving at my new apartment from the psych hospital was depressing and somewhat of a shock. It was a very small studio, courtesy of Social Services. The apartment was so tiny, that it was as if I had to go outside to change my mind. Regardless, I was so grateful for a place to live. On a positive note, it was very clean and bright. The sunlight shone through the two small windows and lit up most of the place. In the far back corner to the right stood a compact refrigerator and a small stove with two gas burners.

There was no doorman and the elevator door was filled with graffiti. The building was run down, but it was my new home for the time being. The block was okay, with several old, red brick apartment buildings and countless stores in the neighborhood. This attracted a lot of people, which in turn brought a lot of noise. I felt safe for the most part but realized that there was no guarantee of safety no matter where you lived.

My previous landlord had been very thoughtful and put all of my things in storage. I was lucky that my security had covered the fees. Briana had the storage facility throw away my previous mattress set. She didn't feel comfortable with me using it because of the possibility of bedbugs and other insects. As a present, she ordered a new bed for me, which was already in my apartment. It was the only piece of furniture I had, and it was more than enough. Briana had no idea of how much she had helped me out.

Social Services also provided me with a cell phone for 90 days. This would make life so much easier on me as it was one less thing I needed to deal with. I placed it on my bed and sat down next to it. Since I didn't know what to do with myself, I took off my shoes and lied down. About half an hour later, the doorbell rang. Not expecting anyone made me wary. I looked through the peephole and saw a man holding what seemed to be a pizza box.

"I didn't order anything," I shouted through the door.

"This is for apartment J320 from Briana, for Evie."

"Oh."

I opened the door.

"I'm sorry, but I don't have any money for a tip."

"No problem, Miss. It's been taken care of."

"Thank you."

Opening the box and seeing non-hospital food for the first time in three months was heaven. It smelled so good and I devoured two slices immediately. I put two slices in the fridge for the next day and placed the rest in the freezer.

Soon after finishing the pizza slices, my stomach began to feel strange. I couldn't put my finger on it but felt something was not right. I then realized that I ate too quickly. Since my appetite had waned, it was too much food at one time. I needed to relax and the best way was for me to call Briana.

"Hi, Briana, it's Evie. Am I interrupting dinner?"

"No, we just finished. How are you doing?"

"First, I want to say thank you for the pizza. That was so thoughtful, but most of all, I want to thank you for being such a great friend. You are the most awesome person ever!"

"You're just saying that because it's true," she said.

Both of us giggled at the same time. It was good to talk to Briana and laugh like that, something I hadn't done in months.

"Briana, I don't want to bother you, but the next time you go grocery shopping, can I join you? There are a few things that I need. Actually, I need everything."

"Of course! Tomorrow after work would be great. Paul has to go out of town for two days, so my evening will be free. I'll pick you up at 6:00 PM."

●

It was my first morning in my new apartment, and I awoke a little stiff since I had gotten used to a different mattress at Heaton Psych. My metal frame was still in storage and this new bed was very low, which hurt my back. I had to get my old bed frame as soon as possible.

Throughout this entire ordeal, I never called my boss to explain that returning to work would be impossible. Whether he knew what happened to me or not, the call to him had to be made. I picked up my cell phone and dialed his office number.

"Bill speaking," he answered.

"Hi, Bill, It's Evie Harris."

"Evie! How are you?"

He never sounded so full of life, which was unusual for him. This made me feel much more comfortable as I didn't know exactly what to say.

"I'm getting along. Sorry I didn't call you sooner, but it was impossible."

"Understood, no problem," was his response.

"I'm not aware of how much you know about my situation. I can't go into details right now."

There was silence for a moment. Neither of us knew how to continue. It was extremely awkward.

"Bill, something so very vile and cruel happened to me and …"

I began to sob and couldn't finish the rest of the sentence.

"It's going to be okay, Evie. Take your time. We can talk as much as you like, whenever you like. I will always be here for you."

At that moment I knew that he was fully aware of what had happened. He never would have spoken to me with such tenderness otherwise.

"I'm sure that you gave my job to someone else. It was the right thing to do. Maybe at some time in the future, I can come back."

"Whenever you're ready, just call me. You're always welcome back here, Evie."

We both knew that I would never return.

"By the way, there is a check waiting for you which includes severance pay. At the end of the year, you will get your bonus check. I hope that will tide you over."

"That will be great. I'll call payroll tomorrow."

"When you feel up to it, ask them to connect you to Frank. He'll talk to you about your pension and 401K account."

"Thank you, Bill. I so appreciate you telling me all this."

"Also, give them your new address and phone number. It was good talking to you. Bye, Evie."

"Bye."

I had forgotten that I was due some back pay and my bonus. Even though it wouldn't be a lot, it would be helpful. I became very tired after making that call, so I had to lie down for a while.

After resting for about an hour, I called the storage facility and made arrangements for the rest of my stuff to be picked up. Other than my clothing, I could only fit a small circular kitchen table and one chair into my new place. I hired a small van and set everything up for the weekend since Briana and Paul were going to help me. Paul would be back from his business trip by then, and that would give me a few extra days to get used to my new place.

Briana was picking me up in the early evening. That allowed me to walk around my new neighborhood and find the local deli and coffee shop.

During my walk, I kept thinking about Sean. Although what had happened to me was very traumatic, I should've been more appreciative of the caring man that he was. He tried so hard to get a hold of me, and after all these months, he still wanted to see me.

Although there was no way for me to be certain, I had a sense that Sean had moved on romantically. At the very least, he deserved a call from me. However, I wasn't ready to have a phone conversation for fear of breaking down in tears. There had been enough crying to last me two lifetimes. Writing a note would be easier for me, way easier.

Dear Sean,

Thank you for your efforts and kind words. You are truly a wonderful person in every way. I hope that in time we can meet up for a cup of coffee. As you can see from the return address, I live somewhere else now. I need some time to myself in order to adjust to my new surroundings.

Take care,

Evie

I mailed the letter two days later and then totally forgot about it. The weekend came and went by quickly. My modicum of furniture was finally in place. Everything was on top of each other because of my small apartment. Briana and Paul set up my modicum of dishes, clothing, and some odds and ends.

Two weeks later I received a letter from Sean. He wanted to see me and made it clear that there was no rush. Even though my new tooth looked real and the bruises on my face had healed well, I didn't look the same. I definitely aged and no amount of makeup would help. To a small degree, I was being vain, but I was also a human being, after all.

I played around with the idea of sending him another letter with the truth about why I was avoiding him. In that way, he would understand that over time, we would become a distant memory to each other. The thought was not appealing, but it was the reality of the situation and we both had to face it. It was possible Sean had already moved on and was planning to end things in his own sweet way. I was very conflicted about what to. Apparently, I was back to my normal self because I couldn't make a decision.

•

As I became accustomed to my small place and new neighborhood, my days were predominantly lonely. Besides weekly therapy and my monthly visits to the OB/GYN, my life was stagnant. I never attended any of the support groups for rape survivors that were recommended by my therapist and Social Services. I would go out only during the day when groceries were needed. Briana constantly tried to get me to meet her for lunch or a walk, but I had no interest in being social. I was functioning but on a very low level. Being six months along was uncomfortable and that only added to my desires to stay in. Also, the phone would ring nonstop because Social Services would always be checking in. I finally told them that they were harassing me, so the calls became almost non-existent.

Sean continued writing to me and I was running out of excuses for not seeing him. Somehow, I needed to get up the nerve to talk to him and deal with the here and now. I went over to the kitchen drawer and pulled out a chocolate candy bar from my stash. They were a great substitute for the wine I used to drink. I woofed down the bar and picked up the phone, not wanting to lose my nerve.

"Hi, Sean, it's Evie. Sorry I took so long to get back to you."

"Please don't apologize. I'm so glad to hear your voice. How are you?"

It was so evident that Sean was sincere, not that I ever doubted it.

"I'm doing better. I don't know how to update you on my situation."

"Evie, you know me. Let's meet and talk for a little while. It could be about anything you want it to be. It would be good for both of us."

"You're so kind, Sean. I don't know what to say. It's not that I don't want to see you, but so much has changed."

"I haven't changed. I still care about you but do understand and respect your feelings. I'll stop sending you any more letters."

"No, you don't understand. I look forward to your letters and like them. The truth is that I'm ashamed of so many things."

"I don't know what you mean. We could meet for a cup of coffee or should I say a latte, your favorite, for a few minutes."

"Sean, I'm pregnant!"

I couldn't believe I just blurted out those words. They brought me a feeling of shame and relief.

"Oh. Congratulations! I didn't know that you were involved with someone."

"Sean, it's not like that. You don't know the scope of what happened. I want to tell you and need to tell you. Can we meet Sunday afternoon?"

"Charlie will be with his mother this weekend so that will work. How does lunch at Arturo's Café sound?" Sean asked.

"It sounds good, but please understand that this is very hard for me. My life has been turned upside down."

"I'm your friend, and that means everything between us will always be okay."

"You are truly wonderful! 12:00 at Arturo's on Sunday. See you then."

That conversation with Sean brought me to life. It was as if I had been given an injection of happiness. I hadn't felt that good in the last six months. It was exactly what the doctor had ordered!

•

Arturo's was a very upscale café. I had been there once before and remembered loving the food. It was more of an intimate type of atmosphere. The servers were dressed in crisp, clean uniforms. Arturo's didn't attract the boisterous and unruly type, and that was exactly what I wanted.

I wore a long, loose sweater and a pair of maternity jeans. Dressing this way distracted from my obvious state. Sean was standing in front of the cafe. He smiled as soon as he saw me. He then ran over and hugged me.

"Evie! It's so good to see you!"

"Good to see you also."

"Let's go inside."

Sean didn't check me out physically. He made eye contact and kept his eyes fully focused on mine. This made me feel as if no time had passed since we last saw each other. We sat down at a table in the back of the cafe near a window.

"You look exactly the same," I said to Sean.

"Look at you, you're beautiful and glowing!" he replied.

Sean was being kind because I wasn't glowing nor was I beautiful. I didn't want to spoil the moment, so I just went with it.

"Thank you. It's nice to hear."

"Would you like menus, or do you know what you want?" the waiter asked.

"Menus would be great, thank you," Sean responded.

"Now where were we?"

"You were telling me how beautiful I am," I said with a straight face, and then burst into laughter.

I wanted Sean to remember that I still had a sense of humor. He smiled that great Sean smile.

"You are beautiful! What would you like to order?"

"The vegetable pasta looks good."

"I was thinking the same!"

I wasn't ready to discuss what happened to me just yet, but I needed to be upfront with Sean.

"Sean, this is beyond difficult for me. Right now, I'm not ready to share with you why I was in a psychiatric hospital and my reasons for blowing you off for so long. If you don't mind, I don't want to say much tonight and would rather hear about you and Charlie."

"We can talk about anything you want to."

And Sean did just that. He talked about work, how Charlie was getting so big and informed me of a new coffee shop that opened up by his building, my former building. I hardly said a word and that's exactly how I wanted the day to go. We spent about two hours together before I became very tired.

"Sean, I'm having a great time, but I need to go to bed. I get exhausted very easily."

"I'm glad you enjoyed yourself. Just let me grab the check and I'll take you home."

"Thank you."

We took a taxi back to my apartment. Sean walked me to my door and waited until my key turned in the lock. He hugged me and gave me a peck on the cheek.

"You're a great guy! You made the day special for me. Thank you."

"No, thank you!"

My heart was filled with joy as I stepped into my apartment. Sean was a wonderful and caring man, but I didn't want to kid myself since there was no hope for a continued relationship.

There were just too many obstacles to overcome and too many hurdles in our way. Regardless of my feelings, I was so thankful that our time at Arturo's went the way it did. I would treasure this memory for a long time to come.

The next day I received a text from Sean.

"I had a great time. When can we meet again?"

His text upset me. I didn't want to lead him on, nor did I want to hurt him. He couldn't possibly be aware of how everything in my life had changed. I had a long way to go to become happy again and didn't want to bring Sean down with me. He was just too good of a person.

Sean continued to text me for the next week, and I wasn't always responsive. He didn't let that stop him because he decided to call me instead. I picked up the phone.

"Hello."

"Hey, Evie. It's Sean."

"I know."

"Are you okay, I mean is everything alright?"

"It's all good."

"It can't be all good. You barely responded to any of my texts and you're giving me one word answers now. Please be honest with me. If you want me out of your life, I'll respect your wishes. Just tell me."

"I don't want you out of my life. It's just that I'm full of so much anger, shame and doubt. I've become a very different person and it's not fair for you to get involved with me again."

"Why don't you let me be the judge of that? Right now we're friends and that's all you need to think about. Stop worrying! I care about you and want what's best for you. Please don't shut me out."

"I'm sorry, Sean. I don't want you to get hurt. You're too nice."

"Well since I'm so nice, then it would probably be nice to see me again, wouldn't it? How about having lunch this Sunday?"

"It's hard to say no to you. Okay, I'd like to go to Pasta On The Avenue. I've been craving gnocchi with a heavy dose of Parmesan cheese."

"That sounds good, except this time I will pick you up at your door. Does 1:00 PM work for you?"

"Yes, I'll see you then."

I was so pleased that he pushed the issue.

•

I was almost seven months along. My bathroom jaunts were becoming more frequent as the baby was pressing on my bladder. Pasta, bread, and cheese were my staples. I couldn't tolerate anything else, so Pasta On The Avenue Restaurant was a good choice for lunch with Sean.

I began to get excited about seeing Sean, yet it was important for me to keep my feelings in check. Regardless, it still felt good knowing that I would be spending time with him again.

CHAPTER 39

Sean arrived at my front door. I didn't want him to come in because the kitchen sink was loaded with dirty dishes. I partially opened my door so that he couldn't fully see the inside of my new place. I tried to squeeze myself out sideways but couldn't do so because of my baby bump. Sean asked me if I needed help and I told him that I was embarrassed for him to see my apartment. He then put his hands over his eyes and told me to let him know once the door was shut. This gave me a much, needed laugh and reminded me of the considerate man Sean was.

The restaurant wasn't filled to capacity, which was great. We ordered two different dishes and shared them. Sean was gentlemanly and sweet throughout the meal, but I had a sense that something just wasn't right. He was less talkative and more on the somber side. I was sure that he realized that it was a mistake to have made another date with me and was regretting it. I didn't want to mention anything at that moment and instead decided to see how the rest of the afternoon would progress.

Sean became very quiet toward the end of the meal. Once dessert arrived, I began toying with the idea of telling him straight out that he could end the date and his agony at the same time. Just as I was about to go with this plan, Sean broke the silence.

"I've been thinking about this since our first conversation from a few weeks ago. We haven't talked about what happened to you and I respect your privacy. But there are some things that we do need to discuss."

"You're scaring me. What is it that you want to talk about?"

"I didn't mean to frighten you. Let's go to my apartment where we'll feel more comfortable. No one needs to overhear anything. I promise there is nothing scary in what I am going to talk to you about."

I agreed to go with him. What could he have possibly wanted to talk to me about that was so important?

Once inside Sean's place, memories of me having lived in his apartment building kept popping in and out of my head. There had been only a few floors between us, and now we were as far apart as anyone could get, figuratively speaking that is.

"Please sit down, Evie. I'm going to put up some tea for us. Is that okay with you?"

That was Sean. He always cared about my thoughts and feelings. Why didn't we meet ages ago?

"Sure. No problem," I said.

I sat down on one of his living room chairs, not wanting to sit next to him on the couch. It was necessary for me to first hear what he had to say before I felt comfortable enough to do that. The baby was kicking me like crazy, so I placed one of my hands on my stomach and began to gently massage it.

Sean came back into the living room with two mugs of hot tea. He placed them on the coffee table and sat down on the chair opposite me.

"The best way to say something is to just say it. I know what happened to you. It was in the news, minus your name of course. I pieced things together and figured it out. First, I want to say I'm so sorry for what you have gone through and what you are still going through now."

"Thank you."

Both of us took a sip of tea and placed the mugs back on the table.

"Since you told me you were pregnant, I couldn't get the thought out of my mind that maybe this child is mine."

My eyes opened wide in surprise. This thought never occurred to me!

"No, it can't be! We had sex all the time for months, and I never got pregnant. It was this horrible guy that raped me!"

I was becoming very agitated. It visually brought that night back to me once again. I started to become anxious and began to breathe heavily.

"I'm sorry, Evie. I didn't mean for you to get upset. What can I do?"

"Just put a pillow under my head. I have to lie down. If you have a fan, please bring it to me."

Sean did as I asked. He spoke in very soothing tones and held my hand. I asked him not to touch me and explained to him that when the anxiety attacks come on, physical contact becomes painful to me. It had the opposite effect of what it should have had. Ever since I was raped, any form of touch made the anxiety worse.

It took me about a half hour to calm down. Sean kept apologizing and I kept telling him it wasn't his fault. In reality, he was the catalyst in this situation. He meant well and I couldn't be mad at him or make him feel guilty.

"I'm glad you're feeling better. Are you okay enough for me to take you home?" Sean asked.

"Yes, please take me home. I need to go to bed."

"Please call your doctor in the morning to make sure everything is alright."

"I'll do that. Please don't worry."

We took a cab back to my apartment building and Sean walked me to my door.

"Do you want me to come in and help you get settled?"

"I'm good. Please don't worry. I'll call you tomorrow after I speak to the doctor."

"I'm sorry about this, Evie. Please call me if you need anything at all," he said and then left.

I took off my clothes and lied down on my bed. I was totally beat. Just at that moment, I felt the baby kick again. Was that a sign to consider what Sean had said? But how could this be his baby? We had so much unprotected sex and I never got pregnant. This couldn't possibly be his baby. Or could it? My head started to hurt from all that had transpired that afternoon to the point where I couldn't think anymore. I needed to take a nap and so I did.

I awoke an hour later feeling slightly nauseous. I got up and drank a glass of water and slowly started to feel better. My thoughts immediately went to Sean's words that this baby might be his. How could I not have considered this possibility?

What if it was his?

I stood up and walked towards the window. This cannot be possible, I told myself. Why didn't I get pregnant all those previous months that we were having unprotected sex? I kept asking myself the same question without coming up with an answer.

I didn't tell Sean that I had decided to give the baby up for adoption and had signed all the papers. The adoptive parents also signed all their respective documents. They had met all the criteria necessary with flying colors, according to their attorney and my state mandated attorney. There was nothing left for me to do but give birth.

Wait a minute, there was something that needed to be done and that was to call Briana.

"Hello."

"Briana, I need your help! I need to see you and it can't wait," I said anxiously.

"Are you ready to give birth?" Briana asked.

"No, it's not that. Please come over. If Paul wants to come too, it's okay. Please hurry," I begged.

"Just tell me if you are hurt."

"No, I'm fine, but I must see you in person. Will you come?"

"I'll get in a cab right away and ask Paul if he wants to come along."

"Thank you, thank you."

I began pacing back and forth and felt so stupid for not having thought this situation through. Granted I was distraught, but someone should have stopped me from being so quick to sign those papers. What was I thinking? On second thought, the social worker at Heaton Psych was very adamant that I should take my time in answering the questions. But at that time, it didn't matter, because I was so determined to give the baby up. There was no one else to blame but myself, and so the struggle continued in my mind.

The doorbell rang. I looked through the peephole and saw Briana. When I opened the door, Paul was standing to her right. I was surprised to see him but was glad that he came along. Even though I thought of him as a pompous ass, he wasn't such a bad guy.

"Come in, come in. Thank you for coming over so quickly."

"What's going on? You sounded extremely panicked," Briana said.

"Briana, come sit next to me on the bed," I requested.

Paul sat on the only chair in the room.

"I'm sorry I don't have anything to offer you unless you want some juice?"

"We're okay. Please tell us what's going on," Briana responded.

Both of them looked very concerned and undeniably didn't want this to drag out any further.

"As you know, Sean is a wonderful man. He tried to contact me several times while I was still at the psych hospital. Once I was released, he continued to send me little sweet messages letting me know that he would like to get together. I finally agreed to see him a week ago but wasn't up to telling him what had happened to me. We met again today for lunch and I finally told him. The problem is that I never got to the part about giving the baby up for adoption."

It was obvious that this conversation was making Paul uneasy. He kept adjusting himself in the chair and cleared his throat a few times. I wasn't sure exactly what was going on with him. I wondered if he was feeling a twinge of guilt because he wouldn't consider the adoption himself.

"The reason why I called you over is because Sean thinks this might be his baby!"

Briana was shocked hearing this. Paul would have preferred to be anywhere else.

"I don't know if I fully understand," Briana said.

"It never occurred to me that Sean could be the father because I was so focused on this vile man who raped me. Maybe I blocked Sean out as a possibility because of how violent this act was."

"What are you going to do?" Briana asked.

"I don't know what to do and that's the problem. The adoption is final. That's what Social Services told me. Everything has been approved. Please help me! What should I do?"

"Evie, you have been through a harrowing experience that no woman should ever have to go through," Paul said.

It was the first time he said anything. He spoke calmly and appeared to be sincere. I appreciated him so much at that moment. I needed all the comfort possible.

"Being upset like this is no good for you or the baby. I think you need to tell Sean the truth, and sooner rather than later. He has a right to know if this is his child, and so do you," Paul continued.

"I agree," said Briana.

"What good can it do? Everything is final."

"Start with one step at a time. Let Sean know your situation and then hear what he has to say. You will feel better and so will he. It might be tough on him to hear this at first, but then he will have all the facts and can decide what he wants to do and how to go about it, or do nothing at all," Briana emphasized.

"You're right! I have to tell him about the adoption and I will."

Briana and Paul both gave me a hug, which made me feel better.

"Are you going to be okay?" Briana asked.

"Yes. I'm going to be okay now. Thank you so much for everything."

"We have to go but call me tomorrow and let me know what Sean said."

"Of course I will, Briana."

With that, they left. Briana and Paul were right. Letting Sean know about the adoption was a step in the right direction. Being with Briana always made everything so much better. In this case, I was glad that Paul was there too.

I took out some cereal and poured milk over it. That was my dinner. It was filling and therefore served its purpose. I had an hour or two to watch TV before going to sleep. It would be hard not to think about the following day, which would come soon enough.

•

I woke up earlier than usual the morning after Briana and Paul came to my tiny apartment. As much as I tried to put it out of my mind, there were two tasks that had to be accomplished within the next 24 hours.

To satisfy Sean, I called my doctor and told him about the anxiety attack. He didn't feel the need for me to come to his office for an examination. He explained that unless I experience pain or note something unusual, everything should be okay. It never struck me that anything might be wrong as I was so used to getting these anxiety attacks for years.

Now it was time to call Sean. I took a deep breath and picked up the phone.

"Hi, Evie. I'm so glad you called. How are you feeling?"

"I called the doctor. He said there's nothing to worry about. I'm tired, but that's to be expected."

"You sound good. Is there anything I can do for you?"

I hesitated for a brief moment.

"No, but there is something I can do for you, or maybe for the both of us. I need to speak to you but don't want to do it over the phone. When can we meet?"

"Anytime today is good. Where would you like to go?" Sean asked.

"Can you come to my apartment? Maybe we can go to the park from there?"

"No problem. I'll pick you up at 11:00 AM. Will that work?" Sean asked.

"That's perfect. It won't be a long conversation," I assured him.

"I'll be there shortly," he said and then hung up.

Revealing the adoption to Sean was the right thing to do. I was not a little girl anymore and had to stop acting like one. I felt so happy at the end of that thought.

I got dressed, brushed my teeth and straightened my hair. There were about 15 minutes to spare before Sean would get to my apartment. I started putting away some of my clothing which was strewn all over the place. That effort kept me from panicking about the task ahead. I picked out a small purse and placed some cash, my keys, and my only credit card in it. I then put on some lipstick so I wouldn't look sallow. My jacket was tight on me and impossible to close, but it would keep me warm.

I stepped out of my apartment and checked the lock on my door three times. Moments later Sean came out of the elevator. He had that same winning smile. I just loved that about him.

"It looks like you're ready," Sean said.

"I am. Let's go. We'll talk when we get to the park."

"I'm good with that."

We went over to the elevator and exited the building. Sean entwined his arm in mine as we walked several blocks together, giving the impression of a young couple out on a stroll. We sauntered slowly since I didn't have the same energy level that I had before the pregnancy.

As we arrived at the park, I was only too glad to sit down on one of the benches. I looked down and found it funny that my feet were not visible to me anymore.

I turned to face Sean. He was such a good guy that I hated having to tell him the truth, but there was no stopping it now. It was time to do it!

"Sean, I have to tell you about something I did. It's going to upset you, but I hope you will understand. The only reason why this happened was because of my state of mind throughout this ordeal, especially during the first few months of my pregnancy."

Sean's face muscles grew tense, and his smile disappeared. I guess he was bracing himself for the worst.

"I signed papers to give the baby up for adoption while I was at the psych hospital. The decision was made before you and I started talking."

Finally, the truth was out, but the hardest part was yet to come … Sean's disappointment.

"It's not a problem. Just cancel the adoption. You don't have to go through with it. Don't sign the final papers," Sean pleaded.

"It's too late! That was already done and I'm so sorry. All I could think of at the time was how I was violated in the most heinous way. I just wanted to rid myself of this whole nightmare. Never in a million years did I think of this other possibility. Please believe me, please!"

Sean looked at me for a few seconds which seemed like an eternity. I continued to speak.

"The adoption is final. I never thought it could be your child. We had sex so many times and I never got pregnant."

Sean stood up and put his hands to his face. He was crying and it tore my heart out. This wonderful human being shouldn't have to suffer for my decision. I stood up and went to comfort him with a hug. He held me so tight and cried like I had never seen a man cry before. After a few minutes, Sean started to calm down. He went over to one of the old, bent oak trees and leaned against it. After taking a deep breath, he walked back over to me. He put both of his hands on top of my shoulders and looked directly into my eyes.

"I need to know if this is my child, our child! I don't care how many papers you signed or what you signed. If this is my son, no one else is going to be his father but me!"

And then he smiled.

"Of course, it could be a girl," he added.

Both of us laughed. It was good to laugh. It broke the seriousness of the moment and relieved some of the tension.

"But there's nothing to do now," I said in a low tone.

"There's always something that can be done! I'll hire a good lawyer!"

"Sean, you have to accept that the adoption is final."

"It's only final if I don't do anything about it. Evie, this baby could be ours. Don't you want to find out for sure?"

I looked at him and all I wanted to do was melt into his arms. He looked so sweet and so innocent, almost like a hurt little boy that needed to be cuddled.

"I do want to find out, but we would just be opening up a can of worms. You're asking to fight the entire adoption system. It could take years and years, and then you may find out that it's not your child after all. And even if it is yours, you still won't be able to get the baby back because it legally belongs to someone else."

"You don't sound like someone who even cares. You gave the baby up and you're done. You don't even want to know the truth."

It was the first time I had seen Sean so upset and speak to me in such a stern voice. It shook me up a little, but he wasn't totally wrong.

"When I signed the papers, I wasn't mentally or physically prepared to raise a child by myself. The social worker assured me that the adoptive parents would go through a rigorous background check. It sounded like the ideal solution to me at the time."

"That was then and this is now. The only thing that makes sense is to get a DNA test as soon as possible and we'll go from there. Evie, if this test proves that I am the father, I promise you that your life will turn around for the better."

And so it began!

CHAPTER 40

Sean hired Candace Fowler as his lawyer. She was a very well-known adoption attorney who specialized in cases such as ours. I didn't want to start an argument but felt it was important to let Sean know how costly this could be. Before I could mention it, he told me that he didn't care how expensive this was going to be because every penny would be worth it.

It was time to let Briana know what was happening. Her support would be my lifeline throughout this process.

"Hello!"

"Briana, I need to tell you something important. Do you have time to talk?"

"I need to get dinner started but go ahead."

"As I had told you, Sean thinks there is a possibility that this might be his baby."

"And ...?"

"He wants to try and stop the adoption."

"Wait a minute! I have to take all this in. He wants to stop the adoption because he thinks the baby might be his! Didn't you tell me that you already signed all the papers, which makes it final?"

"Yes, he knows all that, but it's not stopping him. He wants to get a DNA test as soon as the baby is born. If it's his, he wants to go full speed ahead."

"Wow! So what did you tell him?"

"Briana, Sean is such a good man, but he's blinded right now. He's very driven and on a mission that no one can stop. I explained to him that I would not be able to raise a baby on my own, and that didn't even bother him."

"I don't know what to say. This is going to take a lot of time and money and it will weigh heavily on both of your emotions. Is he prepared for that?" Briana asked.

"He seems to be and doesn't care if it drains his bank account. He has a real need to know the truth. He's going to fight like mad and who can blame him?"

"This is big! What if it does turn out to be Sean's?"

"That's the question of the day. I agreed to back him all the way, but this whole thing scares me more than I can say."

"Evie, imagine if this is his baby! Then you and Sean can become a couple again. It would be a perfect match!"

"I wish it would be as easy as that. Sean is very caught up right now with the belief that this is his child. Eventually, he will calm down and come to the realization that there will never be any romance between us again. It's a fact that I have already accepted."

"Why?"

"Our relationship was easy. There were no hurdles and I knew Sean was everything I ever wanted and needed in a man. But I'm such a changed person now and nothing like the woman he knew me to be."

"Well, you could co-parent with him and take a more active part as time goes by. You'll get stronger and the baby will give you that strength. I wouldn't say this if I didn't believe it."

"We'll see. I guess as of now we have to take everything one step at a time."

"Which law firm is Sean using?"

"I don't know the name of the firm, but he hired Candace Fowler."

"I think I've heard of her. Isn't she that famous adoption attorney?"

"Yes. Sean told me that she is the best."

"Sean is already a good father from what you tell me, and you will make a good mother."

"There's one other thing, Briana. What if this isn't his baby?"

"Then life will go on as usual. He has to know and truthfully, so do you."

"Thank you, Briana. I'm so glad that you are in my life."

"You know that you can call me anytime. Good luck to you and Sean! I have to go. Bye."

"Bye, Briana."

•

My due date was two weeks away. Most of my days were spent sleeping and watching TV. Sean's phone calls to me were incessant. Because he was so on edge, I willingly put up with them.

I called my new social worker and let her know that I wanted a DNA test done. She was not happy and carried on as to how difficult this situation would become. I didn't allow her to deter me or make me doubt my decision. I felt stronger than ever and was determined to see this through with Sean. I owed it to him, myself and especially to my baby.

Three weeks went by and I was seven days past my due date. This gave me some cause for worry. In my mind, this was pointing more towards Sean not being the father. Even though the doctor told me that firstborn children are unpredictable and often born late, it did not ease my mind. The tension was getting to me and I was relying on Briana more and more.

•

Candace Fowler asked for us to meet in her office. I was so tired that it took all of my strength to go.

"This is going to be a very tough case. Your cooperation throughout this matter is essential. It will not be an overnight success. Are there any questions that either of you haven't asked me? Do either of you have any doubts? If there are any, I need to know them right now," Candace said in a very serious tone.

Sean looked at me as I shook my head.

"No, I don't have any doubts. Sean has the right to find out if this is his baby."

"Getting the DNA will be difficult, and that will be the easy part of the case. If it turns out not to be yours, what do you want to do then?" Candace asked.

"If it's not my baby, then there's no reason for me to continue," Sean responded.

"What about you, Evie?"

"If it's not Sean's, then the adoption can go forward as originally planned."

We all looked at each other in agreement.

"I want both of you in this heart and soul. There's going to be a lot of work ahead of us. Everything I ask for has to be done immediately. No excuses and no nonsense! Am I clear?"

We nodded in agreement.

"Wild horses couldn't stop me from this. I feel that this is my child!" Sean said unequivocally.

We then said our goodbyes and left her office.

"How about grabbing a light lunch?" Sean asked me.

"That sounds good since I'm always hungry these days."

A bowl of pumpkin soup with a grilled cheese sandwich and fries put me on cloud nine at that moment. Sean ordered a bowl of Manhattan clam chowder and a turkey sandwich. My feelings for him were still there, even though I was trying to contain them. However, I could tell that he didn't exhibit that same spark of emotion that was present months ago. If this turned out to be Sean's child, he would probably be inclined to gravitate toward me solely because I was the mother. Granted he did have feelings for me, but I could tell that true romantic ones went by the wayside a while ago.

"With some luck she will be able to get approval for a DNA test within the next week or two. If the baby is mine, we will have to be very strong to see it through. You're still with me, right?" Sean asked again.

I took Sean's hand in mine and said exactly what was on my mind.

"I'm still with you and I am going to be as strong as possible. But you have to face certain truths. Even if the baby is yours, we may not be the victors. We are fighting the legal system here. Also, if you're not the father, I'm so scared of how this will affect you."

"I'm a realist. Don't get me wrong, it's going to hurt like hell if it turns out that it's not my child, but I'm prepared for that. I'm so sure that I'm the father, Evie. I have this feeling inside that makes me so certain of it. The other day, I dreamt that Charlie was telling all of his friends that he is going to be a big brother!"

This was the first time that I truly thought Sean was deceiving himself. He was so psyched up, that not being the father could cause him to have a nervous breakdown. He didn't seem to realize what he was truly in for, or maybe I was overthinking everything. Regardless, I was going to support him, not only because he was a good man, but also because I was still in love with him. It was going to be difficult at best. I had been given the opportunity to think of his needs and wants. It was time for me to step up to the plate no matter what obstacles came my way. If this was Sean's baby, then he would be in my life for a long time. That actually worked for me.

•

The weekend came. I was hoping that Sean would ask me to go to the park with him and Charlie. I loved that little boy, and Sean was the perfect father to him. It would be a great afternoon for all of us.

I started to go to the bathroom but did not make it there in time. My water broke and it splashed all over the floor. I stood there motionless, trying to understand what had just happened. Reality set in and I realized that my body was preparing to give birth, with or without my approval. I began to panic, but quickly gained control of myself. I called Sean, but he wasn't in his apartment. I started to dial his cell number when my first contraction came. The pain was horrific. I had no idea that it would be so bad. I doubled over in agony. I was grateful that the pain didn't last long. I continued to dial Sean's cell, but it went into voice mail. I called Briana but she also didn't answer her phone. Approximately 10 minutes later, my next contraction came and I howled loudly from the pain. My next-door neighbor must have heard me because she rang my bell and kept yelling, "Are you alright?"

I made it to the door and opened it.

"I need to get to the hospital. I'm having contractions. Can you help me?"

"Did you call your doctor?" she asked.

"No. I don't know what to do!"

"Don't worry, I'll help you. You need to get your keys and your overnight bag."

"I don't have an overnight bag."

"No problem. Just get your keys, ID, and some cash or a credit card. We'll take a cab and get you to the hospital. I'm just going to lock my door."

I was afraid that she wasn't coming back as I experienced another contraction and again doubled over in pain. Hurriedly, I grabbed my keys and purse. Then, I threw some clothing into a plastic bag. I went back over to my door to wait for my neighbor to return. While waiting, I decided to give Sean another try. Again, it went directly into voice mail.

My neighbor came back with a backpack. She threw my purse and the plastic bag inside of it. After locking my door, she told me to walk slowly with her to the elevator. Once on the main floor, we exited the building together.

"Taxi," my neighbor kept calling out as the cars continued to pass us by.

As this wonderful woman kept trying to hail down a cab, it dawned on me that I didn't even know her name. At that moment my phone rang and I quickly answered it. I was so glad it was Sean.

"Are you okay?" he immediately asked.

"My water broke and I'm getting contractions! My neighbor is getting me a taxi to Metropolitan Hospital. Please come if you can!"

"After hearing your message, I immediately called your doctor to let him know. Then I called Candace. She's going to meet us at the hospital and will try to get permission for a mouth swab of the baby. Hopefully, the doctor or nurse will be cooperative."

"Ohhhhhhh!" I yelled into the phone.

"Hang up, I'm coming!" Sean yelled back excitedly.

A cab stopped at that moment and my neighbor helped me inside.

"Metropolitan Hospital, and don't speed," she said to the driver.

"I don't know your name. I'm Evie."

"I'm Adara. Don't worry. I'll be by your side for as long as you need me."

"Thank you. I didn't know it was going to hurt so much."

"You'll forget about it as soon as you give birth."

Adara had no way of knowing that I would never forget about any of it. She had no idea of the current situation and this was not the time or place to give her any hints.

The taxi ride was uneventful except for my screaming. I tried hard to control it, but it was impossible. The driver was good-natured and put up with it. He offered to walk us to the emergency room. Adara thanked him but told him it wasn't necessary.

Entering the hospital lobby, I saw a number of aides lingering around while on their break. I was placed in a wheelchair and brought upstairs to the delivery waiting room. A nurse took all of my personal history and also called my OB/GYN, although Sean had already taken care of the latter. A hospital doctor examined me and told me that I was six centimeters dilated.

"You have some time to go until you're fully dilated. Your personal doctor will be here in about an hour," he remarked.

"An hour! What do you mean? I'm giving birth in the next few minutes!" I screamed.

He looked at me quizzically and realized that I had no knowledge of the birthing process.

"It doesn't happen that quickly most of the time. You have to be 10 centimeters dilated before you are ready to give birth. Sometimes it happens fast, but it doesn't seem that way here. Don't worry, I'll keep checking on you. Try your best to relax."

Adara came over to me and held my hand.

"Don't worry. Your body knows what to do. It will all be over soon," she said in a calm voice.

"It will never be over," I said as I began to sob.

Adara looked puzzled but did not ask any questions. If only she knew …

Sean showed up and looked as though he had run all the way to the hospital.

"Sean, I'm so glad to see you. The baby is going to be born shortly. What are we going to do?" I asked him.

"It looks as though you're in good hands. Good luck with the delivery. I'm going to leave now," Adara said.

"Thank you so much, Adara. You've been a lifesaver."

She smiled at the both of us and then left.

Suddenly there was a big tumult going on near us. I saw my social worker with two other people in the corridor and a policeman. Behind them was Candace, who was holding papers in her hand and waving them about. As they were coming closer, I let out another loud scream which didn't seem to faze them.

"Evie, these two women are from the State. As soon as the baby is born, they will be the ones responsible for … um, taking care of the agreement," Candace said.

"You have nothing to do but give birth," my social worker added.

Sean stepped forward, and yelled out, "I'm the father! I will make the decisions here!"

The social worker looked at the two women and the policeman. No one responded verbally, but the looks on the faces of the two women were those of utter disdain.

"I'm the parents' attorney. No one will do anything without my permission," Candace emphasized.

That statement created a chaotic scene with everyone talking at once. The policeman did not utter a word, as he must have been used to such pandemonium. Everyone was shouting over everyone else when a nurse came over and told all of them to shut up. She then spoke to me in almost a whisper.

"Your room is ready. Who is your coach going to be?"

"Sean, the father," I said.

"Then Sean can be in the room with you, and this mob can stay in the waiting room."

At that moment, one of the women from the State got involved.

"We're from the State. This baby was put up for adoption and we have every right to be in the room."

The nurse approached the two women and looked directly into their eyes as she placed her hands on her hips.

"What on earth do the two of you need to be in the room for? Only her coach is going to be in there. You are stressing out the mother and the unborn child. I'm not going to allow that on my watch and I don't care who you are. Unless you're also giving birth, you're not going in there."

The women looked at the policeman.

"Can't you do something?" one of them asked him.

"The baby hasn't been born yet. No one's broken any laws," he responded dryly.

"I can't believe this," the taller of the two women said.

Once I was settled, the nurse put a heart monitor on me and hooked me up to a screen. A little while later, my doctor arrived. He examined me and said that I was nine centimeters dilated. He ordered some pain pills and I couldn't wait for him to administer them. All in all, it had been about three hours since arriving at the hospital.

The social worker came into the room. She told me that she was relieved that all of this quarrelling was over so she could get back to work. She walked out right afterward but kept checking my room from time to time. It wasn't clear to me as to why.

The pain medicine was doing its job, although I still felt the contractions. Sean kept holding my hand when he wasn't massaging my back. Both the nurse and Sean tried to get me to breathe the Lamaze way, but it wasn't working for me. I then let out the loudest scream ever. The nurse told us that she had to leave the room but would be back in a few minutes. Finally, Sean and I had a minute when it was just the two of us in the room. He quickly closed the door.

"Evie, we don't have much time. This is what I want you to do when the time is right. You can't make a mistake. I know you can do it. As soon as ..."

CHAPTER 41

"So as you can imagine, Dr. Pennington, my giving birth was as though I was on a movie set with a cast of thousands. It was very stressful time. The social worker behaved as though it was her duty to watch me, as if her life depended on it! She definitely sensed that something was awry; but wasn't sure what it was."

"Go on," Dr. Pennington said.

"Everything was happening all at once. Our attorney was trying to get permission to do a swab test on the baby and the social worker was carrying on. The behavior of the women from the State reminded me of the two evil stepsisters from "Cinderella." Sean was very emotional, yet he kept a cool head for my sake. He made sure that I was as comfortable as possible. My contractions were coming every minute and it was almost time for the baby to be born."

Dr. Pennington was obviously intrigued by my story because she put her pad down and leaned back in her chair.

"Sean gave me the signal and I let out a piercing scream. This unnerved the nurse who was the only attendant in the room at the time. She ran out to get the doctor. Sean shut the door and then handed me a plastic bag with a cotton swab inside. Once the baby was born, the plan was for me to swab the inside of the baby's cheek. I would do this by asking everyone for a quiet moment alone with my baby. If that was agreed to, I would go ahead with the plan. When everyone would return to the room,

Sean would then bend over to give me and the baby a long hug. This is how he would retrieve the bag without being noticed. In that way, we would be assured to have a DNA sample if we couldn't get it any other way."

"I'd love to know if your plan came to fruition, but we only have a minute left. I have another patient immediately after you. Let's leave the rest of this for our next session," Dr. Pennington said.

"Good because I'm drained from talking so much."

I was almost done with my story, but Dr. Pennington had no idea of the bombshell that was to come.

CHAPTER 42

I was at my next session with Dr. Pennington. I couldn't wait to sit down and begin speaking. She told me to continue from where we left off the last time. And so I did …

"You're doing great, Evie. How about giving us another big push?"

"What's wrong? Why isn't my baby coming out?"

"The baby will be born shortly. You just need to continue to push when I tell you," the doctor responded.

My mind started racing with different thoughts. Should I try to fight the adoption, even if the baby doesn't turn out to be Sean's? What if I immediately fall in love with this baby, regardless of how it was conceived? Why did this have to happen to me?

"There's the head!" the doctor said.

And within moments of that statement, my baby was born.

"It's a boy," the doctor revealed in a monotone voice.

He did not make a big deal out of it because he was aware that this baby was being given up for adoption. I was so exhausted from the hours of labor and the birthing process that I could hardly move.

"I want to see my son please," I said.

"We have to clean him up and get his Apgar score. Then you can hold him for a few minutes," the nurse in attendance replied.

Sean didn't take his eyes off the baby and was smiling from ear to ear the entire time. He was asking all kinds of questions so rapidly that it was difficult to understand what he was saying.

One of the nurses placed my son on top of me. I was scared to look at him. I wanted to but was afraid that I would fall in love with him, only to have him taken away moments later. Sean came over and kissed his forehead.

"He looks like me! He looks exactly like me!" Sean said with glee in his voice.

The door opened as the social worker and the two women from the State entered the room.

"It's time to take the baby to the nursery," the taller of the two women from the State said. There was no emotion in her voice.

"He was just born! He can't leave the hospital yet," Sean protested.

"I'm not here to argue with you," she replied.

"He's not leaving the hospital," the nurse interjected.

"He will stay here for three days and then will be released to Social Services to be placed in a foster home," the social worker added.

"Now if you will excuse us," both women from the State said at almost the same time.

"But I'm the father!" Sean stated in an authoritative tone.

"That is of no consequence. Everything was made crystal clear to Miss Harris as to the procedure once the baby was born. She agreed to everything. All that we are doing is following the directive of the State," the shorter of two women responded.

Her words were lethal, as if she had just pierced us with a knife.

"No one asked me!" Sean stated.

"No one knew about you. Regardless, as we said before, all that we are doing is following orders. If you have any grievances, bring them up to your attorney."

"Can I please have a moment alone with my baby?" I asked.

Everyone, including Sean, left the room. I then put our plan into action by swabbing the baby's cheek. Unexpectedly, the door opened seconds later, and a new nurse walked in. I quickly placed the swab under the bed cover. The nurse looked around the room.

"Oh, sorry, wrong room," the nurse exclaimed.

I couldn't believe her timing and my bad luck. The swab was now contaminated.

After a few minutes, the original nurse returned to the room, followed by Sean. While the nurse turned her head to check the time chart on the wall, I quickly placed the swab in the plastic bag. That was when Sean began his part, which didn't fully work out either. Unfortunately, he dropped the bag on the floor and then decided to kick it under the bed. A few seconds later, the nurse looked at me and then eyeballed Sean. She gently lifted my son from my arms and placed him in an isolette. She left the room and took him to the nursery.

It was time to let go.

All this commotion was very disturbing and so I began to cry. Sean tried to protest but to no avail. My baby was taken away from me. It was the biggest mistake of my life.

Sean came over to the bed with his shoulders and head hunched, and we cried to each other. The room was devoid of anyone except for the two of us. Apparently, the doctor and nurses had seen this before. It was impossible to express the emptiness and loss we felt at that moment. The silence that ensued was eerie.

"Sean, I want to leave today! I can't stay here another minute!" I cried out loud.

"I don't know if they will release you. You'll probably have to stay until tomorrow," Sean said.

"Why? It's not like I'm bringing a baby home. I need to get out of here. Please help me get off of this bed," I begged him.

"I forgot about the cotton swab! I had kicked it under the bed when the nurse came in," Sean said.

He bent down and tried to retrieve it. When he pulled the plastic bag out, there was hair attached to it from the linoleum floor. Sean brushed the hair off with his hand. He then found a paper towel in the bathroom, moistened it and wiped down the bag.

"I don't know if the sample is going to be good or not. It might not be sanitary anymore. Nothing is going right for us," I cried.

"The swab inside is still okay. The hair is only on the outside of the bag. I'll take it to the lab tomorrow. I can change the bag and put it into the refrigerator for the night. It's all going to work out, don't worry," Sean assured me.

But I did worry. The cotton swab had been under the bedsheet for a few minutes before it was placed in the plastic bag. There was no doubt in my mind that it was contaminated. Sean was optimistic because that was in his nature, wherein I was pessimistic because that was in my nature. Luckily, I had not gotten off the bed yet, because one of the nurses walked in at that very moment. It would have been a big problem if she realized that I was planning to leave the hospital without checking out.

"I need to do a quick exam to make sure you're not bleeding heavily," she said.

She drew the curtain around me and told me that I would be transferred to another room shortly.

"Okay," I responded in a whisper.

As soon as she walked out, Sean grabbed my clothing and helped me get off the bed. I got dressed as quickly as possible.

"Maybe we should just tell them we want to leave. I don't want any problems," I suggested.

Sean held my hand and we started to walk towards the nurse's station to let them know I was going home. Once there, we tried to get the attention of the only nurse on duty. She was busy writing her patients' notes in a thick loose leaf binder. The shifts had just changed, and this nurse didn't recognize me. Instinctively, I pulled on Sean's shirt which made him bend down.

"Let's go," I whispered in his ear.

We walked towards the elevator and left the hospital.

"What made you change your mind?" Sean asked.

"There is no way they'll dismiss me now and it's just too much for me emotionally to stay here for the night. What are they going to do, send the police and take me back? It's not like I committed a crime!"

"You're right."

"I need to ask you for a favor. Can I stay at your place just for tonight? I don't want to be alone."

"Of course," Sean said.

He flagged down a taxi and away we went.

•

Arriving at his apartment gave me a sense of security. Being with Sean gave me some hope that I would never be alone, no matter what the road ahead held for us.

I sat down on the couch and put my feet up on a small stool. Sean put on a plastic glove and removed the cotton swab from the bag. He then placed it inside a new plastic bag and put it in the fridge. I knew the swab was useless but didn't want to make an issue of it. I just wanted to go to sleep since I was beyond exhausted.

Two hours later, the hospital called my cell phone. I answered only because I didn't want it to become a police matter.

"Hello."

"This is Metropolitan Hospital. We are looking for Evie Harris."

"This is Evie," I said solemnly.

"You left the hospital tonight without permission. The doctor didn't sign you out."

She spoke to me in a loud and chastising way as though I had just committed the biggest felony.

"You need to come back right now, sign paperwork and wait for the doctor to release you!" she continued to yell.

Sean had heard the entire conversation. He came over to me and took the phone.

"Nurse or whoever you are, stop admonishing her and stop screaming!"

I almost laughed because that was exactly how Sean was behaving without realizing it.

"We will call the doctor and take care of everything, but not until the morning. Evie just gave birth!"

And with that, Sean hung up the phone.

"Wow, Sean! I never saw you so angry. I hope we don't end up having trouble over this."

"Don't worry. I'll take care of it in the morning."

"Thank you, Sean. I could not have done this without you."

"You sleep on the bed and I'll take the couch. You need to be comfortable. I have some sweats in the bureau drawer that you can use as pajamas. Let me know if there is anything else you need."

"This might be embarrassing for you, but I'm going to need a package of maxi pads."

"No problem, the drugstore delivers. Don't worry about anything. Just go to bed. You need to rest."

Sean was being very protective and treated me with sensitivity and care. Maybe he thought that our present relationship would be as it was before everything went awry. He wasn't aware of my mental and emotional state at this point, but he would find that out in time.

"My sweet, sweet Sean, I almost had my prince," I whispered to myself.

I cried as quietly as I could and then fell into a deep sleep.

•

I awoke the next morning to the smell of freshly brewed coffee and couldn't wait to have a cup.

"Good morning, cereal or a bagel?"

"Cereal and coffee sounds good to me. I'll take a shower if it's okay, and then head over to my apartment."

"You can stay for the rest of the day, week, or however long you want to. There are some things we still need to talk about."

"Thanks for being so kind. I need to get back to my place and try to figure out how to piece my life together. Besides still being exhausted, I feel very drained and empty."

"I get it. We need to go over some strategy so you will need your strength. Enjoy your breakfast and then I'll take you home."

"Thanks. Can we stop at the grocery store first?"

"No problem."

Sean poured me a cup of steaming coffee and set down the bowl of cereal in front of me. While I was eating, he continued to speak.

"I already placed a call to Candace and to a DNA testing lab. I'm waiting for a call back from both. We're not going to waste even a second of time moving forward," he said.

"I don't want to do anything to stop the momentum. After we go through all of this, realizing that it's going to be the fight of our lives, what happens if the baby isn't yours? What will it do to your psyche?"

"I know we discussed this before and I'm prepared for anything that comes my way. If this is my son, and I believe he is, then every stressful minute will have been worth it. If by some remote chance it turns out that he isn't, I'll resign myself to that. This child deserves to know who his real father is. Don't you agree?"

"I agree, but what if you really do end up being the father? All the rights were signed over to the adoptive parents. I agreed to a closed adoption and don't know who they are. What if we won't be allowed to know that?"

"Evie, you have to have faith, and you have to trust that Candace knows what she is doing."

"I pray that I can go through this with you, Sean."

"That little boy deserves to be with his real father. I'm his real father and he's going to be with me!"

Sean had decided that this was his child, and no one was going to change his mind. Even though he was a realist by his own admission, he was definitely not one in this situation. Desperately wanting something to be true can play tricks on your mind and make you believe it is so. That seemed to be what had happened to him. He was very strong, but the strongest of men can fracture when it comes to disappointment. The greatest fear that constantly entered my brain was that this was not his son. I promised to be in this with him 100%, so I gathered all my inner strength and continued to support Sean. How wonderful it would be if he was the father. It sounded so beautiful and melted my heart, but I couldn't allow myself the liberty of thinking like that. There have been too many disappointments in my life. Just then, Sean's cell phone rang.

"Hello."

"Sean, this is Candace. I need you and Evie to come into my office this afternoon at 3:15 PM. Are both of you available?"

"Hold on a moment, please. It's Candace and she wants us in her office at 3:15 PM today. Are you up to it?"

"Not really, but of course I'll go."

"We'll be there, Candace."

"Sean, I need to be able to sleep until it's time to get there. Remember, I just gave birth yesterday."

"I'll take care of everything. Just give me a list of what you need and I'll get them. I'll make myself scarce and work from a coffee shop. You can sleep or just relax here. There are cold cuts, rolls, and yogurt in the refrigerator. Just help yourself and I'll be back to pick you up at 2:30 PM."

"I'll text you the list. Thank you for being so wonderful to me. I'll never be able to repay you for your kindness."

With that said, Sean was out the door. I placed the dishes in the sink and sat down on the couch, hoping for the day to go by slowly. I owed myself that little bit of pleasure. Sean also deserved my best efforts and so did my son. Yes, my son! It was time that I started to think of him in that way.

The hours flew by, and it was almost time for Sean to come back and pick me up for our meeting with Candace. I started to think about the adoptive parents. We didn't know anything about each other, which was part of the agreement. Of course, I now wished there would have been another option for me, but I had been too distraught to give it any thought at the time.

After three hours, Sean walked into the apartment and placed his briefcase down by the couch.

"How are you feeling right now?"

"I still feel tired, but that goes with the territory. I did have a chance to relax and that does make a big difference."

"Are you ready to go and see Candace?"

I went over to Sean and kissed his lips so hard that I thought I would draw blood. It was impulsive since I had wanted him for such a long time. Sean misunderstood the kiss and thought I was being too emotional.

"It's going to work out for us, you'll see. Don't worry. If we're together, nothing is going to stop us," Sean remarked.

I didn't respond and was only too glad that he didn't embarrass me about my vampire kiss. Besides, I didn't want to appear negative or uncertain as I had exhibited this behavior many times before.

After freshening myself up, Sean and I left to meet our attorney. Neither one of us spoke during the ride to her office. It was evident that we were both nervous.

•

"Come in and have a seat," Candace said.

We both sat down in front of her desk.

"I need every single detail of every event, no matter how trivial. Equally important is that whenever you remember something that you didn't tell me about, write it down immediately. The smallest element could make the difference between winning or losing this case. We are a team working toward the same goal. Are you with me so far?"

Her tone was very serious, and each word she uttered seemed carefully chosen.

"I'm with you," Sean responded without hesitation.

Candace stared at me and I nodded in agreement. Being intimidated by her was a feeling that I had to get over quickly, as it would work against me. After all, if this was how I felt about my own attorney, how would I be able to deal with the adoptive parents' attorneys? I had to grow a stiff spine very quickly. Maybe all this was truly a blessing in disguise.

"Let's begin. We are going to be in touch with each other almost every day, and sometimes more than once a day. If I request something, it must be done immediately. I never want to hear the words, 'I can't do it.' Delete those four words from your vocabulary right now! Understood?"

Sean and I said "yes" at the same time. I think she scared both of us. If her behavior wasn't so serious, it would have actually been funny.

"The State sent me a lot of paperwork explaining in detail everything that pertains to this case: the rape, the first hospital stay, the psych hospital, the therapy provided, etc. But reading someone's report is not the same as hearing it from 'the horse's mouth,' so to speak. Evie, I am going to need you to tell me every detail of what happened. It will be painful for you, but if we are to be successful, we need to be armed with as much information as possible. After all, we are a team!"

I sat up straight and then leaned back in the chair. The last thing I wanted to do was talk about the rape. It would be excruciating to go through every detail of that horror show for the millionth time. I did enough of that at Heaton Psych, but I had no choice in the matter. I remember how I used to lie in bed at Heaton and wonder why this had to happen to me. This meeting with Candace was as serious as it was going to get, and so there was no other option but to get my act together. That's when it occurred to me that my entire scenario of tragic events could be told without me falling apart. All I had to do was visualize that this situation had happened to someone else. That would help me focus on the facts and not on the emotions. I became more determined to move forward in order to show Sean that I was a mature and intelligent woman. I also wanted to believe it myself.

"The first and most important obstacle to overcome is to get permission to take a DNA test of the baby. The adoptive parents will not agree to this. They will fight you tooth and nail. However, we can't move forward without the DNA test results showing that you are the father, Sean. I've already started the paperwork and have sent in the request. The State moves very slowly and I am not expecting an answer before two or three weeks' time," Candace explained.

"Would it be possible to set up a meeting with the adoptive parents? Maybe we could reason with them?" Sean asked.

"We don't know who they are, and their attorney will never disclose this information. Think about it. How would you react in the same situation? These are two people who wanted a baby and got very lucky because of Evie's decision. Nothing is going to make them give up, especially since they have invested years of emotions and money into this process. I don't think their attorney is defending them pro bono. I'm sure they think of this baby as their child in every way," Candace said.

"I need to know if we even stand a chance. It seems everything is against us," I stated.

"The circumstances that led to this adoption are not the usual scenario, but they are also not totally unique," Candace replied.

"Evie almost lost her mind in the psych hospital," Sean added.

"We don't have the upper hand, but we do have a chance, a really good chance. Once I get all the information necessary from the both of you, I can determine more clearly how to proceed. If you're wavering in any way, I need to know that right now."

"I just want to be assured that we have a reasonable chance of winning," I countered.

"If I didn't think this case had merit, I would not have taken it. In fact, I think this is going to be a landmark case. I'm looking forward to a battle royale!"

I was very glad she felt so strongly about our plight. Although, I was wondering how much of it was ego and how much was her envisioning a huge paycheck from Sean and future clients.

"We're going to wrap it up for today. I'll see you back in two days. Sean, I'm not going to need you for the next session. It's going to be all about Evie."

Candace stood up and extended her hand to both of us. We said our goodbyes and left her office.

"Do you feel like you've just been through the mill, or is it just me?" I asked Sean.

"It's not just you. I don't think it's going to get easier anytime soon. We just have to be positive and persevere."

Sean cupped my face in his hands and spoke words of encouragement.

"We're going to depend on each other. If one of us falls, the other one will be there to pick them up. In that way, we'll always be standing tall."

And with that, Sean gave me a delicious smooch on the lips. I was literally in heaven, even if it was for only for a moment.

•

"Dr. Pennington, this was all unfamiliar territory to Sean and the pressure was really getting to him. His persona was that of a strong and together person, but inside, he was a huge ball of stress. I kept hoping that he would not have a nervous breakdown."

"I'm so amazed hearing this, mainly because of your strength throughout it all. Our session has finished, so we will resume next week. See you next Wednesday."

I loved getting everything out of my system and sharing it all with Dr. Pennington. It was shocking to me that I could speak so freely to her, considering how new our doctor-patient relationship was. I couldn't wait for the next appointment to come!

CHAPTER 43

The case continued. Most of the days and weeks flew by, but some of them went by so slowly that I felt suffocated by each passing minute. The procedure of "hurry up and wait" unsettled me. I was having trouble keeping up with all that was going on. On the other hand, Sean was unable to focus

on anything other than this case. Candace always needed another piece of paper signed, yet we were no further along than when we first started. The adoptive parents were not relinquishing any rights, nor were they interested in helping us. The statement issued through their attorney made it clear and final. Candace called us into her office and read the letter she had just received.

LAW OFFICES OF EDWARD P. WORTHINGTON II, ESQ.

22 HOUSTON STREET   Suite 321

New York, NY 10014

Candace Fowler, ESQ.
175 Fifth Ave, Suite 705
New York, NY 10016

Dear Ms. Fowler:

It has come to my attention that your clients, Evie Harris & Sean Graham, have retained you as their attorney. You have

requested a DNA paternity test on their behalf of Baby Boy
Doe, birthed by Evie Harris.

The adoptive procedure is legally binding & final. All
requirements have been met and all paperwork has been signed,
dated and witnessed by all necessary parties.

This is the full and final statement that I am offering to you on
behalf of my clients (names withheld). They do not wish to
acquiesce to your clients' demands now or anytime in the
future. They are exercising their full legal rights under the
closed adoption laws in the State of New York.

At this time, I am putting you on notice, that any further contact
with this office in regards to this matter will be construed as an
obstruction of State Law & harassment. If you disregard this
notice, I will be obligated to inform all parties involved which
may have serious consequences. I deem this matter attended to
and closed from any further obligation.

Sincerely,

Edward P. Worthington, II

Edward P. Worthington, II ESQ.

Sean and I were so distraught after Candace read the letter, that
neither one of us knew what to say. Candace walked out of the
office so we could have a few minutes of privacy.

Words would not come as we sat there drowning in our own sorrows. Our emotions ran high. Neither of us could believe that this legal battle had just started and already seemed to be over. We were so devastated that we weren't even aware that Candace had left the room. When Candace returned, she immediately began to speak.

"I need your full attention. This is not the time to be deflated and we are not defeated. This is just the beginning. There is nothing I like better than a good custody case."

Both Sean and I thought that Candace had lost her mind. We were so dumbfounded that neither of us had time to react before she began to speak again.

"Do you really think that I earned the title of 'The Best Adoption Attorney in New York' because I let a lawyer's letter scare me off? I eat lawyers like him for breakfast, and then for a midmorning snack, I finish off his partners. Ha, ha!"

Sean's facial features changed to a look of pure joy while I thought Candace had a waiting invitation to the looney bin. She continued speaking.

"I expected this outcome. This is exactly the way it begins. Now we're going to get to the meat and potatoes of this case. It is not up to the defendant's attorney and I will continue to petition until we get a yes. I've hired an expert legal team that constantly works with me on adoption and paternity cases. They consist of four top-notch attorneys and their assistants, all who will be working on this full-time. They will be researching every precedent that has ever been recorded and will go over your files and personal comments to me. These attorneys are going to grill both of you over and over again until they feel there is nothing left for you to tell them. Once they are certain that every angle has been covered and each detail has been considered, we will know the best way to proceed. Without question, we will be going to court! It will be a huge battle and will take all that you have within you. Just think of the prize. Your thoughts need only be with that little baby. Leave all the worrying to me."

And then she said the most amazing thing.

"Oh, by the way, my team and I are doing this case pro bono. Consider it an early Christmas present. This, my dears, is going to be a landmark case. Now go home and get some rest!"

My mouth opened up in surprise. Neither Sean nor I believed what we had just heard. We left the office flying high because not only did we have a top-notch attorney, but she was willing to do this case for free. I could not believe our good luck. Sean left Candace's office to pick up his son and I went back to my apartment.

It was the most beautiful of days!

•

"So as you can see Dr. Pennington, even though we knew that there was more to come from Candace, Sean and I were still devastated from seeing the lead attorney's response in black and white."

My session with Dr. Pennington was over, but as usual, I had so much more to say.

"See you next week," Dr. Pennington said with a smile.

•

Sean and I were already two months into it with Candace, and the tension was getting to us. I busied myself by spending time at the library reading about all the ups and downs of raising a child. This continued to give me the confidence that I was lacking for what the future might hold for me.

I also began to take interest in other topics such as Renaissance paintings, especially those by the Old Masters. This subject had always interested me. My evenings were filled learning about Michelangelo, Da Vinci, Rembrandt and so forth. This time period proved to be "the calm before the storm," considering what was to come. Reading these books, but mostly looking at their paintings, helped me immensely. I imagined myself living in that time frame. Maybe I would have fared better then. Who knows?

Early one evening, while stirring the milk in my coffee, I pictured myself sitting in Rembrandt's studio as his model. My gown was green-earth velvet and adorned with pearls. My curled hair was golden, touched by red highlights. Rembrandt took hold of my right hand and placed it gently over my left. He then directed me to rest them in my lap. I watched as he painted me with such voracity and passion. Naturally the phone rang and interrupted my thoughts.

"Hello, Sean."

"Evie, I just got a call from Candace's secretary. She wants to see us tomorrow morning at nine."

"I hope this is not another endless session of the same thing."

"Let's be positive. You knew from the get-go that this was not going to be easy."

"You're right. You know what? I'll meet you there instead of you picking me up. It's time I started to get my life back and not depend on you for everything."

"It's going to work out, you'll see, Evie."

•

I woke up at 6:00 AM the next morning, showered, ate a small breakfast, and got dressed for the appointment with Candace. I wanted to look good, or at least better than I usually did. There was a white and gray sweater hanging in my closet that I hadn't worn in a long time. It was the nicest sweater I owned and surprisingly it wasn't wrinkled. I put on a pair of black slacks and black flats that were starting to show signs of wear. I placed my library books in a canvas bag and left it by the door. Today was going to be a day to be good to myself. After seeing Candace I would return the books, take out some new ones and then go to Bagel Flagel Cafe for a sandwich and a latte.

This was going to be a positive day!

As I arrived at Candace's suite, there were a lot of voices coming from her private office. Sean was already there waiting for me in the alcove. Candace's secretary said that we would be called into her office momentarily. I sat down next to Sean and it was obvious that he was anxious. He gave me a quick smile and continued looking down at the floor. Hopefully, this was not going to be the usual redundant meeting. I stole a few glances at Sean and noticed that his hair was graying and had started to thin out even more. This case was definitely taking a toll on him.

"You may go in now," Candace's secretary said with a smile.

"Thank you," Sean responded as we entered.

There were four attorneys sitting next to Candace with their briefcases at their sides. At least that's who I presumed they were. Candace wasted no time and immediately addressed us.

"Evie, Sean, have a seat. This is our legal team: Emiliano Sanchez, Amber Brighton, Kim Jin, and Simon Bingham."

Each attorney stood up and shook our hands. They looked the part of successful high-class lawyers. The three men were dressed in fashionable suits with power ties. Each also had a gold pin in their lapels and one had a pin of the American flag. Nice touch! The female attorney was also dressed in a smart-looking navy suit sporting a white blouse and a small gold necklace. Mr. Sanchez looked to be in his thirties, while Mr. Bingham was probably in his early fifties. Mr. Jin looked as if he were in high school but was betrayed by a few graying hairs sprouting from his temples. Ms. Brighton was probably somewhere in her sixties. Each one of them was attractive and looked very professional.

Candace continued speaking.

"I called my team in for this meeting. We've already discussed what to brief you on. First of all, the other side thinks that we have hit a roadblock. We have an ace in the hole which we haven't used yet. We needed to see if we could get permission for the DNA test without using it. We were saving this for the court battle which we are destined to have."

I couldn't wait for Candace to come out with what she had to say. The tension was building and I was praying that it wouldn't exacerbate a panic attack. I couldn't even imagine what this was doing to Sean. Candace took a deep breath and continued.

"Unfortunately, the DNA test was denied by the court for the third time."

"Those fucking bastards! Please excuse my French, but don't they understand that this is a human being? This is my son and he needs to be with me!" Sean yelled.

"The court made a decision based on the evidence provided. Now we are going to give them new evidence that they will have to consider. We are all confident that we will be successful, but the courts move slowly so it takes a lot of time," Candace replied.

Sean calmed himself down. He was disappointed and very angry. I was also rattled by this blow to our request. Candace began to discuss the new strategy. She looked directly at me and continued speaking.

"Evie, you have been through a lot of emotional turmoil. Your life has been turned upside down. Every fiber of your being has been touched emotionally, mentally and physically. Your strength and well-being have been challenged on a daily basis. You were powerless over the events that happened in your life that fateful day. Because of it, you acted and reacted to factors that were not in your control. Most important to your case is that the decisions you made while you were so traumatized are not valid. Simply said, you were not in the right frame of mind when you agreed to the adoption. The only thoughts you had were to get rid of anything pertaining to the rape and the rapist. Because of those circumstances, you were willing to give up your baby to make that happen. Am I correct so far?"

I looked at her in disbelief.

"Are you saying that I'm crazy?"

"No. There is quite a difference between insanity and temporary insanity. We have miles of proof that you were seeing a psychologist before that night. Not once were you diagnosed with any form of insanity during that period. You then ended up in the psychiatric hospital because of your inability to cope with the rape. Although the hospital gave you therapy, it failed to meet your needs in this specialized situation. In other words, the hospital did not meet the basic requirements of this case. Did they ever ask you if there was a possibility of there being another father?"

"No, they didn't. I was in such a state of shock that it never even occurred to me that it could have been Sean's. They definitely should have asked me if I was sexually active."

"Exactly! They should have probed more or brought in someone who specializes in these types of cases. Dr. Brown, who initially saw you, is a very good doctor. However, he does not specialize in rape trauma. In other words, the hospital failed you."

"So what happens next?" I asked.

"We need your permission in writing that you will go forward with this information and agree to it. Simply put, we need you to confirm that you weren't in your right mind at the time you signed the adoption papers."

I looked at Sean who seemed to be sizing up the other attorneys. He was paying attention to their body language. He did that in order to get a read on whether or not they were in agreement with Candace's summation of the plan of action.

"Evie, are you clear with what they are asking of you?" Sean questioned.

"I'm clear. I don't like the word "insanity" but if it will help us win the case, why not? I want us to be triumphant, and if this is what it will take, so be it. I probably was temporarily insane at the time anyway. Candace, just tell me what to do."

There seemed to be a silent sigh of relief in the room. I felt it and I'm sure everyone else did as well. At that moment, Sean was assured that I was in it to win it.

The four attorneys opened their briefcases and pulled out folders and tablets. They started to talk strategy and the best way to handle this case. After four hours, the meeting was finished. My plans for the afternoon were going to have to wait until the next day. I was so tired that it would have been easy for me to have fallen asleep in Candace's office.

"Let's go, Evie. I'm taking you home."

"That sounds good to me, Sean!"

•

Our taxi ride back to my apartment was almost too calming. I was totally worn out and devoid of any emotions. I did not have it in me to talk about our meeting at Candace's. Sean seemed to share my thoughts and feelings, even though no words were spoken between us.

When we arrived at my building, I asked Sean to come in. It was a surprise to him, but he accepted the invitation.

"I'm not going to apologize for the mess. Would you like a cup of coffee or tea?"

"Don't worry about anything. Coffee is good if you're in the mood to make it."

"No problem."

I made coffee for both of us and then sat down next to Sean on the couch.

"What do you think the chances are that the court will allow the DNA test now?" I asked him.

"Our chances seem to be very good. Candace is taking out the big guns. Truth be told, if this doesn't work, we're at a dead end. Unless, of course, Candace has something else up her sleeve."

Sean stayed for two hours and we spent most of it in silence. This proved to be quite relaxing. The coffee was having the opposite effect on me, and I became even more tired.

"I have to go to sleep for a little while. You're free to stay if you like."

"Thanks, Evie, but I'm also beat. It's been quite a day. Let me know if you need anything."

"You're the best, but I'm okay. Hopefully, we won't have to wait too long for the response requesting the DNA test. After all, it's the fourth request."

Sean gave me a quick hug and then left. I needed the sleep, but mostly wanted all of this mess over with. Enough of my life had already been stolen from me. I wanted to start fresh, as though none of this horror show had ever taken place. All my bad memories of that night needed to be erased, but I wasn't sure that could ever be accomplished. What was clear though, was that I had to put forth my best effort so that there would be a chance for us to be victorious. I pulled the covers over myself and then went to sleep.

Life was clearly tough. I was the proof!

•

Three months had passed by since my son was placed in foster care. He would stay there until this situation was legally resolved. I developed a nervous stomach from all the anxiety, which made it difficult to eat. Briana was constantly by my side. She gave me hope each time I was ready to throw in the towel. She always reminded me that what was at stake was worth fighting for. What surprised me more than anything else, was that Paul was also supportive. He actually felt some kind of empathy for what I was going through.

Sean had his moments, but we relied on each other for strength. I never thought anyone would depend on me for any kind of support. The reality of life is that you never know what anyone is capable of until they are put to the test.

•

Five months to the day since giving birth, I decided to treat myself to something I hadn't enjoyed in a long time, a glass of wine. Sean had bought me a bottle of Moscato a few days prior, along with a huge chunk of Camembert Cheese. I wasn't in the mood for the cheese, but I was in the mood for the wine. After taking a few sips, Sean called my cell phone. His voice was as jubilant as it could be.

"Evie, the best news in the world has just happened! Candace called and she wants us in her office at 4:00 PM. The court is allowing the DNA test! Can you believe it? If you were here right now, I would twirl you around and we would dance. Evie, our hopes and prayers have been answered! I don't mean to cut the excitement short, but I have to finish up my work for the day. I'll pick you up at 3:10."

"Okay. I'll be ready."

And then he hung up.

Not wanting to be negative stopped me from saying anything further, but I was extremely worried. Once again, that same thought entered my mind … what if the DNA test proved that Sean wasn't the father? How would he react? But there was something else I was concerned about. With all the back and forth meetings at Candace's office and my non-stop discussions with Sean, I began to believe that Sean being the father was in the realm of possibility. How would I react if he wasn't?

We arrived at Candace's office a few minutes before 4:00 PM. Her secretary immediately ushered us into her private office.

"Have a seat, please. Let's get right to it. Both of you know the good news that the DNA test has been approved. The adoptive parents tried their best to fight it, but they lost. However, their identity, where they live, and all other information pertaining to them is still protected by the courts," Candace said.

"I can't believe how lucky we got," remarked Sean.

"We didn't get lucky. This was due to hard work and not giving up, but mostly due to the temporary insanity plea. Also, the courts did not want undue negative publicity surrounding a simple DNA test, which is in the baby's best interests. All this combined with the fact that they do not want group protests, TV footage, etc., is what has made us successful thus far."

"So what happens when we find out that he's my son?" Sean asked.

"I think you need to slow it down. Let's take it one step at a time. There is a letter here and some paperwork for you to sign. This letter gives you the time, date and place where you will be taking the swab test. Make sure you are not late," Candace reminded us.

"I have to admit to something I did just before Evie left the hospital," Sean said.

"If you're going to tell me that you helped Evie walk out of the hospital without being signed out, I already know about it."

"Wow! How did you know that?"

"There is very little that gets by me. That's why you're working with the best."

Nothing like blowing your own horn, I thought. But truth be told, she was the best and I was so glad that she was on our side.

"No, that's not it. There's something else. I wasn't sure if the court would allow the DNA test, so I decided to ensure that we had a sample. I had Evie swab the baby's cheek when there was no one else in the room. Unfortunately, the sample proved to be useless. The lab said it was contaminated. I don't know if the hospital is aware of what I did. What if there were cameras in the room? I'm kind of worried," Sean said nervously.

Candace sighed and then continued to speak.

"I haven't heard a word, and I would have if it was known. Don't worry about it. Are there any other questions?"

"I have one. What happens if Sean is the father?" I asked.

"Then we will work even harder, meaning both of you will have to eat, sleep and drink this case every day of the week. As I had said, this will be a landmark case. There are no guarantees, but I will work it from every possible angle."

It was my belief that Candace would outshine almost any other attorney in her field. I also knew that she would use all the resources possible. However, if this gets to the next level, Candace and her team would have to be able to overturn a contract that was carved in stone. But she was right, one step at a time. We thanked her and left.

"I have to get to my office. My work is piled up to the sky. I'll probably be up all night long. Would you be okay getting a taxi by yourself?" Sean asked me.

"I'm not a child! I'm capable of doing that."

I came off as harsh but that wasn't my intention. I was an adult and didn't want him to think of me as this fragile person who was so dependent on him. Yet truth be told, I was.

"I know you are an adult, and I'm sorry. It's just that there is so much on my mind that I wasn't thinking. I'll email you the address and the particulars of the DNA test. Please remember that we must always show a united front."

"You're right and I'm also sorry. We're both tense and all this stress is getting to me. It's been five months now."

"This is hard on all of us. Please try to relax. I have to go, take care," Sean said as he began to hail a cab.

Sean left and I decided to take a little stroll to clear my head. I had walked about five blocks when I chose to stop at an Italian deli on the corner. I picked up a tin of homemade eggplant parmigiana, a loaf of Italian bread, two bottles of spring water, and a jar of hot peppers. There was enough for two meals if some pasta was added to it. Now dinner wouldn't be an issue for the evening.

I grabbed a cab back to my apartment. Once inside, I placed the food in the fridge and lied down on my bed. I wanted to call Briana but didn't want to interrupt her date night with Paul. I fell asleep almost instantly and awoke at about 3:00 AM. I tossed and turned for a while but could not fall back asleep.

I couldn't figure out what to do with myself, so I began to watch TV. Surfing channels aimlessly was boring and getting on my nerves. I shut the TV off and began to think about the future of this case. Somewhere within me, I hoped that Sean was not the father. It was a terrible thought. However, a positive result for Sean would lead to a nasty, drawn out custody fight. It would probably take years with no guarantee of success. If it got that far and we lost the case, it would drain all that was within me. There was no doubt in my mind that Sean would never give up. I commended him for that, but that type of strength was not within me. Most importantly, I was also the victim.

It was already late in the afternoon and the phone call to Briana needed to be made.

"Hi, Evie!" Briana answered in a jovial voice.

"Hi, Briana, can you talk for a few minutes?"

"Sure. What's up?"

"The court gave us permission to do the DNA test."

"That's fantastic! Why don't you sound more enthusiastic?"

"There's so much more to it. Sean is going to be crushed if the baby isn't his. He's so sure that he's the father."

"Don't put the cart before the horse. Let him take the test and then go from there. Sean is smart. He realizes that it's a possibility, not a given. He's just riding the wave right now. Everything will go in the direction that it's supposed to," Briana assured me.

"I don't know if I can get through this. My life sucks enough."

"Do you trust me?" Briana asked.

"Of course I do. You know that."

"Well, if you trust me then you also have to believe me. Paul and I will support you."

"Is there something else that is upsetting you?"

"Yes. I'm also fearful that if it turns out to be his, he will want to fight for custody. The adoptive parents will also be fighting like mad to win. Then I would be involved in a court battle that might go on forever. There is so much to this."

"You don't think you're up to the task?" Briana asked.

"Exactly!"

"Then you need to be upfront with Sean. If you care about him like you say, then you owe him honesty. He has to know exactly what he is dealing with. I hope you don't blindside him. If you respect him, reveal all your fears. At least then he can make a decision based on all the facts."

"Sean knew I was wishy-washy in the beginning, but now he thinks I'm with him all the way. I can't tell him there are still doubts in my mind. He'll freak out!"

"Think it through carefully. The results of the DNA test will give you direction. You have courage within you. You must search for it within yourself and you will find it. This baby also has a right to know his real father. Paul and I will continue to support you throughout this ordeal no matter how long it takes.

Sean and your psychologist will help get you through it also. And believe it or not, so will your lawyer. Just don't hesitate to tell her how you feel. She will understand. Just trust that you are stronger than you think. You've gone through so much in your young life. You will get through this also."

"Thanks for your support. You just gave me so much confidence."

"When is the test?" Briana asked.

"Next Wednesday at 9:00 AM."

"Okay, everything is starting to come together now. I'm telling you that you have the best support system anyone can ask for. Do you want to come over and have some dinner with us?"

"Thanks, but not today. I'm really tired. Once again, you put me in a better mood."

"Then I'm doing my job as a best friend! Talk to you tomorrow."

There was a lot to think about. Briana had made some good points, but she wasn't living this nightmare.

I was between the proverbial rock and a hard place.

CHAPTER 44

The DNA test had been taken and now it was "hurry up and wait time" once again. Sean was noticeably on edge and I wasn't doing too well myself. The waiting was driving both of us crazy. Sean would call me at least four times a day just to talk about it. The lawyers for the adoptive parents were petitioning to stop the admission of the test results into any court records. Candace continued to give us a blow-by-blow description of all that was going on. I would have preferred to have been left alone until the results were in. Candace said that under normal circumstances, the results could be had in as little as 48 hours, but our case was different. Since there was a court involved, it would likely be closer to four weeks.

At this point, two weeks had passed by and I hung on for Sean's sake.

By some stroke of luck, Sean received a letter from the court three days later. Since he knew it was the paternity results, he called me and then conferenced in Candace.

"This is it! I have the letter with the results," Sean said excitedly.

Neither Candace nor I uttered a word. The tension was high. I didn't realize it, but I was clenching my teeth in anticipation of what those words would reveal. I could hear Sean ripping open the envelope, which sent a shooting pang of fear through me as I expected the worst.

"I'm the father!" Sean screamed at the top of his lungs.

"I knew it! I'm the father! He is my son!"

Sean could not have been happier. I could not have been more surprised.

"That's wonderful news, Sean. Scan and send the letter to me and I will take it from here. We have a case, people!" Candace said happily.

"Isn't it wonderful, Evie? He's our son, our child!"

I could almost see Sean dancing around in his living room waving the letter in his hand.

"It's wonderful, but I do have trepidations."

"What are you afraid of? This is the best news we could have gotten!"

Candace was not interested in hearing about my fears, at least not at this time.

"I'm getting off the phone now. I will call you tomorrow or the next day. We have a lot of work to do," Candace said and then hung up.

"Evie, are you still there?" Sean asked.

"I'm here. I'm very happy for you but we've been through the mill just getting permission to do the DNA test. I can only imagine how tough the road ahead is going to be. I know I've said this before, but I need to say it again. The adoptive parents aren't going to give up without a fight. They've already proven that. Then there's the time frame. This can take years before there is a conclusion. The baby might be one or two years old by then, maybe even older. He will think that the foster parents are his real mother and father. By taking him away from them, it could turn his whole life upside down. I'm just telling the truth as to what the reality might be. It's also possible that we could lose this case."

"You mean I could lose, don't you, Evie? Your heart isn't in this. I need you to see this through with me. If you have all these doubts, then there's no chance we'll win. Don't you want our son to know his real parents? Isn't he deserving of that? What about us? Don't we deserve to know our son? Please, Evie, I'm begging you. Be strong with me. This is our son, ours, a beautiful little boy who was born out of love, not hate. The only reason he's not with us right now is because you were too traumatized at the time to think of the possibilities."

"You're blaming me for giving him away, aren't you?"

"I've never blamed you. You were violated in the most heinous way. You wanted to erase the memory of that day. By giving up the baby, you thought your pain would end. It's not your fault! It was never your fault!"

"I'm so mixed up right now that nothing is making any sense to me."

"Evie, circumstances put us in this position. We can give him a great life and I'm willing to raise him with you in any way you want. I'll send him to the top schools and do whatever is best for him. He already has a brother who will adore him. I need you to be in this with me 100%. I will protect you every step of the way. Please help me to get our son back to where he belongs."

Sean kept on pleading with me and pointing out all of the positive aspects of going forward. It was clear that without me, Sean would probably lose this battle, or maybe the upcoming war. I couldn't believe that my decision could make or break the court case that would ensue. I was in control of something that I didn't want to be in control of. Regardless, it was time for me to come to a resolution and stick to it. My perpetual wavering back and forth must've been so frustrating to Sean. One minute I would assure him that I was fully invested in this fight and the next minute I would express my uncertainty. Needless to say, I still couldn't come up with an answer. Many thoughts were running through my head until Sean said the magic words. At that point, I had no further doubts.

"Do you think this is fair to Charlie? He has a brother whom he will probably never know because the adoptive parents will never allow it. That is definitely clear. How is that fair to either of these boys who are brothers? The stakes are high for everyone, and it's the right thing to do! I'm willing to give up everything. What are you willing to give up, Evie?"

"You know what, Sean, you're absolutely right. With all that's been taken from me, there is still something I can give. These brothers have the right to know each other! No one should be able to take that away from either of them. I'm with you, Sean! Just realize that I'm going to be leaning on you throughout this ordeal. There are going to be a lot of highs and lows. Are you ready for that?"

Sean laughed.

"I'm ready for anything that comes my way!"

CHAPTER 45

I walked into Dr. Pennington's office and continued my saga.

"Hello, Dr. Pennington," I said gingerly.

"Hello, Evie. Have a seat."

"So you now realize how difficult my life had become in those years. I was like a woman who did not know how to swim and kept jumping into the water anyway. If I continued in that direction, eventually I would drown."

"So, what happened after you got the letter denying the DNA test?" asked Dr. Pennington.

"Our attorney had something else up her sleeve, and it worked. I had to admit that I was temporarily insane at the time I signed the adoption papers. By doing that, the court finally agreed to the DNA test. When I arrived at the testing center, I got to see my son for the first time since giving birth to him. Luckily, it turned out that the only people allowed in the room were the social worker who brought in my baby, Sean and myself. It made that day a lot easier for me."

"What was it like to see your son again?"

"It was very emotional for me. I had forgotten that babies grow and couldn't get over how different he looked. Sean was all smiles and wanted to hold him, but the social worker wouldn't allow it. What a bitch! Anyway, they told us that it could take up to four weeks for the results. We got lucky and received them in a little over two weeks. As it turned out, Sean was the father and the court battle began. Our attorney didn't waste any time using all the ammunition at her disposal. She was so driven that it seemed as though she was working 24 hours a day. At first, Sean and I were kept completely out of the loop. We would meet often at Candace's office to sign all kinds of paperwork and take part in conference calls, but that was about it. A month later, all hell broke loose. Candace made it very clear to Sean and I that 'anything goes,' and she meant anything. Our son was almost seven months old at the time."

"Wow, he was already seven months old!"

"Yes, and I couldn't believe it myself. Of course, the sooner he was out of the system, the better it would be for him. Our child needed and deserved to be with us. It meant being with Sean full-time and me part-time. I convinced myself that the means would justify the ends, and went full steam ahead with the custody battle."

"So you found that you did indeed have it in you to forge ahead," Dr. Pennington said.

"I found courage that I could not explain. It was almost as though someone or something took over my brain. I did not need to think as to the 'how and why.' It all just happened in a blur."

"So then what happened, Evie?"

"Candace pulled out another ace in the hole. She leaked what was going on to the newspapers, TV stations, radio stations, etc. There were constant news flashes, panel debates on morning talk shows, etc. It was hard to keep track. Everyone weighed in including women's rights groups and even a couple of celebrities got into it. The pressure was really mounting. I wasn't able to eat properly and had lost a lot of weight. Sean, on the other hand, was eating himself into oblivion."

"Go on with your story, Evie."

"We were so blessed with our legal team, but the adoptive parents also had great representation. They were fighting just as dirty to get public sympathy in the event the verdict didn't go their way. Luckily, our identities were kept private, but that didn't last forever."

"Our time is up. I look forward to seeing you next week, Evie."

Again, I left her office both drained and relieved. Hopefully, my story would be completed by the next session. Even though I had shared all this with Dr. Hunter, I had to reopen this chapter of my life with Dr. Pennington.

•

A few days after getting the DNA results, Sean called with a solemn tone to his voice, which was very unlike him. He said that he was coming to pick me up because Candace needed to see us ASAP. I knew something was up with Sean but chose not to question him at that moment.

He arrived at my apartment building and called me to come downstairs. When I walked out to meet him, he nodded. It was the first time he greeted me without a smile on his face.

"Hi, Sean. How are you?"

"To be truthful, things could be better. Evie, all this pressure has been getting to me and it's been affecting my moods. Please don't take it personally if I don't seem to be myself. I just started taking anti-depressants. Once they kick in, I won't feel so down."

"I knew something was different when you called. I'm glad that you feel comfortable enough to share this with me."

"Don't worry, Evie."

"I'm not worried. You're always going to be my rock."

Sean, who I thought was Herculean, proved me wrong. He was a human being just like everyone else.

We arrived at her office and were immediately told to go into the conference room. Candace was sitting there with her team of lawyers and her paralegal. It was apparent that this was going to be very intense.

"Evie, Sean, you're familiar with everyone here so let's get started. The gloves are off! We are going to war and we will be the victors! We are one team fighting the system and the adoptive parents. It seems they think that they have the law on their side. What they and their attorneys don't realize is that so do we. A gag order was issued and therefore we cannot say anything more to the media or otherwise. There is no doubt that the two of you will be in for the fight of your lives, but the end result will be that you will have your son. My colleagues are going to prep each of you separately and then together. We need you both to be strong and in a positive state of mind. Are there any questions?"

"I can ask a million questions, but all I want is for this to go as fast as possible. Whatever you need from me, you'll have it or get it immediately," Sean stated unequivocally.

Then everyone looked at me and waited for my response.

"If I'm going to be truthful, I have to say that I'm still scared. So many things can go wrong, but I am with Sean one hundred percent."

"There is one question that is of the utmost importance, Evie. Did you ever get specialized counseling on the topic of abortion from anyone at Heaton Psych Hospital?"

"It was mentioned to me by Dr. Brown, but it never happened."

"That's all I need to know. Okay, then let's begin," Candace replied.

Candace, Amber, Emiliano, and the paralegal remained in the conference room with me. Sean, Kim, and Simon went into another room. I needed to get through this mentally intact.

After being prepped for two hours, I joined Sean in the large conference room. There was no way I could absorb any more information that day. I was about to tell that to Candace when she began to speak.

"Today we played make-believe court, but it wasn't make-believe, we were dealing with reality. We want both of you to be well prepared when you testify in open court. You can't stumble or think about how to answer the questions that will be thrown at you. The other attorneys will be merciless. They will try to make the both of you look incompetent, irresponsible, and so forth. And that is why we separated you. We wanted to see how tough you can be and how quickly you can think on your feet."

"I'm almost afraid of the answers," Sean said nervously.

"No need to be afraid. I knew that you would be tough, Sean. But Evie, you surprised me. You held your own. What's needed now is some refinement and polishing."

"I desperately need a break," I said pleadingly.

"Not a problem, Evie. But you must understand, you will be on the witness stand possibly as soon as next week and you are going to have to shine."

"This whole thing is so unfair! I never asked to get raped and now I'm in a position where I have to go through a court battle for my own child!" I yelled out.

"Nothing in life is fair, so it's up to you to turn the wheels of justice in your favor, and you can do it. Always keep your eye on the prize. What you and Sean have to gain is worth it," Candace responded.

I glanced at Sean. He looked very self-assured and was beaming. I had to give credit where credit was due. If it wasn't for Sean's persistence, we would never have known that this was his son.

And yes, this was my son too!

"I'm in this all the way. Nothing and no one will stop us from getting our son back where he belongs," I said with clarity.

Before I could fully stand up to leave, Sean came over and hugged me. I didn't know where all his strength came from. Suddenly, I felt as though I could conquer the world. It had been a long time since I had felt in control of my life. It was at that moment that I began to feel the true love for my son that had been missing in me. I was going to fight for him with all my being! And all my being was exactly what I would need for the next unexpected hurdle to come my way …

•

Two weeks later, Candace called me.

"Hi, Evie, how are you feeling?" she asked.

"I'm okay. I think I know what this call is about."

"Good! The court is ready for all witnesses. It will be you, Sean and the adoptive parents. There will also be psychiatrists, psychologists, and varied medical doctors. In your case, there will also be testimony from some of the staff at Heaton Psychiatric Hospital. They will be focusing on your state of mind at the time you were there. The other side, as I had told you previously, will have all their witnesses to refute the testimony that our witnesses will give."

"Does Sean know yet?"

"Yes, I spoke to him just before calling you. He's very excited to get the testimony started."

"Candace, I'm not scared anymore, but I'm anxious about seeing the adoptive parents, at least for the first time."

"They'll look at you and you will look at them, and then it will not matter. You'll get used to it very quickly. Don't be anxious and leave all the stress to me and my team. If you and Sean have reason to worry, I'll let you know. Until that time, just think good thoughts."

"You're right, Candace. I can't wait for this to be over!"

"Then we're good! Court convenes at 10:00 AM Monday morning. I'd like you and Sean there at 8:30 AM. Dress in professional attire. Everyone will look at what you're wearing because this is a high-profile case. Pay attention to your shoes and your pocketbook as well."

"I can't afford a new wardrobe. I just don't have the money."

"I'll see what I can do, but in the meantime, ask Sean to help you out. I'm sure he'll do it."

"I don't want to ask him. It's too embarrassing for me."

"If you think this is hard, then the other side will annihilate you on the witness stand. Sean is not paying any legal fees, and without you, he has less than a 1% chance of winning. Call him as soon as we hang up! Are we on the same page?"

"Yes, we are!"

"Good! Then I'll see you Monday morning. Eat a high protein breakfast, you'll need the energy!"

After hanging up the phone with Candace, I started to think about the adoptive parents. Are they good people? If they win, will they love my son unconditionally? What if they're selfish, and only want my son so that he will be there for them when they're older? On the positive side, if they didn't already have some feelings toward him, they wouldn't be fighting so hard. Well, I'm going to fight hard too!

And so I made my phone call to Sean.

"Hey, Evie."

"Hi, Sean. I feel a little silly telling you this, but Candace called me and told me to dress nicely for court. I don't really have ..."

"Don't say another word. Go shopping this afternoon and get a few outfits and whatever else you need. It's on me."

"But it will be a lot of money. I don't know how long this case will last."

"Go out and buy whatever you need for yourself. I'll meet up with you and give you my credit card. Just be in the best frame of mind for Monday. Don't worry about the money. And that's an order!"

All the wonderful values Sean possessed from when we first met were still there. I loved him even more at that moment.

•

Let the games begin!

Monday morning came, and it was the first day of court. I awoke at 6:00 AM excited to get the day started. I called Sean to assure him again that I was going into this full steam ahead. He seemed somewhat reserved, and I attributed it to his nerves.

"Sean, now that the gag order has been lifted, Candace said that there will be cameras and reporters all over the place. It's going to be tricky to try and dodge them."

"We're going to have to get used to it. This case has been in the news for such a long time," Sean responded.

"But now they're going to see our faces and the adoptive parents' faces. That makes a big difference to reporters. They're going to be all over us using every media outlet possible."

"That's part of the package," Sean answered.

"We're also going to know who the adoptive parents are. Now they will be real to us."

"The same is true for them. Once they see us, we become real to them. I don't think that's going to sway them in any way. But I'm not worried because we're going to win. Just remember, when the reporters shove their microphones in your face, just smile and say 'no comment.' Then quickly walk into the courtroom as Candace instructed us," Sean emphasized.

"I'm so ready Sean! We're going to bring our son home where he belongs!"

I showered and got dressed in a new navy suit with a cream-colored blouse underneath. The bottom of the skirt and the edge of the cuffs were embroidered with a thin thread of gold. I allowed myself the liberty of a small butterfly pin encrusted with brightly colored stones for the lapel. I knew Sean wouldn't mind the splurge. I took a corn muffin out of the fridge, spread some cream cheese on it and ate it with a cup of strong coffee.

The last thing I wanted was to feel tired and give the other side a leg up on this case.

It was 7:15 AM and I was completely ready. I double checked to make sure that my ID, house keys and wallet were in my purse. It was time to greet this day head on. I was able to get a cab almost immediately and arrived at the courthouse early. The reporters were already there. It always amazed me how the media knew who you were prior to ever having seen you.

I had agreed to meet Sean at the top of the courthouse steps. He was standing there surrounded by two reporters trying to get their questions answered. As I approached the first step, three reporters ran over to me with their camera crew. They barraged me with so many questions that I actually couldn't hear them. I played my role well by smiling and continuously saying "no comment," until I reached the top of the steps.

Sean grabbed my arm and whisked me inside. Both of us saw Candace at the same time and we ran over to her. She immediately ushered us into an empty room. I was so happy that we were able to have some peace and quiet before going into the courtroom.

"Sean, Evie, I know we have been over this ad nauseam, but it doesn't hurt to do it again."

Candace emphasized a few key points that we had already discussed a few days ago in her office. She did not stop repeating herself, and at some point during her lecture, I tuned out. She was just doing her job, but I already knew my role and I was ready.

At 9:30 AM Candace's team arrived. Twenty minutes later, it was time to enter the courtroom. Sean took my hand and smiled. I smiled back and we started to walk in with Candace and the team. It felt as though we were famous movie stars with an entourage. If only that was the case. There were a bunch of people gathered about from the opposing team. It wasn't as bothersome as I expected it to be. As I got closer to where Sean and I were to sit, I looked over to my left.

"Oh, My G-D!!!" I screamed in the loudest voice possible as I held my hands up to my face in shock.

"It's Raquel! That's my sister! She's the adoptive mother? Is this a joke? I can't believe this! This can't be happening!"

My sister didn't even wince. I began to cry and shake uncontrollably. Immediately, Candace and Sean grabbed my arms and escorted me from the courtroom into a private room.

"How could it be my sister? Is this really happening? I don't know what's going on! Sean, help me, please help me!" I begged.

I was hysterical. Sean assured me that everything was going to be alright. Candace was at a loss for words, which was probably a first for her. Amber Brighton, one of the team members, came into the room. She stated that she had requested a 15 minute recess that had been granted. She then left the room.

"What are we going to do? Of all the possible people in the world, it had to be my sister. This is a nightmare! It can't be real! We haven't spoken in years and she hates me so much!"

"I understand that it's a big shock, but this is not the time to be weak. Do you want your sister to win or do you want to be the victor? That's the only question that you need to answer," Candace said.

Sean then put his hands on my shoulders and looked directly into my eyes.

"You can let her win and give up right now, or you can fight and bring our son home. Which one do you prefer?"

I looked up at him and remembered all that my sister had taken from me in the past. I could not and would not let her have my son too. If she got to keep my child, that would be the ultimate insult, the last straw!

"I'm ready to go back into the courtroom. I'm ready to face that bitch!"

I took the tissues that Candace had handed me and wiped my eyes. I stood up straight and took hold of Sean's hand. Together we walked back in stronger than ever. It was finally my day to win, not Raquel's!

Sean and I approached the plaintiff's table where Candace and her team were already seated. We took the only available seats next to her. Candace stared at the defendants' side while simultaneously smiling at them. Nothing like intimidation, I thought.

"Don't let the other side rattle you. If they can do that, they will make you look inept and unfit as a mother. Just stick to the facts and don't say more than you need to. Focus on someone else other than the attorney as you are being questioned. That will help you immensely. Just remember, we're with you all the way to the winner's circle," Candace whispered to me.

I liked what she said. Nevertheless, my curiosity got the better of me and I quickly glanced in their direction. Raquel looked very poised and confident, and so did her husband, who was also my ex-boyfriend. I was hoping that they would show weakness, which would work in our favor, but they looked determined and ready for anything that would come their way. But I was also strong and was going to demonstrate that in the courtroom. I turned to face Sean and gave him my best smile. He returned the favor and blew me a kiss.

The bailiff then called everyone to order and spoke in a loud and clear voice.

"All rise, Judge Benton Broward presiding."

The judge entered the courtroom and took his seat on the bench. The bailiff handed him three large files.

"Thank you, Gerard," the judge said as he began perusing the paperwork.

The bailiff took his position and stood by the side of the bench.

"This is the continuing case of Harris and Graham vs. Balfour in the matter of Baby Boy Doe," the bailiff said.

"We have heard the opening statements from both sides of this case. I see that there are a number of witnesses the plaintiffs' counsel would like to call to the stand. Likewise, I see the same from the defendants' counsel," the judge said.

"Ms. Fowler, you may begin by calling your first witness," Judge Benton Broward continued.

"I call Dr. Elias Brown to the stand."

Dr. Brown stood up and went over to the witness stand where he was sworn in.

"You may be seated," the bailiff said.

"Are you familiar with a woman by the name of Evie?" Candace asked.

"I am," Dr. Brown replied.

"How do you know her?"

"She was a patient of mine at Heaton Psychiatric Hospital."

"What kind of a doctor are you and what are your credentials?"

"I'm a psychologist. I completed my undergraduate studies in my native country of Trinidad. I then continued my education in the United States, where I earned a doctorate in psychology."

"What did you treat Evie Harris for?"

"She was very distraught and frightened when she came to Heaton Psychiatric Hospital."

"Objection, the witness has not answered the question but is trying to gain sympathy for the plaintiff," said Joshua Samuelson, one of the attorneys for the defendants.

"Your Honor, the witness is a board-certified psychologist who is an expert in his field. It is essential that he testify as to the state of mind of the plaintiff at the time of treatment," Candace said.

"Overruled. Please continue, Ms. Fowler," the judge said.

"Go on, Dr. Brown," Candace urged.

"Evie Harris had just gone through one of the most vile and horrific things that could happen to any woman. She had been raped and severely beaten. Her entire being was in acute trauma."

"Did you feel that she could be treated and eventually go back into society as a functional person?" Candace asked.

"At first I wasn't completely sure that this would be the case. But as time passed, Evie Harris began to function on a level conducive with the necessary progress for a person healing from such mental and physical trauma."

"Would you say that you felt Evie Harris would make a full recovery?"

At this point, the lead attorney for my sister stood up.

"Objection, Counsel is leading the witness," Daniel Mackney said.

"Your Honor, Dr. Brown has over 25 years of experience in psychology. His testimony is based on fact and not conjecture. He has no personal stake in this," Candace stated firmly.

"Overruled, I'll allow it," Judge Broward said.

Raquel's attorney sat down and whispered something into her ear. Raquel did not move a muscle, so I wasn't able to discern any information.

Dr. Brown continued speaking.

"After some time, Miss Harris began to communicate with the staff and started to interact positively with other patients. She also spent many hours in the solarium with no incidents."

Candace continued her questioning.

"During her stay at Heaton Psychiatric Hospital, Evie Harris chose to give up her unborn child for adoption. In your expert opinion, Dr. Brown, did you feel that Evie Harris was competent to make important life changing decisions at that time?"

"I can say with certainty that Evie Harris was not mentally capable of making a rational decision at the time she signed the papers to have her unborn child placed for adoption."

"Thank you, Dr. Brown. No more questions, Your Honor," Candace said while looking very pleased with herself.

She walked back to the plaintiff's table and sat down. Then she picked up a pen and began to write down some notes.

"Redirect, Mr. Mackney?" the judge asked.

Mr. Mackney stood up and walked over to the witness stand. He smiled at Dr. Brown, trying to appear friendly and low-key. It's a great trap attorneys use to confuse and gain trust from the witness of the opposing team.

"Dr. Brown, you specialize in psychology and you have many years of experience in that field. Isn't that correct?"

"Yes it is!"

"Isn't it true that you only saw Evie Harris twice a week and not every day as you would have us believe?"

"I saw her as much as necessary to treat her condition."

"Isn't it also true that you told Evie Harris that she did not need to make an immediate decision and could think about it?"

"Well, yes I did, but that was regarding her wanting an abortion. I was not referring to the adoption because ..."

Mr. Mackney did not allow Dr. Brown to finish answering the question.

"And isn't it also true that Evie Harris was not stable before the rape?"

Dr. Brown did not immediately respond to that question. He looked uncomfortable in the witness seat and began to fold and unfold his arms. He did not like the line of questioning from the defendants' counsel. He also did not appreciate being made to look as though he was not being truthful.

"Dr. Brown! You have not answered the question!" Mr. Mackney said in a louder tone.

"And I'm not going to answer your question! The first time I saw Evie Harris was in the emergency room at Metropolitan Hospital. At that point, I barely treated her since she was just raped and traumatized. Therefore, I was not fully familiar with her or her situation before she entered Heaton Psychiatric Hospital!"

"Sit down, Dr. Brown. You must gain control of yourself," the judge said.

"I'm sorry, Your Honor. I didn't realize that I had stood up."

"No more questions, Your Honor," Mr. Mackney said.

Mr. Mackney felt he made his point by showing that Dr. Brown was not a credible witness. Candace was fuming, even though she would have done exactly the same if she were representing the defendants. Mr. Mackney then called up four more witnesses, of which three were psychologists.

When it was Candace's turn again, she called up two additional psychologists. One was an expert in general psychology and the other two worked solely with survivors of rape. Between the questioning and cross-examination, my mind went blank and I tuned the entire thing out.

"It's almost 12:30 PM. We'll break for lunch until 2:00 PM," the judge stated.

"All rise," said the bailiff.

Judge Broward stood up and left the courtroom.

I was so confused and wasn't sure if we were winning or losing. All I knew was that Candace motioned for our team to leave the courtroom.

"Let's go to the coffee shop around the corner. We'll get a table in the back and talk about some points I want to make," Candace offered.

We followed her out of the courtroom and walked in silence to the coffee shop.

"Is there a table in the back that can accommodate us?" Candace asked the host.

"We'll need to push two tables together and add some chairs, but it will be no problem," he answered as he motioned for us to go forward.

We sat down and before I had a chance to remove my jacket, Candace began to speak.

"Dr. Brown held his own, even though he lost a little self-control considering all the pressure he was under. He stood up for himself and in my opinion, he made our case look stronger. However, I don't want any of us patting ourselves on the back just yet. We still have a long way to go. As both of you saw today, the opposing counsel is not a pushover. He made some good points with the witnesses he called to rebut the testimony of our witnesses. However, none of this matters because the key here is the two of you."

"What the hell?" Simon Bingham said.

A mass of reporters and photographers swarmed into the café. They were at our table snapping pictures and shouting out questions at the same time. Sean stood up and began to speak.

"Who the hell do you think you are? This is a private meeting and you need to leave or I'm calling the police!" Sean screamed.

Sean's face reddened and his voice sounded angrier with every new word he uttered.

"Get out of here! Leave us alone!" he continued to yell out.

Finally, the owner came over and rushed them away.

"I'm so sorry. I don't know where they came from. Please order your meals and dessert is on the house."

The proprietor of the café seemed sincere and so we looked at Candace for instructions. She had also stood up and then slowly sat down. Even she was a bit shaken up from the reporters.

"Anyone have a problem with a roast beef sandwich and fries?" Candace asked.

We all shook our heads and the order was placed. I asked for coffee but would have loved a glass of wine to calm me down. A couple of minutes went by and Candace resumed speaking.

"How are you feeling, Evie?"

"I'm okay."

"Do you feel strong and confident in the event you are put on the witness stand this afternoon?"

"Oh, today? I didn't think it would be for a while."

"It probably won't be this afternoon because of time restrictions. Regardless, you need to be mentally ready and fully alert at every moment. We only get one shot at this."

"I'm ready! Should I be concerned with the questions my sister's attorney is going to ask me?"

"Why is that?" Candace asked.

A waiter brought over our sandwiches along with a pitcher of water and a carafe of coffee. The timing couldn't have been better. If I made a fool of myself on the stand, my sister would have one more piece of me to stomp on. I had to remind myself that this wasn't a contest. This was about my son who she was trying to take away from me. That thought angered me, which in turn infused me with more energy and confidence.

"Forget what I just asked. I am prepared for anything that gets thrown at me."

Candace smiled, and so did Sean and the rest of the team. I was fully ready that day and would be the next day and every day thereafter!

Court resumed promptly at 2:00 PM. Raquel glared at me, but it didn't have any effect. She did that to agitate me so I wouldn't be at my best when it was my time to testify.

Since Raquel and I had no relationship, there wasn't any way for me to have known that she wanted to adopt a child. In a way, I felt sorry for her. Knowing her, she probably felt that I didn't deserve a child since she couldn't have one herself. The time had come to stop feeling sorry for my sister. Raquel, you're not getting my sympathy, but I still wish you well, I thought to myself.

The judge gave Candace permission to call her next witness. She called on Tanya Edison. Tanya was sworn in by the bailiff and took her seat on the stand. She looked in my direction with a slight smile. There was no doubt that she was in my corner.

"Miss Edison, what is your position at Heaton Psychiatric Hospital?" Candace asked.

"I work as an aide to the patients."

"Did you work with Evie Harris?"

"Yes. She was one of my better patients."

"What do you mean by that?" Candace asked.

"Evie was personable. It's not so easy to get patients to open up to the aides about their problems. We were able to have in-depth conversations and many times I felt as though Evie did not belong in a psychiatric hospital."

"Would you say that she was a model patient?"

"Objection! Counsel is leading the witness," Daniel Mackney said.

"Sustained," said the judge.

"I'll withdraw the question. I have no more questions for this witness," Candace concluded.

It was obvious by her body language that Tanya was ready to leave the witness stand. I wished that I could have made that happen for her.

"Mr. Mackney, redirect," the judge stated.

"Miss Edison, how long have you worked at Heaton Psychiatric Hospital?"

"It's been almost six years now."

"In all that time, have you received any degrees in counseling?"

"No, I haven't."

"Yet, you proceeded to counsel Evie Harris and make a judgment call as to her state of mental health."

"No, that's not true! I talked to her as I do to any other patient. It's just that …"

Mr. Mackney abruptly cut off her testimony.

"I have no further questions for this witness!"

"You may be excused," the judge said.

Raquel's attorney might have succeeded in upsetting Tanya, but she stood up for herself and told the truth.

☐

Days turned into weeks, as witnesses from both sides came and went. Sean was finally called up to testify.

"Your Honor, I would like to call Sean Graham to the stand," Candace said.

Sean took the oath to tell the truth and sat down on the witness stand. I became very anxious and felt as though my heart was beating out of my chest. I needed to gain control of myself immediately otherwise this whole case would be blown. I forced myself to look over to where Raquel was sitting. I knew that I would gain strength by seeing the hate she had for me on her face. It would fuel my tenacity and there would be nothing to stop me from moving forward. Raquel realized that I was looking at her, so she turned her face toward me and began to sneer. I hoped her face would freeze in that position, but I wasn't that lucky.

"Mr. Graham, do you have any qualms about co-parenting with Evie Harris?" Candace asked.

"Objection! The decision of the court has not been given yet," Daniel Mackey said.

"Granted! I'm warning you, Ms. Fowler. Stick to the facts," the judge said.

"Yes, Your Honor. I'll rephrase the question. Do you have a good relationship with Evie Harris?"

"Yes I do."

"Do you feel she is a good person?"

"Yes I do."

"Has she shown you that she is caring?"

"Yes, in many ways."

"Can you describe those ways?"

"Evie is generous with her time and always offers to help me with whatever I need. She's honest, warm, sweet and caring."

"Do you feel that Evie Harris is a responsible person?"

"Objection! The witness is not an expert to determine that," Mr. Mackney said emphatically.

"Overruled! I'll allow the testimony. You may answer the question," the judge said.

"She is a smart and savvy woman who, before she was raped, was holding down a good job, paying all of her bills by herself and never asked me for money. That sounds responsible to me."

"I have no more questions," Candace said.

"Redirect, Mr. Mackney," Judge Broward said.

Daniel Mackney stood up and walked over to Sean.

"Mr. Graham, do you presently have any children?"

"Yes I do. I have a son named Charlie."

"Isn't it true that you do not have custody of your son because you are an unfit parent?"

A loud spontaneous uproar broke out in the courtroom. This was the exact line of questioning Candace told us to expect from the opposing attorney.

"Order in the court," the judge shouted as he pounded his gavel several times.

"Mr. Graham, you will answer the question," the judge ordered.

It was obvious that Sean was not surprised by that question. He was fully composed and responded in a clear and steady voice.

"I am a very fit parent! I see my son twice a week and every other weekend. I love him and he loves me. I think that defines a fit parent."

"What do you do to support yourself and your son?"

"I'm an energy consultant specializing in corporate cost management programs. I also work part-time for a sports magazine."

"In other words, you do not have a steady income that you can count on."

"As an energy consultant, I am in constant demand and have an excellent reputation in my field. At this point, I can be as busy as I want to be."

"Isn't it true that by taking care of another child, you will not be able to offer him the same extras that you afford your present child?"

"Based on my present position, I could afford ten children with no impact on my income. And that does not include my savings or investments."

"No more questions, Your Honor," Mr. Mackney said.

I didn't expect anything less from Sean, other than for him to shine and be in full control. However, I began to worry as to what this attorney was going to do to me.

Candace was pleasantly surprised at the error Raquel's attorney had made. By trying to negate Sean's financial situation, Mr. Mackney enhanced it without meaning to do so. He gave Sean the opportunity to bring to light his financial security.

When it was my turn to testify, Candace had to show that I was not only capable of raising a child, but that I fully deserved my son to be with me. In this case, I was the weak link.

"Your Honor, I call my last witness to the stand, Evie Harris."

As I walked up to be sworn in, I could feel Raquel's eyes burning into my back. I reminded myself that it was my son's future that was important at that moment and nothing else. My words and my behavior on the stand would count heavily in the judge's decision, so I took a deep breath and hoped for the best. I was then sworn in and sat down on the witness chair.

"What is your name?" Candace asked.

"It's Evie Harris."

"Why are you here, Ms. Harris?"

I thought that was a strange question but answered it anyway.

"I'm here to bring my son home where he belongs."

"I know that this is very hard for you, but can you bring us back to the day of the rape? How did your day start?"

"I was at work. It was like any other day, parts of it were busy, and parts were not."

"Did you have anything special planned after work?"

"Yes, I was going to meet up with Sean, my baby's father."

Candace kept leading me gently into retelling the events of the rape. Her questions became more intense as she continued to speak. I was okay with that and felt comfortable answering them. Then she did something we did not discuss. She began to ask me questions about my past relationships with men. It made me extremely uncomfortable and very angry because it brought my mind back to Ben. I had not thought about him in a long time. He was the last person I wanted to think about, especially at that crucial moment. I was flustered at first and then caught on. She was preparing me for the way Raquel's attorney was going to grill me. Yay Candace!

"No further questions, Your Honor."

"Mr. Mackney, redirect?" asked the judge.

"Yes, thank you, Your Honor."

Raquel's attorney stepped up to the witness stand, looked directly at me and did not speak for at least 10 seconds. Normally, that amount of time would not even be noticeable, but in this situation, it seemed like forever. I knew he did that to unnerve me. While it made me feel uncomfortable, it didn't throw me off-kilter.

"How are you feeling today, Miss Harris?" he asked.

I didn't hesitate for a second, because I knew exactly why Mr. Mackney chose this as his first question. He was leading toward my mental state. It surprised me that I figured it out so quickly.

"I feel good."

"Are you currently employed?"

"No."

So this is the line of questioning you are going to use with me, "Mr. Big Shot Attorney," I thought to myself. Somehow it began to invigorate me and strengthened my resolve to be strong while testifying. I remembered what Candace and her team had drilled into my head, "Answer the questions and don't give anything more than that." It was a great strategy because it kept me more balanced and less emotional.

"How do you support yourself?"

"At this time, I am on state assistance."

"Are you currently getting any psychological help?"

"Yes."

"Please expand your answer to that question for the court."

"I see my psychologist once a week."

"Are you presently on medication prescribed by a psychiatrist?"

"Yes."

"Are you able to function in a normal manner without these pills?"

Mr. Mackney increased the pace of his interrogation. As I barely finished the answer to one question, the next one began. He was trying to confuse me and make me appear to be unstable, destitute and incapable of taking care of myself.

"Objection! The witness is not an expert in pharmacology or psychiatry," Candace said.

"Overruled! The witness will answer the question," Judge Broward responded.

At this point, I became very upset with the way I was being interrogated. My primary objective was self-control, which was essential in this case. That was more important than the answers to these questions. If I lost my temper, Mr. Mackney would be able to show the court that I had no self-control. He would use that to persuade the judge that I was not competent to take care of a child, no less an infant.

I sat up straight and focused on Sean. He was going to be my rock.

"Are you able to function in a normal manner without these pills?" Mr. Mackney repeated.

"I don't know."

"Were you able to function in a normal manner before you were put on these pills?"

"Yes, I was. I was put on these pills after I was raped, not before."

I didn't realize that my demeanor had changed. I responded with more confidence, which was clear to Mr. Mackney. He probably did not like my answer.

"Why do you take pills?"

"I don't take pills. I take only one pill, once a day. It's for anxiety to keep the edge off."

"How large is your apartment?"

"I don't know."

"How many bedrooms do you have?"

"I currently live in a studio."

"How many bathrooms are there?"

"One."

"Is there a backyard?"

"Objection! Counsel is badgering the witness," Candace stood up and yelled out.

"Sustained," the judge said.

"Isn't it true that you can barely take care of yourself? How can you possibly raise a child?"

Unfortunately, with these last two questions, he was able to get the better of me.

"This is my son and he belongs with me!" I screamed at the top of my lungs.

"Are you always this out of control?"

Tears began to stream down my face. I couldn't stop them from coming. He had definitely pushed the right buttons because I reacted exactly the way he wanted me to.

"Objection! Counsel is continuing to badger the witness," Candace thankfully interrupted.

"Sustained," the judge replied.

"I am not out of control," I said in a much lower tone.

Raquel's attorney didn't hesitate and continued his questioning.

"Doesn't it stand to reason that you do not have the funds or the capability to raise and nurture a child? And don't you agree that the adoptive parents can give this child everything you cannot?" he said in a very self-assured manner.

"I don't ..."

He interrupted me before I could finish my sentence and continued to speak.

"And isn't it also true that you have been very jealous of your sister's good fortune in life? Therefore, when you found out that she was the adoptive parent, you were even more determined to try to keep the baby."

"I was not ..."

"Objection, Your Honor. He's still continuing to badger the witness," Candace stated.

"No more questions, Your Honor," Mr. Mackney quickly said and went back to his seat.

He did not let me finish my last few sentences. I sat there flabbergasted. Did I just cause this case to be lost?

"Ms. Fowler, redirect?"

"Yes, Your Honor."

Candace stood up and walked towards the middle of the courtroom floor. She quickly gazed at the judge and then stopped just before the witness stand.

"Miss Harris, you signed an agreement to give your baby up for adoption when you were at Heaton Psychiatric Hospital, correct?"

"Yes."

"Did you have a traumatic situation happen to you prior to signing this agreement?"

"Yes."

"Are you jealous of your sister?"

What! I couldn't believe she just asked me that question.

"I was never jealous of her. All I ever wanted was her love and approval."

"Did you ever do anything to harm her physically or otherwise?"

"No, never!"

"Can you tell me something about your relationship with your sister?"

"I'm the older sister, but it was Raquel who seemed to make the decisions. It was kind of like everything worked in reverse. I was always trying to please her and get her to like me, but she always turned me away."

"What about later in life, when you were in your late teens, early twenties."

"I tried several times to forge a relationship with her but she didn't want any part of me. I could never understand why. And here we are in this courtroom."

"What do you think of her now?"

"I still love my sister but don't like or respect her anymore. I still wish we could have a relationship, but I know that's not what she wants. The only thing I'm sure of is that she wants my child."

"Do you have the means to raise a child?"

"No, I don't."

"Then how do you expect to raise your son?"

"I have everything that my child will need: unconditional love and unlimited quality time to spend with him. I will take him to the library, museums and other places to make his mind grow. I also have the patience that is needed to raise a child. A very horrible thing happened to me, but that has made me stronger."

"What about financially, Miss Harris?"

"I'm not alone since Sean, his biological father, will be with me in every way possible way. He has a great job and savings. Besides being financially stable, Sean is kind, sensitive, caring and very supportive. Together, we will give our child everything he needs. We're the perfect package!"

"What about your mental health needs?"

"I am one of many people with some sort of mental health issue. I am under proper psychological care and my medication is properly monitored by a psychiatrist. I have clarity and am fully functional."

"No more questions."

"You may be excused," the judge said to me.

I was so glad to leave the witness stand. I returned to my seat at the table and placed my hand on top of Sean's.

"Do you have any other witnesses to call to the stand, Mr. Mackney?" Judge Broward asked.

"Yes. I call Raquel Balfour."

Raquel stood up and quickly took her seat on the stand. She looked well put together in her very expensive suit. Raquel exuded confidence, which didn't make me happy at all.

"Please state your name," Mr. Mackney said to Raquel.

"Raquel Balfour," she answered.

"You are in a precarious situation. Your sister is the biological mother of the baby that you and your husband adopted. Now there has been a change of mind on your sister's part. How do you feel about that?"

"My sister has always been jealous of me. Our relationship, or should I say lack thereof, was distant at best. She always wanted our parents' attention and did not deal well if they did not give it to her 100% of the time."

I couldn't believe what I was hearing. Raquel was spewing her usual hate, veiled by her expert way of spinning words in her favor.

"Why did you and your husband want to adopt a child?"

"We tried to have a baby for many years and finally realized it was not going to happen."

"How did you feel when you were told that you could adopt an infant?"

"We were beyond excited! Our dreams had come true. We couldn't wait to prepare the nursery and all that comes with that. We were so thrilled, that we were literally counting the minutes until we could hold our bundle of joy in our hands."

"How did you feel once you found out that the birth mother was petitioning to break the legal contract that she signed?"

"My husband and I were devastated! We loved that child as soon as we found out about him. Even though I haven't had a chance to see him and hold him, I haven't stopped crying every day, thinking that my child might be taken away."

"Objection, Your Honor! No determination has been made as to the final ruling on this case. Therefore, it is premature for the defendant to refer to Baby Boy Doe as her child," Candace stated.

"Overruled! Both parties may refer to Baby Boy Doe as their child until a definite determination has been made," the judge responded.

"Can you please tell the court why you think you and your husband would make more suitable parents than Ms. Harris and Mr. Graham, who want to co-parent?" Mr. Mackney asked.

"The answer is very obvious. My husband and I are just that, 'married.' We do not have any psychological problems to deal with. Our savings are substantial as evidenced by the income on our tax returns that were submitted to the court. We also have continued steady income that can be depended on. Our child would want for nothing. Trent, which is the name we are going to give our son, will be growing up in a loving home. He will have all the advantages of a married couple raising him. We already love him so much!"

Raquel then took out a tissue to wipe away her crocodile tears. I must say she gave the judge a great performance.

"Thank you. No more questions, Your Honor," Mr. Mackney said.

"Ms. Fowler, redirect?" Judge Broward asked.

"Thank you, Your Honor."

Candace stood up and slowly approached Raquel. It was a calculated move on her part in order to agitate her.

"Mrs. Balfour, Isn't it true that you were always jealous of your sister?"

"No, it was the other way around."

"If that's true, then why did you have sexual relations with her boyfriend, who is now your husband, and not even invite her to your wedding?"

That seemed to disconcert Raquel. It was not a question she expected.

"I don't know what you mean. James didn't like her anymore and he always liked me and ..."

"Isn't it also true that you would lie to your parents so that your sister would get in trouble?"

"No, she was always a brat."

"Isn't it also true that you and your husband had separated for three months during your first year of marriage?"

"Well, there were reasons ..."

"And isn't it also true that in the third year of your marriage, you were caught having sex with another man in your bedroom by your husband, James Balfour?"

My jaw dropped. I was so shocked at what I had just heard. Chaos took over the courtroom with everyone talking at the same time. The judge pounded the gavel several times before the courtroom quieted down. Raquel blushed every hue of red as she put her head down.

"Objection, Your Honor! She's badgering the witness. These questions are baseless and not germane to this case," Mr. Mackney yelled as spittle sprayed from his mouth in every direction.

"Sustained!"

"No more questions, Your Honor," Candace said with a smirk.

"The witness may be excused," Judge Broward said.

Candace walked back to her chair. She had made her point loud and clear. It was apparent that Raquel was far from living the picture-perfect life she tried to portray. This undoubtedly shattered her perfect image. I could not believe that Candace knew that Raquel was separated from James during their marriage and that she had cheated on him. Candace probably did not give me this information for fear I might blurt it out in anger. She was correct in her thought process. Kudos to Candace Fowler! She was definitely the best!

"Since there are no more witnesses or testimony, court is hereby concluded. I will have a decision within two to three weeks," the judge said.

He then hit the sound block with his gavel and left the bench.

Everyone began to file out of the courtroom. I purposely didn't look in my sister's direction and turned my back to her to make my feelings clear.

Since everyone was out of earshot, Candace began to speak.

"I think we are going to be in the winner's circle. Just relax as much as you can and think positive thoughts. In fact, don't think about anything. Go out and have some fun tonight!"

All of us laughed as we said our goodbyes.

"How about going to Happy Bar for a drink?" I asked Sean.

"How about going to Happy Bar for a drink and then grabbing some dinner afterward?" he suggested.

"How about yes," I said smiling.

Sean hailed a cab and we arrived at the bar. It was very loud, so a conversation was all but impossible. That was okay with me. I didn't want to talk about the case or anything else for that matter. All I wanted was to be close to Sean and hoped he was thinking the same thoughts. This made me realize that I really was insane during my stay at Heaton. Back then, I had decided to give up two things, my baby and Sean. Now, they were all I wanted in my life. After a glass of wine, both of us began to unwind.

"If we don't win, I'm not going to stop trying to get our son back," Sean said emphatically.

"We're going to win! There are no doubts in my mind!" I responded.

"When did you get so positive?" Sean asked.

"Once you came back into my life. Don't worry, Sean. I'm not getting ahead of myself and am clear as to where we stand."

Sean smiled and took my hand. He raised it up to his lips and kissed it.

"Evie, you're going to make a great mom, and I'm going to make a great dad times two."

Sean winked at me, which made me hot. I didn't think he could arouse me so easily.

"Let's get something to eat now because I am beyond spent. Oh, I just realized that I need to also pick up some groceries," I told Sean.

"I have a great idea. How about we go back to my place, and I make us a great dinner. You can relax there while I cook. I'll take you to the grocery store and then home afterward. What do you say?" Sean asked.

"How can I say no to that?"

We left Happy Bar arm in arm with a real spring in our steps. We behaved as though we didn't have a care in the world, and at that moment, we didn't.

•

Entering Sean's apartment always brought back memories of when I used to live in the same building as him. I dismissed them and concentrated on what was in front of me. I hadn't felt this good in such a long time. Sean immediately went to his refrigerator and looked over what he could put together.

"Make yourself comfortable. Watch some television if you want to. The remote is on the couch," he yelled out from the kitchen.

"Okay, thanks."

Nothing appealed to me on TV, so I walked into the kitchen and took a moment to concentrate on Sean. The love that I always had for him began to stir within me. I was beginning to feel amorous but fought that feeling with everything I had. I didn't want to embarrass myself and most definitely didn't want to ruin the solid relationship we had built.

"Do you want some help with dinner?" I asked.

"It's all under control. How about a glass of wine while the salmon steaks bake?"

"Only if you'll join me."

"Of course!"

Sean took out two glasses and poured white wine into them. He handed me one and we went over to the couch.

"To lots and lots of good luck, to us that is, and to our son who will be with us soon," Sean said.

"Amen to that!"

Both of us smiled as we raised our glasses to a positive verdict. Then we sat there in silence, each waiting for the other to speak. There was nothing else to say. It had all been said. Now it was a waiting game. Sean excused himself and went back into the kitchen.

About 20 minutes later, he came in and announced that dinner was ready. I looked at him and he perceived correctly. My interests were not in the dinner, but they were in him. He came over and took my hands. He gently pulled me up and drew me near to him. He embraced me ever so gently and I melted into his arms. He began to kiss me on my neck and then my shoulders. I kissed him back on his lips and then on his cheeks. This led us directly to his bedroom. Every move that he made was tender and passionate, which tingled every part of my body. I couldn't get enough of him and my hunger showed it. I was kissing and touching every part of him. He understood every move that I made and returned it in kind. This was more than sex. It had to be. He wasn't just going through the motions but was truly making love to me and with me. His goal was to satisfy my every desire, and I wanted to do the same to him. We couldn't have been more in sync. It seemed right that this was the first time I was having sex since the rape. But this was not having sex, this was making love!

It was after 7:00 PM when we were ready to go back into the kitchen. We sat down at the table and began to eat our dinner. The salmon and green beans were cold, as was the pasta. None of that mattered. My mind was on Sean. I didn't know if this was a one-time thing or if we were rekindling our relationship. Either way, it was one of the best nights of my life and that was good enough for me. We ate most of the dinner and then went back to the couch.

"I had a great time tonight, Sean but it's getting late and you have to go to work tomorrow, secretly hoping he would ask me to stay the night.

"It's been a long day and I totally lost track of time."

Sean looked directly at me for a second or two and then began to speak again.

"Evie, you mean a lot to me, but I'm really …"

I placed my fingers gently on his mouth to stop him from apologizing when he didn't do anything wrong.

"Don't finish the sentence. I know this happened because we were both feeling emotional after the trial today, not to mention all the wine we drank. It's okay though. I fully understand."

"I just don't want you to think that I'm using you," Sean said.

"You're too good a guy to do that. I'm clear that we care about each other, but 'it' is not there anymore. I respect you and everything will work out the way it's supposed to."

Sean kissed me on my forehead and then stood up. That was my cue that he was taking me home. I was disappointed but had to be realistic. Our time as a couple had passed. Some very lucky woman was going to be with Sean, but unfortunately, it wasn't going to be me. While I wasn't okay with that, I knew I would be in time. My acceptance of the situation showed that my mental health was improving. I was starting to live in the real world, and disappointments were definitely part of that.

•

The next week and a half seemed to go by very slowly. I called Candace every day and every day she told me the same thing.

"You will receive a call as soon as there is notification from the judge that he is ready to see us," she reiterated.

"Thank you. I'm sorry to call you every day, but I'm so anxious, in a good way that is."

"Just try to relax. The court will let us know shortly," Candace reassured me.

"I understand. Thank you, Candace. Bye."

I also called Sean non-stop. While it was difficult for both of us, he was able to handle the pressure better than I was. Briana was not left out of the loop. I called her every night and vented my frustrations. As usual, she was kind and patient. She should have been put up as a candidate for sainthood.

Tuesday of week three came and Candace called me bright and early.

"Good morning, Evie. It's Candace. I just heard from the court that Judge Broward has made a decision. We are to meet him in his chambers at 10:15 AM tomorrow."

I shrieked out in joy!

"Finally, I'm so happy! Does Sean know?"

"Yes. Let's meet at the courthouse at 9:45 AM to go over a few things. Do you have any questions before we hang up?"

"I don't know what to ask except for one thing. What if we don't win? I couldn't bear it!"

"That's one of the reasons I want to meet with both of you a few minutes earlier tomorrow. Evie, please take it one step at a time. See you tomorrow."

With that, she hung up the phone.

"Please, please G-D let us win. Please give us our son," I said to myself.

A moment later, the phone rang. I answered it immediately.

"Hi, it's me," Sean said.

"Hi Me, I was just going to call you. Promise that you will look the absolute best that you can tomorrow. I want the judge to see that you are ready to take our son home."

"I am ready, Sean but what if we don't win?"

"We are going to win and I already bought a bottle of champagne for the occasion."

"You're so positive. Okay, I'll stay positive too."

"I'll pick you up at 9:00 AM sharp. Bye."

My stomach had tightened up and food didn't appeal to me. Realistically, I had to eat or I would be a wreck the following day. My lunch consisted of half a sandwich and a small salad. The rest of the afternoon was spent deciding what to wear for the big day and watching TV. When it was finally time for bed, I needed to drink a warm glass of milk. That usually helped me to sleep. Before drinking it, I called Sean.

"Hi, Sean, a small favor please?"

"Sure, what is it?"

"Can you give me a wake-up call at 7:00 AM tomorrow?"

"Sure, goodnight."

"Goodnight."

I fell asleep almost immediately but woke up around 2:00 AM. After tossing and turning for an hour, I decided to turn on the TV, but that didn't help. The outcome of this important decision would be known in the early morning, and my nerves were shot. I got out of bed and went into the kitchen. I took out a bottle of wine from the fridge and poured myself a glass and then another. I went back to bed and fell asleep about a half hour later.

At 7:00 AM sharp, Sean called. It was difficult for me to answer the phone as I had fallen into a very sound sleep.

"Hello," I said in a groggy voice.

"It's time to get up, Sleeping Beauty. Today is a big day for us."

"I didn't sleep most of the night, but I'll be fine. I'm already out of bed and I'm going into the shower right now."

"Whatever you do, don't go back to bed for those extra few minutes."

"I promise I won't."

I lied back down on the bed just to relax for a few minutes. However, my eyes closed, and I instantly fell back asleep. An hour passed by when the phone rang and woke me up with a start. Luckily that call happened, even though it was a wrong number. Was it luck or divine intervention? I looked at the clock and couldn't believe it was 8:37 AM. I only had 13 minutes to get ready.

I raced into the shower and finished in record time. Luckily, I had decided what I would wear the night before. I dressed, brushed my teeth, and threw my hairbrush and makeup into my pocketbook.

I grabbed half a donut from the fridge and ate it in the elevator. My heart finally stopped racing when I exited and walked into the lobby. Sean had just arrived and he would not be the wiser. I dodged a real bullet that morning, all thanks to a wrong number. Sean and I went outside and hailed down a cab.

I applied my makeup in the taxi and finally started to feel at ease.

"You look pretty. How are you feeling?" Sean asked.

"Thanks for the compliment. I feel good, but truth be told, I do have some butterflies in my stomach."

"I'm nervous also. The judge is holding all the cards, but I still feel it will go in our favor."

I smiled at Sean and didn't feel up to talking anymore. I just wanted to arrive at the courthouse and get this meeting started. The traffic was surprisingly light, and we arrived ten minutes early. Candace was already there, minus her team. She was standing outside the courthouse talking on her phone. I waved to get her attention, and she waved back as she began to walk toward us.

"Good morning," she chirped in a jovial voice.

"Good morning," we answered at almost the same time.

She motioned for us to follow her inside the courthouse. We all walked in together and then looked at Candace for further direction. She shut off her phone and began to speak.

"Let's go over to the other end of the corridor where it's deserted right now."

We followed her down the empty hallway. It was very odd that there were no signs of reporters in the lobby or anywhere else in the building.

"Did everyone eat something this morning?" Candace asked us.

"Yes."

Again, we both answered at almost the same time.

"Good! Now, this is what both of you should keep in mind. You must be respectful towards the judge. When he gives his ruling you will not react to it. You will not be jubilant or sad or display any other sentiments. Whatever you will be feeling, keep it low-key and in control until we are out of earshot of the courthouse. Is that understood?"

"Actually no, I don't understand," Sean replied.

"Judges are people like anyone else. If you are in control of your emotions, you will show that you are in full control of yourself. You have to show respect, restraint and also maturity. You never know if you will come before this judge again. Regardless of the verdict, you need to show acceptance by being quiet. If you are asked any questions, even if they have been asked before, answer them clearly. And one more thing, which is possibly the most important point that I can make. Evie do not look at your sister, her husband, or her attorney. If the verdict does not go our way, do not under any circumstances say anything to them. I trust that both of you understand the importance of what I just said."

"I do," Sean uttered.

"Yes, I do also," I added.

"Then let's go see the judge!" Candace said.

We went into Judge Broward's chambers. Raquel, James and their attorney were already seated at the only table available. We took our seats on the opposite end of the table. The room was eerily quiet.

Finally, the judge appeared in his black robe with part of a white collared shirt and red tie peeking out from underneath. I must say that he looked very good. The bailiff began the proceedings by asking us to stand until the judge took his seat. He announced the names of the plaintiffs, defendants, and case number.

"Good morning everyone," Judge Broward said before he sat down.

"I have read and re-read all the information in this very lengthy file. It is never easy to make a decision as how to rule on any case that comes before me. In this particular situation, the only ruling that I could make pertains to what is in the best interests of this child. I took everyone's testimony into consideration and reviewed all the laws in the State of New York as well as any federal laws that might apply. I could not dismiss the life patterns of the plaintiff, Evie Harris, nor could I dismiss the ..."

My heart sunk. As the judge continued to speak, the less hopeful I became. It seemed as though our chances of winning were getting slimmer and slimmer. I took a peek at Sean to see if I could read his take on things, but he seemed to be frozen in time. He did not acknowledge me in any way. Candace had her poker face on, so I had no idea what she was thinking. I clasped my hands together and turned my attention back to the judge. I had missed the last few sentences of what he said but knew it didn't matter. What was important was the last sentence he was going to say, his decision.

"I have in front of me two couples that want the same child. The defendants have submitted all the pertinent data and information, including their finances to me. It is clear that this child would not want for anything that money could buy ..."

Why was he dragging this out? It was becoming crystal clear that he was going to rule in favor of Raquel. I folded my arms behind my back to stop fidgeting.

"There is ample love on both sides and therefore the question still bodes. What is in the best interests of this child?"

Say it already so I can run outside and cry my eyes out, was all I could think of. I didn't know how much longer I could take it.

"In conclusion ..."

All of a sudden my stomach began to growl in the loudest possible way. Judge Broward stopped speaking and looked at me.

"I'm so sorry," I said.

I apologized and put my hand over my mouth so as not to burst out laughing. Maybe I should have eaten more than half a donut that morning.

The judge cleared his throat and continued to speak.

"In conclusion, it is the decision of the court that Baby Boy Doe would receive all the love and financial support necessary throughout his life with either the plaintiffs or the defendants. However, in this case, the child would be better off in the care of his biological parents, Evie Harris and Sean Graham. We have seen through the years that the majority of children, no matter how successful the adoptive parental relationships are, want to know who their biological parents are. Evie Harris was not of sound mind at the time she decided to relinquish her unborn child. Although Ms. Harris was provided psychological care, she was not treated by a doctor or counselor who specializes in violent crimes such as rape. Had she received the proper treatment, we most definitely would not be meeting in my chambers today. The child was accepted for adoption due to a legal contract that should never have been enforced by anyone. The child shall be turned over to the plaintiffs within 24 hours. It is so ruled."

The judge pounded the gavel and called the attorneys over. I could not believe what had just happened. Sean and I had our son! We won! It was a good thing that I was in shock, because otherwise I would have fainted. Sean took my hand and squeezed it tightly. He then put his arm around me. We stood there waiting for Candace to give us further instructions. After a short chat with Candace and Raquel's attorney, the judge stood up and left the chambers.

Raquel and James stood as still as statues. Neither of them exhibited any signs of sorrow. Mr. Mackney took off his glasses and placed them on the table. He spoke to them for no more than a minute as they stood up to leave. They began walking out of the chambers when Raquel turned around and yelled out to me.

"Bitch, I hope you die!"

Their attorney rushed them out so as not to cause a further scene. Her words meant absolutely nothing to me. My life could only get better from here on in.

"Let's go back to my office," Candace said to us.

As we descended the stairs, I caught a glimpse of the reporters and photographers waiting outside. They must have been banned from entering the inside of the courthouse and the judge's chambers. They asked the usual questions and snapped photos. This time, Candace stopped and began to speak.

"This has been a long and arduous case. This was not about money or property, but about a human being. It was the wisdom of the court to act in the child's best interests. Therefore, the final ruling is that the child will be returned to his biological parents."

Candace no sooner finished speaking when the reporters barraged her with more questions.

"That's all there is," she concluded.

We began walking away from the reporters at a fast pace. Sean hailed an oncoming taxi and the three of us rode directly to Candace's office.

"I still can't believe that we are going to have our son in 24 hours!" I exclaimed excitedly.

"It's surreal, but the right decision was made," Sean answered.

We went into Candace's private office and sat down in front of her desk. She pulled out a file and began thumbing through it. She stopped abruptly and looked at us.

"Congratulations! I am so happy for you both!"

"We couldn't have done it without you," Sean answered her.

"I think we might have had some divine intervention," she said with a wink.

"I will be receiving a stack of paperwork to fill out which will need both of your signatures. Tomorrow morning, you will get a call as to where and when to pick up your son. There will be a social worker present, and you can ask him or her about special programs available for new parents. I need to know your co-parenting schedules, so please put that together today. By the way, did you name him yet?"

"No, we haven't. Do you have any ideas?" I asked Sean.

"I have a great name picked out but never mentioned it because I was afraid it would jinx the outcome."

Sean turned to me and took my hand as he continued to speak.

"Evie, I would like to name our son Chance Terrence Graham. Chance, because we took a big chance trying to get our son back, and Terrence because it was your father's name."

"That's the name of a winner, and that is the name he will have! Chance Terrence Graham," I said with pride and joy.

Candace clapped her hands. She was so happy for us.

"What about a crib and so forth?" Candace questioned.

"I have everything that is necessary. I saved all that stuff from my son, Charlie. Whatever I don't have will be bought immediately."

"Then we're good!" Candace said with a big smile.

She stood up and shook our hands. Candace then reiterated that she would call us later in the day. Sean and I giggled like little kids as we left her office.

"Let's go to Cafe Allegra for some coffee. We can talk about all of our arrangements and scheduling there. Before that, let's stop at a hardware store so that I can make you a spare key for my apartment and you can do the same for me. Ready?" Sean asked.

"As ready as I will ever be!"

The rest of the day was a whirlwind of planning activity and errands. When I finally got back to my apartment, all I wanted to do was brush my teeth and go to bed. It was late and I was exhausted. But no matter how tired I was, there was something I had to do before I went to sleep that night.

"Hi, Briana, it's Evie!"

"You sound very happy."

"I am so ecstatic! We won! We got our son back!"

"Fabulous! I am so happy for you. That is the best news!"

"Give me a few days and then I want you and Paul to come over and see the baby, I mean my son."

"That will be great. Just let me know when. What did you name him?"

"Chance Terrence Graham, what do you think?"

"I think that you and Sean are the luckiest people. By the way, I'm offering free babysitting services."

"That sounds great. Thanks for your good wishes and all your help. I'll call you tomorrow night. Bye."

•

The morning after our victory, Candace called us back into her office to fill out all sorts of legal forms. We were only hours away from picking up Chance, and the excitement was growing. Charlie already knew that he was getting a baby brother and couldn't wait. All of us were going to be together at Sean's apartment for a celebratory dinner that night. We knew that everything would be perfect.

•

"So there it is, Dr. Pennington. I finally got the big brass ring, my son, not to mention a great father and friend in Sean."

"How old is your son now?" Dr. Pennington asked.

"Chance just turned 23 and I'm so proud of him. He's a wonderful young man, just like his dad."

"What is he doing with his life?"

"He's a mechanical engineer and he lives in Brooklyn. The best part is that we see each other every Thursday night at Café Allegra to catch up."

"It sounds like you've been very successful in raising your son."

"Well, there was a period of time when I wasn't such an amazing mother. When I started co-parenting with Sean, it took no time for me to grasp the concept of responsibility. Everything was going well until I had a major setback. Soon after Chance started kindergarten, I was beginning to have flashbacks of the rape. I then developed PTSD. For six months, I would go long periods without leaving the apartment or showering. Ben even came back into my thoughts during that time frame because I received an unexpected package from one of his ex-girlfriends."

"This must have been a very trying time for you," Dr. Pennington remarked.

"It really was, and on top of it, I had stopped seeing Dr. Hunter on a weekly basis. Things got so difficult for me that I couldn't function properly. Unfortunately, there was no choice but to quit my job. In the beginning, Sean had tried to help me through that period, but I was at such a low point that the only person who could get me through it was myself. I explained that to Sean and told him that until I got better, he had to leave me alone and take care of Chance 100% full-time, which of course, he did. That meant zero contact between me and my son for those six months. Even though Chance was very young, he understood that I had to be away in order to be the best mommy possible to him when I returned. When I was fully back to myself, so to speak, I got a job at the library where I am still working today. I'm really happy there."

"What about Sean? How has he fared?"

"Sean is a great father and friend. We get along really well, but there is no romantic interest on his part. He rekindled his relationship with Charlie's mother, and they have been together since Chance turned three years old. I love Sean and will always love him, but he has made his decision and I respect that. Charlie recently got married and moved in with his in-laws. Chance and Charlie have a great relationship without any sibling rivalry. My son is surrounded by love, three parents and a brother whom he adores."

"What are you doing with your life now?"

"I have a great group of friends whom I met at the library. We get together frequently and play cards or go to the movies and the like. I moved out of that tiny studio a few months after Sean and I won the case. I now live in a two-bedroom apartment with a small balcony, thanks to Sean. Briana and I are still the best of friends, but we don't get to see each other as often as we would like to.

About five years ago, she and Paul moved to a small town in Tennessee. They wanted to get away from everything and plant new roots."

"It seems as though you are standing on your own two feet now," Dr. Pennington said with a smile on her face.

"I finally am, and that is why I have become more selective with men. If someone wonderful appears in the near future, that will be great. If that doesn't happen, I will still feel fulfilled and grateful for the way my life has turned out. I have accepted everything and am thankful for the greatest gift that has been given to me, my son! After all these years, I am not desperate anymore and finally understand what true love is. It has been a long journey with many hurdles in the way, but I've managed to move forward. And, I don't have any problems making decisions anymore. Well, there is one decision I'm having a hard time making. I'm getting a tattoo of a starfish but I'm just not sure where to put it."

"What does the starfish represent to you, Evie?"

"Well, starfish can regrow their limbs."

"That's very symbolic of your triumphs."

"That's true, but mostly, it reminds me of the good times with my father."

"I'm afraid we've come to the end of our session. See you in two weeks."

The End

Made in the USA
Middletown, DE
23 September 2020